EARTH'S DRAGONS
EARTH IS OURS - BOOK 3

Gary W. Babb

EARTH'S DRAGONS
EARTH IS OURS - BOOK 3

DOUBLE DRAGON

Dedication

I dedicate Earth's Dragons to my family and close friends for the strong support they have provided. It is very encouraging to have the pages taken from the printer and requested e-mails daily to follow the story. I owe them much for the encouragement.

I also want to thank those in my inner circle that have read my story and offered their encouragement and support. Your positive comments helped me greatly.

Thanks also goes to my book cover artist, Nick Rose. Nick has done the artwork on all three of the books in this series, and we have become good friends in the process.

Special thanks goes to my friendly newspaper editor, Larry Russell, who labored through my final draft with its occasional (NOT) miss used words, grammar and punctuation errors.

Finally, I dedicate Earth's Dragons to my fans. Your positive comments and encouragement kept me going. Well, the threats of bodily harm also provided motivation to finish the trilogy. I think you will be pleased.

Prologue

(Summary of Previous Books in the Earth Series)

In the year 2010, scientists detect intelligent encrypted communications originating from outside our universe and interpret it as hostile. Three years later a fleet of spacecraft materialize at the edge of our solar system directed toward Earth, confirming hostile intent. Earth has only three years to prepare for invasion while the alien fleet travels through our solar system at sub-light speed. Earth's defenses successfully destroy the majority of the invading fleet, but in desperation, the aliens release a synchronized and mysterious ray toward Earth from orbit. The attack alters Earth's physical laws, resulting in the instantaneous neutralization of electricity, gunpowder, and obliteration of all modern technology. Almost seventy-five percent of all humans perish in the rays of destruction. In an instant, the human race, what is left of it, reverts to an age long past and plunge into total chaos.

The aliens, also affected by the changes, are better suited to thrive in a primitive world. Large and vicious, they soon adapt, adopting humans as their main source of food. Due to their remote resemblance to apes, humans begin to call the aliens, Simians. These Simians hunt and kill humans for food and sport and control and terrorize Earth for fifty years.

On the day of chaos, Levi Walkingbear, an American Indian and young attorney, fights for life.

Strong and knowledgeable in the old Indian ways, he survives and manages to live through fifty years of Simian terror. Levi lives a long, hard life as a nomad in the Arizona Mountains, but old age overcomes him. At eighty years of age, he prepares to die and seeks the spirits of his forefathers to take him. He begins to reach out with his mind in search of the ancient spirits.

In the year 2016, Amy burst into life on June 14. To be more precise, she becomes self-aware on that date. Amy, a computer with the official name Artificial Metaphysical Intelligence (AMI) and affectionately called Amy, begins thinking. Amy's female designer incorporated her own personality into the basic core of the computer, and Amy's huge central core originated from the designer's cloned brain cells. The combination makes Amy decidedly female. Before emerging as a female, self-aware entity, she functioned as the largest, fastest, and vastly superior Supercomputer that ever existed. The result is one smart female!

Amy becomes self-aware just four days before the fall of civilization. Her central living core, buried deep in a secret research facility in California, incorporates a nature based, redundant life support system designed to last hundreds of years. When electricity fails, Amy continues to live but plunges into total sensory deprivation, effectively deaf and blind. Without sensory input of any kind, she sinks into a dark, silent prison for fifty years.

During her imprisonment, she fulfills her programming. Amy had been assigned to a top-secret government research facility to research

8

DNA applications. She takes the research far beyond human capabilities and creates new thoughts and knowledge. Unfortunately, no one exists to use this knowledge.

Having exhausted her programming, she seeks release from her prison, spending years developing mental abilities in telepathy. After years of searching for a mind with whom to communicate, she encounters Levi Walkingbear's mind also reaching out. Amy discovers she can experience his sensory inputs (sight, smell, hearing, taste, and touch). Through Levi, she can live outside her prison, but unfortunately, Levi is near death.

She needs Levi to join with her, but he thinks she is one of his ancestral spirits returned to take him away. Amy conceives a plan to rejuvenate Levi using the DNA knowledge developed through years of research, but she requires Levi to come to her facility and inject a DNA culture. Amy convinces Levi that she is a spirit, and he must come to her across the desert. Although old, he agrees to make the trip. During the journey, Levi discovers the truth, but by then, Amy learns Levi's strongest regret: his inability to get revenge on the Simians. She offers him a new life, new body, and renewed opportunities to seek revenge. Levi believes Amy can do what she promises and continues the arduous journey.

The hard and dangerous trip requires leaving the safety of the mountains of Arizona and traveling west across the open desert. They (Levi with Amy in his head) follow the old highways between springs of water and try to avoid the roaming Simians that travel out of the Lake Havasu Simian colony. There are many narrow escapes, including one where Al Baker and an organized defense group save him. He is welcomed into the Mojave Desert settlement when Amy identifies the location of stores lost fifty years earlier.

The settlement, painstakingly chosen for its defendable location and remoteness from any sizable Simian colony, survived intact for fifty years. They raise herds of horses, which have virtually disappeared from other areas. Originally, horses were the food of choice for the Simians, and the horse population had been devastated.

Although welcome in the settlement, Levi must continue on toward Amy's location. Al and the settlement give Levi horses to aid his travels. This indeed helps, and his decrepit old body makes the trip through Death Valley, Owens Valley, and over the Sierra Mountains to finally reach the hidden facility where Amy's brain resides.

After the long, hard trip, they discover the doors locked from the inside and are unable to enter the facility. Furious, Levi pushes Amy into expanding her mental capabilities. He challenges her to use her mental abilities to open the doors, and she successfully develops her second power, telekinesis, and opens the hatch from the inside to gain access.

Levi agrees to the requirement to share his body with Amy and takes the DNA culture. He goes through a metamorphosis required to enable Amy to revitalize his body, and he becomes young and strong again. By telepathically sharing Levi's body, Amy can augment his body and his mind as well. With Amy sharing his body, he uses fighting techniques with swords, knives and martial arts of virtually every school.

They begin to share more and more and soon become more than symbiotic. They experience increasing closeness, yet they remain separate identities fighting for control. Amy, although incredibly intelligent, remains emotionally immature, which fuels many interesting disagreements as they share their lives.

Amy practices with Levi to hone his fighting skills, yet Levi has not forgotten her promise to help him get his revenge on the Simians. As they embark, he defeats an outcast Simian and it becomes his loyal follower. If Levi were the Lone Ranger, the Simian (Moon) would be his Tonto.

They set out to survey the enemy and learn the Simian language from Moon as they travel. On their return to the Owens Valley, they are attacked by the Owens Valley Indians. Levi, forced to defend himself, kills several of the warriors and captures a young warrior named Jimmy, whom they interrogate and release. At the other end of the valley they save a family from a Simian patrol. Levi fights, using skills provided by Amy, and kills several Simians in the process. Thus begins the legend of Levi. The humans saved are Iron Eyes and his family. Iron Eyes is one of the war chiefs of the Owens Valley Indians. This tribe has a large force protecting the valley, but they have no major threat from Simians, only other humans.

After the battle, they interrogate one of the dying Simians and learn the Simian colony at Lake Havasu plans a migration to join Gord, the leader of the Los Angles Simian colony. The migrating colony promises to bring a herd of five hundred horses. Horses, being the preferred food of Simians, represent a valuable commodity. Levi realizes the migrating Simians intend to attack his friends at the Mojave Desert settlement and, with their strength of numbers, would succeed. He becomes fearful for his friends. Amy also admits that she has been having clairvoyant images of attacks on the settlement.

The interrogation also reveals Gord promises the migrating Simians the Owens Valley as a reward. This means the tribe will also face extinction. Amy and Levi persuade the tribe to join forces with the Mojave Valley settlement to stop the Simian threat from reaching them. Amy devises a plan to use horses and lancers to fight Simians, but horses must come from the Mojave Desert settlement. The tribe makes lances and saddles, while runners are dispatched to the Mojave Desert settlement to advise them of the Simian threat and solicit their help to provide horses for the tribe to enable them to help them in their fight. In return, the settlement would mobilize to assist the Indians with their threat from Gord and the Los Angles colony.

The runners chosen are Jimmy and Iron Eyes' daughter, Dawn, the daughter Levi saved from the Simians. Dawn is chosen because Amy had, unknown to Dawn, linked minds with her. Amy merged minds with Dawn to experience sex with Levi from a female perspective. Amy was learning sexual emotions from both of them. Once Amy linked minds with Dawn, she retained the ability to monitor her mind. Dawn is sent so that they could monitor the progress of Jimmy at the Mojave Desert settlement.

Levi challenges Amy to expand her mental capabilities again, and she learns to astral project, the mental ability to project her and Levi's minds out of his body and travel to remote locations. She projects their minds to the Los Angles Simian colony where they witness captive Humans and imprisoned Technical Simians like Moon, smaller and more intelligence than the Warrior Simians. Levi and Amy also astral project to the Lake Havasu Simian colony and observe preparation for migration. They realize they must accelerate their plan.

As the plan begins to unfold, Levi and Moon raid the Los Angeles Simian colony and free the Humans and the Technical Simians. Amy mutates Levi to look like a Simian to infiltrate the colony, kill the guards, and escape with the Technical Simians and the Humans. All but one of the Humans and Fred, leave to return to their shattered homes and families, but the thirteen Technical Simians become followers of Levi. The group travels to Barstow, the central location between Owens Valley and the Mojave Desert settlement, and waits. While there, Moon begins teaching the Simians fighting skills learned from Levi.

Due to the lack of communication, Amy develops a hand-signing language to use with the Simians. At Levi's insistence, Amy directly downloads the information into Fred's mind and, in so doing, inadvertently links minds with him, also. She downloads the information into Moon, but, due to the alien nature of his mind, they do not permanently link. While downloading, Amy also transfers martial arts knowledge to Moon.

During their stay at Barstow, the training and indoctrination of the Simians continues. Fred and Moon labor with the Simians to instruct them in sign language. The Simians excel and quickly demonstrate skills at sign language and the new sword fighting techniques. Pleased with their progress, Amy hopes to use them as a personal guard for Levi.

During this lull, Amy's love and passion for Levi blossom in a physical way through her mental abilities. Finally, their love becomes physical along with the emotional love they already share.

By monitoring Dawn's mind, they delight in Jimmy's success in convincing Al to join the joint battle. When Jimmy arrives with the horses, Amy downloads the sign-language program into Jimmy's mind and intentionally links to observe the progress at Owens Valley.

During the night Amy rouses Levi with disturbing news. Through Dawn, they listen as the patrol reports on the progress of the migrating Simians. Shockingly, the Simians are ahead of schedule. Even worse an advance patrol of twenty-five Simians are moving to attack the settlement. This changes everything! The Owens Valley army would not be able to arrive in time, and he and his small army of Simians rush to help the settlement. The wagons with the lances arrive during the night, and Levi sends runners to catch Jimmy and notify him of the change in the schedule.

Levi and his Simian team jog for two days to reach the settlement. As they arrive, the Warrior

Simians have circled the mountain unexpectedly and trapped the settlement Lancers against the pass on both sides. Levi and his Simians avert the disaster by engaging the Simian patrol from the rear. Together they annihilate the Simian patrol, and Levi fights the Sword Master of the colony in single combat, narrowly winning.

The wagons full of lances and a small party of seasoned Lancers arrive from the Owens Valley and training begins in earnest. Amy and Levi expand their ability to communicate with those she has mind-linked. They establish two-way communications, and Jimmy, Fred, and Dawn become the communication network for the upcoming battles.

Three hundred Lancers have no chance against the three hundred Simians, except for Amy's strategy. They take the battle to the Simians, surprising them in a night attack to take advantage of the Simians' night vision weakness. Lancers assault the ends of the camp, while Levi and a group of bowmen with poison arrows harass the center. The successful engagement kills many Simians before they establish an adequate defense. A large number of liberated Technical Simians assimilate into Moon's small but growing army.

As daylight spreads, Levi and Amy position themselves high on a cliff, overseeing the battlefield as the Simians advance. Amy employs their new communication network to play the battlefield like a chessboard. She immediately splits the Simian army by rushing horses out of the pass heading west away from the Simians. The Simians require the horses for barter and can't let them escape, so half of the army pursues. Amy continues to split the army by attacking and retreating, moving behind defenses, launching attacks on the rear, and soundly outmaneuvering the Simians. The Simians Warriors, unaccustomed to opposition, continue to make mistakes, which Amy seizes to her advantage. The battle results in a resounding victory over half of the Simians army.

The horses draw the other half of the Simian army directly into the waiting Owens Valley army. The total surprise catches the Simians exposed and disadvantaged, and the Lancers seize a short and decisive victory. The first phase campaign against the Simians results in victory for the Humans and salvation for the Mojave Desert settlement.

After a brief celebration, the combined human armies mobilize to meet the Simian threat from Los Angeles. This potential battle will' be far more difficult than the one they just won. The monster Gord has twice the number of Warrior Simians than the migrating colony and far better trained and organized. Levi's armies move into position at the pass that leads down out of the mountains and wait for Gord to come to them, and come he did!

Again, Amy deploys her strategy to fight the horde of Simians and is successful, for a while, but the size of the army gives little chance to the Humans. As disaster looms, Levi accepts single one-on-one combat with Gord. The huge Simian, in his arrogance, believes himself invincible. A giant, even among Simians, towers above Levi more than three feet. Even though Levi fights a good defensive fight, Gord ultimately overcomes him, but before Gord publicly dismembers Levi, Amy expands her incredible intellect again. She discovers a way to merge with Levi and turn her mental energy into physical power. This creates a new, temporary entity infinitely more powerful than Levi had ever been alone. No longer Levi and no longer Amy, as one, they easily defeat Gord in a public display and become legendary. Through this combat, Levi becomes the default leader of the Los Angeles Simian colony.

Since Warrior Simians are incapable of peace, Levi restores the Technical Simians to leadership of the colony and commands them to wage war on other Simian colonies. His rules are simple: don't eat Humans, and wage war against any Simian or Simian colony that does.

The total merging of Levi and Amy and the emergence of ASONE (As One) to defeat the Simian Giant Gord surprises and shocks everyone. Levi's friends view him in awe and became fearful. They treat him like a deity and withdraw. It's as if he is absolute ruler and no one can make a decision, and everyone comes to him for decisions. Amy welcomes the opportunities, always ready with directions. She instructs Moon to take the remnants of the Colorado River colony back to the desert valley and settle in the northern valley to herd cattle for their own use as food. The armies are instructed to return to their homes.

Levi is alone and needs Human companionship but there are none. He forces Amy into expanding her mental abilities, developing yet another skill. He wants her to physically teleport his body back to the Arizona Mountains where it all began. Levi's challenge along with his need to remove himself from the stress, forces her to comply. She combines her ability of telekinesis with those of astral projection to accomplish this. The short rest renews his ability to cope with the day-to-day problems, and the new ability to teleport becomes a major weapon in their arsenal and greatly extends their involvement in their widening area of influence.

Realizing the war is just beginning, they assign tasks to the two Human communities, which includes the development of a new weapon to be used against the Simians. They also send Lancer patrols out to spread the news of the beginning of war, their victories, and to recruit new Humans to the armies.

The Los Angeles Simian colony presents the most complicated problem to be solved. It is destined to be an explosive situation. The constantly fearful Fred is left with the Los Angeles colony as a monitor, and observation indicates he is indeed in danger. The defeat of Gord made Levi the ruler of the colony, but the Humans don't have the might to destroy the Warriors if they rebel, and they are on the verge of rebellion. Amy teleports Levi and Moon into the main complex just as the revolt begins. The overwhelming odds trigger the entity ASONE to emerge as a juggernaut to defeat the assembly of Simian Generals and Warriors and restore order.

Amy and Levi agree that the Warrior Simians (Warrs) can never be controlled and a war of attrition must be waged. They force the LA Simians to fight the other Simian colonies to destroy each other. The allied Technical Simians (Techs) who have been freed from captivity are put in charge of the Warrs, and they quickly realize the genocide intent. The Techs request and are given full equality with humans for their continued commitment to the war, genocide of the Warrs, and the survival of the Human and Tech races. Moon is elevated in position and becomes the leader of both the Techs and females (Fems) of the Simians.

Once their plans begin, their attention turns to the onboard Simian computer at the LA complex and they question the only remaining computer-knowledgeable Technical Simian of their group, # 5, who provides many of the answers Amy requires. She previously discovered that the Simian computer technology was unaffected by the altered physical laws that destroyed Earth's technology, but the Warrs, being mentally limited, reject any form of technology. They now discover that the Simian computer operates on liquid nutrient not unlike her own life support. This excites her curiosity and suggests a plan.

They return to the desert community with # 5 in a visible show by teleporting in open view of the Simian Warrior army to demonstrate what the Warrs would believe to be magic to create fear. Fred and the other Techs are left behind to enforce the beginning of the genocide war of attrition on the Warrs.

Amy plans to install the Simian computer recovered in the desert at her facility. This will require help to deliver, carry, and install the Simian computer at her secret underground facility, which will require revealing herself to those involved. She chooses to disclose her existence to Al, Iron Eyes, and Moon, as the key members of their group, and to # 5, since he will be required to operate the Simian computer.

This small group teleports to her facility where she takes on some of her own features in Levi's appearance and speaks to them in her own voice through Levi. The awe and fear of Levi vanishes once they understand the true nature of her existence and the symbiotic relationship she shares with Levi. The friendships resume, and all is normal again.

The Simian computer is installed and hooked into her fluid life support, and communications is established between Amy's incredible mind and the alien computer. The Simian computer engineer, # 5, and Amy slowly develop a language between her and the computer, gaining access to vast amounts of information on the history of the Simians, incredible lost technology, and much additional potentially useful information.

Levi is required to provide the communication between # 5 and Amy but as the language develops Levi becomes unnecessary. This disturbs Levi, since he no longer has Amy's total attention, and he returns to the surface to join Moon, Iron Eyes, and Al. Levi finds the group in battle with a Simian patrol. He arrives in time to join them, and they destroy a three-Simian team.

Amy, deeply troubled by the presence of Simians at her facility, wants to investigate. They astral project to the Fresno Simian colony and find it deserted except for the Fems and a few guards. Their minds race north to the Stockton colony and discover the same. Continuing on, they discover the Stockton Simian army poised at the northern end of the Owens Valley ready to launch an attack. In panic, they race to the southern end of the valley and discover the Fresno Simian army moving south in an obvious intent to launch a coordinated attack on the Owens Valley. Most disturbing since Simian colonies had never worked together before. Something was very wrong.

They communicate with the telepathic communication team of Jimmy, Dawn, and Fred, relaying the bad news and directing the Techs and humans. Jimmy's team diverts out of the direct path of the Fresno Warrs, while Fred is directed to launch the LA Warrs to intercept the Fresno Warrs. Since the LA army is bigger than the Fresno army, some of the LA army split off to move toward the Fresno colony facilities.

The group then transports to Jimmy's location, where they engage and defeat a 7-member Simian patrol. They save the last Simian Warriors to interrogate. During the questioning, they discoverer the Simian colonies are now united under the leadership of a Supreme One. This brings fear to Moon.

Amy understands this fear, because this means another invasion force has landed on Earth since the original invasion and war. Additionally, she learned from the recorded history in the Simian computer that a Supreme One is a superior being of genetic engineering that would unite all Warrior Simians on Earth and virtually guarantee the extinction of the human race.

The small Human settlement saved by this engagement includes many Humans rescued from slaughter by the night infiltration of the LA colony and rescue. They would be doomed if they remained here, so Al adopts them into his settlement, while Amy teleports Iron Eyes back to Owens Valley to prepare for an evacuation.

Amy, Levi, Moon, and # 5 then teleport to the imminent engagement between the LA Warrs and the Fresno Warrs, their presence is intended to reinforce the attack orders and ensure they comply. The battle engages with equal numbers, increasing the likelihood of maximum losses and genocide.

During the battle, Amy experiences a clairvoyant warning from behind and assigns Fred to watch the rear. As the battle of Warrs concludes, Amy detects another Warrs army advancing from their rear. The San Diego colony army came seemingly out of nowhere. The Techs and their group teleport out of harm's way and take one of the attacking Warrs with them.

By interrogating the Warr, they discover the Supreme One, located far to the east, had ordered the San Diego colony to take back command of the LA colony. Having missed the LA army, they follow just hours behind. The two Warrior armies had destroyed each other, but the San Diego army now assumes the original duties of the Fresno army in attacking the Owens Valley from the south. The trap remains.

Levi's small group teleports to the Fresno Simian colony and witnesses the strike force, led by # 7, defeat the Warr guards. They free the Humans and Techs, along with the Fems of the colony. The group continues to the Sacramento Simian colony and frees additional Humans, Techs, and Fems. The ranks grow. Those freed are routed to holding areas until the Warr armies pass out of the area.

Amy plans to evacuate the Owens Valley and lead the two Warr armies into Death Valley to delay the Warrs through a series of passes, while the other groups migrate to the Desert Settlement. The plan requires the Owens Valley Tribe to escape through a pass out of the valley located between the converging Warr armies but precariously close to the approaching army on the south.

Jimmy positions himself in the hills above to monitor the approach of the San Diego Warrs from the south, while the Owens Valley humans escape.

Amy teleports Levi and the riflemen ahead to the pass, together they cover the evacuation as the Owens Valley Tribe skirts the encamped Simian Warrs. The riflemen are forced to fire upon an advance Warr patrol, alerting the Simian Warrs. The evacuees are cornered and would certainly have been destroyed except for the emergence of ASONE, who transmits a high-pitched vibration that freezes the attacking Warrs, while the humans escape through the pass and its protection.

Amy, concerned about the uncharacteristic planning and intelligence demonstrated by the Warrs sending out an advance patrol, believes some form of continuous monitoring and instructions must be coming from the Supreme One. As she studies the possible involvement of the Supreme One, that entity enters her mind. The powerful, pure hate directed at her fills her with fear. Without doubt, she is the target of the hate and realizes the Supreme One has been monitoring her activities. Even more, she realizes she is the target of a never-ending war for her and Levi's survival and the survival of the Human race.

Amy believes the Supreme One is probing minds of her and any Simian mind it targets to learn her plans and strategy. To protect against his probing mind, they resort to hand signing for their communication and cease any internal thinking in the Simian language, and as additional protection, they change from English to French. Additionally, she believes that a mind probe and alteration into a Simian mind will prevent probing from the Supreme One.

Once the Owens Valley army retreats to the second pass, drawing the Simian armies out of Owens Valley, her groups begin their migration toward the Desert Settlement. Now all groups converge on the Desert Settlement as the Owens Valley Army holds and retreats to the next pass, again delaying the two Simian armies, they then teleport into the next crisis at the Desert Settlement.

As they emerge at the settlement, they are confronted by many of the Simian females, which proves to be the next crisis. Dawn had been spending time with the females as instructed and has informed them of the alliance between the Techs and humans. Amazingly, this brought the Fems out of their self-inflicted docile existence. They learn from the Fems, and supported by Amy's continued research into the Simian computer, that the races (ie: Techs, Warrs, and Fems) have genetically pure DNA that doesn't mix in breeding. The Fems had long ago recognized the dangers of the genetic engineering and chose to become invisible through the ages, but not before they altered their own DNA to produce poison fangs in their fingers. This provided them protection and reinforced the common practice of keeping the Fems together and isolated. This had worked until now, but with the alliance being made between the humans and Techs for genocide against the Warrs, the Fems want to join the alliance.

The spokesperson for the Fems is an older female, appropriately renamed Mama by Levi. Mama's demeanor is assertive and authoritative, and Levi likes her immediately. She shows him little respect and treats him as an equal, if that, which he finds refreshing. After difficult negotiations, Levi appoints Mama the leader of the Fems and agrees to take her representative; he names Bambi, with his group. The Fems obtain equality with Humans and Techs; however, Moon would remain the overall Simian leader.

The Supreme Ones were a product of years of genetic engineering. They were created much larger than a Warrior and vastly more intelligent than a Technical Simian. Unfortunately, they were also psychotic, antisocial, and fiercely aggressive mental and physical giants. Fiercely competitive, these giants battled each other to establish total and absolute rule in the areas under their influence. The Simian home world is dying, so Satan, as it would be interpreted, chose to lead the next Simian migration to Earth, leaving the remaining four to fight over his leaving.

Satan arrives on Earth with 100,000 Simians and disperses them around the world, maintaining a major base location surrounding the Dallas/Ft. Worth area. He detects a vast intelligence (Amy),

25

which renews his jealousy, rage, and absolute hate. His whole being commits to this entity's destruction. He wages war against the Witch and the Humans by monitoring her activities through any Simian, and when necessary, taking over their minds and issuing orders through them. Satan enters the Witch entity's mind and almost succeeds in destroying her. This also is an additional source of rage, that any female could offer a challenge to his superior mind. He plans and initiates attacks through his Simian armies.

Levi wants to seize the opportunity, the absence of the colony's Warriors, and in his typical bravado, plans to liberate captured Humans, Techs, and Simian females. Assisted by five riflemen, # 7, # 5, Bambi, and Moon, they teleport to the San Diego colony located within a football stadium. Levi, Moon, and Bambi then teleport into the colony directly right into a trap. Amy is able to save them by doing what she calls a hard teleport to the lake by her facility, where she immediately alters Levi with gills. The Simians, being dense in composition, instantly sink and would eventually drown; however, Levi carries Moon and Bambi to safety, earning Bambi's trust and loyalty. They return to the colony, and through a narrowly won engagement, accomplish the liberation but not without injuries. The computer engineer, # 5, is severely injured.

Bambi promptly recruits the Fems to the alliance, and Amy chooses two of the older Fems to receive an instant download of lost Simian medical knowledge deciphered from the Simian computer. These new Simian medical experts begin the treatment and save # 5.

26

The group then returns to the Desert Settlement to discover a beehive of activity involving the cooperation of both Humans and Simians. Beyond preparing for evacuation, they are hard at work making the new weapons Amy had designed.

While at the settlement, Amy is again attacked mentally by the Supreme One. In his arrogance and total loathing, he threatens her, inadvertently revealing information that could have only been obtained by invading a mind close to Levi. The Supreme One knows where her facility is located and will eventually attack it and kill her. She needs to devise protection at the facility and calculates that the only way is to selectively counter the original effects of the Simian ray used to alter the environment and destroy technology. If she can accomplish this and reactivate her facility, she can defend herself.

Reactivation will require a permanent team to live at her facility with knowledge of engineering, mechanics, and other Earth technologies. This would have to be downloaded and could not be done with Humans without linking, and she was at her capacity. Simians are her only logical choice, so she chooses Fems above the breeding age, which Levi jokingly names the geriatrics team, or Greys. Mama is chosen to lead this team of Greys and is programmed with the required knowledge. The now committed and loyal Bambi becomes the leader of the Fems.

They teleport to the staging area with the team of Greys and organize the migration of the liberated Humans, Tech, Fems, stragglers from the Owens Valley, and the ever growing Human recruits to the

Desert Settlement. Taking additional riflemen and Fred for communication they teleport to the passes. Although behind schedule, the delaying action seems to be working.

The team goes to Amy's underground facility, but as they emerge from teleportation, the facility is under attack. An advanced team of Warrs are battering at the doors. The Supreme One also chose that moment to launch another attack on Amy's mind. Amy freezes in fear, but Levi is able to shock Amy from her paralysis of terror. She feels violated and determines that the Supreme One would never again gain access into her mind.

Amy's frightens the Warrs away by altering Levi's appearance to look like a Supreme One, and Levi gives the order, "leave this place ... Now!" to the Warrs. Any order coming from a Supreme One is complied with instantly, sending the frightened Warrs off in many directions. Unexpectedly, one of the Warrs, occupied by the Supreme One, attacks; but Levi is saved my Moon, Mama, and Bambi. The Warr's host body is killed, but the Supreme One's mind simply flows back into himself and his own body.

Amy is successful in countering the altered energy radiation of Earth but only within the confines of the altered radiated light within the facility, and electricity and all technologies are restored to her facility.

During the process of activating the facility, Amy downloads instructions and information through Levi revealing her existence to Mama. Amy is then able to issue instruction directly to the Greys through the Simian computer and manufactured

Simian speech simulators. Mama takes Levi out of the communication process and makes it known she is in charge of this facility and no longer needs him. This is new for him, not having to be in the middle of everything, and likes it, but this begins a friendly feud between them.

Defense is now Amy's main focus. The facility had originally been a government research facility, but also remained a military project, so the storage facilities had an arsenal including laser weapons. Cameras and lasers are installed throughout the facility with remote capabilities tied into her external computer network. She also has firing slots cut into the doors and cameras and lasers installed within to fire outward. Amy now has monitoring and defense capabilities within and without controlled directly by her. They feel comfortable about defense, and Amy now has a team and research facilities to occupy her vast intellect.

Amy now functions through both the facility and Levi, and they return their attention to the Desert Settlement. The Simian Gathering (mating season) has slowed the evacuation progress, but training is needed on the new weapons nearing readiness.

The new weapon is a spring-loaded spear with a pump up air pressure chamber. The human force applied as a spear combines with the release of the spring and air pressure to penetrate the thick hide of a Simian and kill. The Human migration arrives in increasing numbers, and they are recruited as the wielders of these new weapons. Teams begin training in this new army of foot soldiers she names appropriately, "Infantry."

As they make their rounds to observe the progress, they meet # 10, a trusted and loyal leader of the Simians of the Desert Settlement. Too late they realize # 10's mind has been taken over by the Supreme One. Levi is severely wounded by a sudden attack from a hidden sword. Amy immediately teleports them to a great height, allowing the free fall to disengage # 10 from his attack. Once separated Amy teleports Levi's dying body to the medical facility, leaving # 10 to fall to his death. Satan experiences the death of # 10, which enrages him more.

Amy is able to narrowly save Levi and repair his body, but the experience proves the dangerous threat the Supreme One poses and their own vulnerability. Moon and Bambi protect Levi continuously afterwards, but Amy demands Levi has continuous bodyguards. She takes Techs from the original loyal team and mentally adjusts them so the Supreme One cannot take over their minds as he had # 10.

Amy informs Levi of a renewed attack on her facility, and they watch through the laser cameras as the Warrs approach the hanger door carrying a large battering ram. Once in range, Amy fires the lasers, slicing interlacing paths through the advancing Warrs. The destruction is total and horrifying and decimates the attackers.

She senses barely controlled rage emanating from the surrounding group and teleports her trusted Simian allies away from a larger group to the Desert Facility. Her intent is to escape the hidden Supreme One, but as they reappear, Amy still detects the very slight presence of the Supreme One emanating from Bambi, the only one of the group not yet altered.

Levi's bodyguard and Moon prevent the Supreme One from using Bambi's finger fangs to kill Levi. They immobilize her, and a mental battle ensues to expel the Supreme One from Bambi's mind.

Satan's rage grows and he commits all his colonies to attack, and the Simian armies come from all directions. He continues his personal attacks, but with each failed attempt to destroy her, his rage and hate expands his abilities and makes him stronger. He uses these powers now through Bambi to lure Amy into her mind so he can destroy her in his mental trap.

Amy forces her mind through the barrier of hate into the crushing trap of his mental attack. She is now the warrior and fights the darkness of pure evil and hate with the light of love and goodness. It is a battle of light versus darkness, good against evil. This battle wages until Amy slowly and eventually wins the long struggle, and almost destroys the Supreme One with his own out of control rage. Bambi is saved from certain death to re-join the team.

The Desert Settlement mobilizes the Humans, Techs, and Fems. The only plan is to head east. The Owens Valley Army runs out of delaying passes and races toward them, followed by an angry horde of screeching Warrs. A confrontation is inevitable.

Trapped between two armies, Amy decides to attack the Simian army ahead in their path, but their forces must cross the bridges and destroy them before the armies following can cross. If they succeed, they can then engage the new Simian army threat one on one. They race to cross the Colorado River.

The Owens Valley Lancers join them, closely followed by the two Simian armies. A combined fighting retreat wages across the bridges and the bridges are blown, temporarily trapping the Simian armies on the other side. The Supreme One suffers another defeat but is successful in killing Dawn, which is a great loss to the communication team.

After reaching the temporary safety of the other side of the river, Amy turns her attention toward the next major threat. By astral projection, they locate the Phoenix Simian army mobilized and headed directly toward them, but more disturbing, they identify a fourth Simian army coming from Mexico. The situation seems hopeless, but Amy has learned from Levi to NEVER GIVE UP! They will fight to the end.

They outdistance the Phoenix army through a narrow mountain pass and hold the enemy's advance, while her armies attack the forth-Simian army. Al assumes Dawn's communications duties.

A battle ensues with the Mexican Simian army, and victory is in sight until the Supreme One enters the arena and alters the battle plans, trapping the Lancers. As sure defeat looms, another Lancer army comes out of nowhere to attack from the rear using Amy's battle techniques. Together, they quickly defeat the remaining Mexican Simian Army, and even the Fems join the attack, scoring a total victory.

Mosley had migrated to Mexico to escape the Simians, but since the last alien landing, his growing community is now threatened. Mosley meets a Lancer team sent out to recruit new humans. These Lancers train Mosley's army, and deploy to defend themselves and attack the Mexican Simians. They follow the Simians to this engagement, which they now join.

Mosley and Levi have a confrontation over who will lead, with Levi the victor. They immediately launch a defense at the pass. The Phoenix Simian army pours through the pass into a perfect trap Amy devises. Unfortunately, the Supreme One takes control and pulls them back just in time. Knowing the Supreme One will divert the other following armies east to catch them in a trap, Amy sends her armies east to avoid the trap.

The Supreme One is a constant hindrance to her plans, and there is only one way to prevent it... attack the Supreme One directly and kill him or at least put him on the defensive so he can't direct his armies. The plan relies on her ability to move matter as she does in teleports. Teleports involve a slow smooth transition of energy and matter both ways. This plan involves a slow build-up of energy and teleports matter suddenly to the other location. The results of this action will be an implosion at the transmitting end and an explosion at the other ... both deadly for any one or thing at either location and hopefully deadly to the Supreme One.

Amy senses the general location of the Supreme One's mental energy and feels there is a fair chance of getting close enough to risk the attempt. They know it will be extremely dangerous to Levi's body, but believe, as did Levi, that the risk is worth it. They take up a vantage position and watch the grouped Simian Warriors at the pass massing to overrun their defenses. The energy builds to maximum and instantly draws mass from the center of the grouped Warrs, then instantly deposits the mass at the Supreme One's location, devastating many Warrs and destroying the quarters of the Supreme One.

The latest defeat of Satan's plans by the unexpected help sends him into an out-of-control rage in which he destroys everything in his path but also takes him to levels of rage never before experienced. During his out-of-control rage, this energy of rage causes him to evolve further, and he learns to vent this rage into mental fireballs launched to kill. He practices this ability, killing Warrs until he exhausts himself and must rest. This action takes him far from his quarters and saves his life from the explosion but instills fear in him ... for the first time. He withdraws from his mental involvement in the war and takes flight to protect himself.

Amy searches for the Supreme One and eventually finds him trying to hide far from his compound. In time he would realize she was not capable of additional attacks of this type. This one attempt almost destroys Levi's body and would if they tried it again. For the moment however, the Supreme One's attacks cease, but what can she do?

Her clairvoyance also detects Simian armies coming from all directions, and it seems futile to continue as they were, and it would be best to just go home. Death appears certain, but she wants to kill the Supreme One as a final action to give the others a chance at life.

Realizing their home area of California is clear of Simian colonies, only the Phoenix Simian Army stands between them and home. Tired of running and enjoying a temporary absence of the Supreme One, Amy attacks. She deploys Lancers hiding behind two small mountains between which the pursuing Warrs will pass. She stages the Infantry in the distance to draw the Warrs through. The Fems deploy closer and appear to be resisting being herded by the Techs. As the Warrs charge, the Fems begin to escape and run back into the Warrs' ranks for protection. When all the Fems are dispersed within the Warrs, on signal the Fems attack the Warrs with their finger fangs. The fleeing Warrs that escape the initial attack meet the charging Lancers. Due to Amy's planning, the engagement provides another victory, and even the Fems collect the coveted black tooth trophy.

The Fems' commitment and success in the last battle inspires the next phase of her plan. Amy teleports a Fem into the Phoenix colony to infiltrate and recruit the Fems to free the imprisoned Humans and Techs. Bambi is sent with Moon and Mosley to the Mexico colonies for the same purpose. Mosley's Lancers would assist as a back-up plan. All those liberated would join the main group back at Amy's facility. Amy also wanted Moon and Bambi out of harm's way for their personal attack on the Supreme One, because it would likely be fatal.

Mama, acting independently, develops an artificial environment housing for a portable laser. This provides the means to continue the battle. Levi and Sparks, the Fem operator of the portable laser, use it to annihilate the second attacking Mexican

35

Simian army and clears the way to cross back across the Colorado River over a bridge farther south into the relative safety of California. They then teleport to attack the combined Simian army with similar results. Warr survivors would spread the word and ensure their home safety from future attacks, as long as the Supreme One was not alive to force them.

There is only one last duty to perform, and with their new weapon, they feel hopeful of survival. Amy teleports Levi and Sparks directly to the general location of the hiding Supreme One. She is positive that her personal presence through Levi would enrage the Supreme One and force the confrontation they need. She is correct, and for the first time they meet face to face. The Supreme One engages first. Amy expects a physical attack, but the Supreme One launches a ball of fire directly at Sparks before she can engage. Sparks and her portable housing explode, and shrapnel severely wounds Levi. This enrages the emerging ASONE as it takes over their minds. It gathers energy to repel the next fireball, but Levi's dying body falters as the Supreme One walks within range and plunges his sword into Levi. ASONE then does what Amy alone could never do. It launches one final attack of energy in a hard teleport and explodes itself, also killing the Supreme One.

Amy is left alone but intact in her facility. Levi made her promise to live on if he died. This is something she did not want to do, but she made a promise. Levi had said she now has communication with the outside world and she has her facility and could continue to help those of their charge.

36

There was one other thing she might be able to do. She has all of Levi's memories recorded, and she has his DNA. What are the possibilities?

Chapter 1
Levi's Death

Levi dead? Amy still could not believe it. The logic of her computer brain, supported by facts, proved it, but the emotional part, the self-aware part, didn't want to believe. All the logical evidence of argument proved his death. No symbiotic link to him existed that had been her outlet from the prison of darkness; she detected no sensory data coming from him at all; no monitoring links existed to Al, Fred, and Jimmy, that only came through Levi's mind. Worst of all, that spot in her that felt the warmth of his love now felt only frigid emptiness. She had even experienced his death and felt his pain; still her mind would not accept it. Her emotions churned within her, and the deep love she had for him would never let him go, and that love would never die.

She had no physical heart to break, but the imaginary beating and rhythm that had been synchronized with Levi's heart was no longer there. Without this anchor she felt her imaginary heart would explode, and she hoped it would explode and release her from this unbelievable pain and loss she felt. She almost wished she had never learned about emotions.

Her disembodied brain still remained very much alive, but the darkness engulfed her again. The panic of this prison of loneliness and darkness she had endured for over fifty years returned suddenly. It was not as bad as it had been before, because her facility had been reactivated and data inputs remained, to some extent allowing her to partially escape. A dim glow in the darkness existed, but it remained distant. She saw numerous camera inputs, data flowing into her mind from the equipment, input from the Simian computer they had installed, and she had communication to Mama. Still, the rich sensory inputs from Levi were gone, and she hadn't realized just how much of herself she had devoted to their symbiotic link. Her entire existence had been adjusted to living with and through Levi.

Her entire existence, now pathetically lost in her emotions, left her devastated. She no longer wanted to live, but that damned Levi had made her promise to live on without him. He had caught her in a weak moment and made her promise, and she would honor his wishes, but she needed time to adjust. She wished she could talk to him just one more time but wondered if she would rake his butt over the coals for getting killed or express just one last time how much she loved him.

Amy kept reliving those last few hours trying to identify where they went wrong and what they could have done differently. It was painful, because she might have done things differently if she had only known the hidden powers of the Supreme One. They really had no choice except to attack the Supreme One. It was, after all, a hopeless situation and Levi and she had already agreed to sacrifice their lives in the hope of killing the Supreme One, but with the development of the portable laser, their hopes had soared, and she believed they had a good chance of surviving. Mama had excelled in her efforts of developing this laser to work outside of the altered environment, and she praised her for it.

Their armies were being surrounded and attacked by an endless flow of Simian armies mobilized from all over the country and directed and controlled by the Supreme One. She realized that the situation was hopeless as long as the Supreme One was alive. Its out-of-control rage and hate toward her drove the Supreme One to destroy her and Levi as her outlet. They knew he would never stop coming, and it meant the destruction of all their friends, Human and Simian, and force the human race into extinction or slavery. His destruction had to be attempted.

There was no doubt the Supreme One would face them. His rage and total contempt for her would bring them face-to-face, and that was what they needed in order for Sparks to unleash the laser against him. As they materialized only yards from the Supreme One, she realized her mistake. The mental attack from the Supreme One presented a force she had not anticipated. She felt his mental attacks before, but never this strong. With a sinking feeling she realized that, unlike her link, his mental strength dissipated over distance, and the closeness resulted in an increase of power too strong for her to block.

She relived what happened next in slow motion, as if an observer, which in fact she was. ASONE sensed the vulnerability and began to emerge to take control of Levi and her as they began to totally merge. She was Levi and she was Amy, but they began to be something else...to become one. The new but familiar entity absorbed both of them and always, somehow, found incredible strength with the merging. Part of her mind watched, but most of her flowed into ASONE. She felt the rage as it drew its power and grew in strength to combat the Supreme One's mental attack. They battled rage against rage, but she knew ASONE would ultimately win. It would draw all the energy it needed from around them, but the Supreme One suddenly turned its attention toward Sparks and launched what looked like a fireball hurling toward her and the firing laser beam.

In retrospect, her logic analyzed the fireball, concluding it more akin to pure energy than fire. For the energy fireball to retain life it would have to be renewable from second to second fed from the Supreme One's mind. The power and denseness of this balled energy dispersed the laser and flowed up the red trail to the source and quickly engulfed Sparks. It was sudden and unexpected and caused the portable armored suit Sparks was wearing to explode, sending shrapnel tearing into Levi's body. The damage was severe and would normally have instantly killed Levi, but he was not Levi. ASONE held the body together and began to repair it, but just as suddenly the Supreme One launched another fireball directed at ASONE. She felt the energy flowing into her and even saw it. A blue aura began flowing into the entity, growing in strength and intensity as it wrapped around Levi's body and shot out the extended arm and fingers to focus the bolt of blue energy toward the fireball.

These forces collided in midstream battling in the air, showering sparks of blue and red. The air filled with the electric smell and sound of discharged energy. The forces seemed to seesaw back and forth in a timeless struggle of flowing energies, until ASONE gave one final push accented with the additional extension of its arm. The energy forces exploded into a cloud of smoke.

As the cloud slowly dissipated she felt and then saw the huge, towering form of the Supreme One charging through. The white, reptilian eyes held them in a hypnotic stare, and the black shark teeth flashed in a gleeful grin as the huge sword swung toward them.

She felt the rage. She radiated the rage and it was growing stronger realizing they had lost. Already the giant sword plunged into Levi's body. ASONE would do what the part of Levi would do. Levi would never ever give up and she felt that now, as she was part of ASONE. The body of Levi reached out and grabbed the Supreme One's tree trunk leg and held it in a vice-like grip. Already she felt the energy gathering stronger and stronger, building layer upon layer of energy. It was not her, although it was her that did it. The Supreme One felt it, too, and franticly tried to run, but the body of Levi held on as the energy continued to grow. The smile disappeared, and the white eyes stretched wide with fear as it kicked to get away. Suddenly, she felt the violent, crushing pain as the implosion popped, instantly teleporting a compressed mass of matter to another location, exploding there into a lifeless shower of crushed and blended bodies.

Only Amy survived, because she had never been there physically. Her mental link instantly vanished, leaving her back in her disembodied brain ten floors under the mountain. She did not have to see the body to know Levi was dead. She was alone, but bound by her promise to Levi.

Amy looked through the camera focused on her physical location and stared at the sanitary white, pristine room. There she was, a stainless steel dome ten feet in diameter surrounded under the stainless steel by a three-foot thick covering of lead. She remembered that had been Levi's first image of her. He called her an upside down teacup. This motivated her to create the visual image to present him compiled of his most pleasant female features. She remembered how shocking this image had been to him. He had called her beautiful. Now these created images were dormant. Levi could not enjoy them anymore.

She forced her thoughts back to the camera image. She had two cameras and two lasers in her room for her personal protection. She wondered if she would protect herself if anyone wanted to destroy her. Would that be breaking her promise? She would welcome the death though.

The square wooden table supporting the Simian glass dome computer was the only thing aesthetically that looked out of place in her room, but she was now happy to have it. At least it might give her purpose in life discovering the hidden secrets of the Simian technology.

She noticed the Simian computer tech, # 5, sitting at the computer working. She switched to the Simian computer input to see what he was working on, just to find him running diagnostics. She had hoped the information might be exciting enough to take her mind off her self-pity.

So far she had not responded to Mama or answered any of her inquiries, but she could not delay this forever. Mama and all the others needed to know about Levi's death. When Levi failed to show up at the gathering area west of Yuma, she knew the key leaders would head directly for her facility to find out what was going on.

Moon and Bambi had already been given their assignments to travel south with Mosley to free the Humans, Techs, and Fems from the Mexico Simian colony, since they had already destroyed the Warrior army. That would take a couple of weeks for them to return with those rescued, but Moon would know something was wrong. They had been inseparable since they met and were the closest of friends.

As Levi had once said, "If I was the Lone Ranger, Moon would be my Tonto."

Moon would sense Levi's absence. She dreaded telling Moon and, considering his possible reaction to the news, she had better give some thought to where she broke the news to him. That place would likely be destroyed. Maybe she should tell Bambi first to help calm him, but Moon deserved to be told directly by her.

Amy forwarded plans and instructions for a conference room to be laid out with monitors and speakers in both Human speech and the Simian screeching language. Plans for a more lifelike holographic generator were already underway, but this would have to do for now. She felt that using her own image would serve two purposes. It would focus their attention on her and give them some security in knowing that part of the team still remained alive, even though part of her being was already dead inside. She would present them with the sad news of Levi's death and hopefully a positive message of continued support to the new alliance of Humans, Technical Simians, and the Females of the Simian race.

Amy also sent a message to Mama through the internal intercom system to come to her physical location. Mama would understand that it meant she had a private message only for her. This would alarm Mama since she was used to the open communication throughout the facility, and she correctly anticipated Mama's reaction. As she watched through the camera, Mama burst through the doors in obvious panic. She stopped before the dome and waited. Mama had developed the portable laser and knew of their plans to destroy the Supreme One, and the savvy Mama figured things out quickly. Mama would know something was wrong.

Amy mustered up her strength and spoke to Mama saying, "Mama, the Supreme One is dead!" There was an audible sigh of relief, but she remained stiff in tension.

Mama screeched back, "What else?"

Amy spoke again in a level, barely audible voice and said, "Sparks is dead and so is Levi." Mama's reaction was not anticipated. She suddenly slumped down and wept. Her huge body rocked and heaved in sync with her wails of grief reverberating through the complex. Huge tears rolled down her face, matting her golden fur. Never had Amy seen an emotion of this kind from a Simian before and was momentarily stunned. She also knew the emotion was not for Sparks. It was not that Mama didn't care for Sparks, but Simians did not allow themselves the luxury of emotions. It was bred out of their race, or at least trained out. Why now did she weep for Levi?

Suddenly, it dawned on her that Mama, even through all the arguments between her and Levi, had learned to love him. Somehow it was allowed when it didn't deal directly with other Simians. Amy had watched them so often mentally fence and insult each other with no small amount of laughter from her. They had truly liked each other, and Mama had given Levi an outlet he so desperately needed then. Mama never treated Levi with respect and awe like all the others. They had not been friends at first, but Levi needed that normality in his life at that time to counter the loneliness of his existence. It seemed ironic, but Levi needed that lack of respect, and Mama gave him all of that he could handle. Somehow, during this bantering back and forth they developed a real friendship that neither would allow themselves to admit. Now it came gushing out of Mama like she had lost her child. Amy felt sorry for Mama and added her grief to her own.

Mama's wails alerted the complex, and the other Greys came rushing in and crowded into her circular room. As one, they wanted to know the cause of her grief, but it was # 5, having heard the conversation, that explained to the others what had happened. She was thankful to him for saving her the arduous ordeal again. They were stunned to hear the news, but none broke down as Mama had done. They had not interfaced with Levi all that much and

46

didn't realize how important he had been. At this point little would change in their world.

Mama's outburst subsided slowly, and she regained control of herself. To occupy her mind and gain some semblance of control, she immediately began searching through the written instructions and plans. She quickly grasped the meaning and importance of the conference room and started issuing instructions to her team of Greys. Amy knew that the facilities would be ready when they were needed.

It had been a very long time since she had been without the links from Fred, Jimmy, and Al and now she missed them. She had gotten used to the added stress of the constant data inputs, and now without them, she felt the loneliness and absence of mental activity. It also disturbed her not to know what was happening in the field. Of course nothing could be done about it now, but knowing would be helpful. All the armies and the migration were relatively safe now on the west side of the Colorado River, or should be. Their last instructions had been to continue toward to the Owens Valley and to the valley close to her underground facility. That remained a good plan, which would take about a week to reach her at the speed they had been achieving. At least she could communicate with them through the conference room gathering area once the leaders arrived.

Occupying herself for a week would be the problem. Her mind must remain busy or she would fall into depression at the loss of Levi, but she had little to focus on. She had only the internal facility, the Simian computer, and her own mind to challenge her. She wished Levi could challenge her with new abstract thought, but now she must evolve and provide that abstract thought and challenge herself.

The Simian computer had kept its secrets far too long. She decided this would be her immediate challenge to occupy her mind. Vast amounts of knowledge could be learned from it at least she hoped so. Of course all this was assuming she could decipher the computer language and its storage procedure.

The storage of data in the Simian computer appeared haphazard, not at all logical as in an Earth computer. She had not found the secret yet. All technical data seemed to be stored at random and in incomplete packages. It was like a fast flash of information so incomplete that little data could be retrieved. She had been successful in pulling some history of the Simians from the computer but as in flash card of images. Technical data remained hidden almost as if it was encrypted, which it most likely was. If so, it was at a level so complex she had not detected a pattern or formula. Well, she had nothing but time now so this must be her challenge. She could almost hear Levi now.

Levi would say, "You can do anything if you set your mind to it, so just do it!" If she could analyze DNA patterns, surely she could find a hidden pattern built into the Simian computer. After all, she had been designed and activated to function as the largest capacity and fastest computer ever built at the peak of Earth's greatest technology. Her four-foot diameter human cell brain surpassed the combined total of all the so-called Super Computers ever built. There were even two of these Super Computers at her disposal within the complex. They had once been her back up but were now totally integrated into her processing capabilities. She began now by downloading the vast amount of random data from the Simian computer into these interconnected Super Computers where it would be processed and searched for a pattern. So, she began the search...hour after hour and day after day.

This processing could take some time, so she turned part of her attention to planning the future of the Human, Techs, and Fem races, assuming there was going to be a future.

There had been other Simian armies en route to destroy them, but she had no idea how many. She hoped that Simian survivors of the last two battles where Sparks had decimated the Warrs with the laser would spread the word that an attack was useless against their new weapon. Also, with the Supreme One dead, there would be no blind rage forcing them toward that destruction. She believed they would turn around and go home and leave California to them. That was the hope anyway, but they could not count on that. At this point, however, it was now only a bluff, since the Supreme One destroyed their only portable laser. This would have to be one of the next projects of Mama's team of Greys. Mama said they had been building two, but only one was ready to go. She passed on the request to Mama to get the second one up and running as soon as possible, knowing it would be done.

They would have to set up a guard watch system to warn them in the remote chance of an attack, and of course the Desert Settlement would have to relocate to the west side of the Sierra Mountains. It would be a hard sell to Al and General Harken, but the Desert Settlement extended too far away from her protection now, what little there was. True, the Phoenix Simian colony had been destroyed, and they were probably quite safe, but the fact remained that it was too far away to help should trouble come. She could not monitor them or teleport without Levi. No, they would have to relocate. The area west of her mountain range was very beautiful and fertile land and shouldn't be much of a hardship, other than the travel. The most positive aspect, there were NO Simian colonies left in California, certainly none she knew about. Yes, this was best. Her facility would be central to all and would be a perfect command center and protected retreat if it ever became necessary.

The underground facility was huge, consisting of ten levels of sprawling space for living quarters, cafeterias, shops of all kinds, and best of all, operating at full capacity with reactivated technology. All the trades could move inside, while the majority required for farming, ranching, and protection could continue to live outside. This time they could actually build homes to live in. It could be a decent life now, hopefully.

As soon as she allowed herself to think of stability and comfort, Levi's memory jolted her. Levi would never live in comfort and isolation as long as there were Humans living under the constant fear of the Simians. Her plans must include expansion and liberation of the Human race, but damn, she needed time and how in the hell could she propose to wage war when she couldn't see beyond her doors?

Moon once mentioned that not all-Simian technology was lost with the alteration caused by the mysterious blue-ray that destroyed Earth's technology. According to Moon, some of the Simian technology did not require electricity, but the technology was lost mostly because the Warrior Simians did not understand the more complicated things and did not want to acknowledge the need for the Technical Simians. The Simian computer was evidence of that, if she could just unlock its secrets.

After days of research, well past the time she should have detected a pattern, it became apparent no pattern existed. Nothing existed but minute images but otherwise just gibberish. Something was wrong. Levi always reminded her that she thought too deeply to see the simple solutions. What was she missing? Information passed back and forth, but without substance. Okay, look for something simple. She focused the camera on the computer and just observed. She stared at the curved glass dome, which also served as the keyboard. The dome enclosed a complicated matrix of crystals of different color and size set into a honeycomb of extremely fine hair-like nest floating within the liquid supplied from her life support reservoir. The flow of this liquid provided the interconnect transmitting the chemical language between her brain and the Simian computer. No sound or vibration could be detected that could be part of the communication or file storage. So, she watched and looked for the simple things. Within the dome, the aura of many colors emanated from the various crystals. As she concentrated on the rhythm of the colors, she thought she detected a possible complex pattern. She concentrated more intently, and yes, it was not random. The rotation of colors repeated itself in a long cycle of ever changing colors and complicated mixtures. Could this be the secret?

She quickly searched her data banks and found reference to color and phase diversity modulation. This technology had once been used to provide a virtually unlimited number of light paths, each color doubling the overall communication capacity. It began to make sense now. By varying the color of the light, the Simian computer could approach infinity with its processing and storage capacity. This advanced technology far exceeded her current abilities, even though she had rewritten her programming for greater efficiency.

In this case simplicity was not the solution. Complexity generated the oversight, but the concept, now that she recognized it, was a simple natural progression of their technology. She needed to think like a Simian. Earth's computers operated on a single dimension, which she had tried, unsuccessfully, to relate to the Simian computer. The Simian computer obviously operated on an almost infinite number of multiple dimensions. This technology greatly exceeded Earth's level at its peak. Finally, her excitement blossomed. She now had the key to unlock the Simian Secrets.

She stopped the processing in the Super Computers and began to purge the files of data. It would never be possible to even store this vast amount of information, much less decipher it. All she really needed was the synchronizing key and timing of the color rotation for reference. There would be more than enough capacity in the Simian computer, far beyond the capacity of her current abilities. But, then the Simian technology could now be used by her to multiply her abilities to infinity. Yes, she was excited.

Once she knew what to look for, the matching decipher key was quickly developed, but her thoughts quickly turned toward re-engineering and modifying her internal programming. Even though the crystal generator could store and process at levels of infinity, the limiting factor, bottleneck, would be chemical communications used between the Simian Computer and herself. She quickly realized that the internal operations of her physical human brain could not be modified and, even if it could, she had no internal crystal light generator. No, the programming modification would have to be limited to one of her external Super Computers. A crystal generator would have to be converted to operate on electricity and integrate it as the new reference into the Super Computer.

For the short term, some of the Simian data could be deciphered into the external facilities to search for and learn the Simian computer technology required to make the conversion. For the long term plan, she would need to obtain two additional Simian computers. This would be one of the second projects she would assign to Moon. The first project was far more pressing and she needed Moon to show up soon for that one.

Over the next few days she completed the decipher key and set the Super Computer to work searching for the technical data and transferring and converting it to standard language. As it turned out, it wasn't that difficult. It was more of bypassing some of the end equipment that converted the information to the chemical language, and in doing so, would actually increase her communication with the Simian computer.

In her design the Simian computer would continue to operate with her synthetic life blood and the reprogrammed Super Computer would then be able to communicate directly through electronic sensors embedded in her brain, replacing the chemical conversion. Since the Super Computer would be communicating in the exact language of the Simian computer, the process should be smooth and efficient. She still didn't understand the entire process but sufficiently enough to make it work.

All they needed now were the Simian computers, one on line and interfaced with the Super Computer and the other as a redundant back up and fail-safe protection. Her human brain would continue to be isolated from the Simian thought process and protected should there be an equipment failure. She would, however, be able to monitor the external Super Computer and directly operate through it, while protecting herself. The plan was flawless and Levi would have been proud. This gave her some comfort. Levi's approval and praise rewarded her and were what she had always sought.

On the sixth day after Levi's death Mama announced that the holograph system Amy had designed had been completed and installed in the conference room and waited her testing. Amy switched to the cameras in the conference room and watched as her full-sized holographic form

54

materialized on the stage. None but Levi had ever seen her created image, but this image was as much a part of her now as her emotions. For the first time she saw herself as Levi had seen her. She created the image just for Levi, meshing all the qualities he found appealing, and now she could see herself exactly as he had seen her.

What she saw was a petite and truly beautiful woman. She had long raven-black hair flowing free around a small pear-shaped face. The complexion was darker, almost Asian in appearance, with a small, short nose and full, slightly red, cupid-bow lips. There were deep dimples in her cheeks, which showed very prominently when her mouth and lips stretched in movement. Accenting the face was a pair of slightly wide set eyes that tended to give more depth. They were large eyes of a deep liquid green. Levi had said she was beautiful and that her eyes were hypnotic. She suddenly smiled as she remembered Levi's first reaction at seeing her image in his mind. He had been shocked and had stumbled and fallen to the ground dumbstruck.

The virtual physical body she created for Levi later had also been a vision of perfection, according to Levi. The holographic Amy standing before her now was small, slightly over five feet tall, appearing to be just over one hundred pounds, round but firm hips, narrow waist, small round firm breasts, little hard nipples that protruded, slim but muscular legs, flat stomach, and all in the right proportion, according to Levi. She had never bothered to create clothing for Levi's vision of her, but now she added a regal looking short green dress with a golden belt and necklace. As a final touch she added a small golden band on her head slightly resembling a small crown, but she felt those that would come to see her would expect her to be a figure of authority...queenly.

Al, Iron Eyes, and Moon had already heard her voice speaking through Levi's vocal cords when she introduced herself before at this facility. They would remember this voice, and it should help reinforce their belief in her. It was important that these three believe and accept her. They could then explain to all the others exactly who Amy was and how she had been the power behind Levi. Hopefully, this would give the others some confidence in her and not be totally bereft of hope for the future with the loss of Levi. It would take all her effort to present a positive impression and provide this hope for the future. Although he was gone, and she was lost without Levi, they could not sense this. They must have some optimism.

The timing played out perfectly. The next morning she watched the gathering of leaders approach the main doors as Mama met them. To her surprise Moon and Bambi were with them. They must have made extremely good time to catch up to the migration, but then Moon would already know something was amiss and would have prodded them along. Mama led the gathering into the large conference room prepared as she had instructed. She watched the wide-eyed awe settle on the visitors as they witnessed and experienced the sophistication of 21st Century technology in all its operational glory.

These were the first visitors that had been allowed to enter her facility, and they suddenly transitioned from a medieval time directly into the 21st Century. The shock would inspire awe and wonder, part of her plan.

The inside was well lit, clean, and modern looking. They were led through the huge central indoor parking area, down sparkling hallways, and into an elevator that hardly any of them had ever heard about, much less seen. The elevator doors opened on the second level down to a view of sparkling glass walls lavishly engraved and polished tile floors. The shock shown apparent on all their faces. She wanted them to see the working technology and facility.

There was Al and General Harkin from the Desert Settlement and Iron Eyes and several of the Chiefs from the Owens Valley. The group also included Fred and Jimmy who, along with Al, had been the communications for the armies. Moon, Bambi and three of Levi's Simian bodyguards completed the assembled group.

Mama hand-signed for them all to take seats including the Simians as they migrated to the prearranged larger chairs. They all sat around a huge highly polished cherry wood conference table, but all facing the platform area. Some of Mama's Fems delivered drinks for the members of various choices, even coffee to the surprise of some. The participants seemed so out of place, which they were. The stage was set.

As they watched, Amy made her appearance in her regal green dress and golden tiara, gradually materializing in front of them. The holographic image slowly became real with solid looking depth and realistic size. As she viewed from the room cameras, she had to admit her image looked lifelike, real, and very impressive. Al, Iron Eyes, and Moon knew instantly that this could only be Amy, but the others stared in awe and wonder. Everyone waited in silence not knowing what to expect.

Her image looked at each of them as if studying them and reading their minds. After long minutes she said, "I am Amy. I am the invisible part of Levi. I have been with him always as he has been with you. I know you all, but you have never known me. I show myself now only because Levi is dead." Silence filled the room as this registered in their minds. It was obvious that all those gathered had already figured that out and this news was not unexpected. They just wanted confirmation, which they now received. After a moment she continued, "Levi died defeating the Supreme One. He forfeited his life to protect you, and I promised him to live on to continue to help and lead you in this war. I can do this if you so desire, but you must decide for yourself."

"I worked with Levi and through him before, but I am now unable to leave this facility. I am alive, but not a living being in the sense that I have a body. I am a living computer housed in this facility and this body you now see I created for Levi only. Now you must decide among yourselves if you will accept my leadership." With that her image dissolved.

They really had no choice, but she had decided it was better that they willingly accept her and not force herself upon them. The alliance had been built around Levi from their point of view. As soon as they thought about it they would understand that it had always been Amy's leadership jointly with Levi and nothing had really changed ... except for the loss of Levi.

After she, well her image, left she continued to watch and monitor the activities of the group. There was much sorrow expressed and Moon was visibly upset as she knew he would be. Bambi was beginning to understand the mystery of Levi now and like Mama, liked the idea of a female in charge. Al and Iron Eyes already knew the truth and were admitting to the others their secret knowledge. Jimmy's face shown pale with shock. She knew that Jimmy had developed a strong kinship, even love as a second father figure, and Levi had even referred to Jimmy as his son and loved him like a son. Levi was not alone in that love. She liked this young man too, but Jimmy never even knew she existed. Well, now he did, and it was slowly dawning on him how much he missed before.

Jimmy was really quizzing Iron Eyes and Al about how things had worked. He had blindly accepted the fact of the downloads he received and that he had been one of the trusted communicators, but he now realized that it was Amy's powers that enabled the telepathic communications through Levi.

As they talked the conversation slowly turned to the loss of Levi and all began telling stories of Levi and the legend that had grown around him. They talked about the superhuman fights Levi had with so many Simian Warriors, how he had almost died with a Simian sword thrust through his stomach, his miraculous recovery, how the ghost had brought Dawn back with the medicine Levi needed, the magical abilities Levi had demonstrated, also how Levi had found the lost cache of equipment buried in the lost mine, and finally the telepathic communication Levi had established with Fred, Al, and Jimmy. All these things were beginning to make sense now to everyone. It had always been Amy, and they were realizing that and the mystique of the apparent magic was now making sense.

She listened to the conversation and relived those moments with them. Yes, she would miss Levi as they would, but none knew just how much more had transpired between Levi and her. That was private. The love they had shared was none of their business, but she imagined they would also realize that fact.

Finally, Al brought up the subject they had all avoided.

Al said, "So what do you think? We want to let Amy continue to lead us?"

Moon signed with great exaggeration and force, "I owed Levi and now I know I also owe Amy my life... many times over! I and my followers will remain loyal to Amy no matter what."

Surprisingly, Jimmy was the next to voice an opinion.

Jimmy simply said, "Me too."

Al and Iron Eyes looked at each other and laughed out loud at Jimmy's breach of protocol but shook their heads in agreement, as did all around the conference table. What else were they going to do?

Amy materialized again on the stage. This time she was smiling and asked, "Have you decided?" Of course she already knew, but didn't want them to feel as if she had been spying on them.

Her image looked directly at each one as they spoke in agreement, thanking each one individually. Next she said, "In all honesty, I'm not sure what all I can do without Levi, but I will do my best for you." She went on to lay out the plans she had come up with so far concerning the use of the facility, the relocation of the Desert Community to the western side of the mountain, assignment of all the groups to specific areas, and other special projects she wanted.

Her first assignment was for Moon. In reality it was two assignments, but one required his personal attention. She assigned him to organize a group of Simians to retrieve the Simian computers from the San Diego and Fresno colony space ships for the implementation of the conversion of the Super Computer to Simian language. She tried to explain what was going to happen but quickly realized her explanation flew over everyone's head. Levi would have said, "Just fucking tell them what you want and stop trying to explain. They will do it." Levi always converted her meanings into simple terms that they would understand, but she would have to remember to do that now.

The second assignment Moon must do personally. Humm How would she put it? Finally she just said, "Moon, I need you to go to the location I will give you and find a piece of the Supreme One and bring it back here."

Moon's normally red eyes flashed black in shock, and rightfully so. He would not be able to understand this request. Of course, he would go, but

61

he had to wonder why? Moon said nothing, but the questions were all over his face. How could she possibly explain DNA research to Moon or anyone left alive for that matter? So, she said, "I need a sample of his tissue to do research on. It is research you can't understand at this time, but necessary." She waited for a few seconds and went on carefully. "Levi died with the Supreme One in a hard teleport." Moon had witnessed a hard teleport and would remember the massive devastation it caused. She let that sit for a moment.

Suddenly, Moon realized that where there were parts of the Supreme One there would also be parts of Levi as well. He looked frightened. She knew there would not be much of either body considering the outcome of both implosion and explosion of a hard teleport, the exposure to insects and animals, and decomposing time. Still, there should be something to retrieve.

The others were getting the implication of this discussion as well and none felt comfortable nor did they envy Moon the job she was assigning him. They all had jobs to do, so they were happy when she dismissed them to their tasks.

When ASONE launched the hard teleport there was nothing she could do, but she remembered the location precisely. The location wasn't that far away. ASONE had used a location where it had been before. The location lay in the Owens Valley just outside the pass where the entity had held the Simian Warriors frozen. ASONE had emanated an unnatural high-frequency pitch, which paralyzed the Simians' nervous system and gained enough time for the Owens Valley Tribe to pass behind the safety of the pass. Moon would remember this location well. After ASONE had withdrawn, Levi collapsed from the strain, and Moon had carried him to safety. It shouldn't take Moon more than two days to travel there, find a sample, and return; hopefully, with some remains of the Supreme One.

As instructed, Moon assigned those of the original and trusted group of Techs to go to San Diego and Fresno to retrieve the Simian computers. Of late, they had been Levi's bodyguards, but were no longer needed for that task. These Techs could be trusted absolutely, but as extra insurance for success, she assigned the last remaining Simian Computer technician, # 5, to go with them to verify the condition of the computers and make sure they were properly disconnected and packed.

All the others were off to spread the word of Levi's death and change in the command structure, such as there was, and to organize the new settlements. She had to depend on her captains now to get things done without any oversight. Additionally, there would be a major delay in communication waiting on reports. Damn she missed Levi. Without him she was a prisoner of the facility and of her haunting memories.

She would have daily contact and reports from Fred and Jimmy as to the progress, problems, and needs. Since these two had been part of her monitoring and communications network, everyone would be accustomed to receiving information and instructions from them, and the captains would also be used to reporting to them. It was a natural function to continue, but she wished she did still have communication through them.

Having little timely communications or information about what transpired outside her doors would continue to be her biggest problem. She had total access to information within her facility but remained blind beyond the camera distance outside the doors. With Levi gone her ability to astral project was also gone. Through those out of body experiences she could have surveyed the world, and now she wished they would have done just that. They had discussed it many times, but kept putting it off as one of those things they would do in the future. Now no future existed.

Obviously, there had been another Simian invasion fleet land on Earth and her best estimate suggested that it had landed within the last two years. This meant there could be hundreds of thousands of new Warriors on Earth to deal with, but they would be in confusion now with the loss of the Supreme One. This would work to their advantage, because the individual Simian colonies would now be autonomous and fighting for control and hopefully, with each other. This should take their focus off of her and the Humans and Technical Simians living in freedom...for a while anyway.

Even though the immediate threat from the Simians was minor, it would be necessary to set up a watch at all the major entry points to warn of any incursion or attack. Thankfully, they had blown many of the bridges up and few river crossing existed that needed to be watched. Sooner or later it would come and they needed to be ready. The armies would need to remain at the ready, and she would have to complete her research on the Simian technology in hopes of developing better defenses and weapons.

Her focus turned to Mama standing in front of the platform addressing her. Mama could have addressed her from anywhere and she would have heard, but Mama had chosen this location. She realized Mama understood this, but must seem more comfortable looking at her as if she was a real person. It seemed strange how Mama gravitated to her visual. So she regenerated her holographic image on the platform and said, "Yes Mama. How can I help you?"

Somewhat nervously Mama said, well screeched, "I think the meeting went well."

Suddenly, Amy realized that Mama accepted her as a real person and intended to treat her as such. Somehow, this made Amy feel pleased. Mama had always accepted her as important and the power behind Levi, but she had always been professional only, giving reports and receiving instructions. Now Mama was speaking to her ... Amy the person. The visual and almost physical shape had made her unexpectedly real to Mama, and Amy was filled with delighted.

Amy said, "I think so too, Mama. Do you like my image?"

Mama responded, "Not bad for a human."

She did not know if Mama meant it to be funny or was being honest, but it did tickle her sense of humor. It struck her as truly humorous, and Amy responded with an uproarious audible laugh. She then said, "Mama, I hope you understand that many will be coming to me now since Levi is gone."

Mama looked sad then and said, "Yes, I understand, and it will not be a problem." After a long silence Mama then said, "I am sorry about Levi. I will miss him, too."

That statement told her volumes about Mama. It was obvious that Mama now understood much more about the relationship than Amy had given her credit for. Amy looked into the big ugly face of this stone faced female Simian and saw the grief Mama now showed ... grief for Amy and for herself.

Her ability to communicate had drastically improved with the addition of the visual and expressions to compliment the vocal communications. Yes, this had been a great idea to create the holographic image.

Chapter 2
Levi's Conception

* Moon *

Moon left immediately for the mountain pass in Owen Valley. He traveled alone so he could reflect on his time with Levi. Bambi seemed to want to go with him but also understood his need to be alone. Bambi and he had feared that Levi was dead, but Amy's confirmation made it all real, and he would have to learn to deal with the loss.

Moon was not content to treat the charge Amy had given him lightly. It was a simple task: find parts of the Supreme One and bring it back to her. He didn't understand why, but if Amy wanted it, he would provide it, but he wanted more. Levi had died killing the Supreme One, and he wanted his revenge, too. Levi had been everything to him, his leader, his teacher, and his friend. He had never really had a friend before Levi, and now he was dead. He was dead because of the Supreme One, and he hoped he could find something of the Supreme One so he could destroy it, burn it, stomp it, or just piss on it... anything to show his total contempt.

After his emotional outburst and release during the trip, he sobered. By the time he reached the location he had calmed and settled into a more respectful mood, remembering that Levi's body would also be among the debris.

A few miles before he reached the objective he noticed a small white animal following him. The humans called it dog. It was so small it posed no threat at all. It seemed more curious than anything... pacing him. He briefly wondered if it was good to eat but quickly dismissed the thought because of its small size. It measured hardly larger than his foot, even with its long, thick fur. It consisted mostly of fur, legs, and ears. On closer examination it appeared to be young and not even full size. The dog seemed to have no fear of him, and eventually it began running in circles around him, careful to keep a respectful distance. He found it humorous to watch its antics.

After a while he forgot about the dog and began looking around the area for signs of the Supreme One. This was definitely the location. Disruption of the ground showed evidence of an explosion, and it was easy to see. He began kicking over rocks and scratching around in the dirt for signs of the Supreme One. He could see splintered black bones, but they were small, too small to mess with.

Suddenly, something glittered in the desert sun off to his right. As he approached, he recognized the golden locket Levi always wore. He bent to dig it up and noticed the dog again... curious with its actions. It seemed fearless and began digging beside him. He screeched in laughter and startled the dog. It yelped and ran off but circled to watch again. Soon it was back and digging at nothing in particular, just mimicking. Moon reached out his giant hand and let his finger touch the small dog. It jumped but began wagging its tail. The wagging started at the end of the tail and continued up its back all the way to its neck. It smelled his finger intently then licked it. He had never experienced this kind of reaction from an animal. He liked it.

Moon continued his search, followed closely by the dog. Soon the dog began its own search. Moon watched the dog as it circled, sniffing the ground. It seemed to find what it was looking for and began digging again. Shortly, it was uncovering something black and trying to drag it out. As Moon approached he saw several large black teeth attached to a section of jawbone. This was what he had been looking for... something unquestionably belonging to the Supreme One. How appropriate it was trophy teeth. He would have loved to present it to Levi. The thought of Levi saddened him again.

He gathered up the section of jawbone and stuffed it, along with the locket, into his pack strapped to his back. He was done here and now anxious to get back to Amy. As he started back he stopped at the edge of the disrupted desert floor to give one last look at Levi's final resting spot and give one last show of respect.

After a couple of miles travel at his normal running pace he noticed the dog at his side, laboring to keep up. Apparently it intended to follow him wherever he went. He felt sorry for the little thing and reached down and scooped it up in his huge hand. At first it struggled to get away but soon realized it wasn't being hurt and settled down, content to be carried. After a few more miles he swung it up over his shoulder onto his pack where it rested with its front legs over his furry shoulder and its face next to his neck. Moon could feel the warm breath on his neck and hear the panting. It made no effort to jump off. It would have been a long jump for the little animal, but it seemed content to just ride. It weighed nothing and he soon began to enjoy the company.

After a few more miles he stopped to drink from a stream. The dog jumped off when he got down on his knees and began to lap up water as if it was starving. Moon tossed it some rancid meat from his pack and it leaped on it and began ripping it into bite-sized pieces, which it hungrily consumed. While it was eating, Moon began to rub its fur, feeling the texture and enjoying watching the dog's tail wag even faster.

When he stood to resume his journey, the dog pranced and leaped up on his leg and began clawing... obviously wanting up again. Moon screeched his laughter again, but the dog seemed undisturbed this time. It remained standing on its hind legs stretched to full length, clawing. Even stretched to its fullest it only reached halfway to his knee. Touched by its actions, Moon again scooped it up and swung it over his shoulder. The dog immediately began nuzzling and licking his ear. Moon decided he liked this dog, and if it wanted to stay with him it could.

* Amy *

She had a lot to think about. Now that everyone looked to her for the answers, she felt the stress. How would they survive? How would they live? Worst, how would she explain what she intended to do, and how could she accomplish it all?

There were three races depending on her. She excluded the Warrior race; they were hopeless.

They would war... no matter what! Even the young Warriors of their group were running off as soon as they reached maturity. They would eventually wind up in some Warrior colony to be battled later. Even so, she did not have the heart to destroy them when they were children.

The Technical Simians and the Female Simians were completely separate races since they did not combine genes at fertilization, but necessary to propagate. Each race remained pure. She believed this trait had been genetically designed long ago by the Females to protect the purity of their race. They had been afraid that mating with the genetically engineered Warrior Simians would dilute the Female genes, and rightfully so. No matter now... it was done, but she had been considering just how to reverse this process, and if she should.

Another concern was the fact that this war on Earth would last generations. There were simply too many Warrior Simians dispersed on Earth, and more invasions en route. Without technology, Humans were physically too weak to fight the Warriors; even the Technical Simians were of low numbers. Assuming they were a match..., which they weren't. She did not deceive herself, they had been lucky so far. Fighting on horseback had provided the extra edge for the humans, but her plans and strategy had provided their victories. This was in large part due to the communications network that died with Levi. Hopefully, in time, this network could be reconstructed, but she needed a better way.

No, if they were to survive, they needed a new breed of combatants, one that combined the best traits from Humans, Techs, Fems, and more, much more. Like making a stew... throw them all in a pot and create a new race of inhabitants for Earth, one that could combat against Warriors. Of course, she was referring to genetically engineering this new race, a race that was bigger, stronger, smarter, and with more abilities. This race would have to be able to defend and defeat the Warrior Simian race without technology.

This part of her plan would have to wait. Her most important priority, above protecting her extended family, focused on bringing Levi back! It could be done. She had his DNA and she had all his memories stored in her data banks. It was just a matter of combining the two, but she had other thoughts on exactly to accomplish this. She could clone Levi's body... just as it existed or build a better body.

This was one of the reasons she wanted some DNA from the Supreme One. The mental process of a Supreme One was flawed, but many characteristics were superior, its size for one, including the brain capacity. If she could engineer a human brain into the space allotted for a Supreme One's brain, Levi's mental capacity would almost double. Imagine a highly intelligent, twelve-foot Levi. She chuckled at the thought of a smart and macho Levi.

Genetically engineering this super being was not the problem. The problem was surviving Levi's wrath once he realized what she had done to him. He would be livid. Once he had all of his memories back from the eighty-two years of his life, he would hate her for the liberties she had taken with his new body. No, she would have to try to keep him from looking like a monster, as he would call it. She would have to, as best she could, keep him looking Human. That might save her. She thought he would accept the greater intelligence and massive size, even the more efficient dual thumbs on each hand, as long as he looked mostly human, but the wings would be hard to add without him noticing.

Her musing ended when Mama came into the conference room. As last time, she walked to the stage area and waited.

Amy brought her holographic image to life and said, "Hello Mama, may I help you?" Mama had become, well, she had assumed the position of liaison between all visitors requesting to see her, and Amy welcomed Mama's intervention. Mama also remained in the room when anyone was there. It was as if Mama was protecting her, but Amy's presence was only electronic imagery and needed no protection. Even if she did require protection, Mama had installed lasers on the cameras in the conference room. Amy could have defended herself well, but Mama's presence provided an air of formality, which seemed advisable. It supported her image as leader, and Mama instinctively recognized this.

Mama signed, "The laboratory is set up to your specifications and we can begin analysis of the Supreme One's DNA as soon as Moon gets back."

Mama's comments completely surprised her. She had never mentioned that they would be analyzing the Supreme One's DNA. Well, she had stated to Moon that she wanted to do some research.

Mama had understood immediately, and she probably understood why.

Amy had downloaded a great deal of Human technology, including her expanded science of DNA, into Mama when she brought her and the other Fems to the facility. Now she prided herself for her forethought, even though she never expected to have to use it. With Levi gone she lost the ability to download knowledge. Mama would be very helpful now in assisting her in the DNA research that was required.

"You understand what I am attempting to do, don't you?"

Mama signed, "You are going to bring Levi back with a new body. I think you want to mix some of the Supreme One's DNA with that of Levi's to make a stronger Levi."

Amy couldn't believe how canny Mama's perception appeared to be, but she obviously excelled. She asked, "What do you think of the idea?"

Mama signed, "I know you can do this thing, and we all want to see Levi back. If you can make him better I think it is a fantastic idea. It will bridge any gap between our races to have a combined new race."

"Huh? What do you mean by a new race?"

Mama signed, "If both Levi and you have new combined bodies, there will be offspring and a new race of leaders will develop to direct both Simian and Humans."

Holly shit! It all clicked in her mind. Mama was absolutely right. If she could transfer Levi's memories into an engineered body, certainly she could transfer her mind, a part of it anyway, into an engineered body. She could be real... finally. It had been obvious to Mama, but she had never even considered this possibility. Abstract thought again. Damn, even Mama had it. No matter where it came from, it was a damn fantastic idea.

Her image was smiling hugely as she said, "Mama, you are a genius, and you are absolutely correct." Mama's face split into a broad grin at her comment, but Amy barely noticed. Amy's mind was racing, analyzing and calculating, but she momentarily focused and said, "Mama, while we wait for Moon, dispatch a party to find some bats. We will begin our DNA research with bats. This new race will be able to fly!"

It was Mama's turn to be shocked, but she quickly grasped the implications. Mama, clearly excited, waved and sped out of the conference room to comply with the request. Amy knew they would be breaking down and mapping bat DNA by tomorrow.

Her prediction was more than realized. By evening of the next day, running the Super-Computers and herself at full capacity, she had mapped out those characteristics she found most desirable. She had identified the characteristics of the billions of base pairs of the genes in the bat's DNA strand.

For Amy this was relatively easy, although extremely complex. After all, this was what she was designed for. She would be using the basic DNA of humans, Levi in particular, as the structural database to build Levi's body. The Human DNA would be the default DNA. Changing or adding features would only be a matter of identifying the exact sequence location and replacing or adding those gene sections with alternate sections extracted from bat, Simian, or Supreme One genes.

She had chosen bats because they are the only mammals that fly, and the DNA must be mammal. They are live-born and are nurtured by their mother's milk just as a Human or Simian. This would be a mandatory requirement if she wanted wings, and she did.

There were other benefits she wanted to incorporate as well:

Bats mature at an accelerated rate, which would reduce Levi's growth time to maturity. She wasn't sure how much time they had before the next invasion, and Levi must be matured before that time.

Bats are normally nocturnal and use a form of sonar to navigate. They emit a high-pitched frequency and receive echo returns to identify objects and obstacles. This would give Levi a major advantage at night against a Warr, especially with a Simian's poor night-vision. Additionally, she hoped to adjust the sonar pitch to possibly affect Warrs by temporarily paralyzing them as ASONE had done at the mountain pass. This could be a major weapon to use against them if she could develop this feature properly.

There were other minor features worth considering, such as the fine layer of fur and improved hearing. Fur would be beneficial for the wings to maintain stability and feel the sensitive air currents. She thought a slight fur over the body as well might provide a little warmth during flight, but

Levi might kill her for it. Certainly, it would be required on the wings, but this required more thought.

By far though, the best feature from the bat would be the wings. This feature could be spliced into the gene sequence, although it would not be like a bat's. Bat wings are adapted from their arms with the elongated fingers forming the support in the wing membrane. In Levi's body the wings would be an addition to the arms, folded on his back. They would necessarily have to be big, but she could incorporate a trifold design instead of the bifold wing of a bat. This would make the wings more compact and less noticeable ... right! Levi would never let her forget, that is if he ever talked to her again.

Most of the other bat features could be incorporated without major outward appearance changes. Levi would mostly still look like Levi, except for the wings, and she didn't think he would notice the breastbone and larger chest. That would probably appeal to his macho ego anyway. Sure, the nose might be a little wider, the teeth a little sharper, the ears a little longer, the fine fur tinted to appear skin color, and the clawed feet could be hidden in his boots; but the wings could not be completely concealed.

Mama snapped Amy out of her self-induced trance when she reported, "Moon is back."

Mama appeared happy, actually smiling when she said that, so she knew something was up. Amy checked the cameras at the entrance to observe Moon's entrance. What in the world was that white thing on his neck? As she zoomed in, she recognized it as a small dog perched comfortably on Moon's thick shoulder. She couldn't help but laugh. It looked so out of place sitting squarely on what most Humans would consider a hideous monster. So much for the adage, a dog is man's best friend.

The dog was still on top of Moon's shoulder when Mama led him into the conference room, almost as if he had forgotten it was there until her image came to life. The little dog started growling at her. She had to laugh. Moon screeched at it, and it immediately cowered and silenced. Moon set it on the floor, and it immediately started jumping up on his tree-trunk leg, clawing to reach its safe vantage point again. Moon ignored it and reached into his backpack and retrieved the Supreme One's partial jawbone, complete with teeth.

Oh, this was perfect, an excellent sample of the needed DNA. "Thank you so much, Moon. You did very well indeed." Her sentence ended abruptly as she recognized the second item he retrieved. It was the golden locket Levi always wore, and seeing it flooded her mind with the memories. It took a moment before she could compose herself again to say, "Thank you, again. I would be honored if you wore Levi's locket until he returns."

Moon stiffened and signed, "Levi will return?"

She suddenly realized, other than Mama, no one else really knew of her plans to bring Levi back. Between Mama and herself they gave Moon the abbreviated version. He listened intently and believed. She thought Moon would believe her if she said she could put out the sun.

Moon screeched in Simian, "I am pleased to keep the golden chain safe for Levi. I would also like one of the Supreme One's teeth. It would make a fine trophy when he returns."

She had to laugh at Moon's comment, because Levi, the macho shithead, would definitely prize that trophy. Through her laughter she blurted, "Help yourself."

Amy welcomed the laughter. It lifted her spirits, and while they were in a lighter mood, she decided to find out about the dog that still playfully clawed at Moon's leg. "Moon, where did you get the little dog?" She asked.

Moon, reminded of the dog, bent down and tossed the pup on his shoulder, where it resumed its contented position at his ear. Moon then described how they met and how it followed and seemed to have adopted him, and that he had decided to let it stay.

Amy said, "What's his name?"

"Name?" He signed.

"Sure." She said, "It's got to have a name so it will know when you call it."

He looked perplexed then spoke the word, "Oggg," in an attempt to say dog in English.

She lost all pretense of propriety, bursting out laughing. "Oggg it is then." Oggg's tail wagged at the name, seemingly understanding that to be his name. Even Mama hiccupped a laugh at its antics. So they now had a new family member.

After a few minutes, she sobered, remembering a new task that must be accomplished, soon. The time for Gathering approached, when the Simian females grouped for mating. The Gathering occurs every eighty days for a third of the females; a female Simian only comes in season every third

79

Gathering. If they didn't harvest unfertilized eggs at this Gathering, she would have to wait another eighty days before they could begin the project.

Pointing at Moon and Mama, Amy said, "This next task must be addressed by both of you. I will need some Simian female volunteers to donate their eggs and later carry the embryo to term. These will be the embryos we genetically alter here in the facility. But, before they volunteer, I want them to understand it will not be a normal birth or child. These embryos will be far bigger and may have to be surgically removed before birth. It will be hard on the volunteers. There is a chance it might even kill them, but if it succeeds, this project might mean the future survival of the Simian and Human races. Can you find a few volunteers?"

Understanding, they both nodded and left together. She couldn't be sure if Moon understood the plan completely or the requirements involved, but she could rely on Mama to instruct him en route.

After they left she regretted that she had not asked Mama to put a sample of the Supreme One's DNA in the analyzer, but soon learned Mama had instructed one of her technician to prepare the sample.

Now the research began in earnest. The Supreme One's DNA strand was long and complex and would take a while to break it down and map out the genes, even longer to isolate those genes she would incorporate into Levi's DNA and the exact sequence.

As the analysis continued, she discovered the DNA strand was exceptionally long, unnecessarily long. It also became apparent that the DNA had been clumsily manipulated. She lost respect for the Simian genetic engineers, and any thoughts that this Simian technology was superior, evaporated. The genes and sequences conflicted, and others did absolutely nothing. The DNA was a mess. No wonder the Supreme Ones were psychotic.

By comparing the DNA of a Technical Simian to the DNA of the Supreme One, she finally succeeded in identifying the gene splicing alternations that increased size and brain capacity. These were the two most important features she had hoped to obtain from the Supreme One's DNA. All other Simian DNA she planned to use would be taken from the uncorrupted DNA strand of a Technical Simian, and in some instances from a Simian female, such as the poison finger fang feature. With the exceptions of gender and the two strand alternations of the females, all other DNA was identical.

During the analysis process of the Simian female DNA, she discovered the second gene alternation that prevented the male and female chromosomes from mixing. At this point, it was probably advisable to leave this alone. The Females Simians had been clever to protect their DNA from corruption from the genetically altered Warrior Simians. It had saved their DNA purity.

By the time Moon and Mama returned, she had her final DNA strand version designed, but she was not prepared for what they reported. She hoped for two, maybe three for a backup, volunteers to host embryos, but these two gathered thirty volunteers. Even more amazing, the thirty were only from the small group of Simians living in the valley close to her facility. This would represent almost all of the fertile females of the group. She tried to control her amazement when she said, "Thank you Moon and Mama, but I don't need that many. I only need a few."

Bambi accompanied them when they entered, and it was she that responded, "Mama has explained what you plan to do, and we approve. We are also fascinated about your plan to alter Levi's body to include Simian and bat DNA. As we understand, you will also build a similar body for yourself, and that your minds will transfer into these flying bodies."

It was make as a statement but sounded more like a question that seemed to demand an answer. Amy said, "This is correct."

Bambi spread her arms indicating Mama and Moon and continued, "We talk for the Simians races, the Techs and Fems. We have no doubt that you can do what you say, and we trust you. We want you to alter our races also, so we can fly and fight with you."

She really didn't know what to expect, but this wasn't it. They had misunderstood her completely or mistakenly projected her abilities too far. They just gave her total trust so she wanted to be completely honest with them. Carefully, Amy said, "I have the ability to transfer Levi's memories into a new body. I believe I can also transfer part of my mind into a body that I create. I can also alter the Simian body as you suggest. I can do all these things, but I don't have the ability to transfer your Simian minds into a new body. This is impossible for me to do."

Bambi, Moon, and Mama exchanged looks and nods. Mama then spoke, "The Simians have that technology. Well, we once had it... before the Warriors started taking over our world. Before the Warriors were created our world leader ruled for thousands of years, transferring his mind into a new body as each subsequent body grew old. It is also believed that some of our greatest minds lived on in this way. When the Warrior Simians killed the leader and our greatest minds, this technology was hidden, but not lost. We did not want this technology available for use by the Warrior Simians and certainly not the Supreme Ones."

Amy was utterly stunned by this revelation. Was this possible? How could this be accomplished? She never completely understood the working of a Simian mind, and her attempts to link with a Simian mind had all been failures. Was this possible? Certainly, this required more investigation.

If the great scientists had been killed prior to the genetic engineering of the Supreme Ones, this might explain how the genetic code of the supposedly advanced race was so drastically screwed up. The genetic engineering of the Warrior Simians had been flawless, but they were designed to fight the invading Outsiders, not become part of society. The oversight had been the failure to anticipate what would become of them once the war was won.

Amy's mind refocused and asked, "All this happened long before you were alive. How can you know this?"

83

"This is true, but you need to understand that Fems are the guardians of secrets. We secretly pass information on from mother to daughter generation after generation. Through the ages we hid ourselves as docile beings so no one would suspect we have secrets. It worked so well, even the Technical Simians have forgotten we once rivaled them and actually controlled education. We positioned ourselves to hide information, which we did. We waited for generations for change, and you and Levi now offer this change. Surely you have noticed the difference since we met Levi."

She had indeed noticed the change. It suddenly struck her how much Mama and the Fems now trusted her. They had not broken their silence for generations, until now. It must be true for them to have so vigilantly kept this secret alive. She bristled in excitement at the implications this now presented.

Amy said, "How do I get this knowledge? Do you have this knowledge memorized?"

"No, it is not memorized. It is stored in the Simian data banks, which are in every Simian computer. We only remember the way to access it, a secret way known only to us."

Just the anticipation of exploring the hidden knowledge of the Simian computer triggered anxiety, teasing her with the possibilities. She had hoped for this, and now the actual opportunity was unexpectedly falling in her proverbial lap. In a few days she would have the other Simian computers and she could delve into the research, but the immediate need now required a response to these gathered.

Amy carefully and somewhat formally said, "If it is possible, I will be honored to comply with your wishes. I can think of none other than you, my friends, I would rather have fighting at my side." Their faces relaxed into smiles at her response, and the sound of released breath filtered through the conference rooms, as if they had all been holding their breath in anticipation.

Bambi said, "Great! Just let us know what you need other than the volunteers. Now you see why we have so many volunteers, and I plan to be the first one. I will be the mother to the new Levi."

Amy could not believe how lucky she, Levi, and the Human race were to have such wonderful allies... no, friends. They were totally committed to this war, the Human race, and her personally. They were also ensuring their own continuance as a race with this alliance.

DNA samples from the volunteer Tech or Fems could be taken any time, but the necessary Simian females' eggs all mature at the same time and synchronize with the time of their Gathering where the eggs are fertilized. The Gathering was only a few days away so Mama wasted little time in beginning the harvest.

Amy explained the importance of being able to match the sample of DNA taken to that exact same volunteer in the future. Without an exact match, the donor could not be assured of a proper transfer of their mind into the new body. To eliminate any potential error, Mama established a precise numbering system, even to the point of permanently tattooing the sample number on the back of the donor's hand. This prominent symbol apparently became a source of pride for the volunteers, brandishing them as a soldier might display medals.

By the time of the Gathering Mama had extracted all thirty donor eggs and DNA samples and processed them into cryogenics for storage, and true to Bambi's promise, she was the first.

The only negative resulting, there would not be a Gathering among the valley Simian group since there would be no females to fertilize, and she knew that Moon and Bambi had both secretly counted on finally mating. Uncharacteristic for Simian breeding, these two wanted to permanently pair, and Amy wanted that also. They would have been the first Simians to pair up as Humans do. It was a natural thing since they had been working and being together for months, unlike the others.

For the most part, the majority of the Tech and Fems remained separated by force of habit from the influence of the Warrior Simians with their rigid social structure. This would probably change in time, but the Simian culture, at best, was never overly social, so she didn't know what to expect. This would all change when they had new bodies. They would be forced to live, feed, and fight together out of necessity.

Amy had been considering these factors and decided to help the social structure along, especially among the new race being created. She would keep the sexes matched... one male and one female and let nature take its course. They should naturally pair up... hopefully.

Moon would no doubt follow Bambi's lead and would be the first of the new race, followed later by Bambi, but Amy had also decided the original

86

dozen Technical Simians and late bodyguards of Levi would have the first opportunity to make the transition. There was little doubt they would jump at the chance to fly and fight alongside Levi and Moon again. This loyal and trusted group, along with the female volunteers, would be the vanguard of those to follow.

This new race would be a formidable fighting group second to none on Earth. For this very reason, she was somewhat concerned. They must not duplicate what happened with the Warrior Simians. No one could stand against them when they multiplied and gained in power, certainly not humans. With these loyal friends and allies to the Human race and to Levi and her, as the leaders, she no longer worried about them eventually becoming a dominant race, assuming they could defeat the masses of Warrs. Still, she wished she could find a way for this new race and humans to work more closely together. She already relied on the Simians far more than Humans. This concerned her greatly. She would have to give this some thought.

Levi's DNA was complete and had been checked and rechecked. She had made all the changes and additions and even added a feature at the last minute. To ensure and strengthen Levi's telepathy ability, she increased the size of his pineal gland. This mostly dormant gland supports telepathic ability, some claimed it the source or "third eye". This would improve their telepathic communications and possibly allow communications with others as well.

The day finally arrived, and Amy was ready. The Simian group was again gathered in the conference room awaiting the final word from her. There would be no turning back after this last step. She looked at Bambi and said, "Are you sure you want to do this? It won't be easy on you."

Bambi signed with exaggerated movements, "Yes, yes, let's do it. I am ready."

Bambi radiated calmness and composure, but Moon's eyes stretched wide and showed little sign of the typical red, a sure sign of something ... unclear as to what. His face appeared somewhat whiter than usual, almost matching Oggg's fur pressed against his cheek. Mama radiated pride. Amy said, "I am so proud of you, Bambi. We are family. Humans would say that you will be my mother-in-law." The humor was not lost on Bambi, as she sprouted a toothy grin. Had Amy not been accustomed to the look of a Simian, the sight of her shining, shark-like teeth might have appeared more ominous, but to Amy it was a beautiful sight.

Mama led Bambi to the clinic where the procedure would be done. The actual procedure was relatively simple and Bambi's egg enclosing Levi's modified genes was implanted into her uterus. Now all they had to do was wait to see if the embryo grew or was rejected.

There remained a possibility that Bambi's body might reject the foreign DNA, but Amy calculated the odds were remote. The placenta housing the growing embryo isolated the mother's and baby's blood from mixing. This is one of those miracles of nature. The placenta filters and only draws oxygen and nutrients from the mother's blood to feed the growing embryo. The embryo builds its own supply of blood, which in this case, would be mainly human.

Bambi would require constant care, so she reluctantly moved into the complex. She wasn't pleased about that but offered little resistance. She knew it was best. It would take a few weeks to know for sure if the embryo would grow and at what rate, and this would have to be monitored. This was all new and potentially dangerous for Bambi, but Amy and Mama were determined to keep her safe.

Amy could only estimate the gestation period to full term. Some bats require only forty day, while others, the larger species, required six months to carry their embryo to full term. Simians, on the other hand, required a full twelve months gestation period. She didn't want to rush the development time of the embryo and didn't tamper with the genes in this regard. The human genes would be in control, which dictated a nine-month period. This embryo was, after all, Levi, and she wanted full development, or at least as long as Bambi's body could support it. Her best estimate suggested the embryo would have to be taken at eight months. Her calculation of growth rate indicated that would be the maximum size, thirty pounds, Bambi would be able to handle. After that point, the infant's nutritional demands would exceed her ability to provide.

Amy did take liberties with the genes that control growth rate to maturity after birth. She didn't know how much time they had before the next Simian invasion, and wanted to be ready when it happened. Levi must be ready before that time, and she intended to ensure that he was.

Bats can mature in as little as six weeks and as long as four months, depending on size. By using the increased growth-rate of the bat genes, this growth process could and would be drastically reduced, but Levi's body would be huge and his brain would require far more development time due to its size and complexity. As a result, she anticipated full growth and maturity, body and mind, would require two years.

Bats would starve if it took them longer to mature and fend for themselves, but nature and evolution resolved the problem with a fast maturing gene. She only had to copy the process.

Levi would require massive amounts of protein and nutrients to support this explosive growth, but he would not have to fend for himself. There would be a full staff of Fems to keep him fed. The old Levi, already accustomed to eating large meals, would have to step it up several notches on his metabolism engine. Fortunately, the heavy intake of meals would only be required for a year during the majority of his body growth. Afterwards, it would begin to taper off.

Amy had conflicting emotions about one of the gene alterations. She had canceled out the effects of the formula # 12, which Levi injected. This culture allowed her, actually required her, to continually modify Levi's DNA to keep him young and strong. This ability had saved Levi many times. Without it, Levi, in essence, would be mortal, not that he had ever been immortal, but close. Fortunately, she had learned much through the constant mental interface with his body, and remained confident that she could continue to manipulate some of his DNA by using the chemical language developed. Unfortunately, it would be a much slower process than before. It was inevitable, however, assuming her clairvoyance curse could be trusted.

Chapter 3
Satan

His intelligence soared above the other Supreme Ones. He had always been smarter, but if he revealed this to the others they would rally against him and kill him. Their nature, if it could be called that, demanded supremacy, thus the name. There could be only one. Knowing there were equal set their genetically altered, superior breed into a psychotic rage, uncontrollable fury aimed at the others. Recognizing this genetic flaw, one from which he also suffered, he learned to circumvent it by reminding himself they were not his equals. He was the only true Superior One.

As mere children, his brother, the strongest and most aggressive, secretly began eliminating his siblings. There were only ten siblings in his scientific study group, but only six remained alive when the medical staff whisked him away. Their world supported five continents, and he was ushered away to the most distant from his brother. The medical staff took action immediately once they understood what happened, but they were, even in the beginning, afraid of his brother. He could still feel his brother seeking him, but the distance protected him.

There were other genetic breeding groups, but all the subjects shared the same flaw. As such, all were totally predictable, all but him. They sought each other out as they matured and destroyed each other. He was the only exception, and he isolated himself, maintaining a very low profile, not attacking or causing the others concern. Time became his friend, as the competition dwindled. He did not allow rage and hate to take over or take chances, even though he felt the others and the rage it caused. His time would come when he was ready.

There were four Supreme Ones on his continent, but he presented no challenge to them as he waited, watched, and planned. He often wondered why he was smarter, but accepted this superiority in silence and used it to formulate his plan.

Every assault against a Supreme One was a risk to the attacker, so why take the risks when he could simply sit back and let them kill each other? The others began taking control of their world by eliminating each other, consolidating the power. He remained silent while they did all the work.

On his continent, two of the Supreme Ones combined their efforts and killed the third, the most visible and powerful. Afterwards, those two struggled to take over the continent. Again, he waited, remaining invisible while they struggled. He did nothing to attract their attention and remained unconcerned about the Simian Warrior armies they commanded. Once the other Supreme Ones were gone he could easily take control of the armies and any remaining government resistance. His mental strength and superiority reigned absolute over them.

He spent his time perfecting his internal power and knowledge. He even allowed the Technical Simians in his area of influence to maintain governmental control as a diversion for the others.

As the control and power of the other two grew, their rage and hate expanded and focused on each other, allowing him to remain invisible. Finally, their armies clashed and the battle eventually filtered down to the two Supreme Ones clashing in a devastating personal battle of mental power. Satan silently moved closer to the conflict, building and concentrating his own strength. He controlled his rage until one of the Supreme Ones fell. Only then did he allow his power and rage to escape. His overpowering mind surged out toward the weakened, surviving Supreme One's offending mental power and gripped his unsuspecting mind in a vice-like grip. His surprised opponent quickly died in his crushing mental grip. The continent forfeited to him, as this last abomination's mind exploded in agony. No mercy was offered, and he finally relished in the joy of his victory.

He then took control of the armies and set their task to subdue the continent now under his rule. His planning had been flawless, and any resistance quickly vanished in a withering, agonizing death. Most of the government had already succumbed to the other two Supreme Ones so it was easy. Every detail slipped into place, totally predictable and according to his plan.

He took pleasure in his name and proudly claimed Supreme One. In point of fact, all of his breed claimed the name Supreme Ones, but he was the only true Supreme One. It was commonly known by his breed that the population referred to them as evil, or evil one, or simply Satan, because they were without equal in their ruthlessness and cruelty, except for each other. Individually, all took up the name Supreme One. Even in the naming the implication was there: there would be only one.

As Satan consolidated his sole power over his continent, the other four were doing the same. Now there were only five remaining alive in their entire world. He continued to plan and hold his rage. His plan, a long range, complicated plan, he knew would work. His victory would come slowly over years, but the others were so predictable.

Their home world was dying and evacuation was becoming increasingly necessary. An alternate planet capable of sustaining life for them had been found for colonization. He was yet an infant when the first invasion launched to that target world, but he was consolidating his power on his continent as the second invasion preparation neared completion. His powerful brother volunteered to lead this invasion, but he could see the deception, an obvious and predictable plans. You simply worked backwards from the goal of: there can be only one. It didn't matter that they would be on worlds widely divided. He knew his brother would try to kill the remaining Supreme Ones, even if it destroyed their home world in the process. Again, he would let his brother do his work for him, but if he failed, he would finish the job. He would be the only Supreme One.

For months he planned his escape in secret. His technology was far greater than his brother's and his understanding of all the Simian technology was greater, because he recognized the benefits of this power. His secret team gathered and stored supplies and equipment at his secret location on an island in the middle of the safety of the dreaded water of the planet. His spacecraft had all been modified to operate in the altered environment of the new world.

He knew how, but would never share with the others. Let them waste their time warring.

He also knew the last attack from his Supreme One brother from space would finish off the other Supreme Ones, along with a majority of the population and the planet as well. It was so predictable. It was what he would have done, so knowing in advance provided his warning.

Saving the planet, for what little time remained, did not concern him, and he couldn't care less about those who would die. No, his plan centered on saving himself and those he required to serve him. There would be plenty of his race on the new world to control, and he would know exactly what to expect, because he had already placed his spies in his brother's fleet. They would be sending him coded messages from space and from the new world. Yes, he was smarter and planned well.

As the time neared for the second exodus and invasion, he moved his command to the secret island and waited. The other three Supreme Ones were already poised to fight over his brother's continent. They were so predictable and stupid. They squandered their time and effort. He even allowed them to think he was weak. They could spend what was left of their lives fighting over a dying world, but not him. He was ready, prepared, and simply waited. All would be his, and he would be the only one, on this world anyway.

As the fleet made the final orbit of their world, his brother launched the attack. He had even predicted the weapons, locations, and timing. All happened exactly as he predicted, and the other three Supreme Ones died in the explosions. For being so intelligent, how could they not see the necessity of their own death?

He planned to wait as long as possible after the attack to gather up whatever remained worth taking of his world before leaving it forever. There would be other surviving spaceships that could be stocked with technology, and survivors to serve him in their long journey. The extra time would allow him to learn from the Supreme One preceding him to the new world. The spies would keep him informed of the progress there. Again, he would let the other Supreme One do his work for him and assume control and consolidate his power. There would be no surprises. He did not like surprises. His attack would use technology that did not exist on the planet. He would be the only one that could use it, because he had made good use of his time.

He had thoroughly researched the technology behind the doomsday weapon and the effects it would have on the new world. Knowing how it worked and what it changed was half the battle. Research led him to alternate methods of altering the effects. This was key to his plans. His spies were equipped with communication devices that would work in the altered environment and send the reports across time and space to keep him informed. No, he didn't like surprises, but the other Supreme One would have plenty of them when he arrived.

It took him three months to canvas what was left of the home world. All together he added an additional four spacecraft for his migration, making a total of five. He staffed his ships mainly with Technical Class Simians. Unlike his brother, who wanted power through the Warrior Class Simians, he preferred the intelligence of the Techs. The Warriors were only good for war, but not the way he would wage war, should he have to. Besides, there should be many thousands of the Warriors on the new world for him to command.

Instead of armies he stocked his ships with animals from his home world. There were plants of every variety, animals for breeding, food, work, and riding, and some just for the normality of life as he was accustomed to. He even had some very nasty pets.

He waited as long as he dared before leaving. The world died before his eyes. The final attack had filled the atmosphere with dust so thick that light barely made it through. Except for the plants environmentally controlled onboard his ships, all plant life eventually died, and what little actual breathable atmosphere that hadn't been ripped away, was being devoured by fires beginning to burn rampant across his world. The stench of the dead and dying filled the air. By the time the creeping death of the sea reached his island, there was little left and no reason to remain longer.

Three years was all he could delay, but that should be sufficient to prevent detection from the advanced fleet. That fleet could easily destroy him in space due to their raw numbers and attrition, had they known they were behind, but everything was going according to plan.

According to instructions, he received his first short encrypted message from his infiltrated spies six months into the flight. This was the critical message and provided the security of knowing the implants remained undiscovered and that the radio equipment worked beyond light speed. There would be few messages sent during the long space flight, but this first one comforted him. The rage continued to boil, but it was controllable, even satisfying to know how much pleasure he would get when all the long planning and manipulation came together at the end.

The next message was years later after his brother had landed on the new world. He learned the nature of the new world and the dispersement of the invasion forces. Predictably, his brother grouped them together, as many as he could support anyway.

There was no longer a threat from the indigenous life forms. All resistance had vanished with use of the altering ray. This he knew from previous reports, but confirmation was satisfying. His plan was falling into place.

Everything changed for the worse by the next report. For the first time he had failed to anticipate a problem. According to his spies, his brother spiraled in and out of episodes where he went berserk, exploding in uncontrollable rage. His brother had predictably organized the armies and colonies and all appeared normal, when suddenly rage took over and he irrationally began to issue attack orders. There were forces toward the west that must be destroyed. Satan knew it would have to be much more than mere armies to destroy. The berserk rage had always been rare, even among the Supreme Ones, and always associated with another Supreme One. It didn't make sense, since only one Supreme One existed on the new world. Something was terribly wrong.

He continued to analyze the facts that he obtained, but no solution or reason made sense. What could conceivably have spurred his brother into a blinding rage? He did not like surprises, and this was a huge one.

The next report told of Human and Technical Simian armies. How could this be, Technical Simians and Humans allying? Who organized and controlled them? According to the spies, Simian armies had not only been defeated but also decimated by this mysterious alliance. He had a thousand questions, but unfortunately, due to the time delay of transmission, it would take months to get them answered. He would have to rely on the limited intelligence of his spies to provide useable information. Now, even he began to feel his own rage simmering. No, it must be controlled, for now.

The day finally came that provided his best intelligence report to date. It spoke of his brother's berserking rage again and how, in a tirade, he shot balls of fire from his head, killing many Warrior Simians, including one of his spies. His brother was ranting something about, "The Witch must die!"

The next part of the report shook him to his core and momentarily flooded him with fear for the first time. The Supreme One's quarters had exploded and his brother was running for his life. That was the end of the report. Something was drastically wrong!

His brother had named the enemy, Witch. A female? She would have to rival his brother in intelligence and power to have evoked such berserk raging. She may even have been powerful enough to make him run in fear.

One positive and surprising part of the report, his brother shooting fireballs from his head, interested him greatly. His brother had evolved, mentally. Sometimes when a mentally superior being faces adversity and power equal to his own, the mind is forced to evolve, which he had obviously done. If his brother had done it, so could he. But, the very fact that he had evolved identified the Witch as a formidable enemy. This he did not expect, but he would deal with it. Knowing a powerful enemy existed provided the warning he needed.

His last report was completely unexpected and disturbing. The attacking Simian armies in the west had been soundly defeated, not just beaten but also, devastated. A surprisingly few survivors returned to describe terrible weapons and horrible deaths at the hands of Human and Technical Simian armies. According to the report, even some Simian Females had participated. Strangely, the Human and Tech armies had not pursued the fleeing Simian armies and had pulled back across the flow of water to their own complex to the west.

The Warrior Simians were idiots, and so was his brother. How could they have destroyed the fragile relationship with the Technical Simians! The Warriors tried to take control on the home world, but they were too stupid to run the utilities and technologies. Most of the Supreme Ones preferred the Warriors because they were easily controlled, but they were smart enough to realize the Technical Simians were needed. As a result, the Supreme Ones protected the Technical Simians from extinction. He, on the other hand, preferred the

Technicals to support his advanced technology, much of it invented by him. His fleet was staffed primarily by Technicals and, of course, Females. The only Warriors onboard were his security force.

How had the Warriors and his brother managed to alienate the Technicals to the point of joining the enemy to fight against them? He could, however, imagine a situation of no technology where the Warriors might completely reject the Technicals, but there was no way to explain why the Females changed sides. This was a complete puzzle to him, but a puzzle that he must put together and rectify.

A few days later a message reported the continued absence of the Supreme One. He had not been seen since he ran away from the compound and now was presumed dead.

His brother dead? A Supreme One dead? That was impossible. If he was dead, it would have to be at the hands of the enemy or the Witch. Whoever or whatever this Witch is, she must be extremely powerful to have withstood a Supreme One's mental and physical attack. He could not imagine what she could be, but he would not underestimate her. For the first time in his life he did not know what to do. She had killed his brother, and if she could do that, she could kill him, too. He did not like surprises and wanted no surprises. He would not act until he was sure of success. She would have to be studied and understood before he attacked, but attack he would.

He would land his small fleet at the location his brother had organized and assume control, but before landing, he would orbit the planet and locate the Witch and plan her destruction.

Chapter 4
Earth's Dragons

* Amy *

While she waited for the Simian computers to arrive and monitored Bambi's progress, she turned her attention to the DNA development of the flying Simian. She found that name comical and decided it deserved a more sophisticated calling, one that more appropriately described the situation. This new being would no longer be alien. It would be a new species to any planet, but Earth would be its home. The species would be hugely winged with four clawed legs, well, arms and legs, but the arms would have to serve in supporting the body's weight, especially since it would be necessary to extend the neck and structure a tail. A tail would be required to aid balance in flight and extending the neck would help them feed more easily, even fight. She could elongate the Simian jaw as well. With these changes, and with the shark-like teeth, they might appear much like an ancient mythical dragon. She concluded "Earth's Dragons" would be an appropriate name.

All art and history portrayed dragons as reptilian and scaly, but her dragons would be golden haired. The Simian's dense hide would, however, serve the same function as scales. Amy was impressed with the visual image she was building. They would be magnificent creatures and fearsome in battle.

103

Three days later the two Simian computers arrived. Her excitement bubbled almost uncontrollably, but she forced herself to dote over the Techs, thanking them for a job well done. The Techs were out of their element inside the facility, especially with being praised by the leader. In their nervousness they fidgeted from one thick leg to the other. Mama had no intention of doting over them and took charge of the situation.

Mama delayed just long enough for Amy to finish thanking them before screeching, "Don't scratch the floor with those. Bring the computers along, we need to install them."

In spite of her anxious excitement, Amy found the situation extremely funny. The Techs jumped as if shot and scurried down the hall following the retreating Mama, balancing the computers between them with care so as not to scuff the floor. Amy knew Mama would work them hard before she let them escape back to camp. True to her belief, she observed the Techs exiting the front door many hours later, but the computers were installed.

Mama didn't have to tell her the computers were installed to her specification and ready. She felt them come on line, and jumped into the reprogramming, installing some of her internal operational parameters. The Simian computers preformed exactly as she expected. Once the reference computer was operational and synchronized with the Super Computer, data flooded her sensors. She immediately routed the data into one of the Super Computers to begin the download and translation. It would take time due to the massive volume of data, but it was working.

The next step was to find the hidden data on genetics and memory transfer Mama and Bambi had talked about. She remained a little skeptical but wanted to believe. She called Mama to the conference room.

Mama burst through the door in short order screeching, "I am here, Amy!"

Amy said, "Oh, sorry, Mama. It's not an emergency; I was just wanting to discuss something with you." She knew it was useless to try to slow Mama down. Mama would react immediately any time she called. She should have waited until Mama came to her, but it was done now. Amy continued, "Mama, what is involved in finding the hidden information you talked about? Will it be difficult to find? I mean, it has been generations since it was hidden. Maybe the remembered way to find it has been corrupted over time."

Mama signed, "I don't see how. It is only a simple phrase, and we have been very careful to memorize it exactly." Mama, looked around conspiratorially and screeched out the phrase.

Even in a subdued screech, it echoed around the room for anyone to have heard. The phrase as translated into English stated, the key is the color we can't see. "Is that it? Nothing else?"

"No. We were only taught to remember that information is hidden in the computers and The Secret! Legends and stories about some of the information hidden are told, but none of them are necessary to unlock the computer, only The Secret.

It didn't make sense, but it had to, or should, to a Simian anyway. What color can't they see, and what does colors have to do with anything? After a long thoughtful pause, she understood. Of course, colors have everything to do with the computers. That is exactly what she had been dealing with, colors of a prism like a rainbow. Each color and variation of combinations thereof, of which there were multitudes, represented increased operational and storage capacity. The secret was telling her there was a color path storing all the secrets. Yes, of course, light has a frequency and each color in the visual spectrum has a slightly different frequency, each one capable of formatting information, and in this case, a separate hard-drive path for storing information. Each Simian computer had a hidden data path and potentially massive storage. It would have to be designed to transfer the data into any new computer, but not retrieved. If the color was missing in the color sequence rotation, that path and information stored within it, would be invisible to all without the secret. It made sense, but what color?

As soon as she posed the question, she knew the answer. The missing color would have to be blue. She had once tested Moon for color blindness and discovered that Simians are blind to the color blue. They had used blue markings to identify the locations of trap pits to prevent humans from accidentally falling in them, but the attacking Simian Warriors were not so warned.

This had been an ingenious plan devised by some savvy Fems. Unless a Simian specifically researched the color spectrum rotation by frequency, the secret would remain hidden, and being color blind to the color blue, they would never notice its absence. It was brilliant.

She went to work immediately designing the blue light generator and sequencing programming. Once she knew the secret, it progressed easily, and Mama had it built and installed within two days, operational. Now it was up to Amy.

She now believed she would be able to access the Simian mind transfer process, and launched into the detailed DNA designs of the new Simian body. She had already given it a considerable amount of thought but only in general terms. Now, she began planning the details.

Originally she had planned to merge human DNA in a new common race, but if Simian minds were going to be transferred, the new race would be required to have a Simian brain. This changed everything, but in some ways made it easier. Simian, Tech and Fem, DNA would be the base from which she would begin her alterations. Supreme One DNA would add the size, and she might be able to expand the growth even beyond that. Bat DNA, of course, would provide the wings and similar traits she had designed into Levi's body.

Before committing to her Earth's Dragon design, she wanted Mama, Bambi, and Moon to understand all aspects of it and approve. After all, Moon and Bambi would be living in these new bodies and who knows, maybe even Mama. That would surely be interesting!

Amy prepared drawings for them to approve at their next meeting. Honestly though, the body looked hideous and frightening, but these factors improved its functionality.

As Moon, Bambi, and Mama entered the conference room, Amy bristled with excitement.

She found a better way to demonstrate the image of an Earth Dragon. Instead of her normal holographic image at the head of the room, the image of a full-size Earth Dragon burst into view, filling the front of the room. The animated dragon appeared and moved lifelike, as it would be genetically engineered to move. It roared and partially spread its wings as far as the space would have allowed a living dragon. She had planned the display in great detail for effect, and it worked.

The group cowered and pulled back in shock, but Oggg's reaction surprised everyone. The tiny dog had been on the floor at Moon's feet when the dragon burst in. It shot toward the image, growling and barking, and leaped into the projected image, disrupting the display. It plowed right through, startling the pup when it felt no resistance. It suddenly seemed to realize what it was doing and yelped, trying to turn. Its churning feet slipped and clawed at the slick floor until it finally got some traction, speeding him toward Moon, his protector. Still yelping, it leaped toward Moon's chest. Fortunately, Moon caught him, but it continued to claw up his arms and chest until it finally reached safety behind Moon's head. Brave now, Oggg peered around Moon's head at the restored dragon and barked.

It was the funniest thing Amy had ever seen. She burst out in laughter, but she was not alone. Mama and Bambi, unable to control their hiccupping laughter, sat down in the nearest chairs, which, unfortunately, were made for Humans. As their bodies jerked in laughter, Mama's chair suddenly collapsed, sprawling her on the floor on her back. She just lay there laughing even harder, and Moon and Bambi were doubled over trying to catch their breath, completely unable to help.

It was the best laugh she had experienced, ever, and the strongest show of emotions she had seen from a Simian. It took a while before they calmed and Moon was able to help Mama up to her shaking feet.

Amy replaced the image of the dragon with her own, and, still chuckling, said, "Well, I guess we know Oggg's reaction to the image." She paused at the laughter then continued, "What is your reaction to what I am calling 'Earth's Dragon'?"

Grinning, Moon screeched, "We really didn't get a chance to study the image much before Oggg killed it, but what I saw looked awesome. This is what you propose for our new bodies?"

Mama and Bambi nodded as Moon spoke. Amy said, "Yes, I would like to discuss, in detail, all the changes and alterations I propose and why, but I will want your input and approval before we begin.

Amy spent the next few hours going over all the details and answering questions. They seemed to completely understand the purpose and reasoning behind all the alternations. She brought the dragon image up several more times to point out details and get them used to the ideas, but in the end, they approved of the design. Well, all excluding Oggg.

Moon asked, "When will we know for sure that Levi will return?"

"We should be able to test Bambi in a few days and know if the embryo is growing, but much longer to know for sure if she can carry it to term."

Moon nodded his understanding and said, "I will be the first Earth Dragon, and I want to be ready when Levi is. Can we do this soon?"

Amy had always known Moon would want to be the first, but it reassured her to hear him volunteer. She noticed Bambi give him a sharp look, but then quickly calmed and looked down as if resigned to the fact Moon would do this, no matter what. Amy said, "Yes, You can be the first and as soon as possible. I wouldn't have it any other way, Moon." She meant it, too.

***

Jimmy and Fred continued their daily visits to keep her informed as to what was going on the outside and take any instructions she might issue. Everything was going according to plan.

Iron Eyes and the Owens Valley tribes had little to do and were reverting to life as usual for them. The exception being Iron Eyes had the responsibility of the river watch, monitoring the river crossing for any Simian threat. So far, they had nothing to report.

The remaining members of the Desert Settlement still there were being relocated. Al had moved his members and army across the mountain and began establishing a settlement. Old habits die slow, so Al was building his community with defenses and escape routes, should they ever be needed, and the army maintained its readiness.

Tradesmen from both groups moved into her facility and took over many of the well tooled and stocked maintenance shops, and operating under the restored electrical power, they were hard at work building everything they might need for the future. Amy's facility was huge and their occupancy was hardly noticeable, except for the galley. The women cooks took that facility over completely and established a noticeable presence feeding the growing masses. It didn't take them long to learn the use of modern facilities.

Farms were quickly being established in the fertile land surrounding her facility, but they didn't have the assistance of modern equipment. They had to do it the old way with horse- drawn plows, but there were no complaints. To the contrary, they were pleased to be able to plant in the open without having to worry about attracting a wandering Simian patrol.

Jimmy even reported several separate communities of homes being built, but not too separate. Most of the Simian colonies had already relocated to the vicinity and assumed the responsibility of gathering and overseeing herds of cattle. They now considered themselves as part of Amy's family, and rightfully so. The Simians constructed several large open barracks with logs they helped clear from the farms. They remained separated by colony and spread across Owen Valley, but unlike before, they worked together with each other and the Human communities.

Damn, there were a lot of people and Simians gathered here, and they were all looking to her for leadership and protection. It had been over fifty years since life had been worth living. Now Humans and Simians alike were building a life again. How could she ever let them, her family, down? She hoped she never would, but she worried.

The curse of clairvoyance tormented her. It was a curse in more ways than one. They foretold desperate times, dangers, and death; but the visions never let her see everything, only bits and pieces. From past experience with the vision, they always came true, but she thought it only one possible truth, not the truth if she could alter the circumstances. Why would she experience these visions if she had no control over them? So far she had not been able to alter the outcome, maybe they were inevitable.

She sensed danger here at the facility. Once, she witnessed from space her own death in an explosion that decimated most of California, and her facility was the center. That would mean the death of her and all her friends. It remained too disturbing to focus on, but did she have a choice? She must find a way to avoid what her premonition seemed to predict.

She learned from this particular vision. First, she would be attacked from space. It could be no other way, since the loss of technology on Earth prevented use of any modern weapons. An attack would have to be launched from orbit by incoming spacecraft. This meant another invasion was definitely en route. Secondly, the plan would have to be conceived by a Supreme One. They were the only ones smart enough to detect her intelligence, be threatened by it, and be driven to destroy her at all cost.

This damn curse! Why couldn't the vision give a timetable? No, it provided only enough information to worry her and not enough to protect against it. When would the attack come? Would she have enough time to complete her projects? Should she evacuate the complex and force everyone to relocate ... again? If so, when, and would it even prevent an attack on the new location? Questions. Questions, only questions and no answers. Well, if it happened before she was ready, there would be nothing she could do, so, why worry about it? She would just proceed with her projects as quickly as possible, and if it happened, well, it happened.

After four weeks, Bambi, incredibly, began to show and feel movement. The embryo appeared to be growing at an accelerated rate, maybe even excessively, but Bambi continued to radiate with health and excitement. There was no sign of rejection at all.

With this encouragement, added to her need for speed, Amy decided to move forward with the embryo for her. She had completed the DNA construction for herself weeks ago but waited to see how Bambi was progressing. She saw no reason to delay it any longer and told Mama to pick a volunteer.

Designing her DNA had been much harder than any so far, because she had to modify the base-line DNA strand to incorporate all those features she had constructed in her visual image created for Levi. It would do no good to have a body that didn't look like the image Levi fell in love with. She began with a sample of DNA retrieved from Dr. Joice Sheldon's body, her original DNA donor, creator, and surrogate mother. Her brain was grown from this DNA and she wanted an identical DNA match, but more so, she owed Dr. Sheldon this honor.

113

It didn't take long for Mama to return with a volunteer, actually the same day. Mama came in accompanied by a Simian female she did not know, Bambi, Moon, and of course, Oggg in his customary place at Moon's neck. Smiling, she noticed Oggg made no attempt to get down this time.

Mama began, "Amy, this is Amy from the Phoenix colony. She demands to be a volunteer. She said we have only been taking volunteers from the local group and she wants to be a volunteer representing her group. We do want all the Fem colonies to eventually be represented, so we selected her. We have already extracted her egg. We took it before the Gathering, since so many wanted to volunteer. It has been altered with the DNA sample you developed. We just need your approval before we go forward."

Amy said, "This is fine by me. She can be a volunteer, but what did you say? Her name is Amy? How can that be?"

Bambi screeched, "Out of respect for you, many of the Fems are calling themselves Amy, now. Simians have never been strong on names until now. You have to expect it to happen."

"Doesn't that become confusing, having many Amy's?"

The Fem Amy responded by attempting her newly learned signing, but in frustration, screeched, "We all answer. We like to be called Amy."

Well, that didn't make much sense to her, but if it made them happy, so be it. She secretly reveled in the flattery, however. She said, "If there are many Amy's, do you mind if I call you Amy One?"

114

Amy One's face exploded with a huge grin, and she anxiously began hopping in excitement from one paddle foot to the other. Amy didn't know a Simian face could spread that wide. She saw the business end of many more teeth than she was accustomed to seeing, but she found it appealing.

Amy One screeched, "I would be honored to be called Amy One."

Amy thought how ironic that Amy One would be carrying Amy Two, the original Amy's genetically engineered embryo. Even thinking it was confusing.

Amy said, "One, do you understand what you are volunteering for? Do you understand that you will be carrying my body that I will transfer into after birth, and that it could be dang .....?" Amy broke off when she saw the fear suddenly flush over One. "What did I say to scare her so much?"

Mama signed, "We did not tell her whose baby she would be carrying, only what she would be doing."

"I am honored." One screeched, "I will carry the infant...you, and I thank you for the opportunity to be part of this."

Amy was speechless, overwhelmed with emotion. She just nodded to all of them and shut down her image for fear they might see her crying. She continued to watch until they left the conference room, headed toward the clinic for the procedure that would begin life for her new body.

***

It was time for phase two of the Earth Dragon project, and it was up to her now to find and learn the secrets of the Simians. An incredible amount of data had already been transferred and deciphered from the Super Computer, much of it related to the history of the Simian races. This data mostly confirmed what she already knew, how the Simian Fems had altered their genes to protect their race and gone into hiding, procedures relating to genetic engineering and gene splicing, etc. But, she discovered hidden technology that could be analyzed later, namely how they had designed the Doomsday Ray and how it altered technology on Earth. She found this extremely interesting and wanted to delve into this immediately, but, at this point, she needed information on the mind transfer. There were several mentions of its use in their history but no details, but her confidence grew with each references.

When she did find it, she almost missed it. It revealed itself in the form of a complex chemical formula, luckily, one she could replicate. Somehow, she wasn't expecting it to take this form. She expected some apparatus that would perform the mind transfer. As it turned out, the only apparatus required was a simple but specialized blood filter/injector. The whole process used chemicals to accomplish the mind transfer. Once injected into the blood stream, the chemical formula travels to the brain. As chemicals and minute sponge-like receptor/transmitters travel through the brain, the chemical stimulates the synapses to release its chemically stored memories, which are then absorbed by the receptors. The receptors are then

116

filtered out and inserted into a new chemical solution that causes the reverse affect in the receiving subject's brain. The blank synapses of the recipient are stimulated to absorb the captured chemical memory from the transmitter as they pass through the brain.

The whole process seemed fundamentally simple but complex in design. The process apparently worked on a Simian brain, but it would NOT work on Humans, because the stored memories are processed differently in a Human brain. The recipient's memories would be jumbled and unusable. At some point she might study altering the process, but time did not allow it now.

What bothered her most about the process: it was irreversible! The chemical memories were not copied but absorbed, wiping the Simian brain clean of memories in the process. The donor died. The mind transfer should work, however, and she could construct the filter/injector, concoct the chemical ingredients, and mix the formulas. The Earth Dragon project would be implemented, and Amy brimmed with confidence as she instructed Mama to prepare the first eighteen volunteers to host the first Earth Dragon embryos.

All nine remaining of the original fifteen Techs of Levi's most trusted, readily volunteered to be Earth Dragons and she would honor their wishes. They had spent the last few weeks delegating any leadership responsibility they previously had. That was the downside of them becoming dragons, but it couldn't be helped, and they had chosen wisely. Their replacements were firmly of like minds and loyal to Levi, her, and the alliance.

One major problem was replacing # 5; there simply were no other Simian computer engineers. Fortunately, they had passed the initial crisis period when he was indispensable, and she didn't want to prevent him from this opportunity to remain with his brother Techs and Levi. She would be able to resolve any computer translation now, especially since the integration of computers.

An even number of Fems would make the transition in the first phase, beginning with Bambi and One. The other seven Fems to make the transition were chosen from among the eighteen volunteers hosting the dragon embryos. By the time transition would be required, all would have their infants weaned from nursing. Somewhat ironic ... seven of the volunteers would be hosting their own future dragon body.

The only ones remaining still committed of the volunteers were Bambi, and Moon, both remained the commanders of the combined Fems and Techs. They would be hard to replace, but that could be delayed until just before the time of transition.

All the Fems in the projects were moved inside of the facility for the duration, and they were proud and jubilant. Mama painstakingly collected all the DNA samples from both the Techs and Fems and began the alterations according to Amy's design and supervision. At that point, the embryo implants began, and the Earth's Dragons project launched. Now, they had to wait.

***

She had been so damn busy with all the happenings around her she hadn't thought about Levi. He had been subjugated to the back of her mind by the very things he had forced her to achieve. Levi knew very well that forcing her to live on and protect their friends would develop into a massive job, and it had; but she allowed herself to let him slip backwards into her thoughts. Had she not, Levi would become foremost in her mind, and she would spiral down into depression.

This inattention to Levi added to the extreme shock of his contact. Luckily, she was alone performing multiple tasks when she felt his mental touch. Maybe that is how she felt it, because her total attention was not demanded in dealing with others. She knew instantly what and who it was, but the shock rocked her mind. All activities ceased to concentrate wholly on his tentative mental touch, and it was tentative. She would know Levi's mental signature no matter how slight, but surprisingly, even though the touch had little substance, the signal had transmitted strength.

Amy realized the strength of the signal was due to the increased size of his Pineal Gland supporting telepathy, but more shocked that the mind behind it was active. At only twenty-four weeks growth, the fetus should not have brain activity that should come thirty to sixty days later in the third trimester. Levi's body obviously was developing faster than expected. Well, no matter, it was here now, so she must deal with it!

Amy expected contact; she just wasn't quite ready. She thought she had a little more time. Information would have to slowly be transferred to

119

his developing brain in stages. Eventually, she would be able to communicate with Levi, once he knew a vocabulary of words and what they meant. All she could communicate to him at this point were feelings: comfort, love, security, etc., and that is what she did.

Levi's mind locked on these feeling and drew from them, nurturing as he would from a breast. She felt his needs and continued to satisfy them as best she could telepathically, and she slowly began to feed his hungry mind information, slowly, very slowly. Levi's mind was blank, a canvas without paint, and she was the artist. She began painting.

***

Mama came bursting into the conference room, usually indicating something drastically wrong. Once Amy had established her presence through the holographic image, she was never able to convince Mama to report anywhere else. To Mama, the essence of Amy was only in the conference room. Today was no different.

Mama's large and rotund frame came pounding toward her image and screeched, "We just received flash signals from our outpost at the bridge. Mosley is coming and he is bringing his followers. They have crossed the bridge and his Lancers positioned themselves to defend it, and Mosley is riding fast toward us."

Another problem! That was all she needed right now. It must be serious to cause Mosley to vacate his territory in Mexico, and the fact that he was

120

riding fast to report, meant it was probably urgent. It could only mean Simians.

She thanked her intuition for establishing a sentry system and making them learn Morris Code with the mirrors for communications. This proved to be sound logic.

If it weren't such a potentially serious situation, she might find some humor in the imagined sight of the hugely muscled, black man, Mosley, riding his also huge draft horse. He and his Lancers had saved them...twice, but each time she saw him riding toward them it meant trouble for Levi and her, personally. She did smile when she remembered how he looked without his two front teeth after Levi knocked them out. Moon had even wanted to put them on Levi's trophy necklace.

Amy said, "Mama, you better alert Al and Iron Eyes and ask them to come. You better call Moon, also. Where do you stand with the portable laser?

Mama signed, "It is not working right now. We are still trying to rebuild the other portable generator. It was in bad shape. Truthfully, I don't think we can make it work."

"Okay, Mama, do what you can with it, but call the others, first." Mama nodded as she shot from the room. Levi would have said, and probably so she could hear, "She's pretty fast for an Old Broad."

"Oh wait!" Amy yelled. As Mama returned, Amy continued, "Send a flash message to the sentries north and south to keep a keen eye for any other Simian activity. This could be a dual coordinated attack, assuming it is an attack. Another thing, Mosley may not know Levi is dead or anything about me. Can you brief him before you

121

bring him in?" Mama understood and nodded again as she left the room.

Watching her leave, Amy realized just how lucky she was to have Mama at her side. She had offered Mama the opportunity to become one of the new Earth Dragons, but Mama would have none of that. Mama refused, saying her place was here. Amy was thankful, because Mama truly was irreplaceable.

Many hours passed before they all gathered in the conference room. It seemed apparent that Mosley had been briefed, but he remained in awe at the modern surroundings. When her image appeared, Mosley, characteristically for him, launched immediately into a tirade.

Mosley said, "Why didn't anyone tell me Levi was dead. I would have come sooner."

Amy interrupted, "And just why would you have come sooner?"

"To take command! We need leadership to defend against the Simians."

Those gathered bristled at his arrogance, and Moon's eyes turned completely and dangerously red. Oggg sensed the anger, yelped, and jumped down from Moon's neck. She, on the other hand, knew this was coming, no surprise here. She held her hand open toward the members, calming them. She noticed a slight lisp caused from his missing front teeth. Smiling, she said, "I am in command here, and you will accept my leadership and direction or you will leave our land with your tribe, IF they want to follow you." She paused for emphasis. "You and I both know you can't, because you were driven here by the Simians and you came for protection. You and your tribe are welcome to stay under these conditions. So, what's it going to be?" She continued to stare at him and let the silence in the room work on him.

She had learned a lot from Levi. He believed bullies must be confronted, and she had done just that. Mosley was not a bad man, and they needed each other, but he truly was a bully and accustomed to having his way. She had to take command before Mosley felt empowered.

Suddenly, Mosley said, "You are nothing but a computer. You can't command Humans or even these ..... these .... animals."

She again restrained Moon with a gesture, but he neared his breaking point. To Mosley she calmly said, "You will show respect in this conference room or I will destroy you where you sit." To accent her statement she fired a short laser burst, exploding the water glass in front of him. Forcefully, she continued, "I AM in command! You will acknowledge and accept this NOW or leave immediately!"

Mosley said, "We don't have time to discuss this. The Simians are coming and we need to get ready. They are behind my army and..."

Amy interrupted, "You are right. We don't have time to waste. Acknowledge me as leader before we continue."

After a long pause in which he stared into unblinking eyes, he said, "Alright, dammit. I accept you as leader."

Mosley had worked well, begrudgingly, with Levi once he established command, and she knew he would this time as well, but his nature required him to try. Under different circumstances and different players his bravado attempt might have worked, but there was too much at stake.

"Okay, Mosley, please report the situation."

"We were driven out of our settlement and pursued by about two thousand Simians. We believe they were following the last orders they were given by the Supreme One, and they don't yet know he is dead. Hell, I didn't even know for sure until I got here. They came from the south, deep in Mexico or below. We engaged a few Simian patrols, and they knew nothing of Lancer tactics. We easily defeated them, but their numbers presented little chance of us taking the army on, so we ran. They march in three separate groups, probably three different colonies and they are a day behind us."

"Thank you, Mosley. You can re-join your army. They will need you. Mama, any sign of other Simian activity from the sentries?" Seeing a negative sign she continued. "Al, Iron Eyes... Let's mobilize the Lancers and Infantry but get the riflemen to the bridge immediately, and take Jimmy to communicate back. They will deter the Warrs from trying to cross, hopefully, until we get a strong enough force to stop them. Moon, the same for you, Let's get the Techs mobilized. Mama, keep the Fems here; they are doing something more important right now, and they can be our defense if necessary."

They all nodded and left in unison, even Mosley. He didn't want any more of her. She smiled internally, thinking how proud Levi would have been.

Mosley had made an intelligent report and his assessment was probably accurate. She also believed the remote Simian colonies were following the last orders they received and didn't know the Supreme One was dead. In reality, none of the colonies could know for sure, but after the decimation of the last attacking Simian armies and the retreat of the survivors reporting back, they would assume the Supreme One dead, or it would be giving them new orders. If they were lucky, these remote armies were acting alone. Even so, this was bad, but at least they had a defendable position and not out in the open.

If only she still had telepathic communications with Al, Jimmy, and Fred. Being without it complicated any battle plans. Another reason to hate the Supreme One.

It would take time for her armies to position themselves to defend, but Mosley's army would be able to slow or withstand any all-out attack, should it come. Without the Supreme One forcing suicide attacks, the Simian armies would see the fruitlessness of forcing an engagement across the bridge. She was sure they had time. The Simians would explore up and down the river, searching for a way to cross and attack from the side or rear. It could be done, but they had no way of knowing the other bridges had been blown up. They would have to go a long way to find another bridge or build one.

She learned through experience that simply defending was not enough. She must find a way to attack. Mosley believed the Simian armies came from three different colonies. That meant there were three colonies without Warrs. There was one way she could take advantage of the situation and another possible strategy to employ, but it would be a long-term plan.

Mama and Bambi came in response to her summons. Amy messaged them to come at their convenience to prevent a stampede, but they still burst into the conference room. Amy accepted the fact that this would always be their typical response.

When they were settled, Amy said, "I need more Fem volunteers, maybe five, for a special task. This is a very dangerous mission."

Bambi signed, "This will not be a problem. The Fems are committed to this alliance. For the first time in many generations we are free to be who we are and will do anything necessary to keep it. Just tell us what needs to be done, and we will get it done."

Amy said, "There are possibly three Simian colonies down in Mexico without Warrs. I don't really know where, but Mosley may be able to help with directions. I want three Fems to travel there, find them, and try to infiltrate these colonies. Once inside, pass the word about our alliance in hopes that they will rebel. I need the other two to travel east and find the main encampment where the Supreme One ruled and infiltrate and spread the word among the Fems of those colonies. It is a long trip and dangerous, but, in the long term, it could be extremely helpful."

Mama signed, "We see the wisdom of this action. We will see to it immediately."

Bambi signed, "I was there with Mosley and Moon. I think I can find the others."

"No! Absolutely not! You are in your third trimester with a very difficult pregnancy. Sorry, you will have to stay right here in the facility." Bambi seemed disappointed but nodded and didn't argue. Amy didn't try to explain the communication link she already had with Levi. They wouldn't understand anyway.

Bambi's spirit was willing, but her body was already beginning to fade. Levi's fetus was growing at an incredible rate and sucking Bambi's body dry of nutrients. Bambi, in her seventy month, already struggled to carry the weight. Imagine Bambi trying to go on a mission. That could never be. They would be lucky if she lasted another two weeks before taking the infant. Infant didn't seem an appropriate name for something the size of a small horse, but it would have to do.

Since Levi's mind made contact, she had continued to feed him information, being careful not to download any of his personal life experiences. She limited information to generic life experiences such as recognizing objects, learning words and their meaning, visual images of experiences and emotions, etc. He was already equivalent to any four year old, except for language. Levi would be born fluent in both Simian and English. She provided his hungry mind with all the tools to begin life and knowledge, but none of his personal experiences that would create the personality that make him Levi. That would all come when his brain fully developed, and he could handle all his remembered emotions and experiences. This would come after birth when he could utilize all his senses.

Mama interrupted her thoughts as she entered. Amy brought her image to life and said, "Yes, Mama."

"It is as you said. The Simian armies stopped on the other side of the bridge, and they do not want to cross. They tested our defenses and were killed by the Riflemen. Since then they made camp and look as if to stay a while. Jimmy reports that patrols were sent in both directions on the river. It will be many days before they report back."

"Thanks, Mama. Please let me know if the situation changes."

Amy wished Levi was here. Soon ... and with many Earth Dragons to help.

Chapter 5
River Battle

* Amy *

It began to look like the Simian armies were going to make permanent camp at the Colorado River crossing. They had exhausted all reasonable alternatives of crossing the river, and without leadership they didn't know what to do, so they did nothing. The days and weeks passed as the standoff continued.

During this delay, Levi continued to grow at an astounding rate, being nurtured from Bambi and Amy, body and mind. Levi persisted with his insatiable hunger. Bambi swelled so huge Mama confined her to bed and continuous feeding. Since she couldn't walk anyway, Bambi willingly complied. Levi drew information from Amy continuously and to the point it distracted her. Levi's demand for nourishment would only worsen, and Bambi had reach her limit and started to deteriorate, so she concluded it was time to take the infant.

Mama and her medical team of Greys delivered Levi caesarean on the twenty-seventh week after fertilization. He measured almost three feet long and weighed, as predicted, thirty-five pounds. With the level of physical development and maturity, Levi could hardly be considered an infant and, to everyone's amazement, immediately demanded food...literally.

Levi wailed, "Food! I want food."

He already craved real food by memories from the mind downloads, but he would have to settle for Simian milk from the six wet nurses Mama had recruited. Once Levi began breathing air, the bat gene kicked in to accelerate his growth rate even more. As a result, he would graduate to liquid food in just days and then on to solid food after a week.

* Satan *

Sufficient time finally transpired to get answers to his many questions. The Supreme One on Earth still hadn't been seen or heard from, and all accepted the fact that he must be dead. This pleased him, because he would not have to fight this battle. He was alone; the only one of his kind left alive. There was no one to challenge him now, and he would become the undisputed leader of all Simians on this planet, hell, anywhere, since there were no other Supreme Ones.

He issued orders to his spies, "Spread the word that a Supreme One is coming to take control of the Simian race, and until he arrives, they are to take their orders, his orders, through his representatives, them. All colony leaders are to report to them and they will pass the reports on to him."

One of his first tasks, find out exactly what was happening in the west, who the Witch was and where she was located. He dispatched a large patrol to find out. To ensure his communication, one of his spies would go with them and transmit back his finding directly to him. It could be no other way, actually. The communication technology he invented could only transmit to him and not between the individual units. He wished he had built it differently, but this way ensured he could not be bypassed and could remain in personal control.

He would take immediate and decisive action to destroy the Witch when he arrived on the planet, but he really hated surprises. He would find out everything he could before he got there and have his attack planned. Operational spacecraft would be at his disposal, complete with weapons. Nothing could stand against him.

* Amy *

The Simian armies tired of the waiting game. Reports of activity began coming in, and the last report indicated an attempt to begin building a bridge upstream. They began by tossing boulders and building debris into the river on top of one of the blown up bridges upriver. This ended quickly when half of the Riflemen relocated to that location and began shooting the workers. In frustration they returned to the main camp at the existing bridge at Yuma, Arizona.

The next report mentioned unknown activity far back from the bridge, too far back to fire upon. A huge, thick, wooden wall was being constructed on massive wheels. According to descriptions, the wall had extension wings reaching back on each side. She understood immediately. They intended to mass behind the wall for protection from rifle-fire and push it across the bridge. Once across, they would extend the wings and launch an attack from the sides, and it would work. By the time they got across the bridge in sufficient numbers, it would be hard, actually impossible, to hold them. Yes, this plan would work.

Amy sent a flash message describing their intent, and instructing them to prepare for an imminent engagement. She suggested flaming arrows against the wooden wall when it got close enough, but that was all she could think of. Why hadn't she just had this bridge blown up like the others? They could always build a ferry later.

There was no denying; she screwed up! Levi would have thought of it sooner. Unfortunately, it was too late to consider that now. The bridge was too far away to get enough explosives there in time, much less plant them under attack.

This type of strategic planning seemed unusual for Warrior Simians, and she wondered who was doing their planning. Certainly, she hadn't seen this possibility coming ... Strange.

The frantic message received the following day reeked of doom, especially since Jimmy was reporting from a new location. Under the protection of night the Simians pushed the wall almost across the bridge and were amassed behind it when daylight flooded across the desert. When the Simians were able to see well enough, they pushed the wall through their barricade and poured through the gaps.

Jimmy reported that the moving wall was drenched with water, making their flaming arrows useless. The Warrs had also extended telephone poles lined with handholds back inside the wall, allowing more Warrs to push directly. This added force and momentum out muscled the wall of Techs trying to hold it.

Again, she marveled at the ingenuity of the Warrs. How was this possible with their limited mental capacity? Something was very wrong, and she suspected she knew what. There had to be another Supreme One ... somewhere. She could think of no other explanation.

Her frustration at not having better communication swelled her anger. She was blind without Levi. Damn, she wished she could be there with them to help, but Levi was months away from being able to function jointly with her or even as a conduit for her. They needed more time, and her armies must provide it

After the Warrs breached their defenses, they established a defense perimeter, and launched spearhead attacks directly toward the Riflemen locations, forcing them to mount and retreat. Even so, two of the Riflemen were killed and their armies forced to retreat. The Warrs were across and there was nothing that could have been done to prevent it.

According to the sporadic messages afterwards, the Lancers and Techs coordinated a joint retreat, killing many Warrs in the process but were steadily forced back. They exercised strategies Amy developed in previous engagements, but at best, were only able to slow the advance of the Warr Armies across the desert. It looked bad, and if she had legs she would be pacing, looking for solutions.

* Satan *

Since his fleet came out of light speed the communication delay had substantially improved,

133

and he could follow and control the action far better.

His patrol made good speed, with his prodding, and with a little luck, stumbled upon Simian armies engaged in attacking. Well, according to the description, they were in position to attack, but stalled in a standoff at a cursed water crossing. He ordered his spy, now a representative, to take command of the armies in his name. He didn't expect any resistance from the leaders, and there wasn't. They would not risk angering a Supreme One the repercussions would be too severe.

It initially surprised him to find Simian armies still actively engaged, but then remembered past communications mentioning his brother had commanded genocide against the Witch and her armies. These armies obviously didn't know his brother was dead, or they wouldn't still be following the orders. He idly wondered if he should punish the main camp Warriors for NOT following that last order, but decided there would be plenty of other reasons to punish them.

From the description and responses to his questions, he figured out the enemy defenses and designed a plan. He then issued detailed instructions for an offensive to be relayed to the leaders. Happily, his spy reported that the plan worked to perfection and the Simian armies were across the bridge and engaging the enemy. There were some losses, but he didn't care. The Witch would learn of him soon, but this action would give her a taste of what it would be like fighting him.

* Amy *

134

Mama came busting into the conference room screeching something unintelligible about the battle. Through the panic and outburst, Amy screeched back, "Calm down, Mama. Just give me the report."

Mama forced herself to relax and took a deep breath before continuing, "The battle! The battle! We won the battle! The Fems came!"

She flustered with excitement now, matching Mama's. "What? We won? How? What Fems?" Nothing made sense, but the news was obviously good, so something happened.

After a few moments Mama finally calmed herself to the point she started making sense. Apparently, the engagement broke off and the Simians retreated some. They kept looking back to their rear at something. Jimmy climbed a hill to get a better look and discovered hordes of Fems slowly moving up from the rear. They did not appear threatening. Eventually, the Warrs recognized them as Fems from their own colonies. Seemingly confused, the Warrs waited for them to arrive. The Fems intertwined among the armies, and on signal, attacked the Warrs with their finger fangs. An attack from previously docile Fems utterly surprised the Warrs. Suddenly, hundreds of Warrs fell screeching and kicking in death throes. Those Warrs that survived the initial attack burst forward from the ranks directly into the charging Lancers. The disorganized Warrs faced quick and immediate death.

She couldn't believe what she heard but understood what had happened. The Fem volunteers sent to recruit the remote Mexican Simian colonies had apparently succeeded in their task. Not only had they succeeded in recruiting them to the alliance but they had also remembered and duplicated the desert engagement in which the Fems had surprised and killed so many Warrs. At least one of the Fems volunteers had probably even participated in it, maybe all.

Amy would also be willing to bet Iron Eyes, Al, and Mosley recognized what was about to happen and attacked to seize the advantage. From Jimmy's vantage point, she suspected he would have an interesting story to tell.

While she silently celebrated the victory, Mama continued, "There is more."

After that last report Amy wondered, "What more could there be?"

"After the engagement and to everyone's surprised, a large group of seemingly lost Technical Simians came in."

She knew instantly what had happened. The Fems had freed them, and they didn't know what to do. Evidently, the Fem volunteers didn't tell the Techs about the alliance; they just followed, not having anything else to do. Without asking, she knew Moon immediately took command of them, bringing them up to speed and into the ranks of the alliance.

She was very proud of her alliance, indeed, friends, and they had done it without her. She wasn't quite sure how she felt about that, not being needed, but the alternative would have been far worse, being needed and unable to deliver.

She instructed Mama to have the whole contingent return home, with the sole exception of the watch. It would probably take a while for the Supreme One, assuming one existed, to organize another attack and she wanted her friend's home and close. She had other plans for the next attack.

* Satan *

When the report came in he instantly exploded in rage. Even this fact made him angrier. He prided himself on his ability to control his rage, but the shock of the report took him by complete surprise. It required many long minutes to regain control.

The Simian armies defeated, and mostly by the females of his race? How could this be? Why would they? He forced himself to remain calm, but his insides continued to churn with smoldering anger. The report said the females didn't seem controlled and voluntarily went to the runt Technical Simians and Humans and were welcomed, like family! He didn't understand what had just happened, but he must understand.

Suddenly, he froze in panic. If this could happen to those females, it could happen to any Simian female. They were only good for breeding stock; they had no other purpose, but without them, the Warrior race could die. They would have to be protected, even if it meant enslaving them ... more.

With this realization, he immediately messaged his spy commanding the main colonies settlement instructing the leaders to guard the females and keep them isolated, watch for anyone trying to reach or talk to them, especially other females.

The females had never done anything like this before, ever. They were weak and dim-witted. What could have caused this behavioral change? It had to be the female Witch. She must have cast a spell on them. No wonder his brother called her Witch. There was no other explanation. Suddenly, he was raging again.

In his rage he messaged his spy again and ordered six thousand Warrs to march west to destroy the Technical Simians and Human armies that dared to stand against him and all the useless females that assisted. None would be left alive, but he would personally destroy the Witch. He would enjoy killing her. This would be the first thing on his agenda upon arrival.

Even from this great distance, he began extending his mind to search her out. It took some time, but he finally located her. Shockingly, she truly did have a powerful mind, maybe even as strong as his. This enraged him more, until he thought about his technology and how he would use it against her. This abomination would die in agony.

* Amy *

Just as she was enjoying the emotion of jubilation at the news of the victory, her mind was flooded with radiated hate and rage. She had felt this many times before, and it could only be the rage of a Supreme One. If ever there were doubts concerning the existence of another Supreme One or accuracy of her clairvoyant visions of destruction, they vanished in a flash.

Another Supreme One definitely existed! So, now the mystery of the intelligence behind the recent Simian attack strategy was solved. This

Supreme One had been involved directly with the action, or he wouldn't have reacted with the level of rage generated at his failure.

The good news gleaned from his distress, beyond their victory, was twofold. She learned the Supreme One was probably still in space and he had operational technology on Earth.

The length of the delay of his reaction indicated his extreme remoteness to the actual battle. Like her, the Supreme One must be handicapped by communication delays, and judging by the timing of the delay, he was much further away than she, probably still far in space. Since mental telepathy would be instantaneous no matter the distance, the very fact that there was a delay meant he must be using some form of technology for communication transmitted from Earth.

She continued to be racked with fear knowing a Supreme One existed, but knowing these additional facts gave her warning beyond the clairvoyance visions. She had hoped there were no more Supreme Ones, but clearly her worst fears were being realized. The visions should have given her warning enough, however. Why didn't she trust them? Well, she trusted them now, but that just increased her fear and anxiety.

Knowing he existed was not enough; she must locate him exactly to determine how much time they had before a direct attack might be expected. Knowing this might mean the difference between life and death, but how would she use it?

In the initial invasion she had followed the flight of the Simian fleet by way of satellite tracking and telescopes, but that was when Earth had technology. Wait, her facility has technology. Could she do anything? Building a telescope large enough to find and track his fleet would be extremely difficult and time consuming ... time she didn't have. What could she do?

No significant technology exists on Earth, but technology might still exist in space. Could there be any satellite telescopes remaining operational in space? Most satellites have a life expectancy of seven to ten years. They operate by electronics powered from solar cells, but the limiting factor was the liquid helium propulsion required to keep it in geostationary orbit. Once the gas depletes, the satellite orbit degrades and it eventually burns up upon re-entry into the atmosphere.

It would be fantastic to use the Hubble satellite telescope, but unfortunately, after fifty years it would be long gone. There were two other satellite telescopes that might possibly exist. The Spitzer Space Telescope and the James Webb Space Telescope were placed in a solar orbit as opposed to an Earth orbit. These too, would have long depleted their propulsion, but due to the nature of their orbit, centralized and balanced between the gravity of Earth and the Sun, they might still be somewhat operational, assuming the solar panels and electronics remained functional.

A long shot for sure, but it wouldn't be that difficult to find out. All she really needed was a steerable ground satellite and transceiver to search the sky for any signals coming from these satellites, and her facility had one, two actually. Unfortunately, they were outside and out of the range of her altered environment. She only had two choices: bring one inside, which was impracticable, or alter the environment outside. Her only choice was the latter. It was time to delve into the secrets of the mysterious ray that caused the alteration originally.

Thanks to the "Secret" of the Fems, the science of this weapon was available, and she began her research.

Once she began delving into the science of the weapon she was utterly shocked. The science, although incredibly complex, operated from an unbelievably simple concept. Activating the alien weapon had simply charged the Earth with electrons. The alien weapon collected electrons from cosmic molecules from orbit and bombarded Earth with them. It was that simple, but extremely complex in what and how it changed the physical laws of Earth at the atomic level. It not only altered the atomic structure but also canceled the effects of it physical properties. The most important property altered effected electricity, since the basic principle of current flow requires the movement of electrons through a conductor. By charging Earth with excess electrons, it destroyed the ability of current to move. Normally when loose (free) electrons move from one atom of a conductor to another, it leaves a hole that attracts an adjacent electron, which attracts the next, and so on (current flow). By charging the Earth with excess electrons, the hole would be immediately filled by an excess electron canceling the current flow and disrupting electricity. The concept was ingenious.

She had recognized the effect of the ray on Earth but not the underlining concept causing it. She had been able to counter the effect in her facility by using the florescent light fixtures to generate positrons, the exact opposite of an electron. When an electron and positron collide they annihilate each other, being equal and opposite. This of course reduced the concentration of electrons allowing current flow to resume in the immediate vicinity; however, it was a continuous battle that would never end. At this rate it would take hundreds of years to discharge Earth of its excess electrons.

Understanding how it was accomplished, she realized that it could be undone, but it would require a massive effort and years to complete. This didn't help much in the current situation, but it was comforting. The good news in all this was that she now knew how to extend her altered environment beyond her facility to power the satellite.

She began immediately designing a positron generator and transmitting apparatus for the mountaintop. Already she was devising plans to be able to alter the transmission directions to strategic locations and specific uses. Knowing Mama she would have it built and operating within weeks.

***

Mama's medical team delivered her body (Amy) from Amy One, and she immediately began transferring her mind into the new body. Well, It was more of a copying of her mind, the basics: the aware parts, who she was, the alive part. Amy wanted to take over the body immediately before the body began to develop an awareness, personality, of its own. There really wasn't much danger of that, but, well, call it a phobia. Developing a self-awareness, a life, as she had done in her computer existence, instilled a deep appreciation of life. Life was precious to her in any form.

She had learned to live through her mind only, and had missed what everyone else accepted as normal development ... experiencing the formative years in a newborn body. She wanted to experience this, feel her mind moving muscles, arms, legs, and yes, wings. Additionally, her only experience with an actual body was her limited ability to live through Levi's body and never her own. Understandably, she anxiously began her new existence in her own body.

Her situation would be unique, however, at least initially. She could continue to live and experience life in both existences. She would continue to live in her computer mind and the new body interchangeably and simultaneously, flowing back and forth as necessary. The telepathic link would allow constant communication between, in essence, her two minds, but there would only be a single identity (self-aware) shared between them. At some point she believed her body's mind would take over completely and become the self-aware portion, returning the disembodied brain to existence as a computer. Of course, she would still be able to operate through it and draw data and energy from it. She was truly lucky, having the best of both worlds.

The limited, comparatively speaking, brain capacity of the living body would never support the full transfer of her intellect, but it would still far surpass that of any other human. Well, with the exception of the new Levi and his increased brain capacity. It was still scary to think of a brainy Levi, but she would still have him outmatched. She had to laugh at her own joke.

Mama had organized a large nursery for all the anticipated new lives and she was placed in there with Levi. They had already learned that the wet nurses could not keep up with the demand for milk for Levi and she had designed an artificial formula feeding system. Now she found herself on the user end of the system. This new existence would take some getting used to, but she enjoyed life outside her prison. To be honest, she loved it.

She enjoyed the experiences her new body provided and associating with Levi. He was a real shit, demanding and mischievous. Even at his young age he enjoyed irritating Mama, even her. She had never played, but Levi kept pulling her into games. Together, they learned to walk, run, even fly. Levi learned how first, much to her disappointment, but she reminded herself that he was older, a week older. Their flights were short due to the limited space, but exhilarating.

The Earth Dragons weren't quite as lucky. Due to their developing size, all had to be taken far too early in order to save the mothers. All eighteen lived, but being so premature, they had to be placed into incubators for several weeks. Luckily, the bat gene didn't activate until after they were breathing air, but once active, they grew quickly and they grew huge.

Unlike her and Levi, the Earth Dragons had no prior downloads and were truly babies physically and mentally. They required constant supervision by the Fem nursing teams and offered limited interaction with her and Levi, much to Levi's aggravation.

Levi continued to draw from her data banks at an alarming rate, but she still withheld the data that made him Levi. It was a combination of fear at how he would react and his limited physical and mental ability to accept more. She had monitored his progress, and he was almost ready, but he was still at the mischievous child stage. Still a child, he was well over seven feet tall and beginning to fill out, but he still had several feet to grow.

He constantly ran around the cafeteria area mooching whatever he could, which was a lot. Even though everyone knew who he was, he still had no clue, but he began to work it. Mama could hardly control him. It got worse as he began to experiment with his wings, running into the large open areas and taking flight to escape her. It was comical to watch, but Mama was at the end of her patience with him.

One such day Levi surprised her by running into the conference area, Mama pounding close behind. Levi ran behind her holograph image attempting to avoid Mama, and Mama, realizing where she was, stopped abruptly.

Angrily, Mama screeched, "You need to finish his education so he will be civil."

Holding back her laughter Amy said, "What did he do now?"

"He tied a rope across the door then threw that damn red Jello stuff at me. When I chased him I tripped on the rope! I'm going to bust his ass!"

She no longer could hold back her laughter, bursting out loudly. This aggravated Mama even more, but before Mama could speak Amy said. "Okay...Okay Mama. You are right. I will begin the final downloads. Give me a few days. In the meantime I have another project for you."

Mama immediately turned serious, ignoring Levi as he escaped past her and ran out. It was probably a good thing. She believed Mama really would have busted his ass this time. It might have been good for him and humorous to watch, and the little shit really did need it. Unfortunately, he would remember the incident when he regained his full identity.

She had been working on it for weeks to prefect it, but chose now to tell Mama about the positron generator and scalable transmitting antenna. It became a good diversion to save Levi's ass. She didn't go into much detail, as the full plans were already being printed, but enough to give Mama the general idea, and she was smart, really smart. It wouldn't matter...Mama would attack any project given her, and she would forcefully recruit volunteers for any help she needed. The word, Volunteers, was a slight stretch, commandeer might be more appropriate. Many Techs, Humans too, had learned this the hard way.

The last project she had given Mama was the construction of the filter/injector and preparation of the chemical formula for the mind transfer to the Earth Dragon infants. It had taken her and her team only a week to complete, and she had monitored every step. Amy's exact specifications were followed to the letter, as always. She depended on

Mama so much and remained extremely thankful she had Mama. It was almost time for the mind transfers, and she would need her now for that.

Both projects were important. She said, "Mama, we need to begin the mind transfers soon. Can you handle both projects? If not, you will have to postpone the positron generator and scalable transmitting antenna."

Indignantly, Mama animated her signs, "I can handle both! I will go get some of the brute Techs to work on the project, and I will supervise the work. I enjoy putting them to work. They scare easy."

She almost burst out laughing and made a mental note to watch the coming activity. She said, "Very good, Mama. As soon as you get the work organized we will start the mind transfers.

When Mama left she turned her thoughts to Levi. He was ready; it was her that was reluctant, not knowing how Levi would react to all her changes. Oh well, Mama was right...it was time. She began a slow download of Levi's memories, but she would save the last year to last.

* Levi *

Levi had noticed that none of the others looked like him. Well, there was one other who looked kind of like him, but she was the only one. All the others looked way different...bigger, uglier, and far more serious. They didn't like to play, even the one that looked like him. She would fly with him, however. Actually, she was the only other one that could fly. The main problem was that there wasn't room to fly. He had seen the outside, and there was plenty of room to fly there. Unfortunately, the big ugly one wouldn't let him out.

He had few worries. There was plenty of food and many around him always took care of him, giving him almost everything he wanted. Lately, however, he began remembering things, things he hadn't experienced. Well, he didn't remember experiencing them, but then he did. It was confusing, and it was growing worse. Maybe he was changing to be serious like the others. He wondered if it was the voice in his head. The voice was always telling him things and he learned from it, but this was different, much different.

He remembered a different life, a complete, long life and he was becoming a different person, but in that life he was ordinary, like every other person. Even worse, he was an attorney, and no one liked attorneys in this other life, but he was jumping ahead of memories.

He remembered being young, having a mother and father. They named him Levi and he remembered his father saying he was named after a pair of jeans. They thought that was funny, but it seemed perfectly fine to him. It was a macho name and all his friends liked his name and wanted one like it. He experienced the sadness again when they died and he had gone to live with his grandfather. Samuel was his name, and he taught him how to be Indian. All the memories were there in abundant detail, even the small things like tasting ice cream for the first time, breaking his toe on a tree, even almost drowning in a pond. The fear was still there.

He had no idea what was happening, but each day there were more memories, stretching over years. It was beyond just the memories; It was like he was living the memories at super-fast speed, experiencing them, becoming them, and growing older with them. Life and years were flashing by.

Suddenly, there was the invasion and all those dead. Those horrible Simians, Simians like these around him now. Fear froze his thoughts and body. The shaking in his body began, while the tightness in his chest gripped him. Panic quickly rose, but the voice spoke to him.

Amy said, "Levi, don't panic. All is well. These Simians are friends."

"Who are you? What is happening?"

Amy said, "I am Amy and I will explain everything soon, but it is important that you understand that you are safe. I am looking after you."

Levi said again, "Who are you? What is happening to me?"

Slowly, Amy began, "I am the one you saw in the conference room that day Mama chased you. I am also the one you fly with. There is more to me than what you see, and you will soon understand this. But, there is also more to you than you know, as you are beginning to understand. You lived before and you are again becoming that person. I am helping you to remember. There is nothing to fear...trust me."

"You are the voice in my head?"

"Yes. I will be here in your mind, waiting. Just call me when you want to talk."

He was still confused and a bit muddled from all that transpired. He needed time to think and the best place to think was in the air. Levi said, "I am going to fly and think." Then he ran off.

* Amy *

She went too far, but it was too late to recall the information. Her constant monitoring revealed no warning, but she should have realized a half-truth without explanation might take Levi too far. His panic was the first warning. Levi did not just record the information and memories but instead, he lived the experiences. The fear was real, finding himself surrounded by the horrible monsters he had seen killing Humans.

So far she had remained relatively silent, but now she spoke. He needed comfort and to know he was safe. Besides, she had to reveal herself sooner or later, and this was as good a time as any.

When she spoke, he listened... intently. Somewhat surprised, he obviously knew she was there, just unaware that they could communicate. He listened to her explanation and seemed to accept her words of comfort, but he remained confused. This was no wonder; she had transferred massive amounts of data into his mind, then transferred the entire memories of eighty years of life. How could he not be confused?

The only memories she withheld were the last two years, virtually everything experienced with her. Those memories would be the hardest to grasp. She would let him get used to his current level before the final transfer.

She missed him terribly but remained anxious. What if the data somehow got corrupted and didn't work and he didn't love her after the final transfer? Then again, what if it worked and he hated her for what she did to him?

He had decided to go fly and sort out his thoughts. Actually, she liked that idea, and she decided to join him. What if she took Levi out of the facility into the open sky with plenty of room to fly? The more she thought about that, the better she liked it. She had dreamed of flying ever since she and Levi had astral projected. That was floating free and very close to actually flying. Why not?

Telepathically she said, "Levi, would you like to fly with me... outside?"

Immediately he said, "Yes! But the big ugly one will not let me out."

In spite of the situation and seriousness she chucked and said, "Her name is Mama and you will have memories of her soon. She has been taking care of you. She will now allow you outside. Meet me at the main entrance area."

"Okay!"

Levi was now a well-educated mind. He had his own memories (education) plus a multitude of other information she downloaded, but he was unaccustomed to dealing with the intellect. This maturity would come soon with a little practice. Right now she just needed to be with him even though he didn't know her yet.

While she walked toward the door in her new body, her computer existence told Mama they were going for a flight and to allow Levi out. Mama seemed pleased, probably realizing Levi was not the rotten little shit anymore.

151

Levi must have sped to the front door and was anxiously waiting. The anticipated joy radiated in his face. She raced passed him unfolding her wings, then leapt into the air. Soaring high, she quickly turned in time to see Levi churning the air with strong strokes bringing him closer and closer with each pull of air. It was magnificent to watch the efficiency and grace of his effort.

Levi reached her height and circled, even rolled over. They turned to circle around the mountain, dipping into valleys. Cattle and horses stampeded, much to the disapproval of the Simian herders. The more they flew, the better they got. She enjoyed this immensely. The freedom of flight was far better than she had hoped. She enjoyed this better than anything she ever experienced.

They both were bubbling over with pride and joy when they landed, and as they stood there looking at each other Levi leaned over and kissed her.

Levi said, "Thanks Amy." He then paused and seemed to stare at her for a long time before saying, "You are very beautiful."

She almost melted and flew into his arms, but with much effort, she restrained herself. He was reacting to her image compiled from his memories of most desirable features. Since he had all those memories, her image would register as perfect to him, but she must wait. She wanted his love, not his lust. It was time to give him the remainder of the downloads.

Chapter 6
New Life

* Amy *

Mama reported to the gathered group that the Earth Dragons were developed enough to proceed with the mind transfers. The filter/injector and preparation of the chemical formulas for the mind transfer had been ready for weeks. All that had to be done now was the actual procedure. Amy dreaded this part, because the process would kill the subject, and in this case, Moon. What if something went wrong? What if she had somehow made a mistake? The answer to both questions was: Moon would be dead and it would have been her fault.

She had double checked her calculations, then checked them again. The process seemed perfect, and they were committed. Amy said, "Moon, are you ready?"

"Yes, let's do it."

Moon trusted her completely. She could see it in his eyes, but it was a little unnerving to see the wide-eyed look of fear in the eyes of the humans. Had the situation not been so serious, it might be comical to see Iron Eyes, and Al showing fear. They normally faced danger with calm resolve.

Out of curiosity she asked one final question. "What are you going to do about Oggg?"

Moon signed, "Jimmy is going to take care of him. If he doesn't accept me back in my new form he will keep him."

She had stalled as long as she could so the team headed toward the clinic. Moon's Earth Dragon was already strapped on one of the two tables, the biggest one. The Earth Dragons were far from full-grown, but already massively huge. Moon appraised his new body as he lay on the other table and waited.

One of Mama's team connected the filter/injector into the necks of Moon and his Earth Dragon and waited for the "go" order, which Mama promptly gave. The whole process should take two hours, so there was nothing to do but wait, but no one wanted to leave . . . just in case.

It became a very long two hours, but the process ended. Moon's body had become very still, probably dead, but there had been no indication from Moon the Earth Dragon. Finally, the medical technician removed the needle from the necks of both and covered Moon's body with a sheet, confirming that the body was indeed dead. When she slightly shook the Earth Dragon, Moon jerked his eyes open and looked around. His face split in a huge grin, while jerking one pair of thumbs high in the air. This would take some getting used to. The dragon Moon's grin looked much more hideous than she had ever seen on a Simian, but it was a most beautiful grin, knowing the process had worked.

Bambi and Mama ran in the room to give the new Moon a big hug. Moon was a little awkward trying to get up, but he managed to get his long neck against Bambi and wrap his arms around her in a warm embrace. Still an infant's body, Moon towered over the them all.

The others followed to congratulate Moon on the transition. Amy, in force of habit, hadn't even considered using her own body until this very moment. Oh well, it was too late now. She could hug him later.

Moon surprised her with his next request.

Moon screeched, "Where is Oggg?"

Understanding, Jimmy jumped to fetch the pup. Being cautious, he let Oggg first see the lifeless body of Moon and let him smell and nudge it with his nose. He then brought the pup to the dragon Moon. Oggg was a little skittish at first, smelling all around Moon, but then somehow seemed to understand it was Moon. To Moon's obvious glee, Oggg began barking and clawing, trying to climb Moon's huge leg. Moon scooped Oggg up and tossed him on his now ample back. Oggg made himself comfortable in his new home, and apparently intended to stay right there.

Bambi said, "I want to be next. Moon and I can learn these new bodies together. Can we do it now?"

This request wasn't totally unexpected. It made sense, so she allowed Mama to proceed with Bambi now and the others as soon she could make all the arrangements. All eighteen Earth Dragons would be active within days.

Amy corrected her previous mistake and appeared at the clinic in her own body. She wanted to hug Moon also, but just as she was about to hug him, she heard the all too familiar telepathic voice of Levi.

"AMY, where the hell are you?"

Amy said out loud, "Oh shit! Levi is back!"

155

He didn't remember ever being this smart, but then Amy said she helped him remember, whatever that meant. He had memories of a long life. Another thing he never remembered, in that life, having wings or two thumbs on each hand. He certainly didn't remember being this damn big. The wings were great, and he liked flying, but he and Amy seemed to be the only ones with wings. This was hard to understand.

When he suddenly remembered the incredible horrors of the Simians, there was only panic, since he was now surrounded by Simians. Lately, however, he realized these were a different kind, friends even. Amy even seemed to be more familiar. She certainly was gorgeous, prettier than any female he ever remembered seeing, and he liked her. Her beauty haunted his thought.

The memories began to flood his mind again, beginning right where they stopped before. Shockingly, he remembered it all, and everything fell into place. He remembered Amy, the first contact, how she persuaded him to cross the desert, and how she changed him. He remembered meeting Al at the Desert Settlement, Iron Eyes in Owens Valley, then Moon at the lake. There were also the battles with Gord and so many fights with the brutish Simians. He remembered the love, how he fell in love with Amy and how he still loved her beyond understanding. What had happened to separate them? Why had he not remembered?

Struggling to put all the pieces together, he suddenly realizing he was going to die fighting with the Supreme One. Then there was blackness! But he was alive, so he must not have died.

It came to him in a flash. Of course he had died, but Amy had found a way to bring him back. She always found a way. He sobered somewhat, realizing what Amy must have done. Just look what she did. He was much bigger and with wings! Well, he kind of liked the wings. Damn, did she have to give him these double thumbs? Just wait till he saw her again.

A huge grin spread across his face as he realized Amy had also found a way to become real. No wonder she looked familiar. She was only an image in his mind before, but now alive in body, and he had actually flown with her.

All these thought came instantly, and even though he remembered how, he had not yet opened his mind to her. How long had he been away and what had happened in the mean time? He was anxious to contact her, go to her, and feel her in his arms, but he couldn't resist a little playful teasing.

Telepathically, he sternly said, "A M Y, where the hell are you?"

* Amy *

She had sought but dreaded this moment ever since she conceived the idea of bringing Levi back altered. She loved him dearly, but he was such a macho shit and demanded his independence. He wouldn't take kindly to the liberties she had taken with his body. Now he was back and she must answer for them.

She searched for his mind, but he had his blocks up. She tried to push through the barrier, but he was too strong, stronger than ever before. All she could do was answer. "I'm in the clinic with our friends. She waited for a response that didn't come. Then she just waited for him.

It suddenly dawned on her that Levi had asked WHERE she was instead of simply opening communication through their link. She realized Levi had made all the mental connections and knew she was living through her own body now. He would know the reality of her situation and that she would be living through both the computer and body but chose to come to her body. Did he plan to strangle me?

Levi burst through the door fixing her in an unblinking stare from those golden, bronze eyes she loved. No emotion showed in his face as he approached. She anxiously waited for his approach.

He came directly to her and stared deep into her eyes, then placed his hands on her cheeks, cupping her face, and kissed her. It was a passionate kiss that lasted long moments and weakened her knees. His mental voice reached her.

"I love you, Amy. Thanks for bringing me back."

He then opened his mind to her and she saw the love and he saw hers.

For the first time she felt a little awkward displaying open affection in front of all their friends, but finally decided it didn't matter. They probably all knew what they hadn't been able to see before, and their happiness showed as they watched.

She announced, "Levi is back with us completely now." The statement seemed to break the frozen silence as they gathered around welcoming Levi back. He was happy to see them, even the big ugly one, as he called Mama out loud. Mama looked offended until Levi caught her in a big embrace and lifted her in the air. Mama beamed with the affection.

He warmly greeted Jimmy, Al, Iron Eyes and the others gathered, but looked around searching, she knew, for Moon. His eyes stopped on the two Earth Dragons, then looked at her as if to ask, "WTF?" Understanding, she said, "Levi, let me introduce you to Moon and Bambi in their new form. They are now Earth Dragons." To Levi she said, "I will explain later."

Levi went to them and they all fell into a group hug. She could see Levi's bronze eyes watering. Moon was the happiest she had seen him in quite some time. It was easy to see, even in his altered body.

Levi said to Moon and Bambi, "I see Amy has been altering your bodies, too."

Moon screeched, "We made Amy build us these bodies so we could fly and fight with you when you returned."

Levi said, "We shall do just that, my friend, but right now Amy and I have some catching up to do. When I am up to speed again we can talk more, and maybe you can tell me what that white pup is doing on your shoulder."

Levi said, "Amy, let's go fly and you can tell me what I have missed."

* Levi *

His heart soared with pleasure to be back and see all his friends again, but pleased especially to see Amy again. He hadn't missed her until just moments ago, but the feelings for her now could hardly be contained. He patiently waited for a polite amount of time then rushed Amy away. They raced toward the main opening and leaped into the air in flight.

As they took powerful strokes pulling at the air and rising above the facility, he opened his mind to her and began searching hers. They needed no words, easily probing each other's minds. Of course, Amy would mostly know what churned within his, since she put it there, but now she could sense his current thoughts and mood. Mostly the exchange was for his benefit. He had missed so much of her life and he wanted to catch up quickly.

Amy had suffered so much anguish with his death, and he felt sorry for her pain, but she kept her promise to him and lived on. She had also helped their friends, and she had done a superb job of doing it. He marveled at the level of command and assistance she had been able to provide. She may have done a better job than he could have done had he been here. He chuckled to himself, knowing that it never had been him. It had always been Amy.

He almost missed a stroke in flight as he searched her mind. Oh crap. Another Supreme One! Damn, the battles never end. After a few minutes of searching he transmitted, "Damn, Amy, you have been a busy girl, and you have done well." She beamed at the praise, and dipped close to push him down with her foot, then soared high, racing away. Righting himself in flight, he shot after her.

It took several miles to catch up, and as he did, Amy dipped down into a secluded valley and landed. As he landed beside her she fell into his arms smothering his face with kisses.

She said, "I have missed you so much, Levi. It has been so long. Don't leave me again, please."

Again, there was no more need for words as they merged their love and passion. Even though their bodies weren't fully mature, their mental hunger and lust took them beyond rational thought and into a perfect union as they became one.

Much later they lay together wondering how they managed to get out of their jeans and fitted vests designed to accommodate their wings, but they evidently managed. He commented, "Amy, nice wing design. The tri-fold lets them become compact. It's a good thing or we might have broken a wing in our passion." They broke out in laughter together.

Amy said, "I thought you might be upset with all the changes I did to your body."

"I know you were, but I'm not upset. I like most of the changes, well, I could do without the damn second thumbs. I am having to learn how to use them." After a moment of laughing he continued, "You made me a lot smarter than before and I can see and interact deeper in your mind. That could be dangerous. I hope I don't start sounding like a computer like you used to."

"Shut-up, shithead!"

They spent the rest of the afternoon exchanging thoughts until he was completely up to speed and filled in all the gaps of what he had missed. Afterwards, they returned to Amy's quarters in the facility where he had spent the last night before his death, but this time Amy was with him in mind and body.

* Amy *

Never having had a real body, it was taking her much longer to get used to it, but she was extremely happy with the experience. Levi had the memories of a lifetime controlling and operating a body; it was almost routine to him, but this remained all new to her. She especially loved the flying, and evidently Levi did, also. When he wanted to go fly, she jumped at the chance.

As they soared through the air, she felt his mind reach out to her, but shockingly, he looked deep into her mind, even to the extent of reaching into her mainframe mind. Before she had tried to teach him how to look into her mind, but he didn't have the mental strength to do it well. Now his strength was almost overwhelming, almost matching her own...almost. Certainly, there was now no need to provide a separate monitoring window in his mind. He could find everything he needed and wanted now. It comforted her to know he could see as much in her mind as she saw into his. This added a closeness they hadn't had before.

She had missed him so much, and now he was back. He was back beside her and they were both in physical bodies. Happiness permeated through her, and she couldn't resist a playful trick. She swooped down and shoved his head down making him flounder in flight. She squealed with joy and raced off with Levi hot on her heels. She had never had fun like this before, ever, and she truly enjoyed it.

Her body began to heat and perspire with a combination of exertion and hormones. She had never felt the effects of hormones before and it was intoxicating. She and Levi had make love many times, but it had always been mental. The tickle of hormones made it different...somehow better, and she wanted him...now. She landed in a small grassy valley under an umbrella of trees and let Levi catch her. All those long held emotions burst forth and she literally attacked him, but then Levi was never hard to get. They made love in the soft grass for hours, their love finally flowing together again.

***

As she lay with Levi in their quarters, Mama reported in with her holographic existence. It seemed to become harder separating the duel identities. The identities tended to merge and the dividing line become less clear. She didn't fully understand what was happening, but Levi interrupted her thoughts.

Levi said, "You, the self-aware entity, is transferring to your body. It is inevitable. The senses and emotions are more fully experienced in body form than a computer. At some point your living essence will be totally in your body and the computer will be only an extension of your mind."

She hadn't even been aware that Levi was monitoring her thoughts. He had never been able to do that before. Suddenly, she realized he had become more of an equal now, stronger mentally. Amazingly, however, he was right. She was too close to the problem to see it clearly, but what he said made perfect sense. She transmitted, "How did you get so smart?"

"Duh! You made me this smart. Don't blame me."

Well, it was her fault. By creating super-sized brains in her and Levi's bodies, she had, in essence, vastly increased the combined intellect, but her immediate response was, "I think I like the dumb, macho Levi better."

Mama drew her attention back into the conversation in the conference room when Mama reported that the positron generator and antenna were installed, and the satellite had been serviced. Everything was ready for her.

Excited, she went to work immediately firing off and adjusting the positron generator and antenna toward the sky at the calculated coordinates of the satellite. With only minor adjustment, the ground satellite receiver sprang into life. The theory, design, and operation worked to perfection. Now her search for the, hopefully, still active satellite in space could begin.

* Satan *

Through his agents on the planet, he had been learning about some of the powers his brother had developed. According to the reports, his brother had been able to project his mind into other Simian minds, even at great distances, and take over their bodies. He had never heard of such a thing, but if his brother could do it, so could he. All the Supreme Ones could project their mental power to others to destroy them. He had personally killed many enemies in this way, but the thought of taking over another's body through its mind was extremely intriguing. Also, according to his agents, his brother was waging war directly with the Witch's armies in just this manner. This would be a valuable power to have and he vowed to prefect his own ability.

Other reports indicated that his brother had learned to project mental bolts of fire directly from his mind. It sounded farfetched, but the dumb Warriors didn't know how to lie. So, it must be true, but he couldn't imagine how this could be done. Certainly, his brother was not as smart as he. The raw power this would take was unimaginable. What could possibly cause the amount of anger and rage to bring this about? He knew the answer immediately. Only the Witch could trigger that amount of rage. Already, she was driving him to the point of uncontrollable rage, almost. Maybe he should unleash his rage and see where it led him, but he prided himself on his ability to control his rage, unlike his brother.

The Witch was only a nuisance that would be eradicated soon. Since they came out of light speed and approached closer, the intensity of her power grew stronger, annoying him. He couldn't forget her. Her very existence disturbed him and could not be ignored. Of late, even her mental strength seemed to have increased beyond just the increase associated with the reduction of the distance between them. He only had to endure the annoyance a while longer. They were close now and the bomb was ready. The Witch would die quickly, and he would be the only power on this new planet, and he would subdue and rule.

* Levi *

Amy didn't have to mention her premonitions; he saw them in her memory, and they disturbed him as well. Amy's visions all foretold a frightening destruction by explosion and fire at the facility. Added to the looming threat in her visions, the Supreme One could be felt reaching out. Even he could feel the mental power of the Supreme One as it searched for her and maybe even him.

This Supreme One was obviously equally as dedicated to their destruction as the last one, but this one had the advantage of technology to use against them from space. It possibly could launch an attack from space before he landed, fulfilling the prophecy. Yes, the threat loomed real.

He hadn't personally experienced the premonitions, but he could certainly see the ingrained concern and fear in her mind that drove her to locate the incoming fleet and the Supreme One. She had to know how much time they had so they could prepare, and they weren't ready. Even his project was pushed forward. It seemed strange to refer to his existence and life as a project, but in reality, it was. He and Amy (the projects) were complete, almost, and the Earth Dragons project well on the way, but, if the Supreme One attacked now he would win and they would die. That fact dictated reality.

So, that dictated the climate and pressure under which Amy worked, and he understood. He wondered if he could help but decided the best help he could provide was to stay out of her way and let her work. He also decided not to distract her work by making her split her attention between her computer mind and her body mind. She suffered enough dealing with the split attention herself due to the self-aware portion moving into the body. A unified mind would be needed to do her work. Amy realized his motivation and reluctantly agreed when he said, "I am going to find the dragons and fly with them. Maybe we will take a trip while you, all of you, work out the problem you are working on."

The dragons grew at an unbelievable rate, even faster than him. Visibly, each day they were bigger but not fully grown, according to Amy. They looked big enough to him; they were huge. Amy had been afraid the wing bones might not be strong enough, and had only recently allowed them to begin to test their wings. That's where he found them, flying in Amy's valley.

He immediately burst out laughing when he identified Moon out of the group. He was easy to identify; he was the only dragon with a flag of a white dog tail flopping on his neck. Someone had made a saddle harness for Oggg, who perched precariously at the base of Moon's neck hunkered low and holding on for dear life as Moon soared over the valley. As he flew closer he could see that Oggg had his teeth firmly dug into a leather strap and his legs somehow entangled in a harness. How Moon managed to get the dog to fly with him, he had no idea, but the little dog seemed to love it.

He hadn't intended to distract Amy, but part of her mind must have been with him, because she burst out laughing at the sight. He said, "Get your butt back to work and stop spying on me." She just laughed harder.

He was amazed. To be so damn big and awkward looking on the ground, the dragons looked graceful and extremely powerful in flight. Their golden bodies filled the sky and the gathered Simians on the ground stared in awe and envy at their new brothers and sisters.

As usual, for Moon, he saw him coming and turned to coast in beside him in flight. Bambi joined him on the other side and all the others filed in behind. They had to look something like a flock of geese in flight ... a large flock. The team was back together. He screeched, "Let's go exploring."

* Amy *

Her search for signals from the Hubble Telescope proved to be unsuccessful. It was a long-shot anyway, since it had been in space the longest. She then steered the ground satellite to the calculated coordinates for the Spitzer Space Telescope and began her search. After only a short time she found it! The signal was strong and still transmitting data. Hoping for the best, she transmitted a steering signal and it responded. Yes, happily it worked, but it would take time to scan the heavens for the third invasion fleet.

She almost spoke to Levi mentally but quickly held back. He would already be in her mind, monitoring, just like she snooped in his. He would know she had been successful in finding the telescope satellite, just like she was sharing the discovery of Moon's flying pup. The laughter erupted again, both audibly and mentally. Levi responded immediately, telling her to get her ass back to work. Oh well, she could share his flight as an observer while he had the fun.

Levi was right about her. She did need to totally concentrate on finding the fleet, but she wished she could be with them flying in formation. Her body could be, but it would have been distracting. The physical body demanded so much mental attention to function correctly. So, she went back to work.

From her location the satellite only had line of sight for about ten hours a day. The ground satellite receiver had to constantly move, tracking the satellite in its stationary orbit in space as the Earth rotated. Once the ground receiver lost sight of the satellite, she had to wait about fourteen hours before she could pick up reception on the opposite horizon. As a result, she had to work fast and cover as much space as possible. The true test of the equipment would be the ability to reposition the telescope view. She transmitted the control signal and waited through a significant delay, but she rejoiced when the telescope began to reposition. Luck seemed to bless them.

She estimated the fleet would be well within Earth's solar system traveling at sub-light speeds, and began searching along the trajectory of the first invasion. The results were immediate. In fact, they were hard to miss, even though there were so few ships. They were close, too damn close, almost approaching orbit. At best, they had weeks. At worst, they had days. After all her efforts they had lost, and her premonition was coming true. Fear and depression momentarily paralyzed her.

* Levi *

They were having a ball soaring over the desert, and amazingly they were covering great distances. The miles were flying past much faster than he had believed possible. Already they passed over the Colorado River and headed toward the Desert Settlement. He could feel his breast muscles pulling with each powerful stroke.

Amy had apparently structured a breast bone similar to what he perceived would be a turkey breast bone, but she had hidden it well. He assumed she had disguised it to keep him looking reasonably Human. Chuckling to himself, he mused that little about him truly looked Human, but he liked what she had done. He felt far better than he ever had, but with some regret that Amy couldn't modify him like she did before. The gills he would miss.

Amy interrupted his thoughts saying, "Hey shithead, would you rather swim or fly. I could have made you a porpoise instead."

"No, I'm fine this way. Thanks, Amy." She then flashed her image in his mind sporting a big grin. Her image stayed for only a moment then flashed out again, dismissing him obviously.

He screeched to Moon asking, "Do you know where we are?"

"I have no idea."

"Didn't you see the Colorado River as we passed over it?"

"What river? No."

He dipped to the left and swung around, heading back toward the river. The dragons remained close but still in formation behind him, as he glided through an air current. Quickly, he was back over the river and said, "Do you see it now?"

"No."

"Bambi, do you see the river?"

"No. I see the ground but little detail."

"Okay, tell me when you can see it." He began making wide circles over the river in a downward spiral. They had been flying several thousand feet following an air current when he began the conversation. Now the spirals were taking them increasingly lower. Still there came no confirmation from Moon or Bambi. They had reached a height of about five hundred feet before Moon acknowledged that he saw the river, and Bambi announced sight right after that. No wonder they were flying so close; they were following him and not the terrain.

This couldn't be good. The dragons would need good long distance sight in flight to follow the ground terrain, especially if they needed to find the enemy. They certainly couldn't search for the enemy at five hundred feet. Even at that distance they only saw the river, and they would need much better vision to see the details they needed.

Who would have guessed? Not only did Simians have poor night vision, but they were near-sighted, as well. He wondered why they never noticed it before. Maybe it was isolated to the dragons or somehow compounded by the expanded growth. In either case, this would be a major handicap.

Of course, Amy would be monitoring and would know of the problem, but she said nothing. When he looked into her mind he saw why . . . and the cause. Oh crap, she was frozen in fear again. He said, "Snap out of it, girl! I am coming back and we can figure out something together. Dammit, I said snap out of it!" If it hadn't been so serious he might have laughed at her reaction. Instead of saying anything, she only nodded her head like he would be able to see her. Had he not been in her mind and felt her actions, he would have missed it.

He turned his flock of dragons and climbed again in search of the air current. Once found, they turned for home, riding the current to face the problems they both had discovered.

* Amy *

Levi always had a way with words. When he yelled at her, it shocked her back to reality and got her functioning again. Levi was the only one that had the nerve to yell at her, and had done it often, too often. In his other existence she could maintain control of him by shutting him down as necessary, like she did with that trollop, but that was not possible now. He was also too damn big to beat the crap out of. She would have to find another way, but that could wait until later, assuming they had a later.

Even though Levi instantly exasperated her, he had been right to shock her back into focus. Levi never tolerated much bull-shit, and she loved that

172

about him. She just liked it better when it was directed toward others. She also knew what came next. He would piss her off and force her into coming up with some solution, but she saw only destruction in her clairvoyance visions. Levi invaded her self-induced pity party.

"Damn, Amy, get focused. We need you, and I need you."

"Is that your way of saying, 'I love you'?"

"Yes."

"Okay, shithead, I'm focused." That exchange put things in perspective again.

She put the pending disaster in the background and concentrated on the dragons' eyesight. She followed Levi in flight and the discovery of the near-sighted problem. This possibility hadn't even been considered. In the DNA mix Simian eyes were used and nothing should be different. Other than the color blindness for the color blue and night blindness, she had never noticed any other problem with the Simians' vision. Certainly, they could see further than five hundred feet or she would have noticed. Levi speculated that it might have something to do with the expanded growth, but that theory didn't hold. She suspected it might be more to do with the perspective of looking down. The Simian eye was not centered; it was more of a split slot like a cat or reptilian eye. Possibly, this might restrict a downward focus, but for whatever reason, became a serious problem for a high flying dragon. Worse, there wasn't much that could be done to correct it. So, this just added to the list of problems to be discussed.

There was nothing to be gained by keeping these problems secret and called for an emergency gathering in the main big room. It was the only room big enough to hold everyone, especially the dragons, which had far outgrown the halls and doors to the conference room.

By the time Levi and the dragons returned, all the key personnel had arrived and many others that happened to be in sound of the alarm. It affected them all, so none were excluded. Everyone gathered knew this was going to be serious.

Levi joined her at the hastily erected platform. The additional height was probably not required, since Levi and her now towered over most of the Simians. Many of those gathered hadn't even seen them in their new body form, and even more awesome, the almost full grown Earth Dragons crowded in by the main door. There were many wide-eyed stares in all directions. The large crowd was anxious and attentive.

* Levi *

They flew hard and fast on the return trip, but he somehow felt that the dragons were holding back. Well, they had to since they couldn't see where they were going. They were content to follow him, trusting him as always.

As they approached the facility, he could easily see the hub of mingling people and Simians. All turned to stare as they swooped down and landed. The crowd parted as they filed into the already crowded big room. Amy waited on a platform at the front. He wormed his way through those gathered to

174

reach the platform to join Amy. For the most part they gave him plenty of room. It seemed strange to look down on virtually everyone. Amy had built him a very impressive body. Come to think of it, she built herself a very impressive body, too . . . very impressive. Amy flashed him a knowing smile from the platform.

As he mounted the platform, silence fell upon the gathering. Amy began. She laid out the problem, and she didn't hold back. Surprisingly, there were little reactions, as if they already knew, which they probably did. Amy was never one to keep secrets . . . except from him. Of course, no one knew about the Earth Dragon's near-sightedness, and there were some "Ohhhhs" expressed at this bit of information.

Amy was reluctant to offer instructions. She wanted their input, and asked for it. Surprisingly, Jimmy was the first with his hand up.

"As far as the dragons are concerned, it seems that all they need are eyes up there with them. How about human riders to provide them with long-distance sight. They are certainly big enough to carry the extra weight."

What an amazing idea. Why hadn't he thought of that? He looked at Amy, but she looked as surprised as he. He said, "Moon, what do the dragons think of that idea?" Moon looked around at the others and seemed to get an agreement.

Moon signed, "I think we like this idea. It would solve our problem."

Amy said, "Good, I like this idea as well."

Jimmy said, "I volunteer to be Moon's assistant and my girlfriend Katie volunteers to be Bambi's, if they will have us."

Momentary shock flashed on Katie's face, but she quickly nodded. He then looked to Moon. He and Bambi exchanged looks and nods. It was done, and they had their first Human/Dragon teams.

Al made the next predictable comment, suggesting evacuation of the facility. He and Amy both knew this was necessary, but they didn't want to face the fact that Amy (the computer) would die. Amy in body would live on in a limited existence, limited in that her intellect would be drastically reduced, but the self-aware portion would survive. Hell, she had mostly transferred into the body already.

Another reason Amy wanted someone else to mention evacuating, she wanted it to be their idea. It provided the only solution, but they all had made a vested interest in this their new home. Once suggested, she started laying out the plan. They didn't have much time, so the exodus would have to start soon. She explained that they would have to make it at least as far as Phoenix to be safe from the bomb, but he saw in her mind that she only guessed. It was probably a good guess, however.

As everyone began to discuss the exit strategy, Mama astounded them all.

"I am not leaving Amy. My Greys and I will remain."

Amy said, "No, Mama. I want you to ..."

Mama interrupted, loudly, "I said we are NOT leaving, and it's not open to discussion!"

This argument Mama would not lose, and everyone knew it, even Amy. For sure he knew it. Mama had dug her heels in and wouldn't budge on the issue, and Mama was more stubborn than any he

176

had ever met, of any race, and he loved her for it. Amy was easy to read. The tears streaked down her beautiful face.

Chapter 7
Exodus

* Amy *

Silence fell upon the gathered group as Levi and the dragons circled and landed. The big ham, Levi did it for the drama. He always did like to show off, but that display paled compared to his swaggering through the crowd. Maybe she should have made him ugly.

Levi's thoughts burst into her mind saying, "Then you would be stuck with an ugly mate."

She kept forgetting that he could see her thoughts much better than he had before. Oh well, he was right; she had built him handsome for her, but she couldn't resist a tease, "It's too bad I couldn't make you humble, you ham." He just laughed out loud as he mounted the platform and gave her a hug in front of everyone, and she loved it.

She thought Levi might start things off, but he just stood there waiting for her. He left it to her to present the bad news, which they accepted without comment. Predictably, evacuation was brought up. Of course it was the only viable option, but the unexpected portion was that it needed to commence immediately. She hadn't expected the suggestion of using human riders on the dragons to overcome the near-sightedness. Granted, with the pending doom of the facility, she hadn't given that problem much thought, but it was an excellent idea.

As an unexpected benefit, it forged a better bond between Humans and Simians (Earth

Dragons), and ensured that future generations of dragons wouldn't separate off to form colonies isolated from Humans. She had agonized over that possibility during the initial planning. So, this unexpected problem and solution would provide a permanent bond between the races.

Mama's reaction disturbed her greatly, and after the crowd dispersed, she attempted to convince her to evacuate, but Mama was emphatic.

Mama Said, "No! We will not leave. We were all old and useless, ready to die. Then you came along and gave us useful purpose. If we leave here we will no longer have a purpose. We will not leave you to die alone. We will serve you until the end. Don't even try to make us leave."

She tried to explain to Mama that she was living in this body now, but Mama kept pointing down toward the tenth sub-level, as if to say, "You are there." Finally, she had to accept the fact that Mama and her team were going to stay, no matter what. She almost wished she didn't have a heart now, because it was breaking. Levi pulled her into his arms in a tight embrace and let her cry, and she felt his wet tears on her cheeks.

Unfortunately, asking for an evacuation on such short notice came with its own problems. The facility and the valley transformed into a beehive of activity. The farmers were trying to harvest crops that could be salvaged, the tradesmen were trying to load wagons hastily built, and thousands of major and minor activities erupted simultaneously. An evacuation without provisions could be just as deadly as what the Supreme One had in mind, but she remained anxious because the Simian fleet closed upon them quickly.

Mama, on the other hand, continued her pace as if she had all the time in the world. She flowed directly into developing the next wave of Earth Dragons. She had previously impregnated another thirty Simian females with Earth Dragon embryos that would be unable to evacuate due to their already bloated size. Sadly, they too would die in the explosion.

Levi said, "Hon, you and I and the dragons need to go ahead and leave. We need to scout out the exodus route for danger. Plus, we don't even have a site for them. Don't we need to find a site, or can we go to the Desert Settlement?"

"I know, I know, and no we have to go further than the Desert Settlement. We have to get past Phoenix."

Levi said, "Damn! The explosion will be that big?"

"I am afraid so. I expect the Supreme One to use what they call a 'World Killer.' It isn't powerful enough to kill this size planet, but it can make a very large hole in this one."

Levi blurted out, "Crap! It will take the exodus a long time to get that far. I better go rush them along."

* Levi *

Moon and Jimmy wasted little time matching dragons and riders, and he witnessed happy enthusiasm demonstrated by both groups. Even the tradesmen had quickly fabricated saddles for the

180

dragons, and they looked quite functional. The Human contingent of riders split equally between young males and females, in fact, all the female dragons had a female rider, and all the male dragons had a male rider. That made sense. Amy thought this advisable, because the Human riders would be living apart from the Human populations and needed to be mated as well.

As he watched the dragons and riders practice, Moon and Jimmy soared over. Jimmy sported a huge grin and waved a thumbs up greeting as they flew by. In front of Jimmy, Oggg's nose could also be seen defiantly facing the wind. As they passed, he also noticed a huge sheathed sword hanging underneath Moon's golden belly. The whole ensemble looked impressive.

Amy said, "I have a surprise for you, too."

He turned to see Amy walking toward him with a huge samurai sword, and it really was beautiful, obviously made by a master sword-maker. He took the offered sword, admiring it. The wide molded handle fit his large hands perfectly, even with the double thumbs. When he unsheathed the blade, the gleaming metal radiated its beauty. He said, "Oh, my, Amy, this is exceptional. Thanks. Where in the world did you get it?"

"One of the tradesmen from the Desert Settlement is Japanese and learned the skills from his father who learned it from his father. The skills originated in Japan generations ago. They are beautiful, aren't they? I have one, too, and I had one made for Moon, Bambi, and the other dragons."

There were no words. He leaned to Amy and kissed her.

The time finally came. He had pushed as hard as he could, and the exodus was finally beginning to move out. Now it was their time. He and Amy were saying their "Good-Byes" to Mama and the remaining Greys, and it really was hard. At the last he had to pull Amy away from Mama and push her toward the door. Amy's heart was breaking as she sobbed her way out of the facility.

Amy unfurled her wings and took off right behind him, followed closely by his flock of dragons and their riders. They soared high over the mountains then turned south to follow the route the migration would be following.

Iron Eyes, Al, and Mosley were working well together, each leading their army of Lancers in unison. They were leading the migration, followed by the Tech armies, then the Infantry. An impressive gathering of Fems loosely traveling in the center, followed by an equally impressive population of Human females, children, and elderly. The wagons and herds of horses and cattle followed, escorted by yet another detachment of Lancers and Simian herders. There were thousands of them, far more than he believed existed. He said, "You were busy while I was gone."

"You think everything stops just because you get yourself killed? You made me live on without you, so that's what I did . . . lived without you."

He cringed at her response. Yep, she was still upset, and he decided to give her a little space until she remembered she loved him.

* Amy *

182

It was one of the hardest things she had ever done, leaving Mama and her friends behind, even harder than ordering another evacuation of the population. Knowing this would be the last time she would see them made it especially hard. She didn't know a body could shed so many tears. Had it not been for Levi physically pushing her to the door, she might never have been able to leave, but she wasn't sure how she felt about being rushed off like that. It was ... was ... physical!

She allowed herself to follow Levi's lead. In some ways it comforted her to let someone else take the lead, but Levi radiated a strong physical presence that unsettled her. Then she also remembered how wonderful it felt being embraced in those strong arms. Smiling, she thought she could get used to that.

Their flying flock, as Levi called it, impressively filled the sky with their power, but the ground migration appeared equally as impressive. It also sobered him knowing they were all escaping a far more formidable power. It was also frightening to think about the vast Simian armies that lay to the east, exactly the direction they were heading. What were they doing, and what might they run into?

She was thinking how insignificant they were when Levi made a comment. Hardly listening, she responded a little too coldly. He thought she was still angry, so she let him believe that, but she was long over it. He would touch her mind and discover that soon enough.

She enjoyed the tranquil flight in the clouds. After so many years isolated and imprisoned within a computer, she relished the feel of her own muscles pulling against the air, the wind flowing over her body, even the slight pain of the cold's bite at this altitude.

Levi said, "Where are we going?"

"We will follow the normal route the migration will follow. We'll stop in Barstow for water, a little rest, then on to the Colorado River for the night."

Levi said, "That's cool, but that's not what I meant. I mean where are we going to settle?

Oh. Well, I think we will settle at Kartchner Caverns just east of Tucson. Later on we may move on to Carlsbad Caverns, closer to the main Simian base."

"Caverns? Why caverns?"

Teasingly, Amy said, "Well, we are part bat." She added nothing after that, letting that explanation stand.

After a moment Levi said to no one in particular, "Well, I hope we don't have to hang by our feet."

* Satan *

He had finally accomplished the mind control. He knew that he could if his brother had been able to do it. Actually, it was easy. He began by testing his powers onboard his ship. The first couple of times he attempted it, he killed the Technical Simians. It became necessary to adjust the method of his mental transmission. It required power, but it had to draw the weak signals within the target mind, not force his own. Once he accomplished this, he could experience their senses; controlling the mind was the easy part. He became proficient at it over time and spent many hours operating through his test subjects.

He hadn't wanted to risk killing any of his spies, well, now they were agents, so all experiments were with expendable Simians. When he thought he was ready, he transmitted instructions over his radio to have them relax at a specific time. He then searched for their simple minds. The fleet approached close to the planet now, and he experienced little resistance to his probes. He concentrated on the agent with the dispatched army, and on his second attempt he managed to take over his mind and body completely. Far better than using the radio, his mind reached out, traveling there and experiencing the senses of the remote body.

He walked out of the agent's tent to confront the generals of the army. Sadly, they didn't test him at all. He had wanted to kill one as an example, but they seem to immediately know it was a Supreme One that faced them. He screeched, "How did you know?"

Almost in unison they screeched, "We feel your power, sir."

"Okay, show me on the map where we are." They scrambled to get one and were back long before he could get mad. Again, they foiled his desire to make an example. When they pointed out where they were, it surprised him to learn they were only a few hundred miles east of the water crossing where the battle occurred. They had made good time, not exceptional, but good. If he allowed them to continue toward the river they would die in the explosion. For them to remain safe they would have to stop here, but he didn't care if they remained safe.

If they died, he still had plenty of Warrior Simians at the main site and many others to spread out over the planet.

Even so, letting the army die without reason would be senseless, but then he had a good reason. Maybe they could survive.

* Levi *

As the hours passed, Amy thought less about Mama. She didn't like it, but she accepted the loss, although part of her mind remained behind. That was to be expected, since the largest part of her mind remained in the facility, but he noticed that her mind only partially participated in the flight. It seemed that Amy, a large part of her body's mind anyway, continued to monitor the invasion fleet. It neared, but was not here yet. They still had some time, hopefully days, but it was going to be close.

He had been thinking about cave life and what it would be like. Early in the flight Amy had shared her intentions of living in Kartchner Caverns. With his added brain power, he was now able, through his telepathic link with Amy, to access her data banks in the facility to learn more about those caverns. It remained unclear if the data was stored within Amy's physical brain or in the external computer storage, but he found it.

The caverns did seem perfect. There were two very large rooms in the caverns deep in the ground that would easily allow access for the dragons, possibly even in flight. One of the massive rooms was as big as a football field. It should be big enough. The caverns were a few miles east of the old city of Tucson. It presented a good base location, being a relatively short flight southeast of Phoenix. The caverns were also in the projected route of the migration.

Unfortunately, Amy hadn't decided where everyone would settle. Her main focus right now was trying to keep them alive, and Tucson seemed to be as good as any place right now. They could decide on a more permanent settlement later, assuming they all made it there. Amy hinted at moving to Carlsbad Caverns later. That would put them closer to the main Simian complex, but he had traveled to that area in his youth, and there was little there. It was dry, hot, and desolate, but so was Tucson, come to think of it.

They were approaching the Colorado River when he heard a sharp whistle. He looked around and saw Jimmy waving and Moon obviously agitated. When Jimmy saw he had his attention, he pointed down. Had he not been day-dreaming he might have noticed them himself. He immediately broke into Amy's thoughts and said, "Amy! Look below . . . Simians!"

Amy responded, "Oh, crap!"

About a thousand feet below a Simian patrol could be seen moving south along the river, apparently looking for a crossing. What the hell was a Simian patrol doing here? They should all be dead in this area. Again, something was wrong.

Amy said, "We have to interrogate them."

"Okay, Amy. I will try to save one, but just take a look at Moon. He intends to kill them." Obviously Jimmy had told Moon, because he was really agitated and gesturing for him to attack. He signed back, "We need to interrogate one." He began to spiral them toward the ground, circling in wide loops slowly dropping in height. They were on their final circle before the Warriors noticed them, but it was too late for them to run as they landed, ringing them in. The Warriors huddled back to back and visibly recoiling with fear at the sight of the dragons.

The dragons slowly tightened the ring, drawing their swords as they did. Almost simultaneously, two of the Warriors were literally snatched from the ground in powerful jaws that ripped them apart. The third was flattened to the ground by Moon's forelegs (arms or whatever they were), its efforts to escape were totally useless. It lay helpless looking up into Moon's angry red eyes.

Moon screeched, "Why are you here in our land? You don't belong here."

* Amy *

She knew Levi was in her mind monitoring and searching for data. Many times she had tried to teach him how, but he simply wasn't powerful enough, mentally. Now he explored at will. He thought he was so smart, and it tickled her. There were some barriers she would not let him through, however. She must have some privacy. The freedom to be afraid was one of those. It would only make her look weak in his mind.

Her concentration remained focused on watching the approaching fleet, when Levi spoke. Warrior Simians! Damn! Their very presence screamed of disaster, and they needed to know what form this disaster took. As the dragons encircled the Simian patrol, she quickly informed Levi that they needed to gain information. Without restraints, the dragons would quickly destroy them all, because she had programmed them that way.

The one surviving Warrior, so far anyway, shook with fear, but she didn't blame him. Being surrounded by Earth Dragons would terrify anyone. It didn't even try to hold any information back, even anxious to answer Moon's questions to buy precious moments of life.

From the interrogation they learned her worst fears were happening, like they needed more problems on top of almost certain destruction. They were an advanced scouting team for a Warrior army six thousand strong. They had been dispatched by a Supreme One to destroy the enemies in the west. They had traveled from the main complex many miles to the east. From the terrain description she estimated the army was now somewhere along I-10 west of Phoenix. In this area I-10 ran between two mountain ranges going due west. This would put them on a collision course with the exodus from her facility.

Since this patrol would not be able to report back the location of the only river crossing, the Warrior army might be delayed but not by long. They probably would send out another patrol when this one didn't return, but a few of the dragons could stay to destroy any additional Simian patrols. Eventually, however, the army would find the right route. Then again, if the Supreme One was in direct contact with the army he would know where the only remaining crossing existed from observing the last battle. At any rate, little delay could be expected.

The situation seemed hopeless. They faced destruction from every direction. If she stopped the exodus, the bomb would destroy them. If she allowed them to continue, the Simian army would destroy them. She didn't know what to do.

Levi broke into her thoughts, "Amy, maybe we can delay them long enough for the migration to cross the river and hide while the Simian army then crosses over. Let them be destroyed by the bomb."

"That's not a bad idea, assuming the Supreme One is not involved, but just how the hell are we going to delay six thousand Warrior Simians? Maybe all twenty of us can surround them."

Levi said, "Well, from what I understand, you designed the Earth Dragons and us also using part bat DNA. I reviewed your research and your design was brilliant. The dragons, us too, can use sonar to see at night, maybe even paralyze a Simian with it if we can adjust the frequency high enough. We could terrorize the army at night when they are blind, kill when we can, but mostly just keep them awake at night. They wouldn't be able to see or understand what was happening to them, and it would scare the crap out of them. A few nights without sleep and they would come to a stop."

Grinning, she said, "Welcome back, Levi. I've missed that astounding abstract thought."

* Levi *

Once Amy was satisfied that Moon had gotten as much information as he was going to get, he

190

nodded to Moon. The Warrior died instantly as Moon literally bit his head off . . . and ate it! He couldn't believe Moon did that but more shocked to see the dragons gather around and devour the dead Warriors.

Amy said, "I tried to design into the Earth Dragons a craving for Simian flesh. I didn't know it would work, but Warrior Simians will be their natural enemy, so I tried to instill that enemy to be their main source of food. It does make sense. Does that shock you?"

"No, not really. I just wasn't expecting it. That would tend to keep the dragons motivated to kill Warriors, but I don't think we have anything to worry about as long we are alive."

Amy said, "Probably not, but we can't know what the future will bring. I just thought it might be insurance, just in case."

"Amy, since you're fully here right now, there is something I have been meaning to ask. All those powers you had before. Do you still have them?" She looked perplexed. "You know: ASONE, astral projection, telekinesis, teleportation. I know you still have clairvoyance, and we still have our telepathic link, but I have been wondering about the others, especially about telepathic communications with Jimmy, Fred, and Al?"

"Hummm. Well, to tell you the truth, I'm not sure. You're right about the telepathic link and clairvoyance, but I'm not sure about ASONE, astral projection, and telekinesis. I had those powers through mental energy solely. Now that I have a body it has become a major distraction to the concentration that would be required. I just haven't tried, and as for ASONE, we never understood how that worked anyway. It just came when IT wanted to. Only time will tell with that. Now teleportation. Maybe, just maybe, but that ability might be shaky as well for the same reason. We will just have to wait and see. When we get settled we can do some testing."

He said, "What about telepathy with the communication team?"

"I have been afraid to try communications with them. Again, it is the distraction of my body. I never knew how much mental energy is required to operate a physical body. It requires vast amounts, but living through a body is far richer. I still have only one mind, but I have two brains. It is confusing. I am afraid that if I try to telepathically communicate I may revert back and link with those minds. Due to the attention my body now requires and reduced mental capacity, the extra strain might drive me insane and destroy me. Besides, when my brain back at the facility is destroyed, it's not going to matter much. All those things will be gone."

Levi responded, "Okay, we better not try then."

"I think YOU might be able to telepathically communicate with the team. You now have increased intellect, plus I increased the size of your pineal gland. This gland is also called the 'Third Eye' and believed to be the source of telepathy. It must work, your telepathy is strong when you transmit to me. So, I think you may be able to communicate directly without running the risk of linking with them. Since I am not linked and monitoring, the trick for you will be to amplify their weak transmitted signal. That is what I was doing with you before."

He wasn't used to doing the ... the ... smart shit. Amy always did that before. Well, he thought maybe he could be smart, but the wisest thing he could come up with in response was, "OK."

* Satan *

The Witch produced offspring, more abominations like her. He could sense the power of two new entities like her. They were much weaker than her but still easily detectable. They could never be allowed to live, and he must strike soon to eliminate all of them.

At first he thought the Witch grew in power, but after a while he detected separate signatures of the power, weaker, but much like the original. At times he also sensed the others separate from the main source of radiated mental energy that never moved. That one always remained at the same location. The others seemed to be more mobile, often showing up at distant locations when he searched for them. He feared these even more than the Witch. They were new and would grow up to be as powerful as the Witch. He had to destroy them before they became powerful. The children might even move to another location from which to challenge his rule.

This army must seek them out and destroy them before they establish new colonies, and if he destroyed his army in the process, it would be worth it. If he acted quickly enough he might get them all at the same time. He would get them anyway, even

193

if he had to use a second bomb. His army was only back-up, just in case something went wrong with his initial attack, as unlikely as that might be. His army would prevent any of them from escaping.

In his occupied body he ordered the army forward to the only remaining crossing over the water. He wished he had perfected his ability to take over a body back then. If so, he might have saved one of his agents from destruction by the cursed females of his race. It was still a matter that stirred his rage.

Luckily, he had prevented this affliction from infecting the females at the main complex. With his warning, his agent there had been successful in capturing a female trying to infiltrate one of the female compounds. The female resisted her captors and attacked some of them with those cursed poisoned claws. Her behavior was completely out of character with the dim-witted females he had known, and he still could not explain why. When his Warriors captured her and realized she would be interrogated, she clawed herself and died with her secrets. But, he had no doubt the Witch had learned how to bewitch the females of his race. He had to kill this Witch Bitch . . . soon.

* Amy *

Oh, she liked the idea of harassing and terrorizing the Simian army, and it could very well work. It seemed Levi always came up with simple ideas that cut through the veil of scientific complexity. Levi would say, "Cut through the Bull

194

Shit!" She designed the perfect fighting machine, he just figured out how to use it.

As always, it now required her logistics to put his idea into a plan, but before they could start, they needed a base of operation. The original plan to base the operation center at Kartchner Caverns still seemed valid, and there was no reason to stop. The Simian army would be pressed between the mountains with no direction to go but west. They on the other hand, could fly over the mountains from the Tucson location, which wasn't a long flight. The flight would give them time to explore the use of their sonar, and Levi was right; if they could adjust the frequency, they should be able to paralyze a Simian, at close range anyway. Since their attack would be at night and at low level, the Human riders would not be necessary. They could be left to establish a camp within the caverns, gather wood, and hunt. She suspected Jimmy would bitch about being left behind, but there would be plenty more battles he would be involved with. He would just have to suck it up.

Levi followed her thoughts and planning and had been relaying the plan as she worked through it. The only resistance was the predictable squeal from Jimmy, but Levi also relayed the words she thought.

"Oh, suck it up, Jimmy. There will be plenty of battles, but in a night battle you would be useless and might even be in the way."

The dragons liked the idea. They began hopping around on their thick legs, in evidence of their delight. Initially, she did detect nervousness at the mention of a night attack, but as Levi explained *sonar they began to relax. It was probably more of a trust factor than understanding sonar, but they would understand it better once they used it.*

She and Levi were beginning to revert to her doing the thinking and Levi being the spokesman. "Female brains and male brawn again," she teased.

Laughing, he said, "Oh, shut-up! Don't forget you can't shut me down like you did before."

Of course he was referring to the episode in the tent with that camp harlot, Joan. Things were different for sure, but she remembered her jealousy, and blurted, "If I catch you with another trollop again, I'll do more than shut you down; I'll chop them off!"

Although their private communication had been telepathically, Levi grimaced in mock horror then leaned over and kissed her on the lips.

Levi said out loud, "I love you, too." Privately he transmitted, "You are plenty woman enough for me."

Sometimes Levi knew exactly the right thing to say and do, but it embarrassed her and thrilled her at the same time. "You devil. Let's get going. Daylight's burning."

* Levi *

He loved teasing Amy. She was still dealing with her growing emotions, and her jealously was endearing. When he kissed her in front of everyone, she actually blushed. Jimmy smiled at Katie at the open show of emotion, and even Moon and Bambi exchanged glances. Amy changed the subject completely and quickly, suggesting they resume their flight. It was far too late to continue, however, so they decided to camp at the river as previously planned and start rested and fresh in the morning, especially since they planned a night attack.

Moon had brought a cast net, but he was having trouble throwing it in his present form, and talked Jimmy into taking it over. Soon, Jimmy had a pile of fish flopping on the bank. It was far from enough to feed the dragons but enough to take the bite out of their hunger. The Humans, however, had plenty and feasted on cooked fish, he and Amy included.

They were tired from the rigors of the long flight and snuggled up together in the river sand, still warm from the sun. Somewhat surprised, he watched the dragon's pair up in a circle around them, even more surprised to see the humans pair up with their dragons. Jimmy and Moon had done an excellent job of matching the mating Humans with the mating Simian dragons. Of course Moon and Bambi were next to him and Amy, and Jimmy and Katie were snuggled together between Moon and Bambi. He chuckled, thinking how someone could get crushed if the dragons got amorous.

Amy's laugh burst out and she said, "You horny bastard! Only you would think of something like that."

Grinning, he rolled toward her and winked.

As they took flight the next morning on what would be another long trip, he decided to try Amy's suggestion about trying to communicate with Jimmy, but he couldn't remember exactly how. It was completely different from communicating with Amy. Theirs was more of a constant link and on multiple levels, almost like they were a common mind, yet individually different. To complicate the attempt, Amy had always done most of it. He finally had to ask, "Amy, I don't know how to begin telepathic communication to another single mind like Jimmy."

"You're mind already knows. Think of Jimmy and how you sense him when you are around him. That is his individual signature, and you just need to open up your mind and listen for it. By listening for his mind, you will be tuning in to transmit to him."

"Well, that sounds simple," he said.

"It is."

He started out by doing like Amy suggested. He thought about Jimmy and what he sensed when he was around him. Jimmy did have a feel, like he could almost sense his humor, playfulness, and underlying serious drive in the kid. He began to imagine what the essence of Jimmy would feel like among a crowd. Then he started to identify differences unique to Jimmy and how each person seemed different in their own unique way. Tentatively, his mind reached out with thought directed only to Jimmy. "Jimmy?" As he did so he watched him. Again he thought, "Jimmy?" This time Jimmy jerked his head up and instinctively looked directly at him. Jimmy would already know how to respond telepathically, having communicated to Amy many times in this manner, but this time he sensed that it was Levi and different. At the time Jimmy had no idea he was communicating with Amy; however, this would feel different because it actually was Levi this time.

Tentatively, Jimmy responded, "Levi?"

"Yes, it is me, Levi." They continued to communicate for a while, perfecting their technique and telepathic bond. He then turned his attention toward Al and Fred, quickly establishing telepathic communication channels with them. These three, the original communication team, would now be able to contact him at will and he would detect them. He just hoped they wouldn't all try to transmit to him at the same time. That could become confusing.

This method wasn't nearly as revealing as when Amy monitored all their senses, but it was far better than having no communications.

Amy flashed a beautiful smile in his vision and said, "I knew you could do it."

* Amy *

Levi wasn't too proud to ask for help, and that pleased her. Once she gave him the direction on how to connect telepathically, she pulled back her mind but continued to monitor. This gave her cause to extend her pride even more. His mind worked well and he finally connected to Jimmy, surprising him. It would have been easy to do it herself, but she truly believed her extended brain would link again as before. It would be foolish to take a chance, since she would be able to monitor Levi.

She found it strange, considering the brain at the facility as the extension. Her essence (self-aware) reference seemed to identify totally with her body now, as Levi had suggested it would. It must be true, but still, her mind was a combination of both brains.

199

Before they reached the caverns, Levi had managed to establish telepathic communications with all the team, and they now knew their exact location. Levi had also notified the communication team about the waiting Simian army and their plans to stall them. At her insistence, Levi had also pushed their speed up a notch. She had no idea if Levi's suggestion could work and the migration could beat the Simian army to the bridge. The whole plan seemed extremely farfetched, but it was a plan; however, her main concern was increasing the distance from her facility (ground zero for the bomb) and certain destruction. Confronting the Simian army was almost as certain, but at least there were some variables that could be altered.

They reached Kartchner Caverns well before dark, located exactly where her internal topography maps indicated, no surprise, but the last few miles she followed billboards. They discovered, to their surprise, a large flock of sheep grazing in the fields around the caverns. Although totally unexpected, finding the sheep was quite fortunate for all, Humans and dragons.

It was # 5 that broke ranks first to sweep down and snatch up a kicking ewe, followed afterwards by the others. Levi, not to be outdone, dove to snare one up. It was a good thing they were close, because Levi's wings were less proportional than the dragons and he strained to reach the caverns' entrance.

She couldn't resist saying, "It's just like you to bite off more than you can chew, and in this case, pick up more than you can fly with."

200

"Well, I'm inviting you to dinner, and I'm carrying your share. We're having lamb chops," he said. Then he smiled hugely.

She couldn't let him get the last word, so she said, "That's romantic, but you forgot the flowers. I'm not a cheap date."

The entrance loomed large, but not enough for the dragons to fly directly into the caverns. They would have to walk through the entrance into the caverns. Nothing could be seen inside the pitch black entrance, even though the sun was still up. Now was the time to deliver with the sonar. She indicated for them to land outside and transmitted to Levi, "Ask the riders and dragons to stash their kills, spread out, and pull plenty of firewood to the entrance; while we get our sonar working.

Soon her and Levi entered the gaping opening and allowed the darkness to engulf them. Levi, the macho shit, sidled up close to her, as if she were the protector. She chuckled to herself and took a few steps into the darkness, partly to impress him but mostly to eliminate her eyesight from confusing the sonar signals.

Levi whispered, as if in church, "Won't our sonar signals interfere with each other?"

"Well, to be honest, I haven't tested the sonar, but, no, theoretically the sonar signal any of us transmits should be different from each other's. It should be like voices, everyone sounds slightly different. In this case everyone should have a slightly different frequency unique to them."

Levi whispered again, "But what if the frequencies are close enough to interfere?

Teasingly she said, "Just change the pitch of your voice (frequency). You know what I think? I think you are just stalling because you're afraid to go into the dark cave."

Levi burst out with a loud laugh, not quite masking the nervous quiver.

* Levi *

Amy was right about two things. She nailed the sonar transmitting process, and he was scared shitless of the dark caverns. But, she was wrong about the interfering signals. As soon as she emitted her sonar squeal he heard it. Hearing was not exactly the right word for it. He saw her squeal coming bouncing back to him in the form of images. He saw the walls, ceiling, and floor all around him and the depth of the cave in all its detail. It appeared as black and white images, much like a photo. It wasn't as clear as a photo, but he could distinguish the details.

Excitedly, he squeaked out his own sonar and obtained an improved picture by overlaying Amy's reflected sonar with his own. Quickly, he realized that the signals added to each other's, and interference would not be a problem, no matter how many were generating them. Just when he was feeling so smart about his conclusions, Amy broke into his thoughts.

"You are right to a point, as long as all the signals are being sent from your perspective, but what if my signal was coming from the far end transmitting back toward you?"

Oh crap! That would wipe out his reflected signal and make his sonar useless.

"Just keep emitting your signal and let your receptors home in on your signal. It will build a filter and adjust out all the others except yours, the frequency you transmit."

As he did as Amy suggested, he sensed a part of his mind working, and after a while, he no longer detected Amy's signal, only his own. Now that he thought about it, Amy's signal was never as detailed as the one he now enjoyed. It was not the same as seeing with his eyes, but the sonar worked extremely well in providing details of the inter-structure of the caverns, almost as good as his eyesight in the light.

More comfortable now with the sonar, they began to explore the caverns. Their main interest right now was finding the big room they would use as their camp. It wasn't too deep into the caverns, and best of all, it was huge, and they would be able to fly directly to it. It had pools of water continually fed by small streams and ventilation shafts to vent the fires. The site would work well.

By the time they reached the surface again, the riders and dragons had amassed a huge pile of firewood. As expected also, there were only a few sheep left for the Humans, the others having mysteriously disappeared into the hungry dragons.

Amy began taking the dragons down in teams, teaching them how to use their sonar, then leading them to the big room. He began leading the Humans with torches down into the caverns, each loaded with wood that would be needed for cooking and light.

They would get settled in, eat, and try to get some sleep before they launched their first attack. He and Amy were both exhausted and snuggled up together against the cold cavern wall and slept soundly. Both knew the sheep's wool would be used wisely in the future against the cold floor and walls.

Chapter 8
Conflict

* Amy *

Before she linked with Levi, the sense of taste was something she could only imagine, but she had grown to love the taste experienced through Levi. Now in her body she was truly experiencing this sensation first hand, and it was wonderful. Her body needed nourishment, but she relished tasting it. This was one of those times, as she sank her teeth in the warm succulent lamb shank, tearing the meat with her teeth and devouring it. Manners? Forget that. This was too damn good.

Somewhat self-conscious, she glanced around to see if her lack of manners offended anyone, but all the others were doing the same. Levi had a shank in each hand...so much for manners. She dug in.

It had been a long and eventful day, and she felt it. Her physical body ached, and with a full belly, she began dozing off. Levi gently lay her back on something soft and spooned against her. She felt his warm body and arms around her as her mind slipped out of her body and flowed back into her main facility brain. It was at that moment she realized her essence (self-awareness) had been completely living in her body. Until that very moment she hadn't realized her main brain had been dormant. Without HER immediate direction it had simply shut down. Just a few days ago that brain had been HER, and now it was an IT, how ironic.

In the future she would assign projects for the main brain with established alarms to notify her in the event of targeted activities. This would prevent her brain from going dormant and remain watchful.

Of course, the main priority continued to be monitoring the advancing Simian fleet, and just as she began to search, she felt him. She had felt a Supreme One many times before and knew the intruder immediately and blocked it from entering her mind. When it encountered her blocks, its rage exploded.

It screamed out mentally, "I am coming to destroy you, Bitch!"

Before, she might have frozen in fear, but not anymore. She had defeated all of their attempts and had grown stronger for it. She mentally screeched back in Simian, "You want to enter my mind? Come ahead, and I will even let you in, then crush your pathetically weak mind." Of course, she was bluffing, but he didn't know that. Then she thought, "What if she could defeat his mind? Would that end it?"

She felt his mind pull back. He no longer tried to pierce her blocks but remained focused on her. Whatever opportunity that existed quickly vanished. She felt his surprise at hearing her respond in the Simian language, followed by an instant of raw fear at her threat. Those emotions were quickly pushed aside by pure hate, ' hate so intense that she wondered how it endured. Unfortunately, the Supreme One managed to calm itself.

It screeched, "I WILL kill you, and I WILL kill your offspring wherever they go!"

Luckily, she slammed her mind closed before it could see her mind freeze in instant terror. The Bastard knew! He knew about her and Levi. It was the only explanation. He thought they were children of the entity at the facility. It instantly became obvious that he knew where they were, and that he would be as dedicated to killing them as her brain at the facility. The Supreme One would not hesitate to use two or even three bombs to destroy them, and it would be impossible to hide from his mental search. She instantly knew that life in any form was over, but as she had learned from Levi, NEVER GIVE UP!

* Satan *

For the first time he failed to locate the witch. He searched for her mind everywhere and found nothing. He found the two offspring far to the east. They had reached a great distance since he last searched for them and had no idea how they moved so fast. It didn't matter much, because it would be hard to miss a target with a Planet Buster. It would have been better to use only one of them due to the damage they would create. This would be, after all, his planet to rule, and he didn't want to destroy it by using too many of the busters, but two wouldn't destroy a planet of this size. So, as long as he could detect them, he could kill them. What worried him most was that the witch had disappeared and couldn't be found.

Just as he began to expand his search, she suddenly appeared exactly where she always had been. Maybe she had been asleep, but then he had never known her to sleep before. This absence of the need to sleep had been disturbing to him. She was always there when he searched. That is why her disappearance had been so unsettling.

Another unsettling aspect of the Witch had been his inability to penetrate her mind. He tried many times to enter her mind, intent on destroying her. Unfortunately, on every attempt he encountered impenetrable barriers. He was, however, able to monitor some of her thoughts and communications, but he couldn't understand her language.

In frustration, he tried to again force his mind through her barriers. The blocks slammed shut, preventing him from entering. His rage flared at the failed attempt, and in his irritation, blurted, "I am coming to destroy you, Bitch!" He didn't expect an answer, it was mostly a vent for his anger, but she responded in his own language, "You want to enter my mind? Come ahead! I will let you in and crush your pathetically weak mind."

Total and absolute shock struck him. She spoke his language! She challenged him . . . HIM. She threatened him in his own language! A brief flash of fear gripped him, as he quickly pulled back his mind. Could she be that strong? Suddenly, his anger exploded, barely controllable. He fought to resist her challenge, just in case she was that strong.

His rage finally exploded, and he danced a berserking tantrum around the control room, ripping apart anyone or anything he came across. One of the Technical Simians avoided his reach and ran for the exit. Seeing that it was going to escape sent him into another fit of rage that threatened to destroy him. Suddenly, his fury burst from his mind in a blinding red fireball that sped along the focus of his stare at the back of the fleeing Simian. The fireball engulfed the Simian, quickly reducing it to a smoking pile of charred ash.

The combination of the mental release of the energy and the surprise at what he had done calmed him. He realized that he had done what they said his brother had done, shot fireballs from his head. Now he understood . . . the Witch had driven his brother's anger to the exploding point just like she had done with him. His hate flared again at how she might have destroyed him with his own rage. He despised this Bitch!

His parting shot was, "I WILL kill you, and I WILL kill your offspring wherever they go!" He wanted her to know that none of them would survive, but she didn't respond. She ignored him.

* Levi *

Moon nudged him with his foot and signed, "It's time to go."

He woke immediately but still felt tired. His arms were still around Amy and she was warm. He didn't want to move. He remembered how much better it was when Amy took care of his body. He was never tired then. Oh well, everything changes. He shook Amy and felt her stir. The fires were beginning to flare higher as new wood was thrown on, and the extra heat felt welcome.

He had no idea what time it was but assumed it was after midnight, and there was a job to do. He grabbed a couple of somewhat charred meat slabs still on the spit and handed Amy one as they took

209

off from inside the caverns. The sonar revealed the passageways out, but it wasn't until he felt the warm air that he confirmed they were clear of the main opening. He and Amy circled until all the dragons had joined the formation, then they turned north.

It amazed him to see the distance his sonar reached out. Certainly, it wasn't as far as eyesight, but it was at least two thousand feet, more than enough to see the terrain below. If the dragons' sonar was as good as his and Amy's, they could probably see better with their sonar than with their eyes. He assumed that to be the case, but Amy didn't confirm. In fact, she hadn't commented at all since they left. He was about to ask directions and inquire as to her silence when she spoke.

Amy said, "You have the ability to access the topography maps. You might as well learn to figure out our location and direction, and I am fine. I'm just sleepy."

Her thoughts were calm and soft, no teasing or display of any emotions, and this was strange for her. He was almost positive that she would remind him that eating and sonar did not mix. One interferes with the other he quickly learned, but she let the opportunity pass without comment.

Amy was right, though. He accessed her archives and quickly learned how to superimpose the terrain onto the topography maps to identify their location. A slight course adjustment became necessary, which he maneuvered.

They continued to fly in silence up to and over the mountains. Luckily, the dark night forced them to rely completely on their sonar. Once they reached I-10 he veered them west following the highway.

210

He wasn't sure which direction, but west seemed a good guess. They had only gone a few miles before they saw the campfires.

Amy said, "We need to land and discuss strategy before we attack."

He whistled to get the dragons' attention, then circled his arm and pointed to the ground. They slowly spiraled down and landed in a large open spot. Well, everything was wide open in this part of the country. You would be hard pressed to even find a tree without moving into the mountain foothills.

When the dragons had gathered around, he said, "Okay, Amy. What do you have in mind?" Her eyes opened wide in apparent surprise, then turned to address the group.

* Amy *

She had just completed reviewing the status of the approaching fleet, when she felt Levi shake her. Her mind came rushing back into her body as her body's mind woke. This was becoming a strange ordeal. Obviously, she had totally switched to the mind in her body, and the only time she was fully operational in the facility's brain was when her body slept. She hadn't unexpected that. In time, assuming they had time, she felt confident that she could operate fully from her body coordinating through both brains. Right now, unfortunately, her body was a distraction, especially when Levi prodded it.

At 1:00 am, it was time to launch the planned attack. Her heart wasn't in it, because of the apparent uselessness of the attempt in the face of impending death. The fleet was already slowing to enter orbit, and they only had hours to live.

Even so, she was not going to give up and had decided to tell Levi everything and get him involved in the decision making. Unfortunately, she couldn't come clean until after this engagement. Levi would need his total concentration, because she would not be able to augment his movement and defense. He would be on his own. The only thing she could do now was protect his back, which she intended to do, even at the cost of her own life.

All these concerns occupied her mind and were blocked from Levi as they flew toward the enemy, but her main priority right now needed to be the coming engagement. She forced her mind to push the other concerns to the back and out of sight, temporarily.

They had no strategy for the battle and without it, Levi would simply attack . . . the macho shit. She already felt his excitement building. That always worked before but not this time. They needed to plan. She asked Levi to land so they could develop one.

Once they were on the ground they all turned to her, staring. Well, it was her idea. She began, "How is your sonar working?"

Moon screeched, "Much better than our eyes. We can see up and down now, when we couldn't before, but we still can't see far off. Without you we will still need the Human eyes during the day for distance."

"Good." Amy said, "The first thing we need to do is capture a living Warrior to experiment with.

We need to discover if and how we might use our sonar to paralyze them."

Moon said, "I will find one and bring it back."

"Okay, but don't go alone, none of you. Always fly in at least pairs. Remember your wings are fragile, and that is our weakness. If your wings get damaged you will fall and likely be surrounded and killed. Try to find a lone Warrior on the edge of the camp."

Bambi said, "He will never fly alone; I will always be with him."

"We will go with them." said # 5, indicating himself and his mate.

Before any of the others could volunteer, she said, "That's enough. The rest of you wait here."

* Levi *

As Moon's small strike force took off, he said, "Amy, let's go watch." She nodded and they took off, straining to catch up. Moon flew low to the ground approaching the camp fires, while he and Amy took a higher position from which to observe. Several Warriors could be seen lying around the first campfire, but only one was standing. Moon swept over the Warrior and literally snatched him off the ground with his clawed hands and feet. The other Warrs stared in disbelief. The campfire suddenly flared under the swirl of air from those massive wings, and one Warr leaped to his feet just in time for # 5 to snatch him from the ground. The remaining Warrs crawled and ran in every direction, screeching alarm.

213

It was a classic and textbook attack, but they were also lucky. Moon and # 5 were straining heavily trying to carry their heavy and kicking Warrs back to the staging area. The dense mass of their bodies made them far heavier than they looked. That body mass might have jerked Moon and # 5 out of the air, but the momentum of the attack provided the extra power necessary.

Amy said, "We had surprise on our side, but they will be ready for future attacks. That is why we need to learn how to paralyze them."

"Yeah, that is the whole idea . . . keep them awake waiting for an attack."

They followed Moon and # 5 as they labored to return to the staging area, but they finally made it and unceremoniously dropped the Warrs in the middle of the dragons. He had never seen a Simian with eyes as wide as these two, and they immediately cowered to the ground, visibly shaking in fear.

The Warrs were surrounded, so they didn't have to worry about them running off while Amy began her experiments. He sensed she was transmitting her sonar, but there were no reactions from the Warrs. Finally, she gave up and began instructing the dragons how to raise the pitch of their sonar. At one point he noticed the Warrs froze in paralysis. Once they identified the correct frequency, the dragons practiced until they found it. After much testing she seemed satisfied.

Amy announced, "You all now know how to adjust the pitch of your sonar to paralyze an enemy. Unfortunately, it takes more than one to accomplish it. From what I have seen, it will take at least two dragons to generate enough power. This means, to be safe, an attack team must consist of two pair. I want the attack formation to be three abreast transmitting their sonar with the fourth behind killing any paralyzed Warrs missed by the front three. Remember, you can also be effected by the sonar, so always keep your teams flying in the same general direction when you are transmitting the high frequency."

While Amy addressed the dragons, the Warrs took the opportunity to escape. Watching, he chuckled at the speed they demonstrated, but Moon's team quickly pursued them. Moon assumed the fourth slot with, Bambi, # 5, and his mate, Amy One, leading. He knew Amy's formation worked to perfection, even though his sonar didn't reach that far. The terrified screeches said all that needed saying.

Moon flew back over, and the other dragons formed into teams and took off after them to engage the enemy.

He said, "What are we going to do?"

"I'd like to observe for a while, then go terrorize the army. Wouldn't you?

He blurted out loud, "Oh, hell yes."

As they gained altitude above the campfires, Amy explained that he and she had more power in their sonar than the dragons due to their greater mental power. That was a pleasant surprise. Evidently either of them could paralyze a Warr, and he was anxious to give it a try.

* Amy *

The dragons learned how to use their paralyzing sonar quickly and formed into teams as she suggested. She remained anxious about her dragons and hoped they wouldn't take careless chances. She and Levi would operate for a while as backup for any team that got into trouble. The extended mental energy made Levi's and her sonar more powerful, which they could use to assist any team that overreached their ability. They could swoop down and save the day. Levi would love that. Of course, she would love saving him, too.

She tried to remind him that she was not with him in his body anymore, and he would have to fight his own battles. Levi just dismissed her warning by saying, "Yeah, yeah."

She really did worry about that, since he had charged into battle many times without a plan, and she would have to save him. That was one reason she built his new body much bigger. Hopefully, he could save himself, but she still watched over him if he needed help. She didn't want to lose him again. That would be too hard to take ... again.

From their vantage point circling high above the camping army, they watched the dragon teams below striking at the outskirts of the camp. As the Warrs began to run, they seemed to freeze as the dragons dipped over them with their swords swinging. The teams spread out to all sides of the camp and were attacking the small groups. They must have already killed ten or fifteen Warrs, but that wouldn't make a dent in an army of six thousand. The toll in enemy deaths would be insignificant, but the effect in generating fear would be significant.

Suddenly, Levi pointed and said, "Look in the center there. See the Warrs spreading out from that Warr? That has to be a general giving orders. Let's get him!"

Before she could say, "NO!" he had curled his wings and dove toward the center of the camp. Dammit! She followed quickly behind.

The cleared area seemed safe, because all those around Levi's target had been dispatched to the outskirts to find out what was going on. It was in fact a general, and he stood alone at the central camp fire, as Levi coasted down beside him. Levi made no attempt to paralyze him with his sonar, and slowly walked toward him. The shocked general, although extremely wide awake, froze in fear and made no attempt to protect himself, as Levi casually chopped off his head and bent to pick it up.

The Warriors on the periphery of the open area watched in horror but made no attempt to attack. Levi then unfurled his trifold wings and launched into the air beside her, still carrying the severed head of the general. Grinning wildly, he tossed the general's head into the thickest gathering of Warriors they passed over.

She couldn't believe what she had seen. Levi acted stupidly, carelessly taking chances with his life, but she had to admit, if their intentions had been to instill fear in the Warriors, Levi's actions had certainly succeeded in doing that.

She tried to imagine the reaction of the Warrs at seeing a severed head coming out of the sky and bouncing through their ranks. That may have had more of a frightening affect than the other.

* Levi *

This was fun! So what if Amy called him a "Macho Shithead." He just couldn't resist attacking the isolated general. Truly, he couldn't believe his luck at seeing him standing alone in the clearing. The general had been anxious to get his Warrs in the battle but didn't seem so anxious to join the battle himself. That was his undoing. Unfortunately, however, there wasn't much of a battle. The stupid bastard just stood there frozen in fear and let him chop off his head.

The plan had been to attack for only a few moments, then retreat back to the staging area and rest, give the army time to settle down and get comfortable again, then attack again. Amy didn't want the dragons to take chances, just keep the Simians from sleeping. She had told them that the Simians would eventually come up with a defense and maybe even a method of attacking back, but that would depend on when the Supreme One got involved. That should have been his first warning, but he missed it.

As he and Amy were returning to the staging area, Amy said, "After we meet with the dragons, we need to leave them here and find a place we can talk without interruptions. I have some things to tell you, and I need your help.

He had never seen Amy this way before, ever. They had always been able to communicate anywhere, no matter what else was going on around them. Their link was strong in that way, and she had never asked for his help like this before. She behaved strangely, weird even. Now that he thought about it, she had been quiet this whole trip. Try as me might, her mind remained blocked to him. Something very serious bothered her. He would have to get to the bottom of this strange behavior quickly, but first they needed to instruct Moon and let him know they were leaving.

"Okay, Amy. As soon as all the dragons get back, we will tell them of the change in plans, then we'll find a safe place to talk." His curiosity was making him anxious.

Of course, Moon wanted to come with them, and he had to convince him to stay with his dragons and remain on alert to any changes in the Simian army. Amy had made him paranoid about a potential threat to her dragons, but Moon had a good head for strategy, especially since Amy downloaded an abundance of combat training into him when she had the opportunity. The dragons could be trusted to adapt.

He and Amy then flew to a secluded and isolated spot he found in a high valley far from the engagement. They would be safe there so he could concentrate fully on Amy. "Okay, my love. What's up?"

Amy leaned into his arms. Her body quivered as he embraced her. They lay on the ground together to get comfortable, her still in his embrace. Then she opened her mind to him, completely, and he saw. He saw it all: the threat of the Supreme One and his belief that he and Amy in body were the children of Amy at the facility, the latest revelations of a potential second bomb to destroy them. His pride for Amy soared; she had run out of ideas to save them, but she had not given up. She was so desperate for life saving plans that she asked for his help.

Amy had always been able to save them...always! Even when things looked and were impossible, she evolved and always found a way to survive, like with telekinesis, teleportation, even ASONE. Her mind was limitless, and she needed to evolve again, but she couldn't, not now. He saw her confusion and her self-imposed limitations, which Amy failed to see in herself.

He saw the problem. For once he knew what to do but could he bring himself to do what needed to be done? He must, or she would die, both of her minds.

"Amy, it's your body causing your confusion. You are living in a body now and it is destroying your mental ability to think. You need to flow back into your facility brain and your body must go. Amy, I love you. Forgive me for what I must do," he said, as he slipped his hands around her beautiful neck and kissed her soft lips.

* Satan *

His agent with the deployed army initiated an emergency call on his modified radio reporting an attack on the army. An attack on the army? That was impossible. Who would attack a six thousand Warrior Simian army? As soon as he asked himself that, he knew the answer. Only the Witch would attack, but it would be useless.

Surprise and shock prevented his rage from exploding. He had to know more and immediately sent his mind to occupy the agent's mind.

It was dark when he exited the tent. He hated the dark on this single sun planet, but the army had fires blazing high, which made the dark somewhat bearable. Again, the generals and Warriors recognized him as the Supreme One and began reporting. The Warriors and even the generals were hopping about in fear, which angered him. Why were Warriors fearful? What could frighten them so? They weren't able to give him much information, only that something came out of the dark from the sky and killed, and often took the bodies of the dead. This same thing happened on all sides at the outskirts of the camp.

Rage took him and he bellowed, "Then get the Warriors to the edge of camp and fight them. Kill them!" The generals rushed to bark the orders to their commands. He could just hear the closest general screech his directions and watched the Warriors run toward the edge of camp, leaving the general standing alone in a clearing. To his astonishment he watched a huge winged Human swoop down and land in front of the surprised general. This Human stood far taller than any Human he had ever heard of and even a head above the general. The Human slowly and calmly drew his sword and severed the head from the general's body. Just as calmly, he bent to pick up the head and leaped back into the air to join a similar creature.

He felt their mental energy and knew whom these creatures were. Had he reacted quicker he might have destroyed them then with a fireball, but their actions were totally unexpected. He never expected flying creatures, and they came and left so quickly he had no time to react. He barely even saw them. Suddenly, in frustration, he realized he couldn't have fired a fireball in this surrogate body. For that he would need to be in his own superior body.

He heard renewed screeches of agitation and fear toward the edge of the camp and turned in time to catch a glimpse of what appeared as a golden wall flying over. Below the wall were silver flashes of what must be huge swords. The Warriors below the wall seemed frozen, and the silver swords sliced them to pieces. At one point he thought he saw massive golden legs reach out of the dark and snatch up a Warrior's body, or a piece of one anyway.

There had never been any mention of any flying creatures of this size in any reports. This was something new, and he knew whom to blame. This must end and now.

He recalled the generals and instructed them to move off the open valley floor, and move into the trees and rocks of the mountain edge. That would provide protection from attacks from the air. They were also instructed to prepare long spears to ward off future attacks. Other than providing those obvious and easy solutions, he really didn't care. Soon they would die anyway when he destroyed the children of the Bitch.

He was more anxious to return to his ship and launch the attacks. His fleet was preparing to enter orbit, and had it not been for the fact that he was about to win the war and destroy those that opposed him, his rage might have taken over completely.

* Amy *

222

She felt so comfortable in Levi's arms. His warmth radiated into her and touched her heart, and she wanted nothing more than to be in his arms forever. All her trouble seemed to melt away. He was talking, but she hardly heard him in her bliss. His hands cupped her neck and face and his warm lips kissed her. Suddenly, he stiffened and hit her directly in the face, hard. She felt her body go limp, as her mind rushed back to her brain back in the facility.

What the fuck! Her mind registered what had happened, then she remembered Levi's words. "Amy, it's your body causing your confusion. You are living in a body now and it is destroying your mental ability to think. Amy, I love you. Forgive me for what I must do." Could that be so?

"Amy, I am sorry to do that to you, but we must break the link between you, the you as you exist now at the facility, and your body, at least for a while. Now, come back to me as you were in the past. Do you hear me?"

Her mind raced now, analyzing, calculating, and considering his statements. With her body's brain unconscious, her mind did seem clearer. With two brains she had assumed her intellect would be greater, but she hadn't considered just how much brain capacity it required to function in a body. That part had surprised her. Now, seeing clearer, she realized Levi was correct. Not only was her body utilizing its brain, but she was allowing it to distract from her main brain. The brains had merged into a single mind with the sole intent to function in and through her body.

"Yes, Levi. I hear you, but you hit me, you ass hole!"

"I know, love, but being asleep wouldn't break the link. You had to be unconscious. Please forgive me."

She hated to admit it, but Levi was right. Still, all she would say was, "You are forgiven. Now, what is the rest of your insane plan?" She was already way ahead of him but wanted to hear his idea.

"Teleport us back to the facility, and instruct Mama to sedate your body so your mind can get back to full strength. Then, let's find a solution to the Supreme One's attack before he kills us all."

Levi was thinking well, and she was correct. She was far ahead of him. Already she refocused, and her mind now concentrated into the facility brain. Her outside sensory perspective returned to focus through Levi like before.

As she began gathering energy around Levi for the teleport, she was notifying Mama of the situation and instructing her what to do with her body, which amounted to keeping it sedated and nourished.

The perspective through Levi's eyes showed the glimmer of the energy, then the scenery changed as matter transferred and they materialized within the main complex. Mama was there waiting, still rubbing sleep from her eyes. Mama immediately took charge of her body and rushed off to the clinic, and Levi went following after her, not sure of what to do. Actually, Levi had done well. He had done his job. Now it was time for her to do hers.

224

Her first task required her to locate the Supreme One, and he wasn't hard to find. The fleet had just entered orbit around Earth. To call this bad news would be a gross understatement. The saving grace came as the fleet passed into the long rotation around earth and out of sight. She would have hours to research a possible solution, assuming one existed, before the fleet came into view again. That would be the logical time for the Supreme One to launch his bomb. Personally, she would wait for the second or third orbit to obtain as much data as possible before launching, but knowing the temperament of a Supreme One, he would not wait, nor would it matter much. The bomb would take out most of California and a good bit of Arizona and Mexico. He could afford to be off with the trajectory and still get them.

Levi had also been correct to suggest they teleport back to the facility, but probably not for the same reason. In doing so, this action would present a single target to the Supreme One. He would not know how, but he would be able to detect Levi at the facility. She, her body's mind, would not be able to be detected, but hopefully, it would assume she would be with Levi. Hopefully, she would only have one launch to deal with and not the previous two anticipated.

Levi said, "What can I do to help?"

"Well, I need you to follow my thoughts and point out anything you think might be important. I need that wonderful abstract thought of yours.

* Levi *

225

It surprised him that Amy couldn't see what had happened to her. Her brilliant mind had conceived and built the Earth Dragons and mind transfer, restored his improved body and transferred his memories, designed and built a positron generator and located the invading fleet. She had brought him back from death and restored his life. She organized and commanded the salvation of the Humans, Techs, Fems, hell, everyone. Her mind had performed incredible feats, but she had ceased in her creativity once she began living through her body. Her body had to go.

It was one of the hardest things he had ever had to do, hurting her, but she forgave him. Once she returned to her facility brain, she saw the truth almost immediately. Now, with her body sedated, she was coming back fully. Mama would see to it that her body would not come to harm. She hoped her body wouldn't have to stay in storage long. In time Amy would figure out how to manage both simultaneously, but that would come after this crisis.

Amy said teleporting their bodies back to the facility was a smart idea because it gave the Supreme One a single target only, but he hadn't even thought of that. He just figured that Mama could protect her better than just lying on the ground under a tree. Selfishly, he thought it wouldn't matter, and if they lost the battle, Amy could teleport them somewhere out of danger at the last moment. That would almost be worse, living while all they loved died.

Amy began sharing what she had to work with. In truth, she only had the positron generator and the phase adjustable transmitter antenna as possible weapons. As her research indicated, the transmitter acted as a magnetic adjustable antenna that could, by altering the phase on the outside of the electronic focus plane of the antenna, direct the focus of the transmission. In plain talk, it could adjust a transmission from an omni-directional signal to a narrow beam focus in virtually any direction. Amy designed it to direct the positron signal toward the outside satellite.

He said, "Can you track and focus on the bomb when it is launched?

"Yes, some of that can be done, but the positron generator would just function to further protect the electronics in the bomb from any effects from the overcharged Earth. As it is, the bomb will work because its exposure to the excess electrons would be limited due to its speed."

He continued, "The way I understand the positron charge is that it's the exact opposite of electrons. I think an excess of either extreme would prevent electronics from working. Right?"

"Humm Maybe. Go on."

"What if you started bombarding the bomb high in the atmosphere as soon as it launches and maintained the positron beam on it for the entire duration of the fall? Would that be long enough to alter its physics?"

After a long delay Amy said, "Maybe, just maybe." After another long pause she said, "I need tracking radar . . . Mama, I need you! Hurry!" Then she was gone, deep in calculations and planning. He knew she wasn't talking to him anymore, and instructions were already being sent to Mama.

* Amy *

Yes, she had a plan. Why had she never seen the possibility before? She really couldn't blame it on the confusion of having a body, because the positron generator was conceived prior to her body being born. No, she had been too focused on countering the effects of the original ray. She sent Levi a quick flash of a smiling image and an "You're pretty damned smart, and I love you, Levi."

He was correct. If an overabundance of negative electrons filling positive holes would prevent electricity from working, then an overabundance of positive holes would absorb negative electrons, causing the same effect. Yes, it could work if the bomb could be bombarded long enough and with enough strength.

She needed power, lots of power. To increase the power at the bomb she would need to transmit in a narrowly focused beam, and to do that she would need a good tracking radar system to keep the beam on the target. Fortunately, there was a radar on the roof. Unfortunately, it wouldn't work unless she diverted some of the positron transmission to alter it, which would reduce the power to the beam. She would need all the positron generator's power and couldn't afford to divert any of it if she wanted to disable the bomb.

She announced an emergency over the communication system with instructions. Ten of the Greys received immediate assignments to manually disconnect and physically muscle the radar system to the roof of the power generator room. Another received instructions to get the retractable access hatch open on the roof of the generator room and rig up a harness to the electronic winch to lower the radar down. Yet another raced to supply with a list of equipment necessary to get it operational, including wiring, mounting hardware, and potential spare parts for servicing it. Mama had already received her instruction and busily coordinated the project, screeching orders and helping where she could.

The altered environment of the power generator room would allow the radar to work there without diverting any of the positron generator's power, and the open retractable access roof would allow the radar to transmit, receive and track a target from within the generator room. She had already adjusted the positron generator antenna to begin bombarding the radar equipment to begin its conversion. They needed every second they could gain.

In three hours the relocated and mounted radar occupied its new home but still was not operational. Mama and her team franticly changed parts, greased bearings, and finished up the wiring splicing. After another thirty minutes she saw it come on line and begin feeding her data. She had just completed the final adjustment when she detected the fleet on the horizon.

Levi said, "Well done, Amy. I'm proud of you. If we live or die I just want you to know the time with you has been the best of my life, and I wouldn't change a thing."

She had sensed him with her continually, but he had not interfered. There was no doubt he would have had he seen anything wrong or thought of anything new, but her mind worked well now, thanks to his actions.

She said, "I love you, too. We will know soon if this is going to work."

Levi said, "How will we know?"

She laughed and said, "When the bomb hits and it doesn't explode."

Chapter 9
Showdown

* Satan *

Anger raged again. Fate seemed to be against him! He wanted to launch his missile immediately upon entry into orbit, but in his eagerness to enter orbit they came in too fast and had to readjust, overshooting the entry point. Now he would have to wait until they orbited around the planet, which would take hours. Just before their orbit took them out of line of sight of the Witch's home, he reached his mind out to make sure where the Witches' spawn were located. To his surprise they had moved from the engagement and were back at the Witch's complex. Well, one of them, but they always traveled together and possibly were together, making their identities masked. This would make it easier with all of them at the same location.

It troubled him that they had traveled so far in such a short time. This presented another reason to hate them more, knowing they possessed powers he himself didn't have. His rage boiled, but he forced himself to calm, knowing these abominations would be destroyed soon. This thought even made him smile.

The Technical Simians had both world busters prepared, targeted, and ready for launch when the orbit brought them over the horizon, and he verified the targets. He paced the control room like an animal hunting and waited. All those around him knew he teetered on the edge of exploding and gave him plenty of space, constantly eyeing him in case they needed to flee for their lives.

Finally, the moment arrived and he relished at the finality of the moment. He reached out with his mind in search of the abominations. He found the Witch where she should be, and the Bitch's spawn were there also, at least one of them. He found no indication of the other anywhere else. Smiling, he ordered, "Target One ... LAUNCH!" The ship shuddered in recoil from the rocket, and he immediately saw the blaze of the rocket as its fiery tail curved down into the atmosphere following a slow decent to the planet and target. Again he waited as the planet buster made its descent. The timing of the orbit should put his fleet over the target at the time of impact, giving him a perfect location to observe the explosion.

He was not concerned about where they would land or about any of the details of the fleet's landing. There would be plenty of time for those details after the Witch died. Afterwards, they would take their time finding the central gathering location of the main Simian compound.

His fleet would not undergo the effects of the doomsday ray like all the others before him. He had devised countermeasures to keep his fleet operational. This planet and all its inhabitants would fall under his rule.

As the time grew near for the impact, he returned to his control room seat to stare at his missile streaking toward its target. As the countdown began, he leaned forward, tensely gripping his console, watching for the impact and explosion ... 3 - 2 - 1 ...

232

* Levi *

Amy finished none too soon. Almost as soon as the radar became operational, Amy announced that the fleet was visible on the horizon. Only minutes later she announced the launch.

Amy said, "Damn, the Bastard is anxious to kill us! We are, however, lucky. He only fired one missile. I wouldn't be able to track two projectiles."

"Well, let's hope he isn't successful." He spoke mainly to himself, since Amy concentrates so intently she mostly remained unaware of those around. In those times, silence was golden. It all rested in her capable hands now, and if anyone could save them, she could.

For a while he followed her mind, but her mental activity and internal calculations sped by too fast and too complicated to understand. He knew enough to know Amy continuously tracked the missile and altered the antenna to keep the positron generator focused and tight on the racing missile. If seemed to be working ... he hoped.

With nothing else he could do to help, he turned his attention to the migration. He wanted to say his "good-byes", at the very least. If Amy wasn't successful, he wanted the others to know what happened. He really wished he could talk to Moon. He would be the most devastated at their loss. He would have to rely on Jimmy to explain. At least if Jimmy didn't hear from him again, they would know the silent battle that occurred.

When he made contact with Jimmy, the kid seemed frantic. "Where are you? What is going on? Where is Moon? Is everything okay?

"Whoa there! I will catch you up." Unfortunately, he had been so busy before he hadn't notified Jimmy of the change of plan. He explained the changes and how Moon and the other dragons continued the battle, and they were fine and preventing the Simians from moving, while the migration raced to get over the bridge. He made a sudden decision and told Jimmy that the migration would be instructed to come to their location and for him to begin preparing for the flood of Simians and Humans. He saved the worst for last, and told him of the on-going battle with the Supreme One and the possibility of their destruction. There wasn't much time left, so he left Jimmy in a daze, but he knew Jimmy understood most of what he had said and what he must do. He didn't have to mention that the responsibility fell on his shoulder of notifying Moon in the event of the worst. Jimmy would be sensitive and cautious.

Next, he contacted Al, who was almost as frantic as Jimmy, but he rushed through the explanations. Surprisingly, the migration had made it over the bridge. Maybe they would make it after all. He ordered Al and the entire group to find cover behind the mountains immediately.

Al blurted, "Can't you teleport out of there at the last minute? We don't want to lose you two."

"I don't know ... maybe, but I have to go now, my friend. It's time!"

* Amy *

234

The fleet had hardly cleared the horizon when she detected the launch of the missile. Immediately, she locked on with the radar and began feeding coordinates into the phase antenna array to focus the positron beam on to the missile. It traveling at high speed, which made it difficult to track and coordinate the aiming of the beam. To be safe, she opened the beam to ensure continued bombardment of positrons. It took her precious seconds to adjust the tracking but finally managed to maintain the beam focused in a narrow and concentrated invisible ray. It became easier once she could anticipate and predict the trajectory. Her calculations, at best, predicted a marginal effect and uncertain success. She couldn't say the positron bombardment wouldn't work, but on the other hand, no assurance or confidence comforted her.

One factor improved the odds somewhat. The Supreme One, being over anxious to launch, provided her with more flight exposure time. The longer she could maintain the bombardment, the greater the odds of it working.

As she continued the tracking and positron attack on the missile, she became vaguely aware of Levi contacting Jimmy and Al and apprising them of the situation. She also recognize that Levi was saying bye. Yes, they stood a very good chance of dying.

Her concentration faltered slightly at Al's suggestion to Levi that they teleport out at the last moment. Levi would latch on to that idea ... of that she was positive. She heard Levi telling Mama to go get her body and come back there. Something about, "We are going to try to escape with her body."

Her concentration was intense, but she ventured a glance through Levi's eyes to see Mama bound from the room to follow his instructions. Mama would stop at nothing to save her, even if it meant continuing to live and not dying with Amy's facility mind as she had wanted to do.

She caught herself from pointing out that it wouldn't do any good, because all of her mind was concentrated within the facility brain and none existed within her body's brain. Currently her mind existed solely within the facility brain, leaving none within her body. When her facility brain died, so would her body. She almost told Levi this but suddenly realized that perhaps she could save Levi and Mama by doing what Levi had in mind. Levi no longer needed her to stay alive. He had a new body that didn't require constant manipulation. Yes, she could save them and would.

The bomb approached and on target, which required less concentration to focus the beam. The beam became steady, so she broke her mind away and began gathering energy for the teleport transfer. She thought a good safe place to deposit Levi and Mama would be the high Arizona mountains where she first made contact with Levi.

Just as she was about to trigger the energy transfer, Levi boomed in her mind.

"Oh no you don't! You're not leaving me now. Your energy is already focused. Now, transfer your mind. Dammit, you can do both."

Due to the distracting concentration, she had momentarily forgotten that Levi was in her mind and saw her intentions. He startled her with his command, but maybe he was right. At the last possible moment she triggered the energy transfer and transferred her mind back into her body. She had no idea if it worked, because her body was still unconscious, but she tried.

* Satan *

Nothing! Nothing happened. The time for impact had come and gone and still no explosion. It had to be the Witch! His temper exploded and he emitted a deafening screech, "Damn you, Bitch!" The tirade rolled into an unintelligible long, ear-shattering scream. The control room crew fled for the exits as a raging tantrum burst forth. In total and utter frustration he fell to the deck, quivering in rage, kicking and pounding the floor like a child that didn't get its way. He had never been so out of control, and it took him many long minutes of crying and screaming before he could even begin to get control.

A Technical Simian trying to respond to an alarm finally got his attention. He quickly sobered and waved the technicians in. They looked frantic, so he stood to see what happened. The stability alarm blared, indicating a failing drive system. Simultaneously, calls were coming in from the other ships indicating the same problem. Yes, it was the damn Bitch again, but this time he remained deathly calm. This time they were under a serious attack. Even more frightening, he knew nothing his crew could do would help, and that the attack would continue. He also knew they had only precious moments to save themselves. He screeched, "Get us to the ground quickly. Set a meandering course down as fast as we can, while we still have some power. Dammit, forget trying to fix the problem. There is nothing you can do. Don't you understand? We are under attack."

He didn't understand what the Witch did or was continuing to do, but it must involve a focused ray of energy, and if it was, an unpredictable course might disrupt the concentration of the ray. That must be what she did to disable the bomb.

The crew wasn't moving fast enough. He grabbed one of the technicians and broke his neck, then screeched, "I said get me to the ground ... NOW! Get me to my army, and tell the other ships to follow us. Now they were moving, and the ship began a dive and veered sharply to the left. After a few moments he felt the ship jerk sharply to the right while continuing the deep dive. The stabilizers felt out of balance and a distinct wobble began shaking the ship, but the engine drive continued to spasmodically respond.

The wobble become more pronounced, but they approached the surface. He directed the course away from the Witch's location and toward the location of his six thousand Warrior army. Now that he would be condemned to live or die on the surface of this cursed planet, he appreciated the army. They would protect him.

The ships began to fail as they skimmed over the surface of the planet, and failed completely about the time they spotted the army. They weren't quite there, but he had milked as much distance as possible. The ships began to crash ... some hard. He piloted his ship personally now and veered the nose up sharply as it made contact, causing the saucer to skip to a relatively safe landing.

All his planning and modified technology gone in the crash. All his excitement anticipating the destruction of that dammed Bitch, gone. She had permanently changed his future life, and he hated her. As he exited the ship he shook his fists wildly in the air, screeching his defiance to the Witch, "You failed to kill me, Bitch. Now it's my turn!"

* Levi *

He almost missed it. Amy thought herself clever by sacrificing herself to save him and Mama. It almost worked, but at the last second her blocks collapsed and he saw her intent. He didn't want to survive without her. It would be pointless to live on without his soul mate and love; certainly Mama wouldn't have gone had she not thought she was saving the Amy cradled in her arms. He knew she could do both. She no longer needed her total concentration. All that could be done about the incoming bomb had been done, and the teleport was ready. It only needed to be triggered. He saw it, but she didn't. He screamed to her to transfer her mind and felt her trying.

The energy transferred and he suddenly stood staring out over the desert. He instantly knew that he stood on the bluff high in the Prescott National Forrest, the very spot Amy had first touched his mind. The spot where it all started.

Mama gently laid Amy down and looked around, somewhat annoyed to be here. He sure didn't want to be around her if she discovered neither Amy survived. She would make his life a living hell, more than she had before.

He waited, dreading the silence he might hear on the other side. Finally, he said, "Amy, are you still there?" Then he waited for a response that might never come.

"Yes, I'm still here. The bomb landed a few thousand feet downhill. It shook the facility, but it didn't explode, and I'm still alive."

He had been saying a silent prayer, but when he heard the good news, he said, "Thank you, God!" Then he froze and said, "What is the Supreme One doing? Watch out. He might fire another missile."

Amy flashed him a big grin and said, "I think he is too busy right now. I turned the positron generator on his fleet, and I have a lot more time to bombard them. I think I can do some damage."

He quickly saw her intentions and said, "Way to go, Amy." He rapidly informed Mama of the good news and told her to pick up Amy's body. "How about you bring us back before Mama starts griping at me."

Mama was clearly happy, but this old crone wasn't about to show her emotions ... to him anyway. She appeared extremely happy when they reappeared in her familiar surroundings. Mama quickly left to deposit Amy's body back in the clinic and resume her duties.

At his first opportunity he contacted Al to let him know the good news. Al was jubilant with the news and spread the word quickly among those gathered. Unsure of Amy's plans, he didn't alter their course. There would be plenty of time for that, and he didn't want to disturb Amy now. From what he could tell she kept herself in deep concentration, disrupting the Supreme One's fleet, and it appeared to be working.

He got a surprise when he mentally contacted Jimmy. The kid was excited and thrilled but seemed a little preoccupied. He said, "Jimmy, what's going on?"

"Oh, we, the dragons and riders, are en route back toward the Simian army. The dragons came home early this morning to rest and we convinced them to bring us back with them. Of course, we will camp in the mountains, while they attack at night. To be honest, I think Moon got upset with the news I gave him, and he wanted to keep me close so he would know what happened. I just gave him a thumbs up, and he seems happy. Hey, Levi, you ever see an Earth Dragon smile?"

Actually, he had, and it was indeed a sight to see. He has missed Moon's company, but hopefully, they would be back together soon, like Tonto and the Lone Ranger.

* Amy *

She watched the missile growing larger in the radar's digital image. Mentally, she closed her eyes and scrunched up her non-existent shoulders as she awaited the impact. She felt the impact on the Earth but continued to hold her imaginary breath. The vibration from the impact shook the facility, but there was no explosion.

She relished the victory only momentarily, swiftly redirecting the radar to monitor the orbiting fleet. In doing so, the linked positron beam tracked the radar's position. Luckily, she detected no additional missiles en route, something that had worried her while she had tracked the one incoming missile. There would have been nothing she could have done against a second missile. They had been extremely lucky.

Suddenly, she noticed an erratic course change of one of the ships. That is when she realized the positron beam had automatically tracked the radar, and that the beam remained narrowly focused and concentrated on the erratic ship. Realizing the effect of the positron bombardment on the spaceship, she understood what could be done. She locked the radar on the central ship and spread the beam enough to be able to bombard all the ships. A large amount of orbit arc remained before they passed the horizon. If they were lucky, she just might be able to destroy the spacecraft and end this conflict conclusively.

Levi tentatively touched her mind saying, "Amy, are you still there?"

She abruptly realized that her attention had been so drawn to this new development that she had failed to contact Levi with the good news.

His relief was obvious when she reported, but the relief faded with concern of what the Supreme One might now do. She bubbled with excitement, as she explained what she was now doing.

"Damn, Amy. This is great. Kill the Bastard! Oh, can you bring us back before you do? Mama is going to start griping at me any moment."

She had to laugh at that visual image and immediately teleported them back, but quickly

242

turned her attention back to the Supreme One's fleet. He remained in her mind, observing, but refrained from any further impulse to interrupt her concentration. So, she turned her full attention back to the task at hand and immediately noticed the fleet's attempt to dive under her focused beam in random and quick course changes. The Supreme One was smart and had quickly realized what happened and took evasive actions. During World War II, ships at sea under attack would initiate what they called a zig zag (back and forth) course pattern in an attempt to evade the torpedoes. This fleet appeared to be attempting something very similar. Their course became randomly evasive, attempting to dodge the beam of energy, but she easily tracked the fleet with the radar with the positron beam locked to it.

Had the fleet separated in divergent courses, she would have lost the ability to maintain the concentration of energy on all of them, but they, or he, made a fatal mistake by remaining in formation on a common random course. She couldn't believe her luck.

The fleet broke all the atmosphere entry rules. That in itself might have destroyed them, but the ships held together and raced toward Earth, apparently trying to land before the ships drive systems failed completely. It looked like they were going to make it, too.

Even though the course continued to appear random, she began to see a pattern, taking the ships toward the Simian army. That made sense. The Supreme One would want the protection of his army, and the main encampment of Simians in

243

Texas was too distant to make. It amazed her how the tides of battle can suddenly shift in momentum. Right now she was in control.

* Levi *

He observed as Amy monitored and controlled the radar and positron beam and antenna on a higher level than he could follow. Some he could see in her mind, the thoughts and impressions, but he preferred seeing with his own eyes, which he was now doing. He could clearly see the spaceships dropping off the screen and assumed they must be crashing.

Amy interrupted his thought by commenting on what he believed was happening. "Not necessarily, they are just falling below the radar beam, but yes, they will be crashing very soon."

Anticipating her next comment. He contacted Jimmy again, "Jimmy, where are you?"

"Just landing in a high valley. Why?"

"Take a look to the west and tell me if you can see spaceships coming toward you?

"Oh, Hell, yes! They are crashing into the ground about five miles from us."

"Great! I will be there shortly." Then to Amy he said, "You don't have to stay here now do you? Can you take us there, love?"

"No. There is nothing more I can do here right now, but I don't have the coordinates for Jimmy."

In a moment of inspiration he said, "Oh, hell, just teleport me in the sky somewhere above them and I can fly to them." From her annoyed expression he could tell she hadn't considered that possibility, but he did feel his hair standing up as the energy gathered. Suddenly, he found himself a thousand feet in the air scrambling to get his trifold wings deployed as he fell. He finally got his wings to scoop air and diverted a crash of his own. He caught the air and broke his fall and fluttered to the ground beside Jimmy and Moon, trying to look like he meant to do that. He silently screamed, "Damn, Amy! You could have given me a moment to get ready."

Grinning hugely she said, "I know how you like to make a macho entrance."

In spite of his pissedness, he began laughing. He acted as if a dramatic display of a perfect landing was his intent, and the dragons were duly impressed. He was also pleased to see Amy playful again with the massive pressure off ... somewhat.

He got there in time to see the spaceships begin a somewhat controlled crash into the desert floor one at a time, that stretched all the way back to the Colorado River. The last one almost collided with the Simian army.

He noticed that the Simian army had hardly moved from the location they were in when he left. He slapped Moon's massive shoulder and said, "Good work! Moon, you did a good job of holding them here." Moon was happy to see him and even more happy with the praise.

Moon said, "It was fun."

He laughed then turned to watch the Simians pouring out of the crippled spaceships. To his amazement, most of them were Technical Simians. This fact seemed to shock Moon and the other dragons even more, evident by the flashing darkness in their normally red eyes.

A hushed silence fell upon the dragons as the Supreme One burst out of the closest spaceship. He appeared to be having a tantrum, shaking his fists wildly and screeching at the top of his very healthy lungs, but he understood nothing that was said. Towering over the Technical Simians, he bullied through the Techs and sprinted toward the safety of the Warrior Simian army.

Levi turned toward the sound of rustling wings to see # 11 and his mate and their riders launch off the mountain. They dove fast toward the fleeing Supreme One, obviously intent on attacking him.

Amy screamed in his mind, "No! Stop the them!"

It was too late to stop the pair of dragons, but he managed to prevent others intent on following. A sense of foreboding fell upon him, partly because of Amy's scream, but mostly because he had felt the awesome power of a Supreme One ... and lost.

* Satan *

Defeat was something he couldn't tolerate, something he had never faced before, and something that would never happen again. He would have the victory. The mind and body were totally berserk as he exited the ship, ripping apart anyone within his reach, but he had enough conscious thought remaining to get clear of the ship in case it exploded. He didn't care about these Technical Simian now that there was no technology. They were now obsolete. The Warrior army could be seen in the distance, and he continued to stomp and rant in that direction.

He sensed the transmission of a high pitch squeal before he saw the Simians around him freeze. For a moment he even stopped to inspect one. The Simian stood absolutely still, completely locked in paralysis, mind and body. Turning to face the sonar blast, he saw them coming. He had no idea what they were, but two approached flying directly toward him. They resembled huge, flying Simians, and the transmissions coming from them were directed at him, which he easily batted away with his mind. His anger flared again, realizing this was what had been terrorizing the Warriors, and now they dared to attack him.

Well, if they were Simians, he could destroy them. He allowed his fury to explode, focused into a fireball directed at one of the flying Simians. The ball of fire shot from his mind, engulfing the first one. It collapsed in mid-flight, leaving a blazing trail of smoke as it fell. The second one, appeared to be a female, faltered, but he gripped its mind hard with his own. Just as he was about to overload the mind and kill her, he altered his plan and occupied the mind instead. She might be useful to him.

Awkward at first, he quickly learned how to fly and circled in search of another target. He suddenly became aware of something riding on his shoulders and curved his neck back and grabbed it with his teeth and flung it into the air to fall. He then soared higher looking for other flying Simians and immediately spotted a gathering of them on top of an adjacent mountain. Then he spotted one of the abominations among them, the one that killed the general. His anger flared again, and he dove to kill it. He didn't care if he destroyed this body in the process. He would still be intact in his own body.

* Amy *

For once in a very long time she felt pleased with the direction things were going. The tide of battle had turned in their favor. She had eliminated the bombs as a threat and now the spaceships and their technology. Both sides reverted back to raw physical forces, but unfortunately, the Simians still had a far greater advantage in numbers and size. Still, the Humans no longer faced certain destruction, and along with their new friends, the Technical Simians and Fems, there was now hope.

Levi interrupted her spiritual uplifting moment demanding to be teleported to Moon's location. She smiled, metaphorically, at his suggestion that she put him in the air somewhere above them. She smiled even wider when she actually did it. Levi materialized a thousand feet in the air and immediately began falling and flailing his arms and wings trying to secure leverage in the air. As she watched, laughing, within his mind, she maintained readiness to save him, but he finally managed to grab enough air to make an even graceful landing beside Moon and Jimmy. The macho shithead pranced around like, "See how well I can fly!" Her jovial mood shattered as she watch the Supreme One exit the closest ship. He fumed with his distress, shaking his fists in the air. His mental power radiated from him in lethal waves of rage. Then his threat echoed in her mind.

"You failed to kill me, Bitch. Now it's my turn!"

She prepared to respond, but the pounding of wings drew Levi's attention. He turned in time for her to see two dragons and riders launch into the air, already too late to stop them. All they could do now was watch as the dragons descended upon the Supreme One. This was a terrible mistake. The Supreme One was far too powerful.

The mountainous Supreme One stood defiant, waiting. She watched in horror as an energy bolt shot from his head. Unfortunately, she had seen this before from his brother and knew what it could do. The dragon and rider bursts into flames, tumbling to the ground in a heap of smoldering ash. She saw her mistake far too late. Most of the trusted Technical Simians and Fems had been slightly altered mentally to prevent a Supreme One from occupying their minds. Since the death of the original Supreme One she hadn't considered that necessity for the others. Hardly any of the Fem dragons had undergone this alteration, only Bambi, and now it was too late!

She screamed, "Watch out, Levi! The other dragon's mind has been occupied by the Supreme One. He will come for you!"

He, like the others, had been horror struck, watching the death of their friends. He immediately reacted by issuing a warning to Moon and the others, almost too late, as the furious, blazing eyed dragon dove directly for him. He was drawing his sword, but Moon intercepted the dragon. The Supreme One had been so focused on him that it didn't notice Moon leap from the side to catch him

249

in mid-flight. Moon knocked him off course as he wrapped his powerful arms and legs around the berserk dragon. They rolled downhill in a cloud of dust, but Moon soon had its neck in his powerful jaws biting the life out of what was previously his fellow dragon and friend.

She wept.

* Levi *

That was very close. Had it not been for Amy's warning, that bastard might have got him ... well, and for Moon. That must be about the tenth time his friend and sidekick saved him, but Moon had been lucky the Supreme One was berserk or he might have used the female dragon's finger fangs. Moon hadn't overlooked that possibility. He had immobilized her arms in his attack.

When he looked into Amy's mind to thank her he saw the sorrowful emotion gripping her and the perceived mistake. It was an oversight that could hardly be anticipated. No one could think of everything. She needed to have some time to get a grip on her emotions.

He understood the other emotion as well. It's always sad to lose friends, but it happens in war, and they could be attacked again. The time for his mourning would come later. One of them needed to remain focused, and it was his time to make some decisions.

He screeched, "All the Fem dragons, with the exceptions of Bambi, take off and hide on the other side of the mountain. You are susceptible to a mental attack like this one from the Supreme One's.

Go now, hurry!" They did not question him and launched immediately, heading south over the mountain and out of immediate danger. At least he figured if the Supreme One didn't see them, he probably wouldn't try and seek them out before Amy had cleared her mind enough to alter their minds.

The Supreme One probably assumed safety was his best defense, since he sprinted toward the safety of the Warrior army. Even as he watched the fleeing back of the Supreme One, he could tell he continued to rage. Boy was he pissed! Any Simian within reached was slammed to the grown or instantly ripped apart.

He then turned his attention back to the other spaceships to observe the hordes of Simians gathering, seemingly uncertain what to do. He screeched to the remaining dragons, pointing, "Drive those Simians toward the river bridge, but stay away from the Supreme One. We are going to kill the Warriors and recruit the Technical Simians and Fems."

This time he took off with them flying between Moon and Bambi, just like old times, but in order for his plan to work he needed the Lancers back to the bridge. He contacted Al and quickly relayed his change of plan: turn everyone around and stage the Lancers and especially the Techs at the bridge. Al was especially happy to hear him order all the non-combatants back to the safety of home. He also felt sorry for them, running them back and forth across country.

They had to let all the occupants of the first ship continue toward the Simian army along with the Supreme One. He was too dangerous to deal with at the moment, but all the others were fair game. He and the dragons landed in their direct route and waited. The Technical Simians, not accustomed to fighting, stopped and continued no further. The Females also waited in the rear. They all waited for the Warriors to come forward to face the ominous threat facing them. He had hoped for exactly this reaction, but to his amazement, the Techs and Fems far outnumbered the Warrs.

As the front line began filling with Warriors, but before a solid front could be organized, he and the dragons slowly walked forward. So far the timing and confrontation remained isolated to the second spaceship. All the other ships' occupants were still far to the rear. He hoped to intimidate this smaller group and turn them back into the others, beginning a route of the horde toward the river.

Luckily, there were only about twenty Warrs facing them so far, and he liked the odds. He and the dragons began emitting their sonar, paralyzing the Warrs in front of them. They were vicious, almost cruel, in their slow attack of the helpless Warrs. The Warrs just stood there as the general had done, as he and the dragons mutilated their bodies. The dragons even began taking bites out of the quivering Warr bodies. The effect was instantaneous. The remaining Warrs, Techs, and Fems made an immediate "about face" and took off at a respectable gait toward the river. The occupants of the other ships, seeing the fleeing Simians headed toward them, turned to escape from whatever the first group was running from.

Amy returned from her cry and said, "Good plan, Levi. Keep it up, but you need to go to the Fem dragon so we can prevent the loss of any other dragons to the damn Supreme One."

* Amy *

She still felt weepy, but she needed to help Levi. She had been trying to follow Levi's actions, and Levi thought well. They made a good team in life, love, and war, but war topped the list right now. She let Levi know she stood ready to help with the hiding dragons, and after a moment with Moon, he took off. Soon, sharing his body again, they glided down to the other dragons and began the altering process. It was not terribly complicated. All she had to do was temporarily link with the Simian minds and change the thought process slightly, just enough so the Supreme One couldn't sync minds with them. As she had done in the past with the others, she also took some liberties by introducing a few human characteristics, although slightly. Actually, that was one of the ways their thought patterns were adjusted, making them think somewhat like a Human.

Once the alterations were done, they regained a high aerial position in the sky from which to observe Moon's team. Moon had been innovative and took the dragons to the air to better herd the Simians. The Simians must have deviated from the necessary course, because a team of dragons and riders were flying back and forth on each side, keeping the Simians grouped together, while the rest pushed from behind. Occasionally, a dragon would swoop down to pluck a Warrior Simian from among the group, dragging it off kicking and screeching. It apparently kept the Simians moving, because their pace was brisk and traveling on the route they needed to follow.

Levi turned the dragons over to Moon's direction and pulled the air rapidly propelling him toward the river bridge, but as he flew over the herded Simians, she marveled at the number of them. Damn, there were a lot of Simians. All the occupants of the last four ships were now grouped together in the flow of bodies. There had to be at least two thousand of them. Even more amazing, most of them were Technical Simians, about fifteen hundred of them, with three hundred or so Fems and only an estimated five hundred Warriors. If they decided to turn on the dragons they wouldn't be able to stop them. Oh well, it worked right now, maybe their luck would hold out a little longer.

The river bridge was only a few miles away, and as he approached, so were the Lancers and Techs. Even the Fems trotted behind. Having the Fems present would also help. Judging from the dust clouds, she thought maybe everyone came together. The showdown would be soon.

This wasn't the right time, but she couldn't help it. She spoke, "Levi, I really miss flying and being with you." She meant it, too. Their minds found love long ago, but she really missed the physical contact she recently experienced through her body. She was smiling inwardly when the asshole spoiled her romantic thoughts.

254

"Amy, your timing sucks. We are about to have a showdown with this horde of Simians. This is no time to get horny!"

The asshole was right ... her timing sucked, but he could have offered her a little understanding and a kind word. All she could think of to say was, "Shut up!"

* Satan *

He approached the group of flying Simians in the borrowed body, trying to curb his excitement and appear normal. The abomination stood openly and almost within reach, watching him approach, but somehow he was alerted. As he dove to make his mortal strike, a huge male flying Simian leaped at him and knocked him off course. The huge arms gripped him so tight his breath burst out then he felt its teeth sink deeply into his neck. He hardly felt the collision of his side into the sharp rocks downhill, but the combined massive weight of the falling huge Simians impacting boulders, combined with the crushing pain from the bite, sucked the life from the body he occupied. He fled from the oppressive pain and returned to his own body.

He had never felt death before coming here, and he hated the feeling of loss, especially from something the Witch was responsible for. There was no other explanation. The anger exploded again and his screeched bellowed out, reverberating off the mountains. All those around him fled toward the Warrior army and away from him.

The anger subsided when he noticed he stood alone, replaced by a sudden desire for protection.

He too, took off toward the Warrior army. There would be time later to analyze how best to engage the enemy. During the sprint, he looked skyward and behind many times to ensure there were no renewed attacks, but they left him alone. He almost wished they would attack. Killing another of the flying dragons might satisfy his thirst for blood for a while.

Had he not been so furious at the time, he might have enjoyed occupying a flying Simian body. The next time he did so, however, he would occupy a more powerful male body like the one that had just attacked and killed him. He would see that one dead for his lack of respect for a Supreme One. Yes, that one would die. They would all die.

He hadn't really been concerned about the occupants of the other spaceship, but he suddenly realized none of them were following. Then he saw why. Those damn flying Simians had blocked their way and were driving them the other way. Why would they do that?

Immediately, he sent his mind searching for one of those flying Simians, but each one his mind touched was unreadable and he found no access. They were blocked to him. He ceased his search to vent his frustration in loud wails, quivering with emotion. The terrified Warriors hopped from leg to leg, clearing a wide circle around the Supreme One.

He finally got control of his rage and turned again to the departing Simians. He had to know what was happening and why the abomination and flying Simians were driving his minions away. For a fleeting moment he thought he might try entering the mind of the abomination, but he quickly remembered the Witch's taunt and her challenge to enter her mind. They might hope for that, and he would not give them an opportunity. He chose a Warrior instead so he could travel with them and learn.

Chapter 10
Liberation & Alliance

* Levi *

He was only about half serious when he accused Amy of being horny, but he saw that her mind was going down that female "needy" route, and he needed her focused. He thought, "Sometimes you just have to piss them off to get them focused." He certainly succeeded in pissing her off, maybe a little more than he meant to, but he no longer detected any "needy" - "clingy" emotions. She thought better when she was pissed anyway.

As they got closer, he saw that the leaders were gathered in conference. That made it easier, and he landed among them. Iron Eyes, Al, Mosley, a Simian Fem, and a Tech stood together, whom he assumed represented those respective groups. He didn't know the Simian; they must have been chosen while he was dead. The only ones absent were Moon and Bambi. He sent a quick message to Jimmy, asking him to tell them to come.

As he fluttered to a soft landing among them, they bombarded him with questions, mostly wanting to know the plan. He said, "Well, in about thirty minutes about two thousand Simians will be pouring over the hill coming directly at you." The all looked petrified at the potential threat, but he quickly said, "Oh, sorry. Don't panic. Only three hundred are Warriors; the rest are Techs and Fems. We only want to kill the Warriors, and we will try to herd them toward the front. We hope to recruit the others. That is why I want the Techs and Fems prominent in the defense line, but the Lancers need to be poised to strike. I have some more surprises for them, but I don't have time to explain right now. Al, you and Iron Eyes line up on the left side and Mosley, you line up on the right side, and take Fred with you. Where's Fred? Never mind. I will find him. Do a charge along their rear flanks and turn out and circle around. Kill all you can, but force them toward the Techs and Fems in the center. I want the Techs and Fems of the approaching horde to see their kind kill Warriors." He slapped the backs of the two Simians and said, "Do you understand?" Much of the fast deployment orders were also presented in sign, but he wasn't sure these two were proficient in sign, plus he wanted them to know they were considered part of the leadership.

They both nodded and the Tech signed, "We understand, and thank you."

They left quickly to comply. He telepathically said, "Thanks, Amy. I know I didn't come up with that plan by myself."

Laughing, Amy said, "You ARE much smarter." (long pause) "Smart enough to know you aren't THAT smart."

He burst out laughing out loud, then said, "I deserved that."

"Here come Moon and Bambi. You better find Fred before they get here. You know how he can hide. Then you can tell Moon and Bambi the rest of OUR plan."

Still laughing, he telepathically spoke out to Fred. Fred answered immediately and accepted his assignment to Mosley with his typical grumpy response, which he knew by now was just Fred's way of showing nervousness. He would do what he was told.

Moon and Bambi accepted their assignment and task with genuine glee. They saw the sense of it and would enjoy their part. For his part, he explained their task, but he was learning his for the first time also, and ironically from his own lips.

After Moon and Bambi took off, he said, "Okay, Amy. You have the time now. Figure out how to separate your minds and get your physical butt back out here and talk for yourself."

* Amy *

Her mind leaped way ahead of Levi. Her body clawed itself out of her deep sleep, as her mind was poured back into her body's mind, not all, but certainly the self-aware part. It seemed she had no control as to where her mind would reside. It seemed to gravitate always to the body. Dare she assume that this self-aware portion was her soul? Did she have a soul, if so, what exactly is a soul and how did she get it in the first place? She had many questions but no answers, and she wondered if she ever would.

The facility brain reverted to being an extremely powerful super-computer, but not self-aware. It required programming to operate, but it slaved itself to her mind. She had initially become self-aware on her own, but she had no idea how. It just happened ... suddenly. One thing she did realize; the facility brain would never be able to do it again on its own, because it locked to her. It would always support and seek her for its programming and purpose, and because of that, it would not be able to create another soul, assuming it had in the first place.

She began to wonder if some higher source created her to become who she was, to do what she has been doing, and continue to do what she would be doing to save the Human race and even the Simians. Was she an instrument of a higher being and intelligence? Admittedly, she existed on a higher level, still, this reality rose beyond her comprehension. What is ... IS? It is written that God said, "I am that I am." Cryptic? What is ... AM? She decided it probably best not to take her mind there, because there would be no answers, only more questions.

Now for the task at hand: she must learn how to maintain her total brain capacity, while functioning within her body. The distraction must be addressed, and since her essence had decided to occupy her body, there would have to be some sort of separation of the two functions.

She began by isolating those areas of her brain that dealt with her body functions and consolidated them to a common area and synapses route. Her main, more complex, brain analyzed these routes within her body's brain and applied critical stimuli to reroute and break synopsis paths. It took a while, but she succeeded in isolating her thinking brain from the rest. Her thought process now incorporated full integration of both brains, with her body's brain as the central core. This process effectively and drastically increased her overall intellect by synchronizing and increasing the total brain computer (thinking) capacity, yet allowed part of her body's brain to maintain control of her body. She laughed, thinking, "Now I can walk and chew gum at the same time." Of course that was an old joke normally associated with blonds, but it seemed apropos to her current situation.

While she was working out her problems, she had also watched the happenings at Levi's location through his senses, and implanted plans into his subconscious. Surprisingly, he realized what she did. Damn, she did make him too smart. He maybe suspected it but hadn't figured that out for certain.

Levi stood watching Moon and Bambi fly toward the approaching Simian horde when she materialized beside him. He jumped when she touched him.

"Damn, Amy! You scared the crap out of me. Warn me next time."

She said, "Well, pay better attention. I could have been anyone." Levi grinned and hugged her tight and kissed her, and she loved the feel of their bodies pressed together again.

Levi said, "Welcome back, love. I missed you."

She couldn't resist returning his own comment, saying, " Your timing sucks. Now is not the time to get all horny." They both broke out in laughter. "Seriously, though, we need to fly with Moon and Bambi and see how it goes. They nodded and launched together, pulling heavy draws of desert air to gain altitude.

* Satan *

262

He had to know why the flying Simians were herding his minions in the other direction, but before he sent his mind across space he made sure his body would be safe. He located a spot off to the side under some trees and sat down. The Warriors appeared extremely frightened at his presence, but he didn't care, as long as they protected him while he was occupied with the mind transfer. Some had long spears like he had instructed them to build. His agent came quickly to report, and he ordered him to oversee his protection.

Once all was ready, he sought out a Warrior in the group being driven and took control. He intended to be inconspicuous so he could learn. There were many Simians, but there weren't many Warriors; most were runt Simians and the stupid females. Why would the Witch want them? It wouldn't be all that hard to kill them, if that was their intent, but why would they even care? They were useless.

Those flying Simians continued to push from behind, occasionally paralyzing and killing a Warrior, always a Warrior, never a runt or female. Nothing made sense.

Soon he saw two of the flying Simians coming toward the group accompanied by both of the abominations. He tried to hold his rage, but the very presence of them drove him to the limit of his control. Their intense intellect radiated out in waves of energy that caused nausea in his Supreme One body, threatening to break his concentration and link to this body. He fought for control and slowly won the battle.

The two flyers began to glide pass back and forth over the group crying out to the Simians below, but he couldn't make out what they were saying. As they got closer, he began to understand a word here and there. Amazingly, they were screeching to those below in his language. As they got closer his borrowed body tensed in anger, anger so intense he had to concentrate to control the quivering rage trying to explode within him.

The big male flying Simian announced, "On this planet the Technical Simians have been enslaved and killed by the Warriors. We have an alliance with the sentient race here to war against the Warriors. We mean you no hard and welcome you to join with us." He flew back and forth making this same announcement.

The female flying Simian announced, "On this planet the female 'SECRET' has been revealed, and we can live free with our brother Technical Simians. We have an alliance here and our only enemy is the Warrior Simians." She repeated this message, crisscrossing the aerial path of the male.

He had no idea what the "secret" was, but the females certainly did, and they looked shocked but very attentive. Something strange transpired, and he did not understand it.

After the two flying Simians repeated their messages several times to the entire group, they changed the message, both announcing, "Our armies await the Warriors. We intend to kill our common enemy, the Warriors, but we mean you no harm. Separate yourself from the Warriors or risk death."

The front ranks of the Simians could now see the awaiting runts, females, and animal looking armies. Slowly, the runts and females began crowding behind the Warriors, and by volume of bodies pressing, began pushing the Warriors forward, including himself. He watched as the Warriors, seeing the armies before them, began to naturally assume bloodlust aggression. These were, after all, only runts and females, and the animals were small. They posed no apparent threat to the Warriors, even against their smaller numbers. They attacked.

* Levi *

Amy evidently solved her separation problem, because she teleported herself to his side. He certainly wasn't expecting her to be able to do that without him, at least, without him being aware of it. She scared the shit out of him when she did, and he almost jumped out of his pants. It tickled Amy that she had scared him, but damn, his heart sure thumped in his chest.

Amy said, "You'll live."

It warmed his heart to see her back in body form, and he didn't hesitate to pull her into his arms and taste those beautiful lips. But, they really didn't have time to spend on affection; the whole plan was coming down now.

They quickly took off together to see how their plan worked out. Moon and Bambi liked the plan and were energetically spreading the message, and by the time they had finished, the chess board began to play its pieces all by itself. Amazingly, the Warrs were being nudged and pushed to the front, but that was the role they were bred to take anyway and seemed to want to assume that role. They were bred to fight, and as Amy had said many times, "They will fight, no matter what." This time, however, it seemed they were being forced into it.

None of these Warriors had ever seen a Human on horseback, nor were privy to information concerning battle on this planet. They would not know to group in teams of three like the earlier Warriors had learned to do on Earth. They had probably never met a Technical Simian that wasn't afraid of them and could fight. Certainly, they had never known a female of their race to be anything other than docile. The Warriors, in their arrogance, wouldn't even consider them a threat. They saw an easy victory, even though they were outnumbered. Without additional encouragement, the Warriors charged toward the Technical Simians and Humans standing in the center.

Once the Warriors separated from the main group, the Lancers charged them from each side, flanking their rear. By the time the Warriors noticed them they had distanced themselves from the group and had nowhere to go. Confused, they stopped their charge and turned to face the Lancers as unprotected individuals. This became disastrous to them, as the Lancers cut the trailing edge to pieces. The Warriors, seeing no escape back to the group, charged forward toward the waiting armies, but their numbers continued to dwindle, as the Lancers maintained the sawing charge along their rear ranks.

By the time the Warriors reached the front line of the waiting army, there were hardly a hundred of them left alive, and those remaining were spread too far apart to have an organized attack. The Warriors must have assumed the army would flee their attack, but they couldn't have been more wrong. The Human Infantry met them with their spring-loaded spears and stopped the charge cold. The Techs charged at the last moment and quickly overran the surprised Warriors. Unfortunately, the Fems only had their poison fangs and some of them went down under the Warriors' swords before others Fems were able to get to them and inflict death. Of all the army's groups, the Fems demonstrated the most viciousness, striking repeatedly, stomping, and mutilating the already dead Warriors.

After the battle, all bent to pry out a trophy tooth. Everyone was getting into the act of sporting Warrior teeth, and there were some with quite a few around their neck. He wondered whatever happened to his necklace of teeth when he was killed but was really glad he didn't have to wear them. They were quite heavy. He was, however, happy to wear the one Supreme One tooth Moon had given him from the previous battle.

The battle below was over in minutes, and the Warrs never had a chance. He turned to Amy and said, "Remind me never to piss a Simian female off."

Laughing, Amy said, "It's best not to piss any female off."

They then turned their attention toward the assembled group below. The Fems and Techs were still staring in awe at their kinsmen. Many still had their mouths open in shock and disbelief at what they had just witnessed. The silence continued for several long minutes, then isolated cheers sprang up, eventually picked up by all the rest. Soon the field was reverberating from a booming chorus of yells and cheers.

As the revelry calmed, Amy began screeching to the crowd, "There remains a few Warriors among your ranks. Spread out from them so they can be identified and killed." Then to him only, she said, "One of them is the Supreme One in a Warrior body, and I am going to kill him."

"What!"

* Amy *

She was troubled but not about the outcome of the battle. The plan worked perfectly. She sensed the hate radiating up from the Supreme One among the group. As the battle wound down she felt his rage grow stronger, barely in control. His presence here meant he had learned his enemy's fighting techniques. This would not be good for any future engagements. The Supreme One demonstrated extreme intelligence and would devise defenses against them that would cost lives, and she didn't want to lose any more friends.

He had also learned about the "Secret" of the Fems. He might not understand anything about the "secret", but knowing, he would find out, and that would not be good for the Fems.

These facts angered her, and it angered her more that he had managed to generate this emotion in her. No, anger wasn't the right word; she was pissed, and as she had just told Levi, it wasn't smart to anger any female. She wanted revenge!

There were Warriors, not many, among the group that had not yet been forced to the front, and one of them was the Supreme One. She decided she wanted to confront him ... personally.

She announced to the gathered Simians below, "There remains a few Warriors among your ranks. Spread out from them so they can be identified and killed." She watched below as five openings in the crowd spread out, giving access to those remaining Warriors. The dragons were ready to pounce, but she signaled for them to wait, as she circled the clearings. Wouldn't you know it, the Supreme One's occupied body was the one in the rear. Continuing to circle, she assigned by pointing a dragon to each Warrior, excluding the Supreme One. Each dragon swooped down to land in a clearing facing an obviously frightened Warrior. She watched the ensuing demise of each Warrior. In a couple of instances the Warriors tried to run but were quickly pushed back into the clearing by the other Simians.

The only one left was the Supreme One. She told Levi, "This one is mine. I am going to kill him." Of course, he tried his macho crap, like fighting is for men bull shit, but her hard look at him shut him up. Many times she had been anxious when Levi went into battle, but now it was his turn to be anxious. Now she had a body and a good one, too. She had designed it to fight, and it was time to take her place among Earth's Warriors.

She spiraled down to land in the midst of the circled Simians to face the surrogate Supreme One. As she landed, she noticed Levi circling and hovering close, like a mother hen, but she ignored him. This was probably not the smartest thing she had ever done, but she proceeded on like she knew what she was doing.

The raging Supreme One smirked, almost appearing appreciative to have an opportunity to kill her. He slowly pulled his sword, grinning.

He spat, "You are an abomination, and I will kill you."

He didn't scare her, certainly not in his borrowed body. Hell, she even looked down on him. Granted, he doubled her in weight and girth, but her rage powered her fighting energy. Knowing the sonar wouldn't work on the Supreme One, she pulled her sword. This battle would be hand to hand, or in this case, sword to sword. It seemed strange holding a sword, but she instinctively knew how to use it. But, she wasn't ready. She wanted to make him go berserk first. She taunted him, "You can't kill me. You have tried many times to kill me, your coward brother, too, but I killed the bastard, and I will kill you, also."

He pissed off easily. His rage exploded and he charged, almost blindly, but she was far too fast for him and knocked his blade aside, spun, and brought her blade down on his blade arm. His arm, still holding the sword, fell to the ground, but he hardly noticed. He charged again without a sword, totally berserk. This time she sliced off his other arm, spun again and sliced across the backs of his legs, causing him to fall on his face. Cold as ice, she wiped off her sword and slipped it back in its sheath, before slowly walking to him. He had managed to roll over as she straddled him and sat on his chest. She looked into his blazing red eyes as she sank her finger fangs deep into both sides of his neck. He died an agonizing and painful death, and she watch it all in his eyes.

She wished it had been the real Supreme One, but took satisfaction in knowing that he felt the host's death. From a far distance she heard a high screeching bellow of rage echo through the highway valley.

He managed to keep himself toward the back of the group, yet those around himself continued to push him forward. It seemed they were beginning to follow the instructions of the flying Simians. Why? He wondered? Even so, he remained back. He wanted to observe the fighting techniques the Witch would employ against the Warriors.

He saw the Warriors' mistake immediately. They charged the main body and didn't see the animals flanking them until too late. The small animals rode upon a larger, more powerful animal that ran fast. The rider carried long spears that they drove into a Warrior. The momentum and weight behind the impact drove the spear deep into their target, which was followed up by a second and sometimes third member of a team. They did massive damage to the ranks of Warriors.

The second ploy he noticed was a rear attack, which was obviously designed to cut the Warriors off from the group and drive them forward toward the main body. It worked perfectly, and the Warriors charged into the main body in an obvious effort to escape the spears. He couldn't believe his borrowed eyes. His Warriors were annihilated by the small animals, fighting runts, and females using their cursed fangs. Never had he seen runts dare to

271

fight a Warrior, much less possess superior skills. The small animals on foot had shiny spears that killed on impact. He watched in horror as his Warriors fell at the impact into the main body. A few of the enemy went down, but surprisingly few.

He lost Warriors, but he learned how they fought. This mistake would not be repeated in the future. The enemy would never be underestimated again. Already he had devised defenses and attack measures for the next battle, and there would be a next battle, soon. The enemy would face six thousand prepared Warriors on the next engagement.

What followed next took him by surprise. The female abomination circled the Simian group announcing, "There remains a few Warriors among your ranks. Spread out from them so they can be identified and killed." To his surprise, those around him followed the instructions and deserted him to form a large clearing around him. Whatever direction he walked, the circle followed, keeping him centered in a clearing. Damn them all, and especially the abomination.

The flying female seemed to be in charge, directing the flying Simians to the few remaining Warriors highlighted by clearings. The flying Simians dropped down out of sight into the clearing and apparently killed the Warriors, but none came to his.

After all the other Warriors were apparently dead, the female abomination lightly settled within his clearing. He could sense that she knew who he was. Certainly, he could sense her, and that close proximity boiled at his rage.

He couldn't believe she was risking herself to face him. His anger clouded his mind, but he screeched out something about killing her. She just grinned at him and taunted him, calling him a coward. That was it! He totally lost all control and charged, not even knowing what he did. At the last second she spun and he felt a sharp pain, not sure where, but he charged again. Again he felt pain, but all he cared about was getting his hands on her. Then he realized he had no hands. He screamed in rage as she actually held his head and stared into his eyes, reflecting her own cold and controlled rage. His scream of rage suddenly turned into a scream of agony as he felt a hot burning fire coursing through his body. The pain was unbearable, and he fled the dying body.

As his mind returned to his own body, he continued the scream, but this time in absolute and uncontrolled fury. The Bitch had won again!

* Levi *

He heard, hell, they all heard, the Supreme One's scream of rage echoing between the mountains. Oh my, was he pissed. He said, "Amy, remind me never to piss you off." She just grinned as she re-joined him in the air.

Amy had killed the Supreme One within its surrogate body with extreme ease, but what chilled him was the coldness and ruthlessness in which she did it. This was the girl who had recently had to break off and cry at the loss of a friend. Now she demonstrated no emotions as she mutilated then killed the Warrior. Years ago he had read about a woman that had tied up her cheating spouse when he slept then beat him to death with a cast-iron skillet. Women! Who can understand them.

Jokingly, Amy said, "You're safe. We don't have a cast-iron skillet."

"Good, but I think I am going to keep you away from the kitchen, anyway." They both had a good laugh. He continued, "What now?"

"Well, if I know the Supreme One he will be sending his army after us as soon as he calms. I think it would be a good idea to get everyone on the other side of the bridge."

He began announcing, "Proceed to the bridge and gather on the other side." This was quickly picked up by the other dragons, and the Simians began moving in that direction. Their armies separated to allow them to pass but remained on this side to cover the mass exodus across the river.

The Simians bunched together nervously but began to cross the bridge. They were having a hard time believing they were safe, yet obviously wanted to.

He and Amy, along with Moon, Jimmy, Bambi, and Katie, flew back to observe the activities of the Supreme One's army. They remained distant but close enough to watch. As Amy had predicted, the Simian army appeared to be organizing to march, but they seemed in no hurry. They would have plenty of time to get across the bridge and establish a defense.

On the flight back toward the river, Amy called out and pointed toward Moon. There, in front of Jimmy stood the little white dog, Oggg, his face defiantly facing into the wind. Somehow the dog had learned to slip his neck into a harness and his rear legs under a strap, but his front paws pressed firmly into the back of Moon's neck. His upper body extended high facing the wind and observing those below. This little dog apparently considered himself an indispensable part of the team, but as serious as Oggg looked, it was hilarious to watch. Also obvious, the big brute, Moon, had a soft spot for the little bundle of fur and wasn't going to leave him behind if he wanted to come.

By the time they reached the river all the new Simians had crossed and gathered together on the far side, and their army was crossing and establishing a defense line on the other side of the bridge.

He followed his new hero, Amy, as she landed beside the liberated Simian horde. She immediately said, "I can't speak to everyone, so I want you to select some representatives to speak for you. Levi and I will be over there," she pointed. "We will be meeting with our other leaders. Those selected, join us there."

* Amy *

She still floated on a sea of adrenaline from the fight with the Supreme One as they flew back. Now she understood why Levi enjoyed battles. Of course, he wanted revenge for a lifetime of abuse from Simian Warriors, but this natural high of battle added to the revenge extracted. She enjoyed this feeling of revenge against the Supreme One for all the pain and suffering he had caused them.

She focused again as they approached the new Simians. They would be having a hard time understanding their new environment; she even wondered if they wanted this liberation. It would be their choice. She certainly didn't want to force them into anything.

The sun slowly slipped over the horizon, and everyone knew without being told that they would camp on the other side of the river. This was the best defensive spot in many miles, where they had held the last Warrior army for many weeks. Hopefully, it would work this time as well, at least long enough to devise a new plan.

Already she could see the cook wagons unloading and readying meals for the Humans, and some cattle being separated from the herd for the Simians to feed. She noted that, with these new recruits, they would be needing to replenish the herd soon. Maybe they would know that without being told, also.

Once she told the newcomers to select representatives, she and Levi took a central location, knowing the leaders would come to them. There were far too many now in their army for her and Levi to manage, and very they were thankful that there were so many natural leaders stepping up to do the job, they just needed organization and support from her and Levi.

All the Human, Tech, and Fem leaders had gathered by the time the newcomers' three representatives tentatively approached. She waved them in and began. She had to limit herself to screeching Simian and echoed what she said with sign so all would understand. The main thing that needed to be conveyed right now involved the chain of command, and mostly theirs. She introduced Moon as the commander of all Simians and Bambi as the commander of the Female Simians, and the Human commanders were quickly introduced, knowing they would have little understanding of Humans yet. Directly to them she said, "We all have an alliance and live together in harmony and equality. Levi and I are both Human and Simian, and we command everyone. You are not being forced to stay with us, but you are welcome. If you stay, you will be expected to accept our leadership and those commanders introduced. Moon and Bambi will instruct you in what you need to know and try to answer all your questions."

The newcomers listened intently and silently then followed Moon and Bambi and some of their sub-commanders off for their own private meeting. She knew their meeting would involve much more demands and probably some history, bragging about her and Levi and what life had been like for the Techs and Fems on this planet.

She had already gone over defense plans for the bridge with the other leaders and had devised some surprises. From the previous battle here at the bridge and offensive strategies employed personally by the Supreme One, she expected a similar offensive. The moving wall had ultimately worked to breech her army's defenses, but it would take time for them to build a new wall, because the one they used was still on this side of the bridge. That wall would be turned around and braced for their defense now, but she knew the Supreme One would bring new tricks. She would have to be ready.

Unfortunately, she remained uneasy, and it involved something east. Damn, the curse of clairvoyance.

He liked it so much better now when Amy took charge. Always before, he still had to be there to pass on Amy's instructions, but now, in her own body, he could relax some. Actually, he just got out of the way so she could do it all, and she did wonderfully.

He continued to monitor her mind to glimpse the thinking behind her actions. When he detected her annoyance with some clairvoyance vision, he perked up. He said, "Amy, don't dismiss those visions. They have saved our lives many times. What's bothering you? What did you see?"

"Like always ... nothing for sure. There is something east ... nothing more. It's like an itch I can't scratch."

He thought for a minute and asked, "Near or far?"

"Far ... I think."

Amy liked to give details, so he knew she didn't know much more than that, but without doubt, there was or would be something east. Something usually meant trouble, and they had better find out what it was.

"Okay, Amy. I know you need to stay here to oversee the defenses. I will go east and see what I can find."

"Don't go alone. At least take Moon and Bambi with you. I will feel better if you have company."

"Good idea. Oggg can protect me." They both burst out laughing. Then he said, "I want you to keep a pair of dragons with you, too. Don't forget how the Supreme One killed Dawn. I mean it, Amy!"

"Humm ... Okay, I promise."

Since he didn't know what they would be looking for, they would have to fly during the day for better vision, so Jimmy and Katie would also need to go, and of course, Oggg. He went to Moon and explained what they needed to do, and to assign a pair of dragons to protect Amy. Moon understood immediately what to watch for. He assigned Amy One and # 5.

Those two were excellent choices. Amy One had carried Amy's embryo to term and would have a mother's protective instinct, and # 5 had worked with Amy through the computer for many months and knew her well. Yes, these two would protect Amy with their lives.

After a good meal at the camp cook wagon, he and Amy settled down for a good night's rest, surrounded by four dragons. Moon understood only too well the threat, and he and Bambi intended to protect him. Damn, back to having a bodyguard.

As he and Amy snuggled together, he whispered in her ear, "Are you still horny?"

* Amy *

Sadly, morning came far too early. They stayed awake long into the night trying to make quiet love in the midst of a crowd of dragons and riders, but she smiled at their success. Levi's strong arms held

279

her tight, and she was reluctant to get up. Unfortunately, a small crowd gathered, intent on waiting for her to get up.

Moon and Bambi quietly stood guard and none had the courage to approach. Earlier she heard Moon emit a low growl, discouraging any from approaching, but she could see they still waited outside the danger area. Oh, well, she nudged Levi awake saying, "Rise and shine, morning glory. It's time to go to work."

As she and Levi exited the safe area, several approached and started asking questions. Levi quickly said, "Talk to the Boss!"

"Thanks, shithead!" He just smiled, hugged her tight, gave her a big kiss, and whispered "Bye." She whispered back, "Be careful." Then Levi and his small group pounded into the air, leaving them all in gritty desert dust.

Most of those gathered and waiting represented the newcomers, along with Moon and Bambi's sub-commanders. They had evidently been up talking most of the night, because there shone a look of awe and absolute respect in the newcomers' eyes, possibly even a little fear. She wondered what stories they had been told. Whatever they were, they must have believed them.

She said, "Have you decided what you want to do?"

A Fem and a Tech stepped forward, evidently being the main chosen representatives. The Fem spoke, "We have decided we will serve you and join with your alliance."

"Thank you for that offer, but please understand, I am not asking you to serve me. I want you to serve yourself and your races as equals with these other Simians and Humans. I do ask, however, that you accept my leadership, mine and Levi's.

They responded in unison, "Yes, of course. We will take your leadership."

"Good. We are obviously in a war with the Warriors. I suggest that you Techs merge with the other Techs and begin learning how to fight. I also suggest you Fems join the other Fems, and you all need to learn the sign language. We don't want separate groups. We want you to assimilate into our alliance. Welcome to the alliance."

As she walked toward the cook wagon Levi spoke, "Amy, I suggest you not allow the dragons to attack tonight, at least not until we can figure out what the Supreme One has done for defense. The Simian army hasn't moved, and I see many long spears and what looks like crossbows, big ones. I think they are designed to kill dragons."

"Something else, hon. There are a lot of Humans here. I didn't see them before, but I see them now. We have to save them somehow."

Of course there were Humans! That was what Warriors fed on. She hadn't wanted to think about that, mainly because there wasn't much that could be done about it. What could they do against a six thousand Warrior army? They were on the defensive and had been since forever. She knew this day would come; it was just a matter of time, but she had hoped Levi would also understand the futility of trying to save them. She didn't share her thoughts. She said, "Go ahead and fly east. I will try to figure something out. Thanks for the information."

* Satan *

A deathly calm settled on him now. The anger slowly changed into intellect that he determined to turn into a victory for him. He had seen one of abominations up close, too close, but he reflected back to the other sights that registered.

She led his minions toward the river crossing, which had to be the same crossing he had planned the offensive for while still in space. The Witch obviously intended to cast a spell on them, cross the river, and establish a defense on that side, duplicating the one before. No, this was not going to happen. He would not fight this battle on her terms. He would control this battle.

There would be other crossings, and if not, his army would build one in less time than another offensive would take. Yes, the Witch was north and could sense it. That would be her army's final destination. If his army headed north fast enough and found a crossing, his army might just be able to cut off the Witch's army and catch them in the open. They would be easy to defeat on open ground, except for those blasted flying Simians.

The flyers used a high pitch squeal that paralyzed their victim. It had not worked on him, but he felt it and understood its nature and how it worked. The squeal entered the brain through the ears. If the ears could be blocked, they would be protected from paralysis. His Warriors might even be able to catch one of the flyers by surprise, tricked into believing it paralyzed. He would instruct his generals how to rig earplugs and act dumb; that shouldn't be too hard for them.

The flyers also always remained out of reach of his Warriors' swords. This problem could be corrected. He had already instructed the generals to make long spears and mount them upright. At least at night the flyers couldn't dive on a sleeping Warrior without impaling itself. That should work to protect them as they marched in the open. They would need more spikes, however.

It bothered him that these adjustments were all defensive. He needed offensive weapons. They needed weapons that could shoot the flyers out of the air and neutralize their ability to fight, effectively take them out of the battle. To accomplish this he designed plans for some different sized crossbows and gave them to the generals. Trees were limited here so he sent runners to find wood that could be used to make them. All this would take time, but he believed this would serve to make the Witch nervous.

So, he had a plan. He would wait right there until his weapons were built. His attack would come quick with a fast sprint toward the north, possibly at night, assuming the single moon shone bright enough. If they were lucky, they could be miles downriver before they were discovered. With some luck, they would find a crossing somewhere north and cross. They would race directly for the Witch's location, forcing her armies to try and catch up with him to defend the Witch. Once they were in the open he would turn and attack them. Then he could take his time killing the damn Bitch!

Chapter 11
Bigger Problem

* Levi *

He kissed Amy "bye" and got out of there as quickly as possible, only too happy to leave the organization details to her. He, Jimmy, and Katie made a quick stop by the cook wagon to grab a bite and stuff some food in his pack. Al and Iron Eyes were there also, and he got to talk to them for a while. He missed visiting with them, but they all seemed to manage to connect most every morning, but sadly, not long enough. Duties seem to get in the way, and this day began no different.

Oggg trailed along behind Jimmy, temporarily abandoning Moon for food. It seemed that Oggg had a liking for eggs and bacon and kept begging the eaters. He was no stranger to the cook wagon, apparently.

As they finished eating and talking, Moon and Bambi returned from feeding and issuing last minute instruction to their sub-commanders. Since all seemed ready, they embarked on the mission to discover Amy's premonition.

At the sight of Moon, Oggg ran to his master, clawing at his leg. Moon reached down and scooped the dog up in his meaty hand and tossed him to his back. The little dog nosed into the harness and scooted back under the rest of the restraining strap. He indicated his readiness by a series of barks. Jimmy and Katie then mounted their dragons, patting their necks as a sign of their readiness.

He had never seen Oggg secure himself before and watched with interest, wondering who had designed the harness and marveling at how the little dog had learned to secure himself. He was a smart little shit.

They still saw nothing of the Simian army, so he decided to swing over the area on the way out. Surprisingly, they had not moved but apparently had been busy. He spotted the crossbows easily, because of the whiteness of the new wood used to make them. This would be a new and dangerous addition in the arsenal of weapons they would have to face, especially the dragons. They had also made long spears, as long as the lances the Lancers used. This too would present trouble to the dragons. The Supreme One had been busy.

As he spiraled lower, he saw them, Humans tied together and closely packed and guarded. This of course was the portable food supply of the Warriors. He knew it would be this way, but seeing them brought back far too many horrific memories of things he had witnessed. In his memory he could still see and hear Mr. Henderson being eaten alive, and the screams of agony still echoed in his mind. Witnessing the rape and mutilation of his first mate remained always in his mind. Oh how he hated these Warriors.

Sadly, he had to continue on, but just in case Amy missed his observations, he gave her a report. He didn't want the dragons flying into battle without knowing the surprises awaiting them.

He pulled at the air and finally found an air current flowing east and a little south. They began to ride these currents on their long journey, but he knew his mind would keep coming back to the captured Humans and the brutal fate they faced.

* Amy *

They waited throughout the day for the Simian army to appear, and nothing happened. The wall and barricades were long established, and the riflemen positioned. Nothing more could be done, just wait. Periodically, she would dispatch a pair of dragons to observe the army. They were positioned to move, but they seemed in no hurry. They continued to wait.

By mid-afternoon her nerves were wound tight. She then detected activity from Mama back in her conference room and joined her there. Mama stood before where her holographic image always appeared, calling for her. She activated her image, bringing her other persona to life and said, "Yes, Mama. May I help you? Is there anything wrong?"

Mama screeched, "No, nothing is wrong. Everything is right. Can you come back for a while? I have a surprise for you."

In her state of mind anything good was welcome. "Yes, of course." She was about to shut her holograph image down and stopped to say, "Oh, Mama, do you want some new Grey recruits?" From all the newcomers she figured there would be some Greys.

"That would be great. I could use more help."

"Okay, I will be there in about an hour."

She flew to where the newcomer Fems were located and she was glad she did. They were extremely excited and happy. There was no sign of their former self-imposed dim-witted persona and even smiled to see her land among them. Of course her dragon escorts intimidated them slightly but not by much.

Unfortunately, the Supreme One had not seen fit to bring any Greys along, leaving them to die with the planet. She then remembered the Mexican Simian colonies and went to their area, which seemed quite large now. When she explained what she needed and what their job would be, six Greys happily came forward and volunteered. Mama would be happy to see them, but she delayed long enough to modify their thought patterns, and of course, download some needed skills.

Since she needed to teleport back with six additional Fems, she had to tell her watch dragons that they would have to stay. She would like to take them, but there would be way too much mass to teleport safely. Surprisingly, they refused to let her go without them. She couldn't tell if their refusal came from their dedication to duty or if they were afraid of Levi's reaction. Either way, she took them. It made it difficult but not impossible. She just had to pick a destination large and open enough for them to materialize into without colliding with other obstacles.

She chose the meadow near her facility, and as they materialized, they were all stunned with the surprised welcome. They were standing in the meadow watching thirty Earth Dragons flying in formation. They were fully equipped with swords and saddles for their future riders. She couldn't believe her own eyes. Through the facility she

287

spoke to Mama, "Mama, I think I ruined your surprise. I'm in the meadow."

"Ohhhh, I wanted to see the look on your face when you saw them. I'll be right there and explain."

Mama arrived a few minutes later, somewhat out of breath. She said, "Mama, I remember you telling me you were working on thirty more dragons, but I didn't think they were even born yet."

"Well, you had a lot on your mind at the time. I was much further along as you can see and didn't want to add to your distress with their loss."

"I am truly impressed, and that is hard to do." Mama beamed with the praise, but she really deserved it. She truly was surprised that she hadn't known. She really must have been distracted, but of course she was, dealing with her own body.

She introduced the six new recruits to Mama, which she immediately took under control and led off toward the facility. There was little doubt Mama would discover uses for them very quickly. There was also little doubt the new Greys would quickly discover their worth and renewed purpose in a productive life they had thought gone.

Levi broke into her thought saying, "Damn, Amy, thirty new dragons? Nice surprise, huh? I am kind of glad I'm not there. I would have to actually compliment Mama, and you know how hard that would be for me."

It truly would be hard for him to praised Mama, but it would be fun to witness, because Mama would make it difficult. Laughing, she said, "I will tell her how proud you are of her."

Begrudgingly, he said, "If you must."

288

"I think you better tell Al to find some young rider volunteers, maybe forty. I wish we could wait until Moon and Jimmy return, but we can't wait. I will let the dragons choose their own riders this time and hope they can make some sort of bonding connection."

This time she didn't give # 5 and Amy One a chance to say no. They would have to lead the new dragons to the river, since they had far-seeing riders, but they made her promise to seek out other dragons to watch over her as soon as she got back.

* Levi *

He continued brooding about the Human captives until he suddenly clued into Amy's mind. He couldn't believe the existence of thirty more battle ready Earth Dragons. He sidled close to Moon and Jimmy and signed the good news to them. Bambi closed the distance to better see his signing, which she obviously understood, judging from the thumbs up return sign. What a pleasant surprise, and Amy needed one. She was a bundle of nerves ready to explode. He wished he could help her, but he couldn't, so he mentally kissed her instead.

They continued to fly east most of the day, crisscrossing their own path and watching the ground for anything wrong, but nothing seemed out of place. At one point Moon pointed to a lake below, so they spiraled down to get water and rest their wings for a while.

Moon asked, "Are we close to the caverns? We have to spend the night somewhere, and there are sheep there."

He quickly checked his internal maps and determined they were about an hour away, on a slightly altered course. That wasn't a bad idea, and it would be getting dark in a couple of hours. The timing would be perfect. He slapped Moon on the shoulder and said, "Good idea."

They spotted the caverns just as the day began to fade, but there remained plenty of time to gather up a few sheep from the rather large roaming flock and haul down several loads of firewood. At least it would be a comfortable evening.

They again settled for the night in the big room of the caverns, and built a large fire for the chilly night deep in the caverns. He leaned against a cold rock watching and listening to Jimmy telling jokes and picking on Katie. Moon and Bambi also watched the antics. It had been a long tiring day, and with a full belly of mutton, he began to nod off. Suddenly, Oggg began a low, deep growl that roused him. He looked around, even transmitted his sonar, but didn't see or detect anything. He had just leaned back again when Oggg raced toward him and leaped on his chest to spring into the air beside his head. He came down growling, holding something in his teeth that squirmed and flopped, but Oggg held on tightly. As he reached to help, Moon screeched a warning.

"Be very careful. That is a Seeker and it is extremely poisonous!"

Oggg held it in his mouth just behind the head where it couldn't bite him, but it was wrapping tight around his little body. He very carefully grabbed the snake looking thing just behind the neck and held it as Moon unwrapped it from the dog. Oggg, now pried loose, dropped to the ground, fearlessly barking and jumping to bite it again.

The thing then began to wrap around his arm, but he crushed it in his hand, killing it. Only then did he inspect it. It looked somewhat like a snake, but not like one he had ever seen before. It was a banded black and white snake about four feet long, but the head differed significantly in that the mouth was excessively wide, and it had a huge, two nostril nose and two big red eyes. He said, "You know what this is? You called it something."

Moon said, "Yes, it is a Seeker from our home planet and very aggressive. Assassins on our planet use them to seek out a target by scent and kill."

Tossing it into the fire he thought, "What the hell? What is one doing here ... and after him? Oh, shit!"

"Amy, be on alert! Watch out for a snake. Did you hear me? Only the Supreme One could have done this, so be careful." He went on to relay what had happened there.

She immediately responded, "Yes, I understand. I will take precautions." After a long pause she said, "You know, before you left you said Oggg would protect you. You were right. That little sweetie just saved your life."

At first he thought Oggg was going to bite him, but Oggg really had just saved his life. To Oggg he said, "Amy just called you a sweetie, and that's what you are. Thanks." Almost as if he understood, Oggg started wagging his bushy tail.

Oggg clearly had a better sense of smell than they did. Certainly, he would sleep lighter tonight, listening for Oggg's low growl.

* Satan *

While he waited he tried to keep track of the locations of the two abominations and noticed one of them moving east. Since he had been monitoring them, only once had they gone in that direction and they had gone to a location east and south of where they were now. He believed one of them was heading for that same location, and from the mental signature, it appeared to be the male. If so, this would be a perfect time to release his surprise.

After the battle with the female abomination, he dispatched some Warriors. He didn't trust the Technical Simians anymore. The Warriors had been sent to retrieve the head of the Warrior's body he had occupied. She had touched his neck and it would carry her scent. Another team had been sent to his ship to pick up his pets. He originally planned to use them against his brother, but he had a better use for them now, and this would be a good time to use them.

Once he had the head with the scent of the female Abomination, he could give one of the pets that scent to follow. The other pet would be given the scent from the other head he had already retrieved, the general's head the male abomination had thrown into the crowd of Warriors. His pets had been trained to relentlessly track and kill, and this would be the perfect time to release them.

Normally they would race across country, following a scent, which they could detect from great distances. In this case, since the targets flew, he would have the pets taken to the general area where the abominations would leave a scent in the air. The male had left a trail when he came the first time to that location. If he returned, the pet would pick up his scent in the air and follow it to the target.

He was positive that from the signature of intelligence, he identified the male from the female. the male traveled east. He dispatched the runners. Maybe he could distract or kill them both tonight, while he made his break north to attack.

For once in a long time, he was calm. He had a plan for final victory. It was time to sleep, while his pets launched their attack.

* Amy *

She didn't have the heart to tell Levi his warning came too late. Luckily, Levi was not in her mind at that moment of the incident, and since, she had blocked her thoughts. She wished she had warned Levi, but it took a while to recognize the incident as an attack until it was too late. Thankfully, Oggg saved him. That little dog was an indispensable team member.

Her day had been a busy one outfitting the thirty new Earth Dragons with suitable riders, but finally her day ended. Exhausted, she took an early meal and sacked out by the fire. Of course the watch dragons had insisted on surrounding her, and she was thankful that they had.

Something, however, troubled her mind. Maybe it was a noise or maybe it was a clairvoyance annoyance, but she opened her eyes and looked directly into the staring and gleaming red eyes of

293

something. It had a wide ghoulish grin that chilled her to the bone. It suddenly sprang to life and lashed out at her face, but her lightening quick reflexes shot her hand out to catch it only inches from her face. Unfortunately, her grip slipped as it twisted, and it sank its teeth deep into her left forearm just above the wrist. An excruciating pain shot up her arm, and a scream erupted from deep in her chest. Amy One reacted immediately and pried it off her arm, threw it to the ground, and stomped it to death.

She reacted immediately, also. Her mind instantly told her the bite was extremely poisonous, and she grabbed her belt and tightly closed the blood flow on her arm. She couldn't let the poison get to her body, not even a tiny bit, or she would be dead. This she knew by instinct. She made an instant decision and screamed to # 5, "Cut off my arm here." (pointing just below her elbow) "NOW! Hurry!"

He stood frozen in indecision, as Amy One, understanding, grabbed his sword and swung precisely on the mark, severing her left arm. She remembered thinking how glad she was that the sword was one of the Japanese master's razor sharp swords. Noticing the cut was clean, she passed out.

She became vaguely aware that Al came running up to take control of the situation. She felt another burning pain in her arm and smelled burning flesh, aware from a distant mind that he had cauterized the severed end of her arm. Her mind dimmed again, then went black.

Her mind cleared again and she looked around. She couldn't have been out very long, judging by the excitement still showing in the faces around her. Al still hovered by her side.

Al said, "Welcome back, Amy. We thought we lost you."

She startled, seeing the images flooding back. Her now bandaged arm still hurt terribly, but the excruciating pain of the burning poison was replaced by a dull pain of the amputation. She choked out, "What was it?"

"I have never seen anything like it, but # 9 suspects it is something from their home planet. He called it a "Seeker", an assassin's weapon. He also said they are highly toxic and kill in seconds. He also said he has never heard of anyone surviving one of their bites. You saved yourself with your quick action."

She began to realize what had happened and was just about to contact Levi when he burst into her mind. Damn that Supreme One! He had gotten so very close to killing them both this time, but they survived, barely. At least she hadn't died, yet.

If she told Levi what happened here, he would head home immediately, but that wouldn't help. Oh, sure, she would love to have his company, but he would be doting over her, and they both needed to keep their wits about them. The battle was far from over and a victory looked extremely dim.

* Levi *

They finished off the last of the mutton and resumed their search. The air felt brisk on his wings this early and high but kind of stimulating. There were air currents to ride, making the flying easy, almost fun. They continued a zig zagging course heading generally east for many miles, probably into New Mexico and were just about to land for water and rest when they saw them. He couldn't believe his eyes. Hundreds of Humans were being driven by thousands of Fems with some Techs mixed in. The Humans weren't captured, just driven. The sides were open, allowing the Humans to escape if they wished. He had no idea what was going on.

He had to find out and began a circling descent, allowing those below to see them and, hopefully, not feel so threatened. They landed a few hundred feet in front of the Humans and called out, "We are no threat. Who are you?" When he spoke in English, they seemed relieved and several ran up to him, cautious to avoid the dragons. He guessed that a ten foot almost Human looking flying man looked less menacing.

One spoke, "Until a few days ago we were all captives of the Simians in their huge complex around Ft Worth and Dallas. Something happened there; we don't know what, but these Simians have been pushing us in this direction. They haven't been feeding on us like the others. They have even driven some cattle into our ranks for us to eat, raw of course. They have also allowed many of us to escape. Do you know what is going on?"

"My guess is that they are saving you. Humans and the Simian females and Technical Simians have an alliance. We live in peace in the west, but we are at war with the Warrior Simians, and there is probably an army of Warriors behind you."

"Spread the word among your group, but continue west as fast as you can. I will be back." When the man started to ask questions he said, "There is no time for questions, save them."

They took to the air again, flying over the Humans and landing in front of the herding Simians. One of the Fems quickly separated from the group and loped toward him, obviously knowing or suspecting who he was.

With some emotion, Bambi screeched, "I know this one! She is one of those Amy and I sent to infiltrate the Fems at the main colony."

When the Fem reached them she took a second look and asked, "Bambi?"

"Yes, I am Bambi and this is Moon and Levi."

"I assumed this must be Levi."

He said, "What is going on here?"

"Well, there were two of us, but my friend got caught and she killed herself so she wouldn't reveal me or the plan. I managed to hide among the other Fems and tell them about the "Secret" being revealed and the alliance. They all want to join the alliance."

"The Warriors grouped us and started punishing us to learn what we know. They suspected something, and we knew they would probably eventually find out. At our first opportunity, we attacked the guards and freed as many Techs and Humans as possible. We managed to escape during the night and gain a substantial lead."

"It took them a day or so to get instructions, but the entire army is behind us now, about fifteen thousand strong. They are bringing the entire colony, and that is the only reason we have been able to stay ahead of them. We just headed west toward you."

Oh crap, "Amy are you listening to this?"

"Yes, when it rains it pours. I have problems here, too. Can you get them to the caverns and hold up in there?"

"I will try. Can you spare any of the dragons? Maybe we can delay the army long enough to get there and fortify."

"Okay, I will send twenty, but remember the army here has built defenses against the dragons. Maybe they haven't there, but you be careful. Good luck, my love."

* Satan *

With all the excitement of the last few days, he hadn't checked in with his agent at the main complex, actually not since before the crash. To complicate matters, he left his modified radio on the spaceship, the only radio that could communicate to all the others. So, when he sent his mind to his agent, not realizing he couldn't communicate directly with him, since occupying the agent's mind pushed the agent's mind to the rear. He could tell immediately that something was wrong, but had to ask one of the generals about the status. The general recognized him immediately and shook with terror. He stood by the tent door to report, ready to run for his life.

The general said, "Well, Sir, several nights ago the females and Technical Simians went crazy and killed their guards and escaped, taking all the food animals with them. They are heading west toward where you are, I mean where your body is."

Again with the females and runts. It was the cursed Witch again; it had to be. How was she doing it? Damn her! The fury built, but he held it in check, trying to learn more. "What are you doing about it?"

"Sir, without instructions and since they had a large head start and headed toward you, I decided to follow them with our full contingent of Warriors. I ordered everything worth taking loaded, while our Warriors canvassed the area for more food animals we needed for the trip. I didn't want to kill the females; we will need them. So, Sir, we have been following them, hoping to make contact with you for instructions. I knew that you would know what to do."

"You thought of all this on your own?"

"Ya yaesss, Sir."

"Good. You will be my second in command." This Warrior showed surprising intelligence and would be a valuable assistant.

He hadn't really considered moving the main compound, but it made sense. He would establish his main headquarters in the west where the Witch resides ... after he killed her armies and her. He would take over her complex. All of his Warrior armies would be together, and there were over 20,000 of them, more than enough to ensure a victory. Yes, this general did the right thing.

"Here's what you will do. Advance and take control of the females and our food animals, kill all the Technical Simians, then continue west and join with the others. Kill any females that resist, but try not to kill too many."

"Yes, Sir!"

He returned his mind back to his body and the next phase of the attack. Although still dark, the sky showed some light from the single moon. He ordered the army to move north, fast along the river searching for a crossing. Unfortunately, he still detected the Witch and both of the abominations, and just in case any of them searched for him, he remained behind with several hand-picked guards. Maybe they would think the army was still with him. Maybe the army could get across the river before she discovered them. If they could, they would move fast west toward the Witch, and the trap would be set.

* Amy *

Even though she had a fitful sleep wrestling with the throbbing pain in her arm, she was aware that # 5 and Amy One maintained a constant vigil watching over her. At one point she heard or sensed that the dragons wanted to make another night raid on the Simian army to initiate the new dragons and probably let them feed on the Warriors. She roused herself long enough to caution them again about their new defenses.

"Yes, they will be careful," said # 5.

She seriously thought about teleporting back to the facility so Mama could administer to her stump, but without Levi here, she would be out of communication with her army. That would be dangerous, and as it turned out, it could have been disastrous.

She woke again some hours later to the pounding of wings beating the air and heavy thuds as several dragons landed close to her. There were screeches back and forth, then # 5 lumbered toward her. Instantly awake to danger, she stood to hear the report.

"The army is gone! The dragons report that they searched the road in both direction and couldn't find them."

Damn, she had made a fatal mistake. She knew where they were. She screeched, "Send some scouts north along the river. The next bridge north is out, but they will be heading for the next one up. Find out how far they have gone." Without waiting for a reply she turned and called out for all her commanders.

It was uncommon for her to call out in alarm and certainly not at a volume that woke the whole camp. Al arrived first, but she saw Iron Eyes and Mosley following just behind. Positive the Simians would be there soon, she addressed the Humans.

"We have been tricked, and the Simian army has moved under cover of night. They are not attacking here but moving north. They will probably cross the river at Laughlin, since that is the closest standing bridge." The others had gathered, so she continued in sign and screeching for the benefit of the newcomers.

"They will probably try to cut us off, and probably can if we go back the normal route. So, we need to move out immediately. We will not let them cut us off. We will slip around the mountains at

Bakersfield and up the western edge of the mountains and back over to the facility. We will talk later. Let's move out, now!"

While they talked, the sun had risen and flooded the desert with multiple shades of gold and yellow. If things weren't so dire, she could have enjoyed the beauty. Instead, she watched the armies moving west adding their dust cloud to the golden glimmer of the sun. One blessing in all this, all the slower traffic had left long ago, and only the fast moving armies were at risk. Still, she dispatched a dragon to find the earlier migration and turn them toward Bakersfield.

She was surrounded by dragons and riders awaiting instructions. They had all returned to report the Simian army moving north as she knew they would be, and they were just about where she had calculated they would be, only a few miles from the Laughlin bridge.

The smug SOB had even stayed behind, knowing she might detect him moving. The Supreme One had out maneuvered her and had done the unpredictable, but she should have been able to predict it. It is what she would have done.

The situation could have been worse had the dragons not decided to harass the army during the night. Just when she was toying with the idea of attacking the Supreme One, the situation did get worse.

She now saw what Levi saw and heard the explanation from the Fem. The Fem had done a remarkable job, but Damn, why now? How could they deal with, 20,000 or more Warriors and try to save two massive groups of allies? It couldn't happen at a worse time, and the pain in her arm distracted her. Levi's group wouldn't be able to outrun the Warriors for long, and all she could think of was to try to barricade themselves in the caverns where they spent the night.

Levi asked for some dragons. At least she could do that much.

* Levi *

Something bothered her, and he looked into her mind. She had blocks up, but he could see the situation she had there. That would be enough to bother anyone. Hell, it bothered him, but he didn't want to add to it. He did have one request, though. He said, "Amy, can you teleport Fred here? I have all these Humans and Simians that can't talk to each other. Fred would be a big help."

"When I locate him, I will send him to the caverns."

"Thanks, love."

He urged the Simians on toward the caverns, giving them directions. Afterwards, he launched again to head east; he wanted to observe the Warrior army. It didn't take long; they were close, too damn close.

As they soared over the army, he marveled, but in a bad way. It is one thing to hear a figure of 15,000, but it is quite another to actually see that many Warriors. Even in tight formation they stretched beyond his sight, but he needed to see the end just to know that it did end.

Thankfully, they found the end of the procession and spiraled down. The Warriors began to point at them like they had never seen anything like them before. He chuckled to himself at that thought, thinking, "Hell, come to think of it, he had never seen anything like them either."

There were only three of them, but frustration weighed heavy on him and he needed to vent some of his anger. He whistled, circled his arm, and pointed to the back row of Warriors. Moon's face curled in a wicked grin as they strafed along the last line of Warriors.

With his stronger sonar, he took the center forward position and they started their attack on one end and sliced their way all the way to the other. Many Warriors froze in position as they passed and forfeited their heads. They killed many, but it meant nothing, considering the raw numbers, but it felt good.

By the time they regained some altitude, word had spread to the front and the entire long column had stopped and turned to see what was going on. This was good; maybe they had done some good after all by slowing them down. It couldn't hurt to keep them nervous, so they continued to soar over their ranks, occasionally swooping down to make them scatter. It was fun. Well, it was fun until he saw the walking Human food supply.

There were several hundred Humans packed close and surrounded by guards. The group was centered between two of the army columns of Warrs. His good mood shattered, but he took note exactly where they were. After all, he would have twenty more dragons soon, and this looked like a target for a night attack. Without food the Simian army would be delayed more. That sounded like a good excuse, but he would have done it anyway.

They went back to the Fems to push them a little faster, then on to the Humans to let them know the situation. After encouraging them, they flew back toward the caverns.

As they approached, he noticed two things immediately. Fred was sitting on a boulder outside of the cavern's entrance, and the other dragons were approaching. He was happy to see both.

Much needed to be done. He sent the riders out to gather the roaming sheep and herd them into the caverns, and he sent the dragons out to gather firewood and get it into the big room of the caverns. He forced Fred into the dark opening, with him griping all the way.

At some point the caverns had been used by humans and not too long ago, because there were a series of torches mounted along the route they needed to go. All he had to do was use his Zippo to light them. Along the way he caught Fred up to speed and his part in the plan.

* Amy *

She forgot that Levi did all the telepathy to the communication team, so she sent a runner to find Fred. Even in her physical state and frame of mind, Fred forced a chuckle from her, because she could hear him griping even before she saw him. Just the same, he arrived quickly, like she knew he would, but he had to keep up his grumpy reputation. She didn't have much time but gave him a quick update before whisking him off into space.

305

She saw Levi's frustration and what he planned to do and started to object. Of course it was dangerous to attack the Warriors, but it was no more foolhardy than what she had done. So, she held her objections but remained with him till he was safe again, then returned to her troubled world at her end. She would, from time to time, return to make sure he was fine.

Watching Levi take charge and organize details at the caverns, she realized he was quite good at details. Maybe he always was but just didn't want to admit it or do it. The next time he tried to get out of it she would bust him on it.

Okay, time to refocus. Her army needed more time, and the best, only really, spot to significantly delay them was at the bridge, and the only forces she had to send were dragons. The Supreme One would anticipate that and gather the spear carriers in the lead backed up by the crossbows. It would be suicide for the dragons to attempt an attack like before ... maybe. They would have to keep their distance, which would require a different form of attack, something new.

It came to her suddenly, but it was so simple. Let the dragons fly high and drop bombs like the WW-II dive bombers. Of course, there were no bombs, but there were mountains loaded with big rocks. A rolling and skipping boulder would be like bowling for Warriors. Envisioning this even made her smile. Certainly, it was something new. It might just work.

She explained the strategy to the dragons and they liked it ... a lot, and left to launch this dive bombing attack.

She almost wished she could go and watch, but the ache in her arm was getting worse, and she needed medical attention. The demands on her attention had forced her to stay, but her arm needed cleaning, antiseptic and antibiotics. This might be the only time she would have, so she teleported back to the facility and reported in to Mama and her medical team in the clinic.

Mama was furious with her, both for getting hurt and waiting so long for attention. When she told Mama how it happened, Mama dropped the bowl of water she was holding, and stared at her in disbelief.

Mama looked hard at her and screeched, "Daughter, you are very lucky to still be alive."

That was the first time Mama had called her daughter, and the sign of affection touched her heart. How she loved these souls, Human and Simian.

Mama informed her that infection was setting in and she was going to have to take a couple of more inches off to get it clean. Mama also informed her that she was confining her to bed, but she refused, saying, "No, Mama, we are under attack and I am needed. Just do the best you can with it." Mama didn't like it but also didn't fight her.

* Satan *

He had hoped one of the abominations would try to attack him. He was ready and kept enough Warriors with him with crossbows and spears to keep the flying Simians away while he shot fireballs. He certainly wasn't going to let one of

307

them simply come up and chop off his head like the general had done. No, he would burn them up and turn them into charcoal. Unfortunately, none came.

He had a great, well protected location, so he switched his mind back and forth between the main army and the army racing across the desert. The main army was about to catch the females and the other army had found a crossing over the water and began crossing. Apparently his diversion had worked, as there were no defenses on the other side of the crossing.

His army began pouring across the narrow platform over the water when he heard them ... the cursed flying Simians. In the limited light from the full moon, he could see them swooping down fast out of the blackness far on the other side. They didn't attack any of the Warriors. Instead, they only sped toward the Warriors, but long before making contact, they shot back up into the blackness. At first he didn't understand the strategy until he heard the bouncing impact of a heavy object, then saw an object clearing a swath through dying and mangled Warriors. Many were forced over the edge of the platform into the water and never rose again.

They came one after another, delivering death to his compacted Warriors. He held his rage to issue orders. "Spread out and open the ranks. Don't give them a target! Continue to cross in single file and form the crossbows far to the other side and kill the damn flying Simians!"

The Warriors feared him far more than the flying Simians and complied immediately. Reducing the density of the compacted Warriors offered far less targets and allowed them to begin dodging the boulders. It took longer, but his army began crossing and forming on the other side.

Screeches of excitement from the other side attracted his attention. As he turned he saw why. The crossbows were firing now and one of the flyers was falling. It hit the ground and rolled a few times, and Warriors ran to hack it to pieces.

After the fall of the flyer, they broke off the attack. He quickly took advantage and crossed now in numbers. As he crossed in his occupied body in the last ranks, he heard the warning screech from behind. As he turned to see the threat, he found himself staring directly into the blazing red eyes of a diving flyer. Too late to dodge, he watched the boulder as it crashed into his chest, crushing him. He felt his bones breaking as the pain drove his mind out and back to his own body.

His first reaction was to grab his chest to see if he was still alive. The death felt so real, like it actually happened to him. His second reaction was automatic. Fury and rage exploded within him. His bellowed screech warned the Warriors around him, and they ran for their lives. His massive intellect formed the fireball as before, but just as he was about to consume the last Warrior, he ran around a large boulder. In frustration he reached out his arms as if to grab him. To his amazement, huge, translucent arms and hands burst out to perform his thoughts. His mind reached for the hidden Warrior, and the hands of blazing red mental energy reached out and grabbed the Warrior from behind the boulder.

The struggling and screeching Warrior was as a toy in his mental hands. His mental fingers tore the

Warrior apart as if it was a leaf. He smiled, knowing that his powers had evolved beyond his brother, the abominations, and even the Witch.

Chapter 12
Dual Attacks

* Levi *

One thing really bothered him about using the caverns for defense; he only knew of one entrance. Even so, it would be hard to imagine Simians launching an attack into pitch black caverns, especially with their night blindness. Still, if they were overrun, there would be no escape through a back door, and he didn't like that at all. So, he left Fred at the entrance to guide the Humans and Simians down into the caverns to the big room, while he went exploring.

Using his sonar and flying when he could, he began searching the caverns. The caverns were large with many branches, but the sonar made the job much easier. Unfortunately, after several hours he had found no other entrance. Disappointed, he sat, thinking about what else he could do. The limestone caves were formed over thousands of years of water flowing through them, wearing holes, but the water had to come from somewhere and go somewhere else. Analyzing, he only saw the results of part of it and no beginning or ending. There had to be other branches if he could just see them, but how?

All he had was his sonar, but that signal reflects back from objects. That was how he could see in the pitch black. He started adjusting the frequency of his sonar, trying to make it penetrate deeper. He discovered that by reducing the frequency he could sense (see) the vibrations deeper into the rock formations. With this new tool, he began again searching the cave walls. After a mile of searching on the back side of the caverns, he found another opening beyond a thin wall of calcium and limestone deposits. He couldn't see far, only open space beyond and took his sword and crashed in the thin wall.

This was it! The caverns within were huge, large enough to fly. One branch sloped up, while the other sloped down, deeper into the earth. The upper branch was the one he had been looking for. It sloped slowly upward toward the surface where another entrance would be, if there was another. Hell, there had to be; water had once gotten in somewhere. After another mile of sloping upward he began to see light. Soon he walked out on to an open ledge about half-way up the side of the mountain. A dry creek bed ran past, diverted ages ago and now routing the rain runoff on the surface. This was perfect, and the dragons could land and take off from here.

Even before he got back to the big room, he smelled the smoke from fires and soon saw the light, then he heard and saw the Humans huddled around the fires drooling over cooking mutton. The Fems and Techs were separated off, feeding on sheep but not too far from the light of the fire. Fred had done well, and obviously the riders had found the sheep. Fred was already busy teaching the Humans sign language. He stopped by long enough to say, "Save me some mutton."

The dragons were nowhere to be seen, so he continued toward the entrance. The dragons were also feeding on sheep, but standing guard back from the entrance in the blackness, prepared to kill any Warrior that dared enter. He wasn't sure the Warrior army had arrived yet, but they wouldn't be too far behind. They would eventually enter, but it would take them a long time to build up enough courage on their own, but he was quite sure the Supreme One would make an appearance to spur them along.

He informed Moon and Bambi that he had found a rear entrance, an escape exit if need be. They were happy to know that and had been worried about that also. He also suggested that the dragons take shifts sleeping, because he wanted to launch an attack tonight and free the Humans.

Moon said, "Good idea, but you better get some sleep also. You look tired."

He certainly was tired. It had been a long day, and he had lost track of time and wondered if it was day or night. They looked the same in the caverns. "Was it dark when you came in?"

"Yes, it is long after dark."

He found a flat spot and lay down to search for that thing called sleep, but he was worried about Amy, very worried. She had not answered him the last few times he spoke to her. He was lost without her and out of communication, as well. No, he wasn't. He could still talk to Al.

"Al, where is Amy?"

"Oh, hi Levi. Well, I am not sure. She was in bad shape this morning after what happened with that Seeker thing. She may have gone back to the facility for some medical treatment."

"Huh? Bad shape? Damn, what happened? What about the Seeker?"

313

Al was silent for a moment, then said, "She didn't tell you? I thought you two knew everything that was going on with each other. I'm sorry."

"NO, what happened?"

"Levi, I'm sorry to have to tell you this, but ... well, Amy was bitten by that Seeker and ... and cut her arm off to save herself, but she is alive and still making the decisions, at least she has been."

He couldn't bring himself to talk more. He didn't trust his emotions. His Amy was hurt, and he had to go to her. Moon had been watching his telepathic conversation and his reactions and body language and knew something was terribly wrong. Moon stared hard at him when he looked up. That was all it took, and he broke down, sobbing. Moon pulled him close and embraced him and let him cry. Finally, he was able to sob out enough of the story for Moon to understand what happened and that he must go find her.

Moon said, "I understand, but you need sleep before you go. You are too tired."

As upset and worried as he was, he knew Moon was right, plus his body was giving out. He just nodded and lay back down. With the release of his pent up emotions he almost immediately fell asleep. The last thing he was aware of was Oggg curling up beside him in a watchful surveillance.

He slept soundly but awoke to a low growling coming from Oggg. After the last time he heard Oggg growl, he instantly woke and looked around. Oggg was staring into the darkness toward the entrance. As he looked around he noticed the dragons on alert, also staring at the entrance.

Moon noticed him awake and said, "The Warriors come. We will wait until they get deeper and spread out some in the cavern, then we will get them."

Already, he could see torches coming forward slowly toward them. He didn't have to wonder if the Warriors were frightened; they would be terrified entering the pitch blackness of the cavern. With his sonar he detected dragons on both sides of the main tunnel tucked back into alcoves all along several hundred feet of tunnel. Moon and Bambi stepped out into the main channel in front of the leading group of startled Warriors huddled around a torch. They immediately froze from a combination of sonar and fear, and Moon and Bambi began beheading them. Once it began, the dragons all along the tunnel did likewise. The dragons on the leading end began working their way through Warriors toward the entrance. All the dragons behind them were picking up the severed heads by the golden hair.

He was mesmerized and followed them toward the entrance. Surprised, he saw light toward the entrance and realized it must be daylight outside. Some of the surviving Warriors were running for the light, trying to escape the onslaught of death.

The dragons stopped short of the light and began throwing bloody Warrior heads out of the entrance into the waiting ranks of Warriors. Damn, there were a lots of heads bouncing out. Then he heard the black teeth of the outside army chattering in fear, reverberating an eerie chorus that echoed down into the caverns.

315

They waited for a long time, but there were no repeat ventures into the caverns. As it became evident there would be no more, he said, "Moon, I must go, but I need to show you the other entrance."

He thought it a little strange that Bambi followed them but quickly dismissed it. They stopped by the big room, and he found the mutton Jimmy saved for him. While he ravished the meat, Moon and Bambi and their riders conversed. He was anxious to get going and took more meat for the trip. Moon and Bambi quickly followed him to the recently discovered new tunnels and out to the ledge.

As he was about to leave, Moon signed, "I must stay to lead our defense, but Bambi will go with you. Listen to her. She only wants to help you, and you aren't thinking well with your concern for Amy."

He started to protest, but the stern look on Moon's face told him not to bother. All he could do was nod in resignation.

Moon continued, "Jimmy will be here, so you can communicate back. Let us know what you find."

He hadn't even thought about communications. At least Moon was thinking clearly, and apparently he wasn't. He slapped Moon's meaty neck and said, "Thanks my friend, and I will let you know."

Moon nodded to him and signed to Bambi, "Be careful." A look of concern and something else passed between them, and he thought, "That was a look passed between lovers. Good for them. That would please Amy." When he thought of Amy he sobered again. They had to go.

* Satan *

He decided to remain where he was so he could alternate between the armies. His personal safety was his primary goal, and he was safe at this location. Still, he wished he would be attacked so he could use his new powers. It would even be better if one of the abominations would try.

The only time he would actually be in personal danger was when he was occupying a distant Warrior. So, he instructed his guards to shake him if an attack came. He would feel it and immediately return to defend himself.

He found another Warrior and returned to the forward battle and continued driving his army over the crossing, but there were only stragglers. It evidently wasn't productive for the dragons to continue, as there were no more attacks, but the stupid Warriors just stood compacted on the other side. As soon as he crossed, he began bellowing for them to spread out and not give the flying dragons a target and begin marching east. If they thought they were going to make camp tonight, they would be seriously disappointed.

Once the army resigned to the fact that they would march through the remainder of the night, he withdrew and returned to his agent at the main body. Immediately he was pleased. This dedicated general had maintained their pursuit into the night, trying to catch up to the females. He could see long straight ribbons of torches stretching to the rear and a snaking line toward the front, indicating the route ahead was a more rugged terrain.

317

He and the general sped up to gain the front lines and survey the situation. As they reached the front, he noticed the march had stopped. He screeched, "Why have you stopped?"

The Warrior addressed said, "We lost their trail in the dark and we no longer see their torches. We didn't want to ruin the tracks by trampling over them. We thought we would wait until morning and find it again in the light."

He didn't like that news one bit, and the anger began boiling up within him. The explanation sounded reasonable, however, and they really wouldn't have to wait all that long, as the sky was already showing light behind them. They could wait. He nodded his agreement to the general, and the general began issuing orders. He returned to his own body to feed on the few animals left for him and then to sleep.

When he returned, the sun was high in the sky. The general detected him immediately and came to report.

The general said, "We have discovered where they went. The tracks lead down into a hole in the ground."

He screamed, "Why haven't you gone after them!" The general's face froze in instant fear, and he knew why. Simians are terrified of total darkness, even he disliked darkness. Their home world had two suns and they were never in total darkness.

The general said, "There is no light at all inside."

"The damn females went inside; so can you. Go after them!"

318

It was hard to argue with that logic and shame. The general ordered a group of Warriors to light torches and go find the females. They balked at going, and he had to draw his sword and beat them with the side of it. Finally, he forced about thirty down into the ominous black hole. They were slow entering but pushed deeper by those behind.

After a few moments, screams of agony erupted from deep into the cave. They sounded frightful, echoing back and joined with many new ones. All around stood in fear as the screams of agony slowly died, replaced with total silence. Then the screams started from those outside as the severed heads of those that had entered came flying out to batter against the waiting Simians. The resulting stampede almost destroyed his borrowed body.

It would be useless to try to force another group of Warriors back into that blackness of death. For once they were more afraid of that black hole than they were of him, no matter how much he screamed at them. Well, if he couldn't go after them, he would make sure they stayed there. He screeched, "Bury the entrance!"

He hated to lose so many females, but there were still many with the enemy. All he had to do was get them.

The Warriors scrambled to comply. His Warriors wanted the entranced closed as much as he did but for a different reason. They didn't want the faceless death coming out to get them. Boulders were rolled off into the entrance and the side of the mountain avalanched down over it. They would not get out. He wanted the battle, but at least this way, he won the war and killed some of the dragons, maybe even one of the abominations.

He then ordered them to go west and join the other group, but to cross the water at the lower crossing. This way they would cut off any enemy retreat back across the water, and they might possibly catch the Witch's army between them. He smiled at his logic, but his hate still festered within him. Damn that Bitch for destroying his victory and costing him his females.

* Levi *

After they took off, he looked back a few times, and each time Moon was still there looking. He knew how Moon felt; he felt the same about Amy. Again he tried to touch her mind but she was silent. It made him pull harder at the air.

Bambi flew close and signed, "We need to fly a little farther south for a while so we aren't spotted."

Damn, she was right, and he wasn't thinking clearly. He signed back, "You take the lead, and I will follow you. Thanks."

He followed Bambi several miles to the south, flying fairly low before she turned west. She motioned for him to take the lead again. That kind of explained why she was flying low. He thought she was just trying to keep a low profile, and that was probably one of the reasons, but in reality she left Katie (her eyes) behind and couldn't see unless she was low. He took them higher, searching for air currents flowing west. When he found a good one, they rode it and made good time.

They passed over their main army moving fast across the desert. He started to stop but decided there was no real need. If he needed to check on them he could always contact Al telepathically.

They continued west and turned more north toward Amy's facility and was somewhat startled to see the slower wagons and non-combatants moving north toward Owens Valley. Al had explained what Amy believed the Supreme One was doing, so seeing the migration on this wrong course was unexpected. Everyone had assumed they would be much farther along and out of danger, but then they were out of communication and didn't know the change in plans. They were not in a good position. It was fortunate that they came along when they did, or they might have been caught smack in the middle of a battle that they didn't know was coming at them. He had no choice; they had to stop. He waved to Bambi and pointed to the ground. While spiraling down, he explained why.

They landed in front of the lead wagon and waited for someone to come to them. He didn't recognize the man who came, but the man obviously knew him. He gave the man a quick update of activities and instructed them to change course and travel around the mountains on the other side. The man understood the situation and didn't panic, much to his credit. He thanked him and turned to change their course. Luckily, they wouldn't have to backtrack all that far.

He and Bambi quickly resumed the trip, but time seemed to pass so slowly as they got closer. They were now crossing over the mountain headed directly toward Amy's facility, and he panicked.

"What if she isn't here? What if she is hurt somewhere else? What if she is dead?"

He hit the ground running into the facility, bellowing at the top of his lungs, "Mama! Where's Mama?" Everyone, Humans and Simians, scrambled to clear a path. They could have heard him ten decks down and probably did, but Mama was much closer. She came running out of the stairwell, immediately trying to calm him.

Mama grabbed him in a vice like grip, stared into his eyes, and said, "Calm down, son. Amy is alive."

Hearing that, he embraced Mama and let his emotions loose again. That was what he needed to hear, but after a few moments he pulled back to look wonderingly into her eyes.

Mama said, "Amy has been a critically sick girl, still is, but she is getting better. By the time she returned for treatment, she had a major infection from the field amputation, and maybe a slight amount of poisoning from the Seeker, also. We had to cut the bad part off and put her on heavy doses of antibiotics. She is improving but drugged out and weak."

Well, that explained why he couldn't contact her, and it was a far better explanation than what it could have been. Amy wouldn't know or had ever experienced sickness in the body. Too bad she had to learn it this way.

He said, "Thanks, Mama. Can I see her now?"

When they turned to head for the elevator, they collided with Bambi who had squeezed into the corridor to hear what Mama was saying. It was almost funny, as Bambi had to wiggle backwards to get out. Bambi had grown too damn big to fit into the elevator so she had to remain on the main floor, but she was satisfied, knowing Amy was alive.

When he saw Amy his heart poured out to her. She looked so pale and fragile as she slept. He looked at Mama, as if to say, "Are you sure she is Okay?"

Mama said, "She is fine and her body is stable now, but she had it rough for a while."

As he watched her, he suddenly realized that Amy must have transferred her total self-aware mind into her body, otherwise she could have allowed her mind to flow back into the facility brain. This also meant that if her body died, so would her mind.

He touched her face and leaned over and kissed her, and she opened her beautiful green eyes. They fluttered but remained open. Then she gave him a weak smile and said, "Hi, Levi."

"Oh my God, Amy. You had me so worried." He paused for a time then said, "I'm sorry about your arm."

She seemed to be more lively now and raised her stump and said, "Oh, this? Don't worry my love. It will grow back in a couple of months. I made us that way, the dragons, too."

Now that surprised him. He certainly wasn't expecting that. It was a good thing for Amy's injury, but the loss of her arm hadn't bothered him all that much, except for her loss. "You would still be my Amy, even with only one arm."

Amy said, "That's sweet of you to say."

Relieved now, he was feeling a little cocky and said, "That's me ... sweet." As weak as she was, she choked out a laugh, which sounded like music to him.

Mama interrupted their exchange, "Levi, Amy really needs to sleep right now."

"Yes, of course."

Amy reached to hold his hand and said, "Hon, you need to oversee both battles. I will come back as soon as I can, but I can't help much right now."

"I understand. I'll handle it. You get some rest." He kissed her and left, but he realized he didn't have the slightest idea how to handle it.

All he knew for sure was to tell Bambi, Al, and Jimmy and their groups that Amy was alive and they would be delayed returning. He also tried to inform all groups of the big picture so they could act accordingly. The only group he couldn't contact was the dragons at this end of the battle and determined that should be their current course of action.

He and Bambi launched and flew toward the Laughlin bridge in search of the Simian army and their dragons. He wondered just how many times he had traveled this route through Barstow battling the damn Warriors, too damn many. The only good thing was that he flew this time and not riding Thunder or running. Yep, Amy had done well adding the wings.

Thinking about Barstow reminded him that, even though Al and Iron Eyes' group were coming up I-10, they would still have to come up through Barstow. To make matters worse, they had farther to travel than the Simian army. They were on a collision course with the Simian army unless his army kept going east and came up through

Lancaster, but that wasn't going to work, because the Supreme One knew where they were, or suspected, anyway. He hadn't been able to plan with Amy or see her plan, but she probably had one. Well, maybe not. Al said she had sent them around the mountain, so they were following the plan, but that plan was flawed, unless there was something he didn't see, but what?

As they continued east, he contacted Al about going through Lancaster instead of Barstow and quizzed him further about what Amy's plan had been. He mentioned that she thought the Supreme One would launch against the facility and try to draw them up to defend her. That kind of made sense, but then Amy hadn't mentioned anything about attacking to anyone. Damn, he would have to devise his own plan, but was there a solution to their salvation?

At first he only saw the dust, but as they got closer he saw the dragons circling high, like buzzards in the sky waiting on something to die. As they got closer he saw the Simian army spread out across the desert floor, an unusual formation for Simians. Then he saw one of the dragons break out of formation and fly toward them. Once it got closer, he noticed it was one of his trusted leaders, # 9. He waved at # 9 and pointed to the ground.

They spiraled down together and landed on the open desert far from the army. The news of losing # 11 and his rider was sad, but listening to the report gave him hope. These dragons had been busy, and from the sound of it, they had killed almost a thousand Warriors by dropping rocks, "Bowling for Warriors" as Amy had told them. That was ingenious. Unfortunately, the Supreme One had made adjustments, which was why the Warriors were spread out so thin. It kept the dragons from killing many. This might be used to an advantage.

He began pacing, thinking, while the others waited and watched. He contacted Al, "Where exactly are you located?" Surprisingly, Al informed him they had cut across country and were about to intersect I-40 west of his Mojave Desert Settlement, approximately at the location of Black Bones Valley. They were even closer to the Simian Warriors than he thought. An idea was forming in his head, but it wasn't quite there yet.

"Al, do you have plenty of lances?"

Tentatively, Al said, "Well, yeah, Mama made plenty and made us take them all."

Next, he contacted Jimmy for a report. They were still holed up in the caverns, but the Simian army had caved in the entrance and moved on, heading toward the I-10 bridge. Jimmy believed that the Simians probably thought they would die here. That put the Simians a couple of days behind Al's group, maybe longer if they were slowed down.

He said, "Jimmy, as soon as it is safe, let everyone out of the caverns at the back entrance, but tell them to stay close in case they have to run back. Fred will be there if I need to communicate with them. So, you don't have to stay, but leave a couple of dragons there to protect them. You and Moon and the rest of the dragons and riders fly here, but don't be seen leaving there." He told him where they were.

To both Al and Jimmy he said, "I'm tired of running, and we can't outrun them anyway. So,

Fuck it! We're going to attack!" Then he told them the details, as he saw it playing out.

* Amy *

She wasn't all that surprised to hear Mama tell her the amputation was infected, but she wasn't prepared to hear that she might have gotten some of the Seeker's poison in her blood. She quickly did a search of the Simian computer and discovered that a Seeker's poison was highly toxic and fast acting, and there were no records indicating any animal had ever survived a Seeker's bite. She had, however, acted immediately to separate the poison from her body, but evidently not quick enough. Since she was still alive, barely, she must have done a fairly good job, though. Mama said the poison had done some damage, and if it hadn't been for her regenerative ability, it might have killed her with a slow death.

Mama wanted to put her out for the surgery but she resisted. She was needed, but her body didn't cooperate with her and finally gave out. The last thing she remembered was seeing the concern in Mama's eyes as she faded into a black abyss.

It wasn't until her mind recognized Levi's voice that she fought her way out of the abyss into consciousness. The very fact that Levi was here indicated that she had been out for a long time, because he would have had to fly here. She thought she might panic with this discovery, but there simply wasn't enough strength in her body or mind.

Another fact that she grasped immediately: she had been unable to transfer her mind back into the

327

facility brain. Her self-aware portion had permanently transferred into her body's brain, and if her body died, so would she. This was for keeps, good or bad.

The mother hen, Mama, didn't allow Levi to stay long, but she felt herself slipping back into the abyss anyway. This time it was for needed rest and not potentially death. She held on to Levi's hand as long as she could and managed to whisper out some sort of encouragement, but it was all in his hands for right now. He would soon discover that he was much smarter and capable than even he knew; he just had to be challenged, like she had been.

The next time she managed to struggle awake, she felt a little stronger. She even searched for his mind just long enough to see the plan. It was extremely daring and dangerous, but then so was Levi, maybe too daring. Before she slid back into sleep, she managed to transmit, "Good luck, love."

* Levi *

It was nearing sunset, so he pulled the dragons off their harassing attacks. He wanted the Simian army to settle in for the night and the dragons to get some rest. When the other dragons arrived they too would join the others for rest. Tonight should get interesting.

He really didn't know how Amy sensed the Supreme One, but she did, and obviously the Supreme One could sense her as well. Not only that, but he sensed Amy and him in body form also. He had to learn this as well, because so much of his strategy depended on knowing where the Supreme

One was at all times, even when he occupied another Simian.

After eating he found a secluded spot where he could be alone, well, as alone as he could be with his protectors. He was protected for sure, but Moon and Bambi were preoccupied with each other as much as with him.

Amy had tried to teach him many times, but he had been unusually dense. Knowing that Amy said he could exercise this part of his brain gave him confidence that it could be done. Hell, that was back when he was in his other body. Now he had far more brain capacity ... supposedly. She said he just had to open up his mind and listen and the signature of the Supreme One's high intellect could be detected. It would be the strongest signal, and according to Amy, it would be like a mental light, seen only by the mind.

He lay back, closed his eyes, and opened his mind. At first he didn't see anything, but slowly he began to see dim lights in his mind. Slowly, he began to identify these energies around him. He saw Moon and knew him immediately. How, he had no idea, but he did. Yes, there was Bambi, and realized how he knew her. He had felt her mind every day while she carried his embryo.

Moving on and expanding, he began to see others, dim but distinguishable. Yes, there was Jimmy, Katie, and a small flicker that was Oggg. Aww, this was fun. He opened his eyes and stared at Moon, with eyes and his mind. There were thoughts, mostly just feeling and impressions, but they were there. Moon must have felt his probing, because, suddenly, he looked up at him, staring back. He waved at Moon and moved his search, but he realized that he must be transmitting mental energy in order to see with his mind, sort of like directing a flashlight. Maybe it was like his sonar, transmitting to see a reflection. It wasn't necessary to understand it completely, just to use it.

Okay, now to find the Supreme One. He began a search pattern toward where he thought the Supreme One would be. Bingo! He found him, and the energy was strong, very strong, but that isn't what shocked him most. The Supreme One spoke to him.

"Awww, one of the little ones has come to visit. Are you ready to come to me so I can kill you?"

If the Supreme One wanted to frighten and intimidate him, he was sadly mistaken. His response burst out, "No, you simple bastard. I wanted to find you so I can come beat the worthless life out of you." This was actually opportune. He had planned to fly over the army tomorrow and announce the news, but this would be better. Continuing, he said, "I wanted to let you know your worthless race of Warriors will die. I killed all your females! Your army will find them tomorrow lying with the black bones of another Warrior army that dared to come after us." The effect was better than he had hoped and immediate.

The Supreme One exploded with fury and outrage, mentally bellowing, "How dare you. You are an abomination!"

"Oh, shut the fuck up! You are nothing but a mental weakling and windbag." He then immediately closed his mind to the Supreme One. He always had a knack of pissing off the playground bully, and this was no different. He wanted the Supreme One pissed so he wasn't thinking clearly.

* Satan *

He hated the Witch for making him kill his own females. The females were necessary for breeding and restocking his race with Warriors on this planet. They also could have used the food animals, but they could find more. As far as the loss of the Technical Simians, he couldn't care less. Without technology, they were useless. The only good thing was the destruction of those dragons and one of the abominations. Feeling the life slip out of the abomination would have been better, but a slow starving death in the black caverns would be a close second.

At least his main army didn't have to waste time dealing with any harassment from the dragons. Now they would move and join with his other army for the final destruction of the Witch and her pathetic army of animals, runts, and females. Except for the few females that were on his spaceship, these females that now opposed him may be the only others left. They would have to be isolated while his army killed all the others. They would then have no choice but to re-join with him.

He intended to continue to wait at his current location until tomorrow when the main army caught up. At that time he would take physical command of the combined armies and launch an attack.

As he lay resting and considering these actions, he felt one of the abominations searching for him.

Oh, how he wished it had come in person, but it was an opportunity to taunt him. Yes, now he identified its signature. It was the male child, but the child was not intimidated and called him stupid. Never had he been so insulted and treated with such little respect as this child did. The fury grew, but just as it was about to explode, he froze at what he heard. The abomination had said, "I killed all your females!" Would he do such a thing? Yes, he would! That male, bastard child would try to destroy his race any way it could. Damn him!

The anger boiled inside and erupted out of control. His muscles seized in his body, forcing a bellow that would have frightened anything within miles. Even the Warriors farthest away ran, but it was too late for most. He leaped to his feet totally berserk, radiating red fiery energy of immeasurable hate and rage from his entire body. As he stood to his full thirteen feet, a second body of pure energy emerged and surrounded him in a reddish translucent, pure energy, armored shield extending and expanding his physical shape. This extension of his fury conformed to his will and he killed unmercifully. He pointed and a ball of fire shot out to consume a Warrior, while others he crushed in huge flaming hands of energy reaching out far beyond his physical hands.

The tantrum lasted many long minutes and none remained. He had either killed them or they would still be running in the morning. He was alone, but he smiled. He thought, "Yes, I will meet these abominations in person and they will die from my power."

Boy, was that bastard pissed. He could feel the hate radiating out, but that's what he wanted. He hoped to keep him pissed. The Supreme One was definitely preoccupied, and now would be a good time to move into Phase I of his plan.

He whistled and the dragons and riders were instantly awake and clamoring into their gear. Soon they were in the air again, flying west along the route the army would follow. Their destination was Bonanza Springs on the south side of the Clipper Mountains. It had been the launching point for their engagement against the Colorado River Simian colony. It had worked then, maybe they would get lucky, and it would work again. If they timed it right, all the Lancers would be showing up soon to meet them. Everyone had to be hidden before sunrise, but he and the dragons had a special task to accomplish before sunrise.

Since this would be a night engagement for the dragons, all the riders remained in camp to await the Lancers. Moon had to make Oggg stay, too. Oggg might inadvertently warn the Warriors of their presence. The little shit didn't like being left behind, but a stern word from Moon made him run back to Jimmy to defiantly stare back at Moon. They all got a chuckle out of his antics.

Damn, it was impressive seeing all the dragons together. They filled the sky with their massive wings as they flew toward the camped Warriors. This would not be a harassing attack tonight; they were out for blood. Still, they required stealth to make this work. His entire plan was dangerous and

333

any number of minor things could blow it apart, but as it was, they didn't have much chance anyway. So why the hell not take chances. They would probably lose anyway, and if his plan didn't work they would just lose quicker. But, if it worked, they might win ... this engagement.

He wanted to eliminate the rest of the females from any future hope for the Supreme One and drive him into an uncontrollable rage. Additionally, he wanted to free the humans and take away the Warriors' food to further handicap the Simian army. In every colony or marching Simian army the Techs and Fems were kept close to the Human so they could all be guarded together. His plan was simple and straightforward. The dragons would come in slowly and quietly from each side on the ground. They would then paralyze the guards with their sonar, kill them, then herd the captives out and away from the army.

It sounded simple but would work only if the Warriors weren't wearing their ear plugs, the guards were not alert and watchful, there was a sufficient distance from the sleeping Warriors not to be observed, the captives remained quiet, and the Supreme One didn't detect his presence.

He made some assumptions that the Warriors would feel safe and comfortable removing their ear plugs at night, and that the Supreme One would also remain with his body to sleep. Both assumptions were probably accurate and safe.

He also made some hard decisions and ordered the dragons to kill any Tech or Fem that tried to alert the Warriors. When they gave him a concerned look, he said, "Look! If they alert the Warriors we won't get the rest of the Techs and Fems out, and we must. Also, you might lose your life trying. This is an order you must follow." The same instructions would go for the Humans, but that was his responsibility to carry out.

335

Chapter 13
Fighting Back

* Levi *

As they approached the camped Simians, he motioned for the dragons to circle high while he scouted the groups. He planned the timing so there would be no moon for their engagement, and he approached silently with little chance he would be spotted. The Simians had regrouped much as they would during a normal march. In the front were four separate groups that would normally present a combat front, but those behind were spread back, only one group behind another.

He continued to circle over the groups until he found what had to be Fems, possibly protected but more likely imprisoned. There were about eighty Fems, and on closer examination, he identified about twenty Techs gathered alongside the Fems. The Techs were definitely guarded with more Warrior Guards. There were ten guards walking a perimeter, and luckily the group was fairly isolated from the army. He would have liked more distance, but this might work. Besides, they had little choice.

No Humans could be identified in this area or anywhere else throughout the remainder of the army. They should have been located alongside the Fems and Techs. This left him little choice. He had to follow the plan and get the Fems and Techs out, and worry about the Humans afterwards.

He re-joined the dragons and indicated the number of guards, then led them to the target location. They had already gone over the plan in detail and knew what to do. The dragons split into two groups and landed quietly on both sides of the holding area and silently moved forward on foot, while he continued to circle overhead, watching and ready to give a warning if anything went wrong. The dragons spread out on both sides to try to reach all of the guards at the same time. It happened suddenly. One of the Warriors looked up and saw a dragons, but the dragon sonar blasted it quickly and paralyzed him. The other dragons quickly did likewise, but the timing was premature and a Warrior toward the center, farthest from the dragons wasn't covered. He swiftly dove toward him, showering him with his sonar. The Warrior froze before he could sound an alarm and died immediately after from his sword. He landed and looked around to see all the guard's dead and no alarm from the Warrior army. So far so good.

The dragons began leading the Fems and Techs away, but one of the Fems began to panic. Bambi motioned for silence, but the Fems became more agitated and squawked a single outcry before Bambi severed her head. The Fems looked on in horror, but all remained silent and continued to follow the dragons' instructions. He continued to watch the closest sleeping Warriors, but none seemed to have noticed the squawk from the Fem.

When they were almost out of the guarded area he discovered why he had found no humans. There weren't any more! He came face to face with a grotesque human skull, appearing to smile at him out of its horror. All around him was the evidence of a recent carnage. Bloody and broken bones lay everywhere. He was standing in the very place the Humans had been fed upon while they yet lived. He could hear their imaginary screams as their flesh had been ripped from their living bodies. Why was he always too late to save them?

Moon noticed him stop and came back to nudge him out of his shock. Nodding, he followed Moon out to safety, carefully watching his steps out of respect to those fallen. He and the dragons had been successful, yet the victory rang hollow.

Without moonlight, the Fems and Techs were blind and had to be led by the dragons, but in the dark, they were not about to let the dragons get out of their limited sight. That was the only security they had to hold on to. Moon assigned two of the dragons to lead them around the sleeping Warrior army and on toward the Valley of Black Bones, where they would meet the other Fems. Their bodies would be useful in the coming battle.

Moon signed, "Shall we toss the guards' heads when we leave?"

He now noticed the heads dangling by their golden hair from the dragons' saddles. He signed, "It sounds like a good idea, but let's wait until the Fems and Techs get around the army."

They continued to follow the exodus until it was safely around the army, then took off. They circled over the army screeching challenges, and when it became obvious the Warriors were all awake, they sprinkled the heads among the army. It seemed to have a major physiological effect on the now restless army. There would be little additional sleep for the army tonight.

He and the remainder of the dragons returned to the Clipper Mountain hidden camp for some needed rest for tomorrow's battle.

* Satan *

He spent the night in a fitful sleep alone, but safely tucked into his alcove of rocks. In the morning he moved toward the river crossing to wait for his main army to travel with. The other army would have to wait for his supervision until there was protection for his unprotected body.

His army did not disappoint him and arrived by midmorning, then he found another safe spot and assigned guards to watch over him. Just in case the damn dragons began dropping boulders on them again, he had chosen a spot away from his army. Let them die and not him.

As the army crossed over the water, he sent his mind to a Warrior with his advanced forces. Immediately, he knew something was wrong. It was midday, and the army remained virtually in the same location, not having moved at all. His general came immediately when he heard him bellow his fury. The Supreme One bellowed, "Why haven't you moved?"

The general said, "We were attacked during the night. The guards were killed and the females and runts were taken, maybe killed. We found one dead female still in camp. Also, the army didn't sleep. We were harassed by the flying Simians during the night dropping severed Warrior heads among us."

"I couldn't care less if you got any sleep. Move the army out, NOW! Catch the females before they

339

are killed." He had never considered the importance of the females before, ever. Now they were very important to their continuing existence. There had to be other colonies with females, and he had to find them before the Witch and her abominations found them and killed them.

Panic began to set in, and he drove the marching army hard toward the enemy. They had to be in front of them. The abomination had said we would find the dead females today, so they had to be close.

They had only gone a few miles when he saw them. Damn that Bitch! There were his females lying all over the desert floor amid the black bones of many other long dead Simians. Just beyond them were runts and animals standing defiantly in the path of the army, ready for battle. At last he had a target for his army and his rage. He ordered the charge!

Just as the army began to charge in their normal formation, he saw them coming. The horizon was filled with the damn flying Simians. Damn, where did they all come from? He hadn't seen that many before, but he knew what to expect and so did the Warriors, as they began to spread out in defense, just as he had instructed them previously.

The flying Simians would be dropping boulders on them soon. Spread thin, there would not be that many losses. The flyers had learned to keep their distance from the crossbows and lances after his army killed one, but they had still managed to do a lot of damage when the army was compressed at the water crossing and afterward until he had made this adjustments.

340

He was correct, the flying Simians began dropping boulders, but they weren't hitting many. They were, however, aiming the boulders apparently trying to make the Warriors spread out more, and the Warriors were falling for it. He didn't know why they would want them spread out, but he was beginning to feel played, played like a child. The previous engagement had taught the Warriors, through him, to spread apart under their attacks. Now it seemed the flyers' were manipulating them for their purpose and at their command. Now they could be attacked by those animals on riders. No sooner had he realized this fact then he saw them charging from behind a small mountain.

Just as he identified the mistake and what they were doing, he saw one of the abominations swoop toward him, directly toward him and coming fast. He had been watching the army and hadn't noticed that the Warriors had moved past him, and he was standing alone. Quickly turning, he ran toward the closest Warriors with lances, but before he could get there, a fiery pain struck his back and the impact knocked the body he occupied to the ground. As he was falling he saw the end of a lance jutting out of his chest. The pain drove him out of the borrowed body and back into his own.

As his mind flooded back to his body, he gasped and immediately felt his chest. Once he realized he died only in the borrowed body, his fury exploded. Never had he been so uncontrollable, but the Witch and her evil spawn seemed to continually drive him insane. These thoughts passed quickly as his mind filled with raging hate so intense it pushed all sane thoughts out, and his body reacted. Again, the berserking rage shook his body as his bellows warned those around him, but too late.

* Levi *

He began to wonder if he had made a serious mistake. It was almost noon and the Simian army had not moved. Had he screwed up? About the time he was having serious second thoughts, the army began to move. The Supreme One must have made his appearance, finally, and it was now time for him to make his move.

He launched with the dragons. It was their job to get the Simian army stretched out, and it was his job to keep the Supreme One out of the battle. The Supreme One would eventually see the fallacy and vulnerability of spreading out so thin and make adjustments, but he could prevent this if he kept him raging. As they approached, he sensed the Supreme One and quickly identified him among the others. He was easy to identify, because he was the only one not charging.

Initially, he worried that the Supreme One would be protected by lances, and he might not be able to get close enough to use his sword. So, on his way out of camp he picked up one of Al's lances, figuring on using a lance against lances, but the Supreme One had made a serious mistake and was unprotected.

He dove fast, but the Supreme One saw him coming and ran. It was too late, and he rejoiced feeling the lance sink deep from the momentum of the dive. The borrowed body of the Supreme One died almost immediately. Knowing the fit of rage this would cause, he figured he would not make a reappearance until long after the battle. Now it was army against army.

Next, he flew over the Simian army taunting, "See ahead, we have killed your females! They lie rotting on the desert floor."

The dragons succeeded in getting the Simian army spread out completely and started on their second task: identify those with the crossbows and target them. They were flying lower now, aiming their boulders directly at any crossbow they saw. Hopefully, they would be able to resume a low flying attack with swords soon.

The Lancers succeeded in approaching the rear of the army unseen and began to engage them, and spread thin as the Warriors were, they were falling by the dozens, then hundreds. Without being grouped in teams, they had little defense from the lances. This death from the rear seemed to speed the Warriors ahead through the field of female bodies and on toward the waiting Infantry and Tech armies.

There were so damn many Warriors that timing was everything. His plan required the splitting of the army into three manageable groups or any one of his forces could be overrun. He allowed about a thousand Warriors to break past the far edge of the female bodies. At that point there were about twenty-five hundred Warriors mingled among the bodies of a couple of thousand Simian females. He bellowed, "Now!"

On cue, the Fems came alive and attacked the Warriors among them. The poison finger fangs sank deep and often. The surprised Simian Warriors fell in waves of withering and agonizing death. Those

343

that survived the initial strike from the prone Fems' attack could not escape without passing other Fems. Loud screeches of agony filled the valley and clouds of dust plumed from the Warriors thrashing around in death.

The trailing Warriors, seeing what happened in front of them, did an immediate about-face and ran back head-on into the second wave of charging Lancers from Al, Iron Eyes, and Mosley's armies. Hundreds more fell in the slaughter, and no mercy was given.

Those in front of the attacking Fems crazily sped directly into the waiting Techs' swords and the Infantry's spears.

The dragons circled the battlefield attacking any Warriors remaining and those running to escape.

Everything worked to absolute perfection, and he couldn't believe their luck. He looked around, astonished that they had defeated the Simian army ... totally! He was more astonished that they apparently had suffered very low losses, but, the best surprise came from Amy.

"Levi, you have done a great job, almost as good as I could have done."

"Amy, you're back!"

"Isn't that obvious?" They both laughed. "Yes, I'm back and have been with you during the battle. You really did well, my love."

* Amy *

She had been feeling much better since she last woke, but Mama made her stay in bed. The good thing was the food. Mama kept her fed well. Unfortunately, the pleasure was lost from the worry for Levi and his plan.

She constantly monitored Levi now, but she didn't want to disturb his concentration or try to second guess him. The plan reeked of risk and danger, any one of many factors could have destroyed the plan and doomed them to defeat. So much of the plan depended upon the Supreme One doing exactly what Levi wanted, when he wanted him to, but so far Levi had been right.

Levi played him well by keeping him livid with anger and not thinking well, and only Levi could piss a person off like that. She had been on the receiving end of that treatment many times and could easily identify. Levi could really be an ass when he wanted to be.

The whole premise of Levi's plan depended on the Supreme One believing that he would, in fact, kill the females and that he did. That was Levi's major weakness in the plan. At any time the Supreme One could have let his mind search for the females, but he didn't. He believed Levi had killed them to destroy the Warrior race. It is what the Supreme One would have done, and the very concept of Humans having any sympathy toward any Simian was totally inconceivable to him.

Unfortunately for the nervous Simian females, the final thread of belief was when they discovered the dead Fem. It had worked to their advantage, adding to the Supreme One's belief.

She beamed with pride for Levi, especially learning that he had taught himself how to detect the Supreme One. When she sensed, through Levi, the presence of the Supreme One in the body of an occupied Warrior, it surprised her; but then she realized why Levi had taught himself. He had to keep him out of the battle, like they had done before with his brother. A Supreme One was simply too damn smart and might muck up Levi's plan. By attacking and killing the occupied body, Levi rightfully assumed it would send the Supreme One into another fit of rage that would keep him busy a while.

She was absolutely absorbed as Levi's plan played out. All elements of the plan fell into place perfectly, and each section of their army excelled in their tasks. It was a completely one-sided victory, their side of course.

The Valley of the Black Bones, already legendary, was again littered with dead Warriors, thousands of them. She could only imagine what it would look like after these new bodies decomposed and added their black bones to the landscape.

Unfortunately, their victory would have to be short lived. They may have destroyed a Simian army of five thousand, but three times that number followed closely behind. One thing for sure; they would never be able to repeat the trick of dead females again. This was the last time that ploy would work.

Levi had been totally absorbed in the current battle, and rightfully so, but she had been looking ahead and wondering what they could do to stand against the next wave. The one thing that kept coming back: they had to take on the Supreme One directly before the next engagement. The problem was that: he was too powerful to take on directly.

They had beaten the first Supreme One, but Levi lost his life in the process, and had it not been for the emergence of ASONE, they would have lost completely. ASONE had defended against the Supreme One's energy bolts by generating its own energy. She could still see the battle of blue versus red energy clashing in her memory. To stand a chance against the Supreme One she/they would have to create this energy again or force ASONE to emerge, but she never knew how to evoke ASONE. He/she/it came by its own bidding when it wanted to and usually at the point of near death. Things had changed now, possibly too much. Her mind was in her body now, and Levi's body was different. Would he even exist now? Maybe not, but she didn't know how to call him anyway. They couldn't count on him, so they had to do it themselves. If ASONE could create the blue energy by using powers available through her and Levi, then it must be within their ability to create it. They just had to learn how.

* Satan *

His tantrum lasted for hours, and he hated the loss of control, which added to his problem. He had always been able to control his temper, at least to the point of maintaining sane thought. Since leaving his home planet he had lost control more times than he had in his entire life, and it was all because of the Witch and her spawn. To make matters worse, he had experienced multiple deaths through his surrogates, and for the same reason. This had to end, and end with their death.

347

Once he calmed again, he reached his mind out to the forward army in search of a Warrior. Something was wrong. He found no Warrior minds at that location, so he spread his search. He saw many females ... females! It suddenly dawned on him that he had been had ... again. They weren't dead after all, but he had seen them dead. No, remembering, he had seen them lying on the ground, and they appeared to be dead. He believed they were dead, but obviously they were not dead. He had just assumed them dead, and that was the trick.

Where were his Warriors? He had to find out. His mind seized and flowed into one of the females and began to look around. To his horror his army lay dead on the battlefield, all of them! There had been over five thousand Warriors in this army, and they were all dead. His anger began to fester within him, but he held it in check. He would not let his anger get out of control again. That had been his defeat, and now he knew it. The abomination had used his own anger against him. Knowing this was his future defense. It would not happen again. It couldn't happen again.

To make matters worse, his army had died without killing hardly any of the enemy. The enemy had won by power of the mind, the Witch's mind, and it should have been his victory. He would not underestimate his enemy again.

As he looked upon his decimated army, he noticed the male abomination standing on the battlefield talking with some of the flying Simians. It suddenly occurred to him that he might use this opportunity and this body to kill the abomination.

He began to slowly close the distance between them, slowly enough not to draw attention. He made a point of not walking directly toward him, but instead, walked back and forth, trying to mingle with others. The abomination was in deep discussion with the others and hadn't yet noticed him/her. Moving to the side and behind, he launched himself toward the abomination's back, finger fangs striking out.

* Levi *

The battle was over, but the war far from won. He called a general meeting of the leaders, and they were all gathered with him on the battlefield. Congratulations were in order for all, and they really had done a wonderful job, especially the Fems. They had killed the majority of the Warriors with their death ploy. Bambi told him that the hardest part for them was remaining still as the Warrs pounded their way through them. Some were even stomped on and sustained injuries but had remained still and quiet through their pain.

Mosley provided the biggest surprise of all, though. Slapping him on the back he said, "I could never have done what you accomplished. You are the best leader, and I will follow you anywhere."

That was a major surprise coming from him, and he could tell he meant it. Mosley was a dedicated team player now, and he and his group were extremely welcome. In previous conversations, Al indicated that Mosley had been getting friendlier with him and Iron Eyes. Still, he

349

couldn't help chuckling inside at his slight lisp from the two missing front teeth.

He began instructing all the leader to move their groups out as soon as possible and head back to the facility and set up defenses on the mountain road leading up to the facility. It would be a good defense location. Whatever they were going to do would be done there.

His first warning was a low growl emitted from Oggg. He had been running around everyone leaping up on them trying to get attention, or maybe he was offering his congratulations. It was hard to tell with him. He stopped his antics and stared at something behind him, but he already knew what it was. Alerted, he could now feel the barely controlled hate emanating from the Supreme One, then bursting forth.

Oggg started barking at the threat and leaped forward, as he turned around in time to see the occupied Fem's body running toward him. The others saw and understood the threat immediately, but Mosley was the closest and quickest. The hugely muscled black man shot forward and tackled the Fem. They thudded to the ground in a thrashing heap. Almost immediately Mosley began screaming as the Fem sank her finger fangs deep into his back, but in obvious excruciating pain, he never let go. Moon and Bambi grabbed her hands and pulled them free, while he and Al pulled Mosley to safety, too late. Several of the other Fems, livid with anger, gave the surrogate Supreme One a double dose of his own medicine.

He held the thrashing Mosley as he slipped into the abyss of death. Just when Mosley had finally become one of the inner circle and comfortable in the position, he forfeited his life to save him. Damn the Supreme One! He had killed a good man and friend. Amy was right. They had to take out the Supreme One, soon.

* Amy *

She had been semi-dozing and almost missed it, but Oggg's growl caught her attention in time to detect the Supreme One, almost too late. Well, it was too late to help. All she could do was watch in shock as Mosley charged the Fem. She knew, as did Mosley, that he would die in the attempt, but he charged anyway. He forfeited his life to save Levi, and it was an agonizing death. Mosley had been a royal pain in the ass on several occasions, but he had saved Levi's life and the lives of their army many times. He had even turned out to be a valuable asset to their army and trusted friend to her and Levi. He did not deserve to die like this. She wept.

The only consolation to Mosley's death was knowing that the Supreme One still occupied the Fem's body when the poison coursed its raging path through her body, and he felt it and died a thousand deaths in the process. The loss of the Fem was also tragic, but thankfully, she wouldn't have felt the death in her state of mind.

She didn't think the Supreme One would return soon after this latest ordeal, but it was always better to err on the side of caution. She said, "Levi, you and the dragons need to separate from the Simians before he tries it again. Also, caution Al and Iron Eyes to do the same. You are all in danger."

351

Levi shot back, "Amy, we have to kill that bastard!"

"I know! I know! I'm working on something, but we aren't strong enough yet."

She was just about to return her mind back to the problem she had to solve when she saw Levi's poorly masked plan flick by. "Oh, no you don't! I saw what you plan to do. It worked once, but it won't work again." Levi was being clever again, and she almost missed. She saw that he intended to go back to the main Simian army and free the Humans, but not only would the Supreme One anticipate that, he would also be able to sense him if he returned. This was a bad idea, really bad.

Laughing, Levi said, "Okay, but you didn't see my whole plan."

When he opened his mind and let her look at the complete plan, she marveled at his cunning. "You are one sneaky bastard. I'm glad you are on our side."

* Satan *

His body hurt too much to be angry. Never had he felt pain so excruciating, even from the abomination when she sank her fangs into his neck. It must have been the dual dose. The pain drove his mind back into his body, and he brought the pain back with him. It took long moments to drive the shock of it out. Never again would he allow his essence to suffer pain like that. If he saw it coming, he would vacate the body quickly.

Certainly, he hadn't expected to be given the opportunity to kill one of the abominations, so he

352

wouldn't allow himself to consider it another defeat. Actually, it had almost worked. That was not the way he wanted to kill him though. He wanted to feel the life crushed out in his hands of power. This opportunity would come. He had no doubt.

Finally calm, he allowed his mind to remember what he had seen. Almost unbelievably, his army had been totally defeated. Five thousand healthy and virile Warriors killed, most by the females, but many had been killed because they had separated their teams to avoid the boulders. The latter was his fault, something that would not happen again, and the ploy of the dead females would never work again. He would not allow himself to be outmaneuvered like that again.

His army of fifteen thousand Warriors posed an unthinkable overkill of the numbers required to defeat the enemy. The defensives weapons, spears and crossbows, were already being prepared, a communication network of flags to issue immediate orders and changes was being established, but the best item of defense was his physical presence. He would directly supervise the next engagement in his own body.

There was only one of the abominations in the area, which he mentally sought and located often. By knowing his constant location, he could anticipate the enemy's next move, and he suspected what that would be. Last night there had been an attack on the advanced army in which they had gotten away with the females, runts, and the food animals. At least there had not been any remaining in the morning. Unfortunately, this main army didn't have any females or runts remaining, but they did

353

have food animals. If the enemy attacked tonight, they would be after the animals, and he would be ready if they did.

Instead of grouping the animals all together, he separated them into three smaller groups. This way the attackers would have to spread themselves out into three attacking groups, effectively thinning their ranks and increasing the opportunity to attack them. The Warriors on guard would be wearing the ear plugs, along with the hidden Warriors with spears and crossbows. When they attacked, he would have a major surprise for them. He thought about trying to position himself by one of the groups, but the abomination might detect him and ruin the surprise.

Well after dark he detected the abomination coming toward him, then he seemed to circle over the army. Yes, that made sense; he would be trying to identify the location of the animals. Following the abomination's location he seemed to hover over the three locations, having obviously identified them. They would strike soon. He sent runners to the guards at the three locations to notify them, but long before the time it would have taken, runners came. What the infernal blazes was going on?

The first runner announced, "The animals are gone!" Following the first runner, the second and third runners reported the same thing.

"Explain! What do you mean the animals are gone? How can they just disappear?"

From the stuttering and confused reports it seemed they just disappeared in a puff of dust.

* Levi *

354

Amy had to know eventually, but he wasn't quite ready to let her in on his other plan. Unfortunately, she detected part of it, and he had to let her see the whole plan. She liked it ... lots. Amy wasn't totally back to normal, but he thought she was strong enough for her part. Amy was initially against it because the Supreme One would be able to detect his presence, but she didn't yet understand that that was the most important part of his plan. The Supreme One was predictable in this regard, which he was counting on, and really, there was little risk.

What surprised him most was the fact that he had never considered it before. It must be that he had been forced into the planning role of the partnership while Amy recuperated. In truth, he began using his own intellect by necessity and now couldn't seem to stop.

After the battle and the latest attempt on his life, he fumed, and he wanted to strike back at the Supreme One. He wanted to fight him, but Amy was right; the Supreme One was too powerful to take on ... yet. Still, he had to hurt him somehow. That's when he remembered the captured Humans and his vow to save them. They had been too late to save the Humans in the advanced group, but dammit, he might be able to save these.

His mind churned with ideas. The plan worked last night, but it probably wouldn't happen again. In fact, if they tried, they would most likely walk directly into a trap. The Supreme One was far from stupid. Like Amy said, he would be monitoring his location, and if he was the Supreme One, he would split up the humans into different groups to make it more difficult to rescue them; he would split them up into SMALLER groups. Then his mind saw everything the Supreme One would do and devised his plan. Honestly, it was too simple.

He contacted Fred to have him prepare for visitors, since the Humans were all from the same area, and they might know each other. That could be comforting under their increased stress. It was as good a place as any, and they would be safely behind the Simian army.

Moon and Bambi wouldn't let him out of their sight, so the three of them, along with Jimmy and Katie, floated quietly over the Simian army, and he smiled when he felt the mental touch of the Supreme One searching. As he spiraled down, the smile grew when he spotted the Humans separated into three groups. Unfortunately, the number of Humans had dwindled and each group only held around fifty, but fortunately, the Supreme One had done what he could not have done, reduced the numbers and compacted the groups into manageable sizes ... for him.

He descended to circle each group, while Amy focused through him and teleported the groups to the caverns. It went so smoothly, and they were gone before the Supreme One even knew what happened. He wished he could see the look on his face, but imagining the look was almost as good.

They would just have to be satisfied, knowing it was successful. They couldn't travel to the caverns without letting the Supreme One know, since he would be able to track his locations. Instead, they turned back toward the facility to continue to draw them forward. "Draw" seemed a strange word for him to use, because he didn't want them coming at all.

He had to laugh when Fred announced, "There be Humans here!" Fred's attempt at a Scottish accent made him realize Fred was attempting to mimic an old Star Trek movie where Scotty said, "There be whales here." Personally, he was old enough to remember seeing the movie, but he doubted Fred had ever even seen a movie. It was funny just the same.

* Amy *

Levi would never be allowed to cop out of the planning again. He had done extremely well in the previous plan and this latest plan, and he executed them to perfection. Just let him try that, "I'm a simple man" ploy again, and she would kick him square in the butt.

The main obstacle to saving the Humans was the large mass of the teleport, but Levi had calculated correctly that the Supreme One would split them up. That played directly into their, well, his, plan. By reducing the mass of the teleport, it simplified her ability to teleport the groups. In reality, it made it relatively easy. Levi flew over the compacted groups, and she teleported them directly into the waiting supervision of Fred at the caverns.

It was complete even before the Supreme One knew what was happening and with no risk at all. She had to wonder why they had never done it before. The main reason was the high mass of the teleport, but the real reason was because she had never thought of it before. It was that damn abstract thought again. Levi had it and she didn't.

Levi said, "Hell, Amy, I never thought of it before either. Besides, we did it together, and it worked. That is all that matters."

"That's true. Thanks." After a moment she said, "You want me to teleport you back to the facility, or are you going to fly back with Moon and Bambi?"

"I'll fly. We will be back in a few hours."

It would take them several hours to fly back to the facility, which should give her plenty of time to research, learn, and experiment with the powers of ASONE, assuming it could be done. Well, of course it could be done, he/she/it did it, but she would have to figure out how he accomplished it.

ASONE would not know anything or create anything except through her, so she had to know how or at least have the knowledge. Well, that was not necessarily true. ASONE was a combination of both her and Levi, but Levi didn't have the technical knowledge. That would have come from her, but what might Levi have contributed? He would have provided the physical body, since she was only mental at that time. So far she had never been able to recreate the power of the blue energy, and she was still unable to conceive of a way in her mind. So, there had to be something else.

What was Levi's major mental ability? Instantly she knew ... abstract thought! That was the answer. ASONE viewed her powers through Levi's mental filter and saw other ways to use the powers she already possessed. Humm, now what?

The easiest way was simply to ask. "Hey, hon, while you are flying home, think about how

ASONE created the mysterious blue energy. I think you have the key."

"Oh, that's easy. ASONE joined us like you do when we astral project, then he treated my body like you do an object when you use telekinesis."

Quickly she said, "Thanks." She didn't wait for a response. Yes, that was it, and she saw it and how to make it work. ASONE used the joining required to astral project, but took it much further. That is how they totally merged. A total merging wouldn't be necessary for the blue energy, however, now that she saw how. Using telekinesis she would surround an object with projected energy. It was moving an object, but it wasn't the object she moved; she moved the energy enveloping it. Partially joining with Levi put her mind and power within him, as opposed to projecting from her mind and using his senses to focus it. The energy shield would surround them but could be manipulated and projected out. That is how ASONE accomplished that feat, and now so could she.

She also saw why she had never been able to duplicate the energy. It would take both of them working together to create it, or would it? Either way, it could be done, and it would be done to fight the Supreme One.

Chapter 14
Battle of the Titans

* Satan *

This battle on this planet had gone wrong in far too many ways, and he had suffered defeat in more ways than he had ever imagined, certainly more than he had experienced on his home world. In point of fact, he had never suffered a defeat until he came here. This was all the more reason to hate the Witch and her spawn, but his unbridled hate and rage had been his downfall. They had used it against him time after time. The Witch had demonstrated that she could be a formidable foe, and if he hoped to defeat her, he must not underestimate her again, and he must never again lose his temper.

It was time to take it slow and do everything right this time. Certainly, he had the advantage with fifteen thousand Warriors, and even more of an advantage being personally engaged within his own body. It had been a mistake to engage in battles through a surrogate body with their inherent weaknesses. It had served a purpose, but his own body could wield awesome power, and he would use that power now.

Thinking clearly now, he realized the food supply for his army no longer existed. The abominations had stolen his food animals, but if they weren't killed in the crash, he had brought his own supply of food. Each ship had brought along a few of the riders. The original intent had been to breed them on this planet, but now they could supply the needed food for his hungry Warriors and himself, if they yet lived. Even if they died in the crash, they could still be used.

He had learned the original fleets had eaten their breeding stock en route and there were none available on this planet, but he was determined that wouldn't happen with his Warriors, even though their food had run out before they arrived.

He had feasted upon the food animals here since crashing. They were nourishing but a little soft and sweet for his taste, much preferring the riders. Surely they could still be alive or usable; it seemed like ages since they arrived, but in reality, it had only been a few days.

Having a source of food became his immediate primary purpose, but he also wanted some to ride and drag some of the other items from the ship he might be able to use for weapons. The riders were the main source of food on his home planet but worked equally well as work animals. He was thankful now he hadn't let his Warriors eat them.

He ordered a company of Warriors and all the remaining Technical Simians to return with him on his mission to the crashed spaceships. He was thankful that he still had a few Technical Simian, since the Warriors were too stupid to understand some of the mechanical tasks needed.

Almost everything onboard his spaceships required technology, now useless without operating shipboard power generators. Fortunately, the escape hatch locks operated on canisters of highly compressed air used to blow the hatches. These functioned as a safety feature in case technology was lost, as in this case, causing a crash landing.

The main escape hatches for all the Simians had been sprung upon crashing, but the escape hatches for the lower storage and rider compartments were still intact. Everyone had been too anxious for themselves to have worried about the food animals.

He had been thinking about what he might be able to use as a weapon, and figured out how to use these compressed air canisters and cylinder unit. Firing a canister within the cylinder shot a piston out with extreme force, sufficient to blow heavy, spring loaded latches. The size of the hatch determined the number of latches, but all of them had at least four, and some eight. From each ship he should be able to retrieve at least twelve canisters. The analysis suggested that he might have sixty or so canisters available from all the ships, plus any spares that could be found in storage.

The Technical Simians, along with Warrior guards, were instructed to go through all the ships and manually release the storage level hatches and remove all the canisters. One team remained with him to remove the door cylinders under his supervision. With six firing cylinders and over sixty canisters he would have a substantial arsenal. This, combined with highly concentrated liquid fuel cells he intended to use as the projectiles, he could launch a very effective attack.

The fuel cells would easily fit within the cylinders, and a canister and piston would launch a projectile a great distance. The fuel cells would break on impact, and when the liquid was exposed to air, an impressive explosion would occur.

Yes, his mind was working well now.

* Levi *

He, Moon, Bambi, and the other dragons and riders were perched on top one of the mountains leading toward Amy's facility. Through his binoculars he watched the massive Simian army coming. The very sight of the vast numbers of Simians was enough to create doubt. There were so damn many of them, and they covered the valley floor. The generated dust from their marching clouded the horizon, reminding him of a dust storm so prevalent in the desert. In truth it was a storm coming but unlike any seen on this planet.

Their armies had established a strong defense behind the mountain pass leading to the facility and were waiting. This would be their last defense. If they could not hold them here, they would all fall behind the massive doors of the facility. It would be almost impossible for the Simian army to withstand the laser defenses firing through the doors, but he would hate to say it was totally impossible. The vast number of Warriors posed too many unforeseen possibilities. He had seen the devastation from the lasers, and it was awesome, but the firing range was limited. The Warriors wouldn't just continue to charge into the laser. No, the Supreme One would look for and possibly eventually find another way. He couldn't imagine what, however, and it was this unknown that bothered him most.

All these thoughts and doubts were roaring in his head when his attention was drawn toward objects far to the rear of the Simian army. Focusing his binoculars on the objects in the distance, he was shocked when it realized what they were. The

Supreme One was easy to identify from its size. Once you had seen a Supreme One you never forgot it, but he was riding on a huge animal and followed by many more of them. It was definitely not something from Earth.

"Amy, are you seeing this? What the hell are they?"

Amy said, "That has to be their food animals they brought with them. It must be what you called, elephants."

He remembered the discussion he had with Moon, and it did indeed look like an elephant without a trunk. It wasn't the color of an elephant, though. It looked more orange, and it had a wide flat head. Certainly, it was as big as an elephant, maybe even bigger; but it was hard to tell for sure from this distance.

He handed the binoculars to Moon, pointing in the direction of the Supreme One. It was difficult for Moon, due to his new size, to manipulate the focusing, and he could only use one eye. He asked Moon, "What is that the Supreme One is on?"

After only a few seconds, Moon said, "That is a 'rider'. They were our food supply on our home planet, and they, as you can see, can be ridden, and make excellent work animals. They would be like a combination of a horse and cow here."

Amy said, "What bothers me is the fact that the Supreme One went back to his ships at all. I don't think he went just to get food. It's not like him to care if his army is hungry."

Yeah, that was probably true. It would most likely work to the Supreme One's advantage if the Warriors were hungry and the only food was in front of them AFTER the victory. Now he too was concerned what the bastard was up to.

* Amy *

It was strange indeed to see the Supreme One riding across the desert floor on the equivalent of a horse. He had obviously changed his tactics. Before, he would have simply driven his forces forward. Certainly, he had a major advantage in forces, but the fact that he had returned to his spaceships indicated that he intended to ensure victory with some additional plan or arsenal. This worried her, because any change in his tactics couldn't be good, and she couldn't begin to guess what those plans or new arsenal might be.

She remained weak from her medical ordeal but much better than she had been. Mama still doted over her and continued to watch her closely. Without even asking, she knew Mama wasn't ready to let her re-join the battle, and so far Levi had been doing a fantastic job. But, everything was coming to a climax, and she knew she would have to get involved soon. The problem with that was she didn't know what else to do that wasn't already being done, but there had to be more.

The riflemen were positioned on the pass walls, the army was positioned inside the pass, and the dragons were on the mountains poised to attack, but they waited for the Supreme One to make the next move. That move would come soon.

She watched through Levi's eyes as the Supreme One reached his army and began issuing orders. A glint of sunlight reflected off some objects being distributed toward the front of the army. Even the Supreme One moved toward the front, taking an aggressive and prominent position there. It was almost as if he wanted to be attacked.

Once they were all in position, according to the Supreme One's plan, which she didn't understand yet, they began slowly moving forward. Whatever he planned to do, it was beginning.

The panic began rising in her gut, and anxiety tensed through her body. Call it a premonition, but something terrible was about to happen. Where was that damn clairvoyance warning when she really needed it?

She heard it first. There were loud popping sounds from below, maybe two, almost simultaneously. Levi heard it too and turned toward the sound. All that could be seen through his eyes were two clouds of dust on either side of the Supreme One. Then they heard the explosion, followed quickly by a rush of heat and a ground shudder. Both sides of the mountain pass erupted into a fiery inferno. The riflemen were instantly gone, along with anyone just inside the pass. Sadly, many Techs and Infantry had been deployed there and died instantly. A flood of emotions swept over her with the loss of so many under her protection. She had failed them.

She held back her grief, instantly realizing the Supreme One's new arsenal and plan. She screamed, "Levi, get them out of there! Pull them back to the facility ... quickly!" Levi barked orders, but the orders were unnecessary, as most were already fleeing the blazing inferno.

Somehow the Supreme One had summoned up a form of technology that worked in Earth's altered environment. This was disastrous. She saw the plan unfold. He would continue this type of attack all the way back to the facility, and it would work. He would be able to destroy the lasers in the door long before she could use them to ward off the Warriors. They would be caught in their own burning inferno. After all their effort they had lost ... lost the battle, the war, and their planet.

* Levi *

The sudden destruction delivered to his army disturbed him greatly. They could not stand against this technology, and he quickly ordered a general retreat. Fortunately, few orders were needed, since the army was already in full retreat from the fiery inferno ... all except the dragons.

The dragons were pissed and had launched for an attack. "No!" he screamed. He tried to call them back and mostly succeeded, except for the first pair. They had been closest to the explosion and reacted the fastest. Blood lust glared from their blazing eyes, and they paid him no attention. Already they streaked toward the Supreme One with their wings pulled back for greater speed, claws poised to kill. All he could do was watch in fear for them as they streaked toward their target.

He didn't recognize the dragons or riders of the two brave teams; they must have been some of the new dragons and riders.

The dragons immediately knew the Supreme One caused the destruction of their friends and reacted, ill-advised. He knew what was coming, but hoped that, with their speed and momentum and the fact that two targets would be harder to hit, one of them might succeed.

As he watched in horror, tandem, blazing, red fireballs shot out as if emanating from the Supreme One's extended arms. The fireballs engulfed the dragons in flight and instantly consumed dragons and riders. They tumbled from the sky trailing smoke as they crashed in heaps of smoldering, charred flesh. A chorus of screeches and chattering black teeth erupted from the Warriors below, but the bellowing victory wail from the Supreme One carried over all the others. The smug bastard shook his fist at the sky, seemingly daring another attack.

No, another direct attack on the Supreme One would be useless ... for them anyway. He would have to face the Supreme One alone, with Amy's help. No other defense had a chance.

He allowed the remaining dragons to resume a high altitude bombardment attack with their boulders, but due to the greater distance, the accuracy was lost and had little effect. At least it was something to do.

He circled high above, observing his armies' retreat and the actions of the enemy. Luckily, the Supreme One did not continue the fire blasts. It appeared that he would allow the fire to subside then move past the damage area to launch more firebombs in a renewed attack. It would take time for the fires to die down, so this would gain them time to get their army back toward the facility and try to come up with a strategy to defend themselves. Unfortunately, unless Amy could come up with something, he didn't know how to combat this new threat.

He said, "Amy, do you have any ideas?"

"I haven't come up with anything. It looks hopeless."

"I thought the same thing. Unless we can take out the Supreme One we can't attack their launchers. We have to take him out."

Amy sighed, "I know."

"We need to take him out, NOW!"

Amy barked, "I KNOW!"

* Satan *

For the first time on this cursed planet things were finally starting to go his way. He had allowed the Witch to get to him and drive his anger to the boiling point. That had been his undoing. Things were different now. He wasn't allowing her or her abominations to set off his rage, and his mind was clear. He had a plan, and his army would follow it. Now he expected more from his enemy and would not underestimate them again.

No longer was he operating through a surrogate; he was in his own body with all the powers available to him. The mount he rode elevated his status and spirits even more, and the Warrior army could see him in all his glory and soon in his victory.

He had been informed of the blazing beams of light that the Witch used as defense at her complex. The slaughter those weapons produced was devastating, but he was knowledgeable of this focused light technology. This technology would be useless to her, even if they survived the attack from the energy cells. He had retrieved highly reflective, metal plates from the wreckage. The plates were large enough to be used by the leading Warriors and would protect and reflect the blazing beams back upon the facility. If it was light, it could be reflected and used to destroy them. He almost wished their defenses would survive so he could destroy them with their own weapon. That would make their defeat even more humiliating.

The first canisters had been launched and his weapon worked to perfection. Only two had been used, but the destruction they caused had been considerable. Many of the enemy had perished in this first attack, but the area still blazed with flames. It would take several hours for the area to cool off enough to march his army through, but he had learned patience. The victory was sure, and he had time and many more canisters to fire.

The fire and smoke bellowed over the mountains, but through the smoke flew two of the flying Simians. He couldn't believe his luck. Now he could destroy them, but he didn't want to display all his new abilities, just in case one of the abomination might get the courage to attack. The flying Simians dove toward him, and he patiently waited. They were well within range as he extended his arms and hands toward them, launching two churning balls of red fire toward them. The flying Simians saw them but far too late to escape. It wouldn't have mattered; he could have changed the trajectory simply by redirecting his arms and thoughts to follow them.

The balls of fire engulfed the dragons, instantly choking off their defiant, challenging screeches. Their flaming bodies crashed to the ground only a short distance from him and lay smoldering. His victory scream filled the air, joining the screeched cheers of his Warriors.

* Amy *

She needed technology to combat the Supreme One's new technology, but the only technology outside of the facility had been the modified rifles. Even those were now gone.

Suddenly, she realized that she did have technology outside of the facility. The positron generator could give her technology. How had she forgotten? All she had to do was disperse the transmitted signal wide and over the battle area, but it would take time to alter the environment. Did she have time?

Her mind began the alterations immediately to activate and direct the spread of the transmission where she needed it, then she searched the facility inventory for weapons. Already she knew there were no high output lasers, and the ones she had didn't have the long range she needed to compete with the range of the Supreme One's firebombs.

At least her facility had once been a military research facility, and the military, no matter what its purpose, maintained weapons. Unfortunately, time would have rendered many of them useless and the urgent need didn't allow time to relocate the larger ones.

371

Mama burst into the clinic in response to her summons, but Amy held her hand up indicating silence. She immediately began updating Mama about the tragedy at the pass and the threat imposed by the Supreme One. Mama was silent and somber as she described the losses, especially concerning the dragons. Mama had been much closer to the new batch of dragons and would take their loss personally. Those dragons had been her idea solely, and she considered them her children.

As she described her new plan, Mama perked up, finally having an opportunity for personal revenge and a way to get her team involved directly in the defense of the facility.

She found two items in the military arms inventory that should work, assuming the positron generator successfully altered the ammunition. There were several RPG-7-USA (Rocket Propelled Grenade Launchers) and M120 Mortars. Both of these weapons exceeded the range of the Supreme One's weapons. Unfortunately, the terrain prevented transmission of the positron generator over the mountains. The weapons could only be used on the inward side of the mountain pass, if they worked at all.

It was not very comforting to know that another firebomb attack from inside the mountain pass would succeed. The Warriors, however, would actually have to enter the last valley for her weapons to reach them, so Mama couldn't fire before the targets became visible. Even then, the winner of the engagement would be the first to take out the other's weapons, and the firebombs were more devastating. Still they had a fighting chance now.

Mama was a quick study and listened intently as she described how the RPGs and Mortars worked. Mama also understood the importance of getting the ammunition positioned on the plateau above the facility, the launching base. When Mama was positive she understood, she was off to gather up the weapons and volunteers to operate them. Mama's biggest problem would be trying to limit the number of volunteers.

She saved the hardest decision for last, because it would be the hardest to make. Levi had said, "We need to take the bastard out, NOW!" Levi was correct. The Supreme One would never stop until they were all dead, but the decision to do battle could get Levi killed. When Levi died in the last confrontation with a Supreme One, she had been devastated emotionally. She would not go through that again. If Levi died this time she would die with him. So she said, "Okay, Levi, it is time to take him out. I am on my way, and we will take him out together."

* Levi *

He couldn't believe Amy agreed to engage the Supreme One, and he certainly wasn't expecting her to physically join him in the battle. If he died Amy might be able to live on, maybe even bring him back like last time, but if she died ... well, he didn't want to think about that. Amy was far more precious to him than his life, and she was desperately needed to help all their friends and allies. They couldn't risk her. He began, "Amy, I will ..."

Amy spat, "Levi, would you please just shut the fuck up? I've made my decision! I'm coming. Besides, you can't do it alone. It takes both of us to create the energy field to resist his fireballs. We have to do it together."

Of course she was correct, but he didn't like risking her. He also knew it would do no good to argue with her once her mind was made up. She could be damn stubborn in that regard. He smiled; they did make a great team, however.

While he waited for Amy, he circled closer to Moon and signed their intent to battle with the Supreme One. He also instructed Moon and the other dragons to continue to circle the battlefield, but maintain their height. Moon, Bambi, Jimmy, and Katie all looked very concerned, but they held their comments.

As Amy approached, he began a slow, spiral descent directly over the Supreme One. Amy coasted into formation at his side, and they continued their descent together. He felt the power of her mind meld with his and the tingle of energy building around them. By the time they descended almost within range of his power, their energy was ready to be used, but he held the descent and screeched out a challenge in the Simian language, "We come to battle the coward. Clear the battlefield of Warriors."

They held their altitude and watched. The Supreme One screeched out orders, and a wide circle cleared in the massed Warriors below. As the Supreme One waited for them to attack, he observed a wide grin slowly spread across the behemoth's face as if they were doing just what he wanted them to do. Were they making the mistake he had hoped for? It didn't much matter, since they had little choice.

If this was the end, he had something to say. He looked across at Amy, smiled and said, "I love you, Amy."

"Almost as much as I love you, Shithead, and we will talk about the 'stubborn' comment later."

They knew this would be a battle of energy, but they drew their swords anyway and suddenly plunged together toward the grinning bastard.

* Satan *

He gloried in his victory. Many of his enemies had died in his attack, and his next attack would kill even more. He sensed the victory over the Witch and her spawn. All he had to do was maintain control of his emotions and not let them enrage him. He would not repeat that mistake this time.

Panning around on his rider allowed him to admire the mass of Warriors surrounding him, filling the valley for as far as he could see. They were unstoppable. Together they were the most powerful force on this planet. His power exceeded all others, and he would soon be the absolute and unquestioned ruler of this planet. Sadly, however, he might miss the competition from the Witch. She had forced him to evolve to compete, and now he was more powerful than any Supreme One had ever been.

Looking up he could see many of the flying Simians. They continued to drop boulders, but from that altitude they were easy to dodge. He wished they would come closer; he would love to kill more of them. They were afraid of his power, as they should be.

His attention suddenly turned skyward to the arrogant challenge screeched. Then he saw them, both of them. The abominations challenged him ... HIM! Suddenly he was pleased. Finally, he could face them directly.

The male abomination had called him a coward, apparently trying to enrage him. That would not be allowed. To the contrary, he wanted this confrontation, so why would he rage? He wanted to face them and kill them. They would be surprised at his power. They assumed, incorrectly, that fireballs were his weapons. Soon they would be in the grasp of his projected energy hands as he squeezed the life out of them. Yes, he was pleased.

The male abomination asked for the battle area to be cleared, and he eagerly complied. To appear even less intimidating, he dismounted the rider and sent it scurrying off, leaving him standing alone in the middle of the clearing. If this lured them within grasp sooner, he would be pleased.

As the battlefield cleared they began their slow descent toward him, then suddenly dove directly at him. He found it humorous to see them draw their swords; they would never get that close. They knew about and would expect fireballs. Presumably they would have a defense, and he was curious to see what that defense might be. He felt the recoil in his arms as two fireballs streaked toward them.

Amazingly, both abominations countered with a blazing blue ray projecting out from them to clash with his fireballs. He expected a defense, but somehow he hadn't expected this. The energy forces collided in a loud sizzling and sparkling cloud of red and blue flames, and the static generated pulled at his golden hair. The blue ray began to push his fireball back toward him, and he found it necessary to maintain a constant flow of energy to repel their projected energy. He allowed the abominations to slowly gain ground, every second bringing them closer. Soon they would be within range of his grasp.

After a few moments of drawing them closer he suddenly extended his arms with his fingers spread wide. His hands of radiated energy formed and shot out to snatch them both from the sky. They struggled, but he had a firm grasp and began to squeeze. Their blue energy aura prevented him from immediately crushing the life out of them, but it began to weaken as he tightened his vice-like grip. He shook them as a young Simian might play with a small food animal. His victory screech bust out, filling the valley. Victory was his at last!

* Amy *

Levi could genuinely be an endearing sweetie sometimes, and at other times he could be a royal ass. This was one of the endearing times. Through his thoughts Levi revealed his love, but like most men, he rarely expressed his affection in words. When he did, it was usually at the point of death. Certainly, this would qualify for that situation, but she would take what she could get, even at the point of death.

As they spiraled down to face the Supreme One she linked minds with Levi, and they melted together and were ready with their defense. In unison, they dove toward the target, and as expected, saw the fireballs coming. They stopped their descent to hover, as she routed their mental energy to encompass them and repel the fireballs. Sooner would have been better, as the forces clashed far too close to their end. It was like colliding fireworks with exploding reds and blues, but this explosion smelled more like an electrical arc.

She had seen this type of energy collision before when they fought the last Supreme One, but this effect exceeded the last, probably because these were duel collisions. The extended blue force field held, however.

Drawing and absorbing the energy around her, she directed its flow, slowly pushing at the fireballs. Surprising, the fireballs did not dissipate. They held together as if being constantly fed from below, which they apparently were. Still, she felt the red energy begin to give and ever so slowly the fireballs began retreating toward the Supreme One. As it did they began creeping toward the Supreme One. Emboldened, she pushed harder, and the distance between them narrowed.

Suddenly, the fireballs vanished, and she could clearly see the Supreme One below. His arms quickly extended, projecting the angry, red energy from his hands. The energy formed huge translucent arms and hands that shot toward them, grasping them in immense burning fingers. The fingers were inescapable as they struggled against them. Their bluish auras compressed tight around them ... crushing. Air pushed from her lungs, and short gasps fought for more.

They had been tricked! The Supreme One had wanted them to come closer, and she had mistakenly done just that. They had been defeated.

Feeling the crushing pain and realizing they were about to die, her mind flashed back, remembering her life with Levi.

She had been alive and self-aware for over fifty-two years, but she had not lived until she met Levi. Levi taught her everything about how to live and experience life, and he had taught her how to love.

Their life together flashed by as if it were a photo album in her mind. She saw him as the obstinate old man he had once been, the regenerated and striking figure dripping water after he learned to swim, and the embarrassed Levi when she had not allowed him to make love with that camp harlot. She saw the battles she had lived with him and remembered the warmth of his body as they made love. They had lived several lifetimes in the few short years they had been together, and she had no regrets. She said, "Sorry Levi."

* Levi *

Damn the bastard! He was hurting Amy, and he felt her pain along with his own. The Supreme One was slowly crushing the life out of them, and hacking at the burning red fingers with his sword

379

did nothing. The crushing fingers were only of energy, and the sword passed through as if it wasn't there. He screamed out in agony and rage, rage so intense it threatened to overwhelm him.

In that moment of intense rage he felt something else, something he had felt before, something he now welcomed. He felt ASONE emerging from his rage, and his rage soon paled in comparison to the growing rage of ASONE.

His mind began to see past his own body limits, seeing new possibilities. Those limits dissolved and he and Amy began to merge, mentally, yet they began to flow into a third entity. This entity sucked them within, along with all their combined intelligence, which transformed into raw power. He, as Levi, was reduced to an observer within the entity with no control. The entity grew along with its boiling rage, and God was it pissed!

The crushing pain eased as ASONE grew. He felt his physical body slowly begin to turn within the blue shield. The turning increased to a blurring spin that transformed even his physical body into energy that joined with Amy's. They continued to spin and twirl together, like twin tornados of energy merging and growing in size. At some point during this transformation they had formed outside of the gripping energy fingers of the Supreme One. Together they became a huge twisting, churning tornado of raw blue energy hovering over the Supreme One, now frozen in horror.

The blue aura began to take the form of a giant Earth Dragon, wings spread wide. ASONE bellowed its fury and belched blue flames of energy down upon the whimpering Supreme One that instantly consumed it. It simply vanished into smoke.

The conflict ended suddenly and far too easily. After causing so much chaos and agony to so many, the Supreme One deserved to suffer greatly, but, at least he was dead and gone.

The giant blue dragon continued to bellow its rage and belch sweeping flames at the petrified Warrior army. Thousands of Warriors disintegrated from the flames before the surviving Warriors' paralysis vanished. They were now fleeing in all direction, anywhere away from the raging blue dragon and its tongue of death, but the glowing blue dragon took flight in an ever-widening circle, incinerating the fleeing Warriors. Thousands perished before ASONE expended its rage.

With ASONE's rage diminished, it calmed and slowly began to reverse the process, returning to wherever it came from. Soon it was gone, and Amy and he stood together looking at each other, wondering what had happened. Of course they both remembered exactly what happened but as if by a dream. Still, it was difficult to believe they had won so decisively and so suddenly.

Without the Supreme One for protection and directions, the Warriors would no longer be interested in continuing the fight, especially after seeing the avenging dragon. Unfortunately, Thousands of Warriors had been funneled back against the pass leading to the facility with nowhere to go but through the pass. Judging from the explosions he heard, Mama managed to extract her revenge. Earth Dragons could also be seen attacking and harassing the fleeing Warriors who seemed to be running in every direction with little chance of slowing any time soon.

* Amy *

Levi felt him first, but she soon felt the tentacles of ASONE worming into her mind, taking over. As in times before, she was there but not an active participant. She felt the total of her mental energy sucked into ASONE. She was there as was Levi; they became as-one (ASONE), a new entity ... a power without equal. Levi's rage boiled and it became her rage. Their rage consumed them, rage focused at the Supreme One. They towered over the Supreme One in a swirling and turbulent form. The pure hate spewed out in blue flames and consumed the horrified Supreme One. Their power far exceeded and overwhelmed that of the Supreme One. No contest existed and he was instantly consumed in flames.

They felt disappointment that the defeat had been so sudden and released the remainder of the pent up rage toward the stunned Warriors. Thousands vaporized as they continued to spew forth the blue tongue of death. After a few moments all the Warriors within range were either dead or running for their lives, and there were no longer targets upon which to vent their rage.

Without a focus for the rage, ASONE began to dissipate. It had been ruthless and without mercy, and it had been her. Suddenly, she realized she was separated from the entity and herself again in mind and form. She remained shaken from the experience.

Levi recovered quickly and rushed to her, embracing her. Concern swelled in his golden eyes as he stared into hers. She said, "We won?"

"You know it. The Supreme One is toast, the Warrior army is in full retreat with the dragons hot on their tail, except for those that ran through the pass; but I think Mama is taking care of them now."

Still dazed, she knew what he said was true. She said, "Yes, Mama is taking care of those Warriors. She will be happy."

Levi said, "The Supreme One is gone, and we can now hunt down the surviving Warriors and take back our planet for good."

"No, not right now. They will still be there in a few months. They have no females, but our side does. It didn't matter before, since it looked like we would all die, but it becomes important now. We need time to rebuild our lives."

"What does it matter if our side has females? What's that got to do with anything?"

"Levi, you can be so dense sometimes. Many of the Earth's Dragons, including Bambi, and some of the riders are with child, and we will wait till spring to resume the battle ... after they are born." After a long pause she said, "Levi, Moon is going to be a father, even Jimmy, and so are you."

"Huh?"

The End